THE
CHASING
COLLECTION

ZOMBIE TAGGER EDITION

R.M. HAMRICK

THE CHASING COLLECTION

ZOMBIE TAGGER EDITION

R.M. HAMRICK

THE CHASING COLLECTION

A SHORT STORY PREQUEL
CHASING A LEAD

BOOK ONE
CHASING A CURE

BOOK TWO
CHASING REDEMPTION

BOOK THREE
CHASING EXTINCTION

CHASING A LEAD

A SHORT STORY PREQUEL

R.M. HAMRICK

CHASING A LEAD

In her SUV, Lisa was a large, strange beast crashing through the thick Georgia pines, kicking up dust and gravel on the highway's rough patches. With intersections few and far between, this road – like most leading into Victory – saw little traffic. Still, it seemed to Lisa that the rest of the world must be eerily preoccupied, and so, had left her on her own.

When something unseen struck the side of her vehicle, Lisa let out a panicked scream. Her passenger side tires slipped off the road's narrow shoulder. Keeping the steering wheel straight, Lisa let her vehicle grumble to a stop. The pounding in her chest drowned out even the engine's hum. Whatever had hit her window had fallen away, but had left a wide track of fluids streaking the glass. The small amount of gore she glimpsed turned her stomach and her mind tossed with fear. Had it been a deer?

Lisa was surprised the window held. Her entire body shook with adrenaline and fear as she searched for the release on the seatbelt. When it struck the window again with nearly the same force, Lisa did not think she'd ever stop trembling.

This time she had seen it, but knowing the truth did little good now.

*   *   *

LYSENT CORP: INNOVATIVE HEALTHCARE OR INNOVATIVE MONEYGRUBBING?

While Lysent Corporation is in the end-stages of developing a targeted antiviral to combat the Zari virus, many in the science community believe these rapid focused treatments might actually be accelerating the viral mutations we've seen in the last decade.

The Zari virus is so far milder and less deadly than last year's influenza, and targeted elimination of it may pave the way for far deadlier bugs. Many outside of Lysent Corp recommend using non-targeted methods to lessen symptoms while allowing the virus to run its course.

Lysent products may bring relief, but the company remains focused on profits within the medical industry with little thought to patient education or to global health as a whole.

Inside the gray cubicle, Lisa Pearson drummed lightly on her keyboard. She knew there was no way the *Southern Gazette* was going to publish her article. Dawson Gentry was her editor and he'd assigned her an update on the newest and best antiviral, not a piece on the economics of private healthcare. Still, the thought of just copying and pasting Lysent Corp's press release made Lisa feel as if she were dying a little bit on the inside. Lysent Corp and the private health sector in general had no incentive to improve the overall health of the demographic they claimed to serve. Maybe that was why their scientists were creating an antiviral for something that added up to a cold.

And while Jacksonville Florida's *Southern Gazette* didn't typically publish articles like this, Lisa felt it really should. The newspaper had been running for over a hundred years on nothing but local events, AP news, and high school sports – the same superficial dribble that had killed nearly every other newspaper. If anything, Lisa was helping the paper evolve, stay relevant, and dig deep for the truth behind the schmaltzy stories.

With a couple impulsive clicks, Lisa sent the article to Gentry. Within two minutes, Gentry had replied.

GENTRY: What is this? See me now.

If Lisa thought she could temporarily ignore the message, the appearance of Gentry's bearded head from his office declared otherwise.

Rising from her desk, Lisa shook her shoulders out as if to ready herself for a fight. This wasn't their first argument they'd had over assignments. Gentry didn't take any of her opinions seriously, probably because he didn't take her seriously. Thin, blond hair, blue-eyed, Gentry had asked in her interview if she knew the *Southern Gazette* was not a television news station. The articles he'd ask her to write since he hired her had been nothing but fluff. To Gentry and the newspaper, that was what she was — fluff in a pencil skirt, peach sleeveless blouse, and tiny black kitten heels.

Several staff writers had noticed the subtle exchange between journalist and editor, and Lisa purposefully ignored the stolen glances and tiniest of smirks as she marched over the worn-bare spots of the high traffic carpet between the cubicle rows. If her officemates could have sniffed out a story like they could an office squabble, the *Southern Gazette* would be an entirely different newspaper.

Before reaching the cheap hollow core door, Lisa had already managed a dozen reasons Gentry should print her article. She could do an entire series on "Profit over Welfare." She had an interview with the public relations specialist for Lysent Corp's Victory branch tomorrow. There she'd be able to get Lysent's response to the argument. If Gentry was concerned about offending the giant, she could include articles on government organizations and policies as well. It shouldn't all be on Lysent...

Preempting with an empty knock, Lisa slipped into the room, which was more like a desk with walls around it than an office. Behind the desk, Gentry sat with his hands steepled. The man was an age-enigma with brown skin that had refused to wrinkle and a short fade that had prematurely grayed. Whether the salt in his pepper was from stress or accumulated wisdom, Gentry retained all the classic traits of a newspaper editor. He was excitable and authoritative, and Lisa refused to sit down until she learned which it was today.

"I'm not going to fight you over every article," he said as he motioned to the ancient chair to Lisa's left.

His voice was calm and apologetic, so Lisa gingerly lowered herself into the upholstered chair, where she promptly sank. The staff had taken bets on when the chair would fail underneath a staff member. If Lisa hadn't overheard she'd been given good odds due to the frequency in which she was called into the office, she would've broken the chair just to sit in a less precarious one months ago.

Gentry leaned back in his chair, becoming partially obscured by some paper stacks and an overflowing inbox. "This is not the *New York Times*. It's Jacksonville's *Southern Gazette*. Write the articles I ask of you or leave."

"Did you even read—" started Lisa. She broadened her shoulders and put her arms on the wide armrests in an attempt to counter the feeling of shrinking.

"Did I even read which part? The part where you dismissed the fifty-some-odd deaths from the whatcha-virus? Or the part where you insulted Lysent Corporation, who has more money than the newsprint business as a whole?

A lot of fantastic local businesses advertise in our paper, but if they withdrew, we'd be OK because we have one national advertiser. And that's?"

"Lysent." Lisa was tempted to let the chair and its scratchy material swallow her up. She couldn't remember any of the arguments she had ready.

Appeased, Gentry raised his eyebrows. "Now are you going to re-write the article or should I assign it to somebody who can?"

* * *

Lisa sulked back to her cubicle under more than stolen glances. Too angry to begin rewriting the article to Gentry's specifications, she opened her email application and checked her messages.

The first was an AP news alert which never had to be opened as the subject line told all. "Zari virus spreads: first confirmed cases in New Mexico."

There were several requests to cover local events – the bowling alley's summer block party and the farmer's market requesting another story, rather than buying advertising like all the other businesses. One that had just come in looked as if it had slipped through the spam filters. The sender's email address was a meaningless jumble of characters, but "Important: Lysent" was the subject line. Crossing her fingers it wasn't an advertisement for Lysent Performance Products, Lisa opened the email out of curiosity.

It only contained a single sentence and an attachment.

"Dig deeper in Victory tomorrow. – Mo"

Lisa racked her brain for a 'Mo,' but couldn't come up with one. Whoever it was knew Lisa was visiting Victory, Georgia tomorrow for an interview. Lisa surveyed her coworkers in their cubicles – could one of them be pulling her leg? It didn't take long to realize she didn't know anyone well enough to take any guesses.

Opening an unknown attachment and infecting the entire office with a computer virus would consume any last bit of goodwill Gentry had for her, so Lisa scooped up her laptop and brought it to Branson, stationed a few rows down. Branson wrote a tech help column and solved the office's constant networking problems, which apparently gave him the latitude to keep his brown hair and beard scraggly and his clothes casually flannel.

Meanwhile, Lisa now owned three pencil skirts.

After a few minutes of Branson's tinkering and scanning, a map of the United States with many, many labeled dots and arrows appeared on the screen.

"No idea why this was encrypted. It's just a bunch of public info – looks like data for all the virus epidemics…"

Lisa gave a noncommittal shrug, but she remained intrigued. The data might be public, but it was highly relevant to the story she had been told to delete. Not to mention, the map was watermarked with Lysent's logo and the words *Innovative Healthcare*.

Her phone buzzed a text notification in her pocket.

MOM: 911

It probably was not an emergency. Knowing Kelly Ann, it definitely wasn't an emergency – but it was still difficult to ignore such a message. Thanking and ditching Branson, Lisa slipped out the back door of the office, startling a few smokers on their break. Lisa turned the corner and leaned against the aging red brick, soaking up its warmth to replace that which the office's air conditioning had zapped from her. Even in just these few minutes, she could already feel her skin baking pink or worse in the Florida sun.

Kelly Ann answered on the third ring. "Hello!"

"I got your text. Is something wrong?"

Having greeted her brightly, Kelly's voice suddenly went hoarse. "I'm not feeling well. Did you hear about that virus going around?"

Lisa shrank farther down the wall.

"I have. Do you have a doctor's appointment?" It was always easier to go with Kelly Ann than against. Lisa hadn't even discussed her recent assignments as her mother often adopted stray symptoms and suggested illnesses.

"I do but it's not for weeks. They seem very busy. I think I should try some new supplements. These aren't working. Lysent just released a new pro-health regimen…"

"Mom, it's the same vitamins and minerals you're taking now. They're just repackaged."

"Now, don't start this again. You can't distrust the government and health companies," Kelly Ann chided.

"Yes, you can!" Lisa said with exasperation, startling the smokers again. She lowered her voice. "Get what you need to feel healthy, Mom. I gotta go – I'm at work."

"You really shouldn't be on the phone at work, dear."

"Yes, mother."

*　　*　　*

Back at her desk, Lisa pulled her laptop close as she studied the secret and anonymous file. Of all the newspaper staff – the file had been sent to her – and she was going to figure out why. First, she zoomed in to Jacksonville. She recognized the name of several viruses that had come through, and some she didn't realize *had* names. The map must have been created recently; the up-and-coming Zari virus had already been identified and marked with an aquamarine label.

Back to the map's original scale, Lisa began to distinguish the individual colors. She could see epicenters for the viruses and how they blossomed outward, like fireworks. It was actually kind of pretty. In areas with sparser population, the viruses didn't overlap as much, so it was easy to spot the large burst of aquamarine centered over Albuquerque, New Mexico with tendrils creeping toward Santa Fe, Amarillo, and Flagstaff.

Hadn't she seen something about New Mexico recently? Pulling up her email, Lisa found the news alert.

"Zari virus spreads: first confirmed cases in New Mexico."

Even if this map was very up-to-date, the news alert reported the first cases – this map represented much more. Were these projections? It seemed unlikely. If Lisa had been tasked to predict Zari's path, it wouldn't have been through New Mexico. This map showed that most viruses skipped the Southwest entirely.

"What's this about an encrypted file?"

Lisa jumped back. She had been so focused on her screen that she hadn't heard anyone approach. Gentry stood partway in her cubicle, beads of sweat collecting on his collar and his mouth drawn into a heavy line.

"It's a mapping of viruses. I thought it'd be relevant to my story."

"It's not," said Gentry firmly. "I just needed seven lines that said, 'There's a virus, but hey, here's what you do about it,' so that the layout on page 4 would work. Instead you pursue a story with no regard to your duties or your job."

"But no, you have to understand. That map—" Gentry's tired eyes and head shake stopped her. Lisa felt a twinge of guilt – she was making Gentry's job rather difficult.

"I'm sorry, this is not working out. You need to collect your things."

Embarrassed, Lisa mumbled an apology and her appreciation for the opportunity. She stuffed her laptop into her bag and stupidly looked over the cubicle empty of all but some dusty plastic flowers that had witnessed another birth and death of a journalism career at the *Southern Gazette*.

*   *   *

Driving back to her apartment, Lisa should've been brainstorming job opportunities and calculating rent payments. Instead, she couldn't get the map and the note out of her head. Was that map official Lysent documentation? Did 'Mo' work for Lysent or for someone else?

Lisa focused her attention on the road as the light traffic began to react to something happening just ahead. Cars swerved to avoid a forest green pickup truck making its way across lanes with abandon. The light truck clipped a sedan before taking the righthand shoulder quickly, scraping along the heavy metal guard rail that separated highway travelers from marshy land. The rail did as designed, and the truck slowed to a stop against it.

Two cars, a blue truck and the white clipped sedan pulled up onto the shoulder behind the crashed vehicle. The occupant inside thrashed about, having some sort of fit. Blood splattered the window and windshield in some violent, bloody seizure.

Unsettled and not knowing how to help, Lisa drove on. A few minutes passed before she thought to call emergency services. She dialed 9-1-1 as she searched the side of the road for a mile marker to explain where they were. Even from here, she didn't dare look in her rearview mirror.

The busy signal from the emergency line startled her. Lisa hadn't heard such a thing in a long time. Others must be calling it in. Dozens of cars had passed the accident by now. Lisa tried one more time, but still received the uncomfortably loud and abrupt screeching noise.

Lisa was still trying to calm her nerves when her phone rang through the car's stereo system. It was a Georgia phone number, but not one she had saved on her contact list.

"Hello, this is Rosie with Lysent Corp. I was calling to confirm your interview with Mr. Randolph Ludington at our Victory location tomorrow at 8AM."

Her *Southern Gazette* interview was still lined up.

Lisa's mind rocketed back to the map. She considered her questions might only be answered at the facility itself. She could get in a lot of trouble if she performed the interview under false credentials, but if she uncovered illicit activities by the global corporation — credentials wouldn't matter.

All the thoughts and what-ifs bounced around in Lisa's head, but what came out of her mouth was, "Yes, I'll be there."

*   *   *

The next morning, Lisa crossed the Georgia state line then reluctantly exited onto a two-lane state highway. The dense forest of pine trees crowded either side of the road and the noise from the interstate was immediately silenced.

The scenery remained constant with only an occasional lone mailbox to mark a hidden residence. An hour passed before the forest abruptly ended for plowed farmland where brown shrubs squatted in rows. The remnant tufts of missed cotton on the thin branches should've given proof of earlier abundance, but instead somehow added to the area's desolation. A few older model trucks shared the road with her. They pulled to the side when she approached, letting the flashy SUV move on to its destination, which surely wasn't here.

They were correct. Lisa had spent her first eighteen years in Victory, Georgia — and she wasn't about to set up residence again.

She turned onto another state highway which was unmarked. This one only differed from the other in its evenly spaced signs warning pedestrians of their proximity to electrical train tracks. Lisa vaguely remembered Lysent choosing Victory based on some tax incentive. They had further negotiated federal funding, promising clean and sophisticated infrastructure. The silent electromagnetic trains fit that bill, although Lisa saw neither pedestrian nor train.

Most Lysent employees were not commuters, but lived with their families on campus. Campuses had gyms, schools, rec centers, childcare, and even a fantastic cafeteria to entice employees to stay long hours with little excuse to leave.

Lisa parked in the guest parking, and entered Lysent's pavilion through the gated entrance. Across, a white three-story building stood, modeled after traditional southern plantation mansions. The stately building with its tall columns and correspondingly tall windows had graced more than one Lysent magazine cover as the face of innovation and wellness. On the outer edges of the complex, massive factory-like buildings detracted from that image. Their white painted brick was too industrial. Large cooling towers interrupted the sky.

Between her and the Lysent mansion stood an almost overly tall cherub-ed fountain. The sprays of water appeared chaotic, but were cleverly and uniformly distributed. At the pool's edge, she picked up a small white pebble from the ground and dropped it into the pool. The jets pushed it this way and that until it settled on the bottom, anchoring her wish among the coins. She wasn't alone in the plaza, and one of the employees who walked behind her surprised her.

"Meet me in Lab E after your interview."

Lisa turned to catch a glimpse of the woman with short cropped brown hair as she walked away. When Lisa had replied to the email yesterday, she'd only earned a prompt 'undeliverable' error. It seemed Mo was this woman, and an employee of Lysent. Respecting the woman's dedication to covertness, Lisa didn't chase after her, but instead tossed another wishful pebble into the fountain for good measure.

Through the mansion's double-doored entrance, the lobby was just as bright and extravagant as the fountain outside. It was also largely empty with expansive white and gray marble covering walls and floor alike. A long, rich mahogany desk obstructed access to the building's deeper interior, outfitted with a shapely woman with straightened black hair, a wide nose, and eyes that cut sharply.

A formidable guard.

"How may I help you?" the woman asked as she set down a rather large stack of papers to her right.

"I'm Lisa Pearson with the *Southern Gazette* in Jacksonville. I have an appointment with Randolph Ludington."

The woman shuffled through a few papers scattered to her left, then looked Lisa up and down. "Ah, yes. He's running a little behind schedule at the moment. You can wait over there."

"Thank you... Rosie," replied Lisa, spotting the name plate underneath its shelter of fluorescent post-it-notes.

Rosie smiled at the effort, then teetered between the stacks of papers, perhaps trying to remember what she had been doing when Lisa walked in.

Thirty minutes and two offerings of coffee by Rosie passed before a waft of cologne preceded a man in the main entrance. He first spoke with Rosie, his back to Lisa. His professionally coiffed hair complemented his expensive business suit.

This had to be Randolph Ludington. And by 'running late,' Rosie meant he hadn't yet bothered to arrive. Lisa stood up and straightened her skirt just as Randolph turned in her direction. He smiled with bright white crocodile teeth and soon she was being directed out of the building with a heavy hand against her back.

"Ahh! The Zari virus. I'll show you how we're fighting back against the bugger."

Randolph escorted her around the fountain and into a large square building with frosted glass woven into a design among the white bricks. On the first floor, he opened a door to a darkened room and urged her inside, where a long two-way mirror partially lit the high tables and stools in front of her, most likely a setup for potential investors.

"Zari's a nasty one – head and body aches. In rare cases, there's brain swelling. That's unfortunately led to some of the deaths. One in St. Louis. A few in New York City. Developing a treatment is our highest priority," Randolph declared.

Lisa perched onto a stool and looked into the room on the other side, which had standard laboratory fare. Two scientists worked together, one using a microscope and the other doing work under an exhaust hood. They communicated quietly to each other, but Lisa expected it was a byproduct of their delicate work and not because they were being observed.

"These scientists are trying to isolate and study the Zari virus. By understanding its structure, we can create a treatment that will attach directly to the Zari viral particles for a targeted attack."

"Why can't people take a generic antiviral?"

"The public doesn't want generic medication anymore. They want something specifically for what they've got. We're still paying the price for the previous generation's over-prescription of general antibiotics. It created an environment for superbugs to emerge and thrive."

"What problems might arise from your current practices?"

Randolph laughed. "You don't have to worry about that. Under Lysent's umbrella of research and care we've learned so much about disease and the human immune system. Once a virus is identified and isolated, we can curb any potential epidemic in just a few short months." Even with his solid PR answer, Randolph seemed to sense the shift in the interview's tone. He ended with, "What paper are you with again?"

Before Lisa could form her answer, rapid footsteps echoed in a nearby stairwell, followed by a woman frantically rushing into the laboratory. Randolph was instantly at the door, flicking on the lights to their room so that the people in the laboratory could see he and Lisa were on the other side. The newcomer muffled noises of surprise before half croaking, "Mr. Ludington, I was going to see you next. We need you upstairs."

"—seems important," Lisa remarked before offering her hand. "Thank you for your time. I really appreciate it."

The alarmed scientists abandoned their work. Scanning their badges at the door, they disappeared up the secure stairwell. Randolph escorted Lisa out of the building, making mention of global healthcare standards and serving and protecting their customers, before joining the woman holding the door at the stairwell.

Once outside, Lisa recovered her bearings. Laboratory E was a squatty building which looked more like an afterthought than a planned annex of the larger laboratory complex. As Lisa wondered what she'd do once inside besides ask, "Does Mo work here?" a woman sitting on a nearby bench motioned her over. The woman had dark cropped hair – the same woman who'd spoken to her this morning – this was 'Mo'.

Mo had petite features which seemed to be melting with anxiety. She stood up before shaking Lisa's hand. Lisa was a head taller, but they both carried the same thin frame.

"Millo Cromwell," she squeaked. "Sorry for all the cloak and dagger," but even as she apologized she hurried around the bench and farther into the greenspace behind it.

Partway inside the miniature park, Millo confessed. "We weren't supposed to get promotions at the same time. It's against company policy."

"We?"

"Me and my husband, Stuart. It was just some oversight. We didn't bring it to anyone's attention, because we earned the promotions independently and hey – it's extra money, right?"

Millo paused for reassurance or maybe permission. Lisa nodded.

"I was modeling infection rates through populations. On the other side of the campus, Stuart was performing profit analysis for antiviral treatments, but we were both working on the *same project*."

"Sure, both those tasks seem appropriate for a company like Lysent—" started Lisa.

"That's what we said, but when we combined our data we got *those lines* for the Zari virus."

"No," Lisa asserted. "The chances of that… they'd have to actually *use* your data to…" She didn't even want to finish the sentence.

Millo nodded, ominously encouraging her.

Confusion and doubt shadowed Lisa's face. "The company is distributing viruses then selling their cure? Is that even profitable?"

"Financially, the worst thing Lysent ever did was eradicate those chronic diseases. Healthcare used to be an eight-trillion-dollar business. Now it's what, three? Yes, according to Stuart's profit analysis – the sector has a lot of potential."

"Why are you telling *me*? You know I'm just with a city newspaper, right?" – not to mention, she wasn't.

"I know, and you're so young too," she hesitated, her face wrinkled in worry. "You look even younger than your staff photo, but I didn't want to risk reaching out to anyone else. We have a daughter. We live here. Lysent owns the internet service, the phone service. That cell tower over there belongs to them. God, maybe this wasn't a good idea…"

If Millo's accusations were true, it made sense that she couldn't trust getting the word out safely. This was a story worth more than Lisa's 9-5 job. When it broke, the whole world would be watching. "No, I can do it. But, I'm going to need more than that file."

"Why?"

"Because if I post that map, people are going to assume it's just aggregated and predicted data. Then, Lysent will modify their strategy so that the 'predictions' don't even come true. It's going to be near impossible to convince people that the company that makes them feel better is making them sick beforehand. We need more proof, and I need you and your husband to speak out against the company. You need to report what you've seen and what you've been asked to do."

"Ohh, no, I can't do that." Millo pressed her hand to her mouth as if she were silencing herself even now. "Maybe if we didn't have our little girl, but we do. We just can't."

There hadn't been a lot of opportunity at the *Southern Gazette* to learn persuasion techniques. Never had she had to convince someone to do an interview or to provide information considered proprietary, but she had argued plenty with Gentry over their duty to uncover any truths, no matter how uncomfortable it made anyone else. Hell, that's why she and her mother had such a bad relationship.

"Lysent is manipulating the country's health – your daughter is already in danger. This is beyond your job, where you're going to live, where your daughter will go to school—"

"No, I've given you the file. I've talked to you. That's enough. Besides, maybe I'm wrong. There's no way my company would do this…"

"I didn't think the military would lie about my father's death, but it doesn't mean the entire military is bad. I'm sure Lysent is the same. They do a lot of good, but anything that's wrong needs to be rooted out. Help me find more," Lisa pleaded.

The woman shook her head and began walking out of the park. Not wanting to burn the bridge – her only bridge – Lisa caught up and gave her a quick hug. "Thanks. I know you risked a lot sending me that file. I'll do what I can."

Millo, surprised, left in a nervous daze.

*　　*　　*

Lisa immediately returned to the building she'd toured with Randolph. It wouldn't be long before Millo noticed her access badge was missing. With a quick scan, the stairwell door opened and Lisa closed it quietly behind her. The second floor appeared identical to the first, so Lisa opened the door marked *Observation* and found another darkened room with a two-way mirror overlooking the circumstances that required Mr. Ludington's attention.

Everyone in the room wore more protective gear than a surgeon might wear, but Lisa still recognized some of the faces behind the masks. Randolph stood behind several scientists gathered around a single subject, a man writhing against thick restraints strapping his wrists and ankles to a gurney.

Lisa's first thought was to rush in for a rescue, but his behavior soon frightened her more than the presence of his sinister caretakers. Drenched in sweat and overcome by massive coughing fits, he arched his back, contorted his shoulders, and craned his neck, jaw reaching for his captors.

"And you say they're all acting like this?" Randolph chuckled.

Pulling out her phone, Lisa began recording.

"Some of them, yeah. We think the virus has mutated somehow. What should we do?"

"People are going to lose their shit when their kid comes down with this. We'll be able to charge anything for our antiviral."

The others in the room exchanged some pained glances, but nothing more.

"OK, this is all the ketamine we have in-house. It's enough to kill two of us, and maybe a small horse," said someone from the corner of the room, drawing clear fluid into a syringe.

Several scientists, including the spastic messenger who had fetched Randolph, closed in so that the drug could be administered. Another violent fit took over the subject, knocking several people off balance. The messenger, an Asian woman, was knocked into the top of the gurney. She threw out her arm to catch herself, and the mouth finally found its captive.

Her coat sleeve was coated in blood and saliva when she yanked her arm free. Holding her injured arm, she made a mad dash out of the room as she had also lost her respiratory mask in the scuffle. Randolph only laughed at the scene. Moments later the drug was administered and the subject stopped fighting, sedated and confused but clearly able to handle the supposedly large dose.

This footage alone would prompt an extensive investigation by the government, not to mention the public outrage. Trembling, Lisa slipped out of the room, down the hall, and into the stairwell.

Before she reached the first floor landing, a shout came from above. Instinctively Lisa looked up right into Randolph's face, red and contorted in anger.

Damn.

Lisa rushed for the exterior door, but Randolph was fast. He caught up to her and dug his meaty fingers into her arm. She squealed in pain and twisted from his grasp as they stumbled through the doorway and into the plaza.

Having caught the attention of a couple eating lunch by the fountain, Randolph hesitated. Lisa took the opportunity to sprint to the parking lot. In the distance she could hear Randolph shouting to nearby security guards.

Lisa's tires squealed as she pulled out of the parking space toward the lot's exit. Heaving heavily, she fought a stitch in her side and adrenaline's desire to eject her stomach's contents onto the dash. Without warning, a figure darted from among the parked vehicles and Lisa's windshield caught the mangled body of a woman. Lisa slammed on her brakes in an awful delayed reaction. As the vehicle lurched to a stop, the slumped body slid off the hood and onto the road with a heavy thunk. Shocked, Lisa stared, unseeingly, through her cracked windshield. Everything seemed silenced – senses on hold.

Slowly, a bloodied head rose into view. Arms reaching over the grill, the woman pulled her body back onto the hood. Even with injuries, Lisa recognized the scientist who'd lost her mask. She'd since lost her lab coat too, but it was her. Or, something like her.

Now crouched like a spider, the woman launched herself onto the windshield and began her attack, bashing head, limb, and body. She clawed and jawed at the glass, seeking out Lisa. Her eyes had grayed over, except for bloodshot vessels that visibly pulsed. Her behavior was undeniably like the man on the gurney. Was this the Zari virus?

Suddenly the woman jerked her head as something else caught her eye. Leaping off the SUV, she ran deeper into the parking lot. Alone, Lisa could now hear shouting. Despite all her senses telling her otherwise, little time had actually passed. Not knowing what else to do, Lisa pulled onto the highway, leaving Randolph, Lysent, and whatever had just happened in the dust.

*　*　*

Lisa teetered on the edge of panic. Her heart threatened to pound out of her chest. Her hands and limbs had gone clammy with sweat. She couldn't think about how the Zari-infected shared some of those same qualities. She'd lose it, run off the road, and into some embankment or tree. She had to stay calm. Other disturbing thoughts rose to take its place. She'd given Millo her business card, but had never received contact information in return. Lisa couldn't warn her that Randolph could connect them, or that the virus was morphing into something truly terrifying.

The streets narrowed, the houses shrank, as did the spaces between them. Without anywhere to go, Lisa was halfway to her mother's house before she realized where she was heading. There was no way she'd be able to drive back to Jacksonville in this condition, and there was no chance of driving back to Lysent – her childhood home seemed one of very few options.

The little grungy white box of a house looked like it always had, although now a thin layer of grime coated the bleached vinyl of the window awnings. Lisa always imagined they were originally bright blue, but the sun had faded them long before her father, Peter moved a pregnant Kelly Ann into the house. By the time Lisa had arrived, Peter had already been deployed and killed in an 'area of conflict.' Kelly Ann didn't have any other ties to the town – or even the state, but she considered it too difficult to leave with an infant in tow.

And twenty-three years later, that's where she'd remained.

Lisa pulled in behind her mother's sedan on the gravel ribbons that served as the driveway in the front of the house. It wasn't until she switched off the ignition that she considered that going inside might not provide any sanctuary or rest.

Her mother already had the front door open. "Have you ever heard of calling?" she scolded.

Kelly Ann was simply an older version of Lisa, which seemed fitting since her father wasn't in the picture. They were the same height and both a bit too thin. Kelly's blond hair had lightened a bit and her complexion had earned a few more sunspots, but they were near the same.

"I'm sorry. I was in town for a story, and I need a place to regroup. Could I come in for a bit?"

Kelly Ann didn't answer, but she left the door open as she disappeared inside. Lisa was surprised she received that much of a welcome.

Stepping inside, a swirl of relief and discontentment flooded Lisa. The house was tidier than she remembered, which might have something to do with the absence of a messy child. The thin plank hardwood floor had faded and aged, and still made the same dry creaks when she stepped on it. The worn runner that led to the kitchen had been replaced with a new one. Its bright colors and plushness contrasted with the rest of the town. It would take years for it to earn its place. The kitchen overlooked the small white plaster living room. There, a television with bunny ears and an ancient loveseat rested.

With no further greeting, Kelly Ann busied herself in the kitchen making a fresh pot of coffee among the numerous plastic bottles that helped to combat Kelly Ann's often lingering illnesses. Having been gone for five years, Lisa couldn't help but wander the narrow hallway.

Her mom's door was closed, like always. Lisa had very few memories of being in there. Her father's death should have brought them closer, but Lisa had always felt the distance keenly. The door to her former room was also shut. Lisa pushed on it firmly to get past the sticky point that had always prevented a good angst-filled slam.

Her room was exactly how she'd left it – or exactly how it'd been when she was kicked out, if Lisa was being honest. She didn't know what she expected, really – that maybe her mom had redone the room for a different purpose, or at least had tossed a bunch of junk in the room over the years. Instead, Lisa could have very likely been the last person to go through that doorway. Lisa wasn't sure if it being forgotten was better or worse than it being replaced.

Lisa put a hand on the bed's pink flowered quilt. It was dusty and its edges were fraying, but still the bed looked welcoming and Lisa's body felt heavy, so she sat. This bit of comfort tugged at Lisa, and she blinked away a couple of tears. This was no time to rest. Millo's family was in danger until the story broke. The truth had torn Lisa's family apart, but it would keep Millo's family safe.

Lisa couldn't recall when she first started doubting the story surrounding her father's death. She was young, and it was something she thought about constantly as it had shaped her life before she even had life. If her father had survived, maybe they'd have been a normal, happy family.

Graduating high school, Lisa used her father's GI Bill benefits to secure admission to a school in Florida, as well as buy a laptop for her studies. It was with that laptop that Lisa was able to investigate the story that never quite added up in her mind.

The US Army had told her mother that Peter had died in combat, but after months of research Lisa found he'd been shot by friendly fire and hadn't even died immediately. He was taken to a Lysent care facility. When he passed away there, Lysent and the US government covered up the accident, giving Kelly Ann a noble story to cling to and tearfully declare.

When Lisa uncovered the truth, she thought her mother would want to know. Why wouldn't she? But she didn't. She preferred the story the government had told her. Worse, she believed Lisa was slandering their family – dishonoring her father to deliberately embarrass Kelly Ann. She kicked Lisa out of the house weeks before school began. Lisa bummed rides and then slept in a tent outside her school until it opened up for classes.

There she was able to get some reprieve. She studied journalism, and eventually got her job at the *Southern Gazette*. Her experience uncovering a US military lie while in high school should've impressed Dawson Gentry, but he thought along the same lines as her mother — she'd revealed something unnecessary for her own gain. Lisa couldn't reveal something for truth's sake, but that was going to change now.

Hard-lined into the house's ethernet, Lisa entered her credentials to log in to the *Southern Gazette's* file server. She was promptly denied. They must have removed her from the system. She didn't have time for this. She called Gentry's direct office line.

"What the hell is going on?" Gentry near shouted when he realized Lisa was on the other end of the line.

"Sorry—" Lisa wasn't sure what she was apologizing for, but she had done a lot of things out of line today. It wouldn't matter in a few moments.

"You took that interview with Lysent!" It was more of a statement than a question.

"Oh, that, yeah—"

"And now we're under fire for that woman you hit with your car! The police are looking for you. You need to turn yourself in."

Lisa almost dropped the phone then demanded Gentry explain.

"There's footage of you running over a woman!"

"That's not what happened," Lisa stuttered. "I have video for you. Lysent's experimenting on humans and releasing viruses. That woman—"

"Stop. I do not want to hear it. You're wanted by the police. The police! In another state. We released a statement that you were fired yesterday and weren't authorized for any interviews. No one is going to take your story. Please turn yourself in," Gentry said before hanging up.

The world was falling apart around Lisa, and no one cared to listen.

The police would be there any minute, causing Kelly Ann great embarrassment. Her arrest in the house would be the end of their relationship. She could at least go outside. Lisa returned to the kitchen. Kelly Ann was holding the coffee pot in one hand and a small remote in the other. The television set displayed security footage of a black SUV in the Lysent Corp parking lot striking a woman, then a clip of her driving off.

"I didn't—" Lisa started.

"Get out," Kelly Ann finished.

Lisa was quick to obey, and surprised there were not police officers surrounding the house when she stepped out. Driving off, she began to work out the nearest police station to turn herself in. No one cared about what truth she knew. Like Gentry said, her only story could be hit and run until her name was cleared – and by then, it might not matter at all.

When Lisa's phone rang, she recognized it as a local number, but not one she had saved.

"Lisa? It's Millo," said the panicked voice on the other end.

"Oh God, I've got to tell you someth—" blurted Lisa, but Millo cut her off.

"They took Ryder," Millo whimpered. "My daughter... they took her."

A pit grew in Lisa's stomach.

"You stole my badge and now they think I'm involved. Mr. Ludington is demanding all his intellectual property be returned. He's keeping Ryder safe until then. I didn't want any of this! You need to get back here and do everything that man wants."

*   *   *

Lisa sped back to Lysent. The SUV kicked up dust and gravel as it rumbled through some rough patches. The road was eerily quiet when Lisa thought there should be emergency services, state troopers, and field teams for the Centers for Disease Control. With no one to listen, there was no one to help, and Lisa felt a bit like a strange, large beast crashing through the thick Georgia pines.

A few miles south of corporate headquarters, something else hit Lisa's vehicle, slamming into the driver's side window with a startling crack before falling away. Lisa let out a scream in surprise, but managed to keep her steering wheel straight as her passenger side tires slipped off the narrow road. Her vehicle grumbled to a stop and she couldn't hear the engine's hum over the blood pulsing in her ears.

Lisa stole a fearful glance to her side. A wide track of fluids streaked across the cracked glass, encouraging the acidic taste of bile to creep up the edges of her throat and rest beside her tongue. Her entire body shook with adrenaline and fear as she searched for the release on her seatbelt. She wasn't about to be charged with another hit and run. She needed to know.

She hadn't yet found the courage when it slammed itself against the window with nearly the same force as before.

This time, Lisa saw.

She screamed as the body charged her window again.

"Please, stop! Let me get you help."

The former scientist made no gesture of understanding, and she did not stop. The thunk and crack of head or window filled Lisa with helpless terror. She started her vehicle and attempted to get back on the road, but one of her tires spun to no avail.

As the woman pulled back again, the impact on her face and on the window could be seen. The crack in the laminated glass had spread, patterned like a spider web. Blood seeped along its edges like thin tributaries. Beyond the glass, two grayed eyes stared empty and wild, hedged with liquified mascara. Her jaw hung awkwardly, and her swollen, mangled nose had drifted to one side. With another strike even those features deteriorated.

"STOP!" Lisa screamed. She cried. Tears coursed down her cheeks. She reached into her bag for her phone to call someone – anyone. She found her phone and a small round canister.

Pepper spray.

The screech of a busy signal was all Lisa received from dialing 9-1-1. Perhaps that's why the police had not apprehended her already. Here was her proof she hadn't killed this woman, and little good that did. Pressing through the break in the glass, the scientist's face was arguably within the vehicle now. If Lisa did nothing, she'd be physically assaulted in due time. The news report had called her a liar, a thief, and a killer. Those words burned inside her, like all the lies she'd fought. Her father didn't die in combat. Why didn't Gentry listen? Why didn't her mother care?

But it seemed this was the only way she was going to survive. She would have to become some of those lies. And she'd have to turn in the footage to Lysent, leaving her with no proof this woman had been infected by something in Lysent's lab, or even that Lysent had motivation to defame her.

This was it. Her chance to survive. Her chance to protect something other than the truth.

Lisa pressed the button on the pepper spray, shooting it directly into the woman's face. Spray-back came fast. Lisa shut her eyes tightly and turned her head, but she was determined to keep spraying until she heard the other woman retreat or until the canister emptied. Soon the stream diminished, and the remainder ran down her hand and arm.

Her face swelled and burned like hell. She wanted to rip out her own eyeballs. Dropping the canister, she grabbed her bag and wiped her face with the leather, then her right sleeve, then her headrest. She kept her distance from the window as her attacker had not left.

Eventually Lisa was able to crack an eye open. The other woman's eyes were bulging from their reddened sockets, any remaining soft features had swelled – much like Lisa had imagined hers had. Lisa had had enough.

Finding the keys in the ignition, Lisa started up the SUV. Immediately air blasted through the vents, exacerbating the spray's effects. Lisa slapped at the vent before realizing how close she'd come to her attacker. Leaping back, she grabbed her leather bag and positioned it in the hole. She could feel the woman jawing at the bag. Lisa gave it a little punch, hitting an open mouth but securing the bag's position.

Fear shook her body, and she came down on the gas pedal harder than she intended. The passenger tire spun. Lisa clenched the steering wheel and tried again, pressing on the gas in intervals to cause the vehicle to rock forward and backward. Eyes screwed shut, she worked by feel, and soon the wheel climbed out of its ditch.

Lisa did her best not to consider what was happening on the other side of her car door as she inched her vehicle down the road. Growls, snaps, and snarls of all sorts featured, and with each thump, Lisa started. Eventually the woman fell.

With a bit of gas, her back tire eased over the mass, and although Lisa had now managed to open her eyes, she didn't dare look back. Picking up speed, she arrived at Lysent Corp a few minutes later, her bag still sticking partly out of the window. Lisa stumbled into the Lysent plaza, where she promptly stuck her head into the fountain. She could feel the left side of her face was swollen, despite it all feeling aflame. She scrubbed. It got worse before it got better, and it didn't get better by much. But eventually she could breathe freely and her eyes opened enough to see the coins shimmering at the bottom of the fountain.

"Ms. Pearson?" asked a voice behind her. Lisa wobbled as she tried to stand, and Millo grabbed her arm.

"Did you really hit that woman with your car? What's going on?" demanded a man beside Millo, likely Millo's husband.

"The virus has mutated – has made people go crazy. I'm going to get your daughter then you're going to leave this place." She grabbed her keys on the fountain's wall and shoved them into Millo's hand. "It's a bla—, oh, you'll see. Bring it here."

Without another word or question, Millo and her husband rushed to comply.

* * *

Lisa found Randolph Ludington in the observation room on the second floor, which looked into the laboratory that formerly housed the first Zari-infected Lisa had seen. Now, it held several. The man who'd been tied to the gurney had been upturned. He writhed on the floor, reaching for the ankles of his captors. However, they were no longer performing experiments. They seemed just as ill, and paced the room, disoriented.

Beyond Randolph, a young girl was seated at a corner table. Her back was to the mirror and a book had been placed open in front of her, but she mostly quivered in fear. Lisa was unsure of her age, but she looked petite for it, like her mother. Her hair was a dirty blond, but it likely would match her mother's someday. Ryder stole a glance at the newcomer, but Lisa was only another stranger.

Randolph remained fixated on the two-way mirror.

"It's not too late to help them – to fix this," Lisa said, breaking the silence.

"Oh, it was too late decades ago. Lysent managed the most innovative scientists and the very best doctors for a time. We cured several chronic diseases that had plagued the modern world. And because we were good at our jobs – other companies and even government healthcare fell to the wayside. And when we decided to invest in other industries, the government told us we were obligated to provide care, and more so, we needed to lower the prices of our more profitable treatments. They admired how we grew and prospered, then told us to continue that model would be amoral. Typical government, right? But Lysent adapts."

The newcomer and conversation had riled the other room's occupants. They pressed upon the glass, upon each other, and eventually they'd break through the glass. That much she knew.

A shiver wound up Lisa's spine. "You *meant* to do this?"

"Well, not entirely. And this new vector of transmission is… exquisite. We've never seen behavior like this, but in retrospect, it makes perfect sense." Randolph spoke with adoration, almost awe, evoking a peculiar fear in Lisa. He pulled back his dark suit jacket sleeve to reveal a quickly deteriorating bite wound on his arm.

He only laughed when Lisa gasped. "You forget, I've got the antiviral, soon to be flying off the shelves in a store near you. Now, do you have my video?"

She did. Lisa wondered what the impact would be if she turned around now and posted it online. If people knew where the disease had started and how it might spread – millions of lives could be saved. The deep pit in her stomach that had taken up residence hours ago told Lisa one life could be saved – now. And it was far more important than any broadcast.

She'd reached Ryder by now. The girl slipped her small hand into Lisa's and gripped it fiercely. Her body pressed into Lisa's as if she could disappear and find safety. The potential to save lives, to clear her name, to declare the truth – none of it mattered. It didn't matter one bit.

Lisa set her phone atop the child's open book.

Their movement toward the door seemed to empower Ryder. "He did this," the girl accused.

"I know, but we can't do anything about it here."

"I'm afraid you can't be anywhere *but* here," sneered Randolph, grabbing Lisa's arm, digging into muscle.

Lisa used her reaction time to push Ryder out the door. "Your parents are at the gate. Go! Go without me!"

The girl wailed as she bounded down the stairs.

SCHWACK!

A body hit the window…

SCHWACK!

It hit again.

* * *

Once Randolph had barricaded the door, he returned to watching his keep. Lisa sat at a table, looking through the exterior window. The plaza was not any less chaotic as the illness began to claim its hosts. Lisa had achieved nothing she'd set out to do. She had meant to broadcast the truth, instead she'd been attacked and discredited. She'd wanted to break a story, but stories didn't matter anymore.

By the time Lisa managed an escape, her vehicle was long gone. The family was safe. Lisa started on foot toward her mother's house. She'd help and protect her, no matter what it cost.

BOOK ONE

CHASING A CURE

R.M. HAMRICK

1 Forest

Audra looked past the makeshift shelter to the soft drops of rain. She knew it could devolve into a sudden storm and bring down their hovel of fence sections and tree branches. But for now, it was almost pleasant. Audra imagined the place would not be much smaller with a collapse. The three inhabitants already crawled on top of each other. For a moment, she took a deep breath and appreciated the structure's ability to hide them from the biters, and the rain's patter to mask her mom's quiet groans and her older sister's whimpers.

Now was as good a time as any.

In the isolated wood with no biters in sight, Audra turned her attention to her mother's leg. The pant leg had been cut to her high thigh weeks ago to dress the wound. It had been redressed several times now, but it was still difficult to separate the flesh from the dressing. Her dad's quick actions had stopped the bleeding at the scene, but now Audra wished upon everything it would bleed again. Instead a smelly, hot ooze had taken over. Dad was gone now, but Audra did not need his life's wisdom to know the same incident that took his life would also take her mom's.

As Audra cleaned the wound, her dark auburn hair fell over her green eyes, despite its sticky dirt and grease. Her mom allowed her to help today. A few days before, she had sent them away, in order to cut out the dying flesh and drain the wound herself. She had wanted to protect her twelve- and sixteen-year-old girls from the harshness of near-death, but Audra would have been able to handle it. She was always stoic, even before all this happened, never crying over scraped knees or unfair treatment. But still, her mother had insisted that she did not need to cut dead tissue from a wound. Now Belinda lay in her mother's arms, positioned away from the injured leg. The daughter gazed into her mother's face, searching for comfort. She didn't notice how warm her mother had gotten or what was unfolding around her.

It wasn't even a bite.

It was just an infected cut, maybe from a poor machete swing. No one remembered in the frenzy of the attack. And wandering through the woods with no supplies, it was impossible to keep it clean. The cleaning and re-wrapping were a futile effort. No sterile sutures or bandaging, no antibiotics. They did not even have clean water. Audra assessed the wound one last time and decided. She met her mom's eyes. The infection had not taken the grit from them. She nodded her agreement above Belinda's head, out of her sight. It was not supposed to happen this way. As a family, they had survived the initial outbreak. They were surviving. Their days had become routine, normal. Audra packed without a word to her sister, careful to hide items of comfort behind for their mother.

Now a new normal would take over.

It was not long before Belinda noticed the change in routine and her panic floated to the surface. It was never far. The mom held her oldest tight and gave her small kisses on her forehead. Belinda's cries only got louder. Once again, she looked to her youngest.

"Take care of your sister. You're all she has left."

Audra nodded her promise and continued packing supplies. The rain might stop soon and they would need plenty of time to set up camp before night fell.

A noise stopped her rummaging.

Belinda whimpered and her mother hushed her. Outside, one crept past, none the wiser of the lean-to in the rain. Audra watched from inside. The zombie's jaw, unhinged and off-center, gathered water. The skin on his face was swollen and distended from his time spent exposed. His pant leg caught on a root as he walked past. With his leg dragging, the mirror image of her mother soon wandering the woods came unbidden.

*   *   *

"Look, dude. I saw him first," Audra shouted into the woods toward the man.

She caught side glimpses of him through the brush. He was easy to spot with a large green backpack slowing him down. Her first pursuer was directly behind her. All six feet of him seemed to lean forward from his ankles to reach her. A blood stain darkened the arm of his business suit. He was a perfect specimen aside from a small tear at the corner of his mouth. Nothing a few stitches couldn't fix. His shambling chase did not worry Audra. The man running alongside them in the isolated woods did. She stole another glance and tried to size him up. She did not recognize him or know his intentions, but he was trying to cut them off.

This newcomer could foil her plan to take off around a hill bend and come back behind the zom to tag him with her biometric reader. He could cut over to snipe her find. Whoever scanned first received Finder's Rights. All was fair in the game of tagging, but that didn't mean she wouldn't be pissed. This was her find.

She would at least make it more difficult for him.

Audra picked up speed and teased her zom to follow. Soon they were moving at a quick pace. She could hear both men in the heavy woods laboring to keep up, tripping, and bumbling. The backpack was too big for chases through the branches and brambles. No wonder he was trying to poach her find. And this was a good one. He looked like he came from a wealthy family. Someone could be looking for him.

She heard a big "Oomph" followed by a crash. One of them had tripped hard. Audra glanced back again. The zombie, nonplussed by the sound, still focused on her backside. With his visual and olfactory senses locked in, hearing became less important. She veered to the left, away from their fallen pursuer. A minute later she looked back and saw no signs of him. She noticed her zombie's shoe had fallen off. His black-socked foot stomped over rocks and sticks.

She did not want to damage the goods.

She took off into a sprint and disappeared behind a big oak tree. The zombie grunted in anger and continued in his same direction, not having enough reasoning skills to change his mind. As he passed the oak tree, Audra was ready with her silver handheld reader. She scraped the sharp comb along the back of the neck, above his falling suit collar. He turned, and she fended him off as she retracted the comb into the device for analysis. She elbowed him. When he twisted around, she kicked the back of his knee. He fell to the ground, face smashing first.

She sat on his back. Her foot contacted the back of his head, more to muffle his angry noises than to keep herself safe. She pulled out a prickly pear pad from her bag to munch on while she waited for the reader to analyze the DNA.

BING, BING came the beautiful sound, the sound of money.

"Let's see who wants to pay for you, my friend," she directed toward the zom underfoot with a renewed smile on her face. The thought of his torn mouth flashed into her mind. She should not push his face too far into the ground. He was worth money now, and the better his physical condition, the better the payout.

The readout display had text stats on her find. Every person's DNA had been cataloged for almost 25 years before the outbreak. And now that information was used to determine if your corpse body would be awakened or if you would continue to roam the countryside, a remnant of your former self. Today was her and Randolph Ludington's lucky day.

Name: Randolph Ludington
Gender: Male
DOB: 5/29/2043
Status: Deposit paid

There were three potential status findings: No Inquiries, Inquired, and Deposit Paid. A deposit started the wake-up process - if, by process, you meant negotiation.

Audra punched the FOUND key as she settled onto her zombie seat. The usual survey followed, documenting body condition, difficulty of capture (in this case, already captured), and distance from Lysent headquarters. Audra typed in the answers as she chewed on the end of the cactus pad. It was her last prepared one. She would have to be on the lookout for more.

It would take a while for Lysent to contact the depositor and negotiate a price. She surveyed her surroundings. Was the stranger still lurking around to snatch her zom? Technically now that she had pressed FOUND, she was the only one entitled to the corporation's payout through Finder's Rights. But there were always loopholes. If poaching was enticing earlier, it was now even more tempting. Any zombie with 'No Inquiry' status would be left to roam with a yellow serial tag on his ear. Audra's attachment to him showed his value. It was time to find a camp, away from here and close to water.

She leaned forward, moving from her rear to a kneel, pushing each knee into a shoulder. She inched the bartered handmade leather mask over his face, taking care that her fingers did not slip near his teeth. One bite and she would be infected and wandering the woods, too. Some taggers removed the teeth, and the awakened person would be given dentures afterward. Keeping him intact would yield a better payout. Audra tightened the lacing of the mask and finished with a Carrick bend like her father had taught her. She got off the zom's back and pulled up on the knot to bring him to his knees. The mask had an eye slot, but for now, she threw a small cloth sack over his head to block his view and calm him. He could still smell her though. The mask muffled his noises, but his arms reached wide to find the source of the smell. She grabbed and bound his hands in front of him with soft, wide cloth to prevent injuries to his limbs. Prices dropped fast with amputations. The cure could not regrow limbs or extensive tissue. She hitched a long lead to his binding.

With his arms bound and his nickname chosen, Audra pulled the cloth sack off Randy's head so they could walk without stumbling - too much.

Audra knew the Georgia woods, or what was left of Georgia. Really, the only townships this far south belonged to Lysent. The goal was a secluded spot where she could start a fire and have a nice campsite without being found by others. If she was stuck with Randy for a few days, at least she should be able to enjoy it. Sometimes she would travel with a zom toward Lysent before a negotiation's end, but the date of Randy's deposit was old. His family's circumstances may have changed. She wanted to be out here if his deal did not go through. The land near Lysent was already well hunted. Besides, Randy was so demure, she could handle at least one more zombie if she found it in time. She was sure Randy would love another travel buddy.

Audra was stuck working for Lysent. Most of the time, money never exchanged hands between her and the corporation. She had indebted herself to them as an indentured tagger. She could ask for a payout when she needed to buy items, but it lengthened her employment. It seemed like a never-ending battle anyway, as she incurred more debt each day.

Audra tried not to think about it.

Randy grunted as he caught on a high root that Audra had missed. The rope gave a quick tug and Audra jumped ahead to miss his fall. Over the last two years, she had become adept at feeling the tautness and looseness of her lead. His cadence, the vibrations of his steps, his unfortunate scent all gave her information.

They walked eight miles plus another two to find a good camping spot. Audra controlled most of the conversation. She tried to guess Randy's occupation before his unfortunate accident (Were you a stockbroker, Randy?). His suit gave away that he was in the initial outbreak. Once people learned there was a disease sweeping the country that turned you into a cannibal, they stopped donning suits. She complimented him on his obviously successful efforts to stay in one piece. Most of his colleagues had since decomposed beyond what was salvageable.

The conversation ended for a while as Audra set up camp. She tied him to a thick sapling, threw down her pop up tent, and gathered wood for her fire. As she roasted her found hickory nuts, the sun set behind the trees and the woods darkened. She set her eyes on the fire, but kept her ears on the forest past the fire's crackle and Randy's shuffling. Was someone out there? Another zombie would be nice, another tagger would be bad, to wildlife she was neutral. Any large predators had plenty to eat with the zombies walking around. They were easier prey.

"I wish we had marshmallows to toast, Randy. Do you remember marshmallows?"

Zombies required nutrition, but marshmallows wouldn't cut it. The virus stimulated the brain's hunger response only toward non-infected humans, as a way for it to spread through the bodily fluid exchange of bites. The virus attacked higher brain structures, leaving parts responsible for survival and basic movement functioning. The heart pumped. The lungs breathed. And the five senses seemed intact. But it all happened at a slower pace. The slowed breathing and heart rate diminished the amount of oxygen delivered to the body. The bodies began to look dead, sagging and decaying. With their bodies running at such low capacities, it took an extended amount of time for them to starve to death, over a year in fact by Lysent's estimations. The cure couldn't awaken the actual dead, only those infected with the virus.

When had Randy eaten last? She wondered.

* * *

"I wish we had marshmallows to toast," said Audra.

Her voice tried to lighten the mood, but her eyes remained dark staring at the sparks coming off the fire. Belinda hunched over the fire Audra had built, crying like she had for the last three days. Her blond hair clung to her face with the wetness, her peripheral vision lost. Audra did not know you could shed that many tears and still maintain your eyeballs' shape. At least the tears streamed without noisy broadcast, only an odd sniffle timed with footfalls as she followed Audra through the woods. Audra offered her water again to compensate for the continual dehydration from her eyes. Belinda swiped and yanked the bottle from her hand. Her eyes like wet ice, flashed with anger.

"How can you even think about sweets?"

Audra ignored the comment. She had ignored a lot of comments in the three days since they had left their mother. Despite that having been their mom's idea and insistence, Belinda blamed Audra. She had forced Belinda to desert her mother and now they were alone. Audra did not cry, and that angered Belinda, but Belinda did enough crying for the both of them. Someone needed to stay aware and her mom had chosen her.

No reason to set up their crappy makeshift tarp-on-sticks. There would be no rain tonight. Audra took all their soft things and put them on the ground in a pile. The navy sky filled with stars and planets. That was one of the few good things to emerge from the loss of the modern world. No more light pollution. Satellites flew through the dome of visible space. They kept their orbits, useless and irrelevant.

Belinda moved from her spot and curled up against Audra. Her head felt heavy on Audra's chest. Her hair tickled her nose. Her body felt warm and soft.

"I love you, Audra."

The words were whispered into her chest, almost inaudible. It was hard to stay mad at her. Her blue eyes would go wide at any sign of trouble and her body would freeze. She bubbled with emotion and fear. The new world only amplified these characteristics. But it was easy to care for the beautiful girl with the sweet smile. Audra often forgot herself that Belinda was four years her senior. She cared for her like a younger sister.

"I love you," Audra repeated as she closed her eyes and enjoyed the brief reprieve.

*   *   *

Audra's eyes opened with the dawn. She could not imagine sleeping through the deafening roar of the birds. Even the late ones woke with the sun. Audra peeled herself off the floor and threw her pack outside. She broke down the tent and put it in her bag. Even having a "camp" meant being ready to run at a moment's notice. It had taken months to find a tent, and she was not about to abandon it because of some damn zom herd. She said good morning to Randy and asked if he would like any coffee. He declined, which was a good thing because she had none. Coffee beans were expensive as hell. And not fresh.

Audra disliked coffee as a child before the outbreak. She had not grown to enjoy it as an expensive, watered-down luxury.

Audra pulled her food down from where she had hung it from a tree. Despite plenty of slow-moving flesh, bears still went for easy picnic baskets. She opened the pack and did the math. Math and food had become second nature to her. She knew how much she needed to eat each day to be comfortable. She did not double-check her math when she came up short. She was always short, but she did not need much today - no running if she could help it. She decided to forage for breakfast.

She told Randy to guard their empty camp spot. On second thought, she dropped him to the ground and bound his feet. She did not want him making too much noise with another runner around. Pain in the ass Randy. He was such a good walker though. She secured his limbs and let him rest on the forest floor. She pulled on her pack and began exploring.

The forest exploded with nuts and berries with the late spring weather. She collected her favorites along with some greens. She snacked on them as she continued around the area, looking for signs of another zombie or human. A mile out, she saw signs of trampling as if a zom or a careless hiker had passed through… or both. The question was soon answered.

The unmistakable "Rawnrerr" of a zombie and the grunts of a human echoed through the forest. The human sounded like he was struggling. Audra deftly maneuvered downhill to the source of the noises. Her scent was upwind, but Audra would have been surprised if anyone noticed. They were busy.

Audra could mind her own business, but if the human failed, there would be two zombies to check out and cash in. And even if he did not, Audra wanted to know who was so close to her campsite. It was probably that idiot trying to kidnap Randy from her. Audra already felt annoyed, and she had not even met him yet.

She got to the bottom of the hill and there he was, big-green-pack guy. He had a stick in one hand, stabbing at the zombie, putting holes in the merchandise. In the other, he had a brand new, shiny reader. Any safe distance he gained with the stick thwarted his ability to retrieve a DNA sample.

The zombie was much more decomposed than her Randy and getting worse by the minute. The big-green-pack guy continued to yell, causing the zombie to flail about and further the damage. He did not know he was within arm's reach of a woman standing behind him.

"Wow, this looks hard," she said in an amused voice, announcing her presence.

The big-green-pack guy swung around in surprise. His brown curly hair cut short on his head, his eyes wide like a deer's. No longer held back by the stick, the zombie wasted no time. Its feet left the ground as it lunged for the curly hair. The full weight of the zombie hit the guy's pack, and he fell forward with a panicked yell. Audra rolled her eyes and sidestepped the disaster. Her boot met the zombie's ribcage to roll him off the pack. The pack was bloodied by the holes the tagger had poked into the zom's body, but otherwise had protected its human underneath.

The human stumbled forward and away. His wide eyes darted between her and the zombie who was struggling to get up from its back like a turtle. Audra remained unimpressed. She ate more berries from her hand.

"Well," she said, "tie him up."

The tagger, still in an attack posture, had fear in his eyes. He looked like he might run away. His eyes searched for an escape into the forest.

"It's your zom. Tag him," she said again to encourage.

He gave her one more look, trying to read her, then straightened his posture and removed his pack. He was much taller than Audra, but his demeanor yielded to hers. He pulled out duct tape, an expensive supply, and tore off a big strip. He slunk around Audra toward the zombie's head. He attempted to cover the zombie's mouth but did not find the subject cooperative. It opened its mouth so that the tape was not wide enough. It rolled left and right. He managed to get the top lip, but the jaw opened and closed on the edge of the tape. At least the top teeth were covered. He took another piece of tape and did the same to the bottom. Feeling more comfortable, he pushed the jaw closed and employed more tape, but almost got his eyes clawed out. Maybe he forgot it had arms? Another piece of tape tied up the wrists. It was a tedious affair, and Audra watched with both amusement and impatience. Pack guy sat down next to the zombie and took a break, trying to slow his heart rate and catch his breath. Audra considered leaving once more out of boredom.

He finally rolled to his hands and knees to search the ground for the biometric reader lost in the frenzy. He sighed in relief when he found it in one piece.

This guy was a dummy.

The reader let out a long, low-tone "boop". Audra already knew what it meant.

Name: Andrew Smith

Gender: Male

DOB: 12/1/2056

Status: No inquiries

"Damn," he said, collapsing back onto the ground, too tired to stand.

"Did you expect to get something for him?" she asked, still trying to figure this guy out.

"What do you mean?"

"Dude, I don't mean to help my competition… but look at this guy! He's wearing farmer clothes - his family was poor before the outbreak. They are still poor. He looks like he was ugly, before, ya know, he got uglier. No one is missing this guy. You picked a bad one and wasted your time."

Pack guy looked at his ugly, poor zombie covered in tape, and sighed.

"Damn," he said again.

2 Initiation

"All you have to do is scrape this part along the skin…" she recalled from her orientation. The short lecture and demonstration on the reader; the note to secure their hands and mouth with no explanation of how; none of it seemed like training as she stood horrified, staring down a quick and nimble zom in the overgrown field. The little girl lurched forward, almost trying to get Audra to pick a direction like she enjoyed the chase. Audra responded with a high-pitched yip and a backward jump. She tripped. With the girl at her heels, she pulled herself up with a flurry of feet and curse words.

Audra had been running from zombies for a long time now, but she had never teased one with a reader before. She stole a glance behind. The girl, just six or seven years old, was running like a crazed, murderous maniac. She was hungry, and she was not about to let her prey escape. Audra dashed into the woods hoping to navigate branches and roots more efficiently than her chaser. The girl tore through without a care, earning deep gashes on her face and arms. A thick branch lodged in her chest did nothing to stop her.

Their speeds were matched, but not their stamina. Audra's lungs ached and her left calf twinged with every undetermined number of steps. With adrenaline flowing, she realized her previous survival successes had been contingent upon not purposefully inciting trouble. She caught sight of a clearing. She forced a deep inhale and went for it. Maybe she could sprint away and gain some distance.

She got ten feet into the field before she realized her mistake.

Twenty zombies sprinkled the forty yards of field. Twenty. It must have been a camp that got overrun. Audra veered left, but it was too late. Ten had seen her, and the rest would follow their lead. Several cut her off, and the girl was on her ankles. Panic set in. She kept away from zombies for this damn reason. Who the hell did she think she was to chase zoms? This was how she died, she was sure of it. She ran toward a pine. And while it was a bad idea, it was the only idea she had. She shimmied up the tree, gaining vertical distance from her zoms. She climbed high and caught her breath as she assessed her situation.

There were no low branches for the zombies to pull on. She was twenty feet off the ground with twenty surrounding the tree. Her pack? She'd left it in the first field. To be more agile against the girl, she thought. Now she was stuck up a tree with no pack, no help, and no hope, just a dagger and a useless biometric reader. Audra resisted the urge to throw the reader into the field. It was more trouble than what it was worth. Instead, she sucked in all the air she could, then sipped in some more. She turned her face to the blue sky and let out an angry outburst against the tall pine branches above her, against a fate that had brought her here - alive up to this point, for no reason at all. The noise only sent the birds in the tree flying off and made the zombies below her spike in energy.

*　　*　　*

"You were trying to poach my zom yesterday, dude," she said with a head tilt, trying to read him.

He felt like fresh blood, new to the tagging game. But, he might also be a good actor, trying to get Audra to let her guard down. The zombie he had damaged did not appear valuable, and his pack had kept him protected when he turned. This guy could be playing her.

Instead of answering, he continued to look ruefully at his prize.

"You think if I can take the tape off, I can use some of it again?" he asked half to himself.

Audra let a smirk escape. He was good, but she would not let him change the subject.

"Yesterday?" she asked, confronting him again.

"Poach? I don't even know what that is. I thought you were in trouble. I didn't realize there were…" he hesitated, "girls… out here, tagging and stuff. I thought…" he trailed off.

"Poaching is taking someone's zombie they've targeted, stalked, and positioned. It's a jerk move. So the question is, are you a jerk?"

"No, I'm Wilfred," he said.

"I'm not calling you that," Audra said. "It's the damn apocalypse. No one remembers your name, you can pick a new one. And yes, there are girls out here," choosing his diminutive term. "We don't have enough people to be picky about genitalia."

"Ok, I'm Dwyn?" he asked.

Audra responded with a furrowed brow and a confused look. A guy that would flip and change his name was someone worth suspicion.

He continued, "You seem to know what you're doing… will you teach me?"

He then reached for something in his pack on the ground. Audra's hand covered the handle of her knife. He resurfaced with a grain bar purchasable in the village. When he looked up, he was surprised that he had put her on the defensive. He offered her the bar. Audra let it fall to the ground but took her hand off the blade. Audra still had trouble believing he was dangerous. He scrambled for it with unnecessary motion like a teenager still growing into his limbs. He stuck it back out to her again with a smile on his face. His clean and straight teeth revealed a history of safe shelter for most of the outbreak.

Still refusing to acknowledge the food, she countered, "Who are you out here trying to find?"

"I'm just out here to help."

It was as rehearsed and as awful as his Wilfred name. If he did not want to tell her that was fine. So far, he seemed too optimistic and idealistic to be out here. Everyone had their secrets. Dwyn could have his for now. Whatever his end game, Audra figured she could handle him. A short partnership to carry out more complicated tags might just be what her ledger at Lysent needed. Afterward, she could ditch him and be that much closer.

"I get all your zombies during training," she said, seeing how he would react.

"Deal."

"You tag along, help when I need you, and then leave when you've had enough," she spouted.

"Deal," he said with increased energy.

"Touch me or my stuff and I kill you."

Her eyes narrowed and her face turned sharp with dark shadows that the sun could not erase.

"Yeah, no problem. Want a grain bar?"

Audra rolled her eyes as she turned back to camp. Randy needed to be checked.

"What about Andrew here?"

"You tag him," she called out over her shoulder.

"Will you show me how?"

What had she gotten herself into? She mustered the patience she imagined she would need for weeks to come, spun on her heel, and returned to Dwyn. After they tagged his zombie with a fresh number, she showed him how to type it into his reader. They untied his feet and did their best to remove the tape from his face without removing flesh.

"Maybe duct tape isn't the best way to go…" he concluded as he crumpled the wasted tape and flesh into a ball.

Turns out there was a lot Dwyn didn't know, including reliable ways to build a fire. Audra taught him the basics. She had nothing else to do. He was excited to be sitting next to a warm fire that evening, which kept away the bugs that plagued them most hours. They would wait on Randy's negotiations and tag more zoms in the morning. For now, it was quiet and the night undisturbed.

Audra wouldn't admit out loud that it was nice to have company for a change, but the evening was pleasant as they lounged luxuriously against a log by the fire. Audra looked up at the sky. Satellite 867, as she called it, was flying by. She and Belinda often had dreamed of escaping off this earth to what remained in the sky.

"Audra?"

She came back from space, her eyes dropping to the fire.

"Yeah, dude?"

"How cool would it be to have marshmallows?"

*　　*　　*

"We have reached a pivotal point in our lives, in our history, in our evolution."

The train had brought people in from the nearby towns to hear the important announcement. It was rumored that Lysent had figured out something monumental, maybe even how to fix the electric generators which had been down since the initial outbreak. They were doing well in the towns, keeping clean water and clean people with hard, daily work. A way to store power to run water purifiers and keep the lights on would mean a leap in their redevelopment.

While Lysent promised to improve community infrastructure for all, they still found the time to clean the front of their tall, white building and to replace the extravagantly sized glass windows in the front. Sandwiched between two uniformed guards, a small, regal woman spoke to the crowd from behind her podium. Her gray hair slicked back into a bun. Her eyes sharp.

"We confirmed this advancement several months ago, but much thought was needed to implement it in the world in which we live. While we hope this will not always be the case, it is the only way to use this advancement AND maintain our current level of living. No one wants to struggle like we have before…

"We have a cure."

The crowd broke out in incredible noise. The pause written into the speech was much extended as people shared skepticism, celebration, even screams of terror. Some cried for their dead loved ones who would never be cured. They shouted questions to the speaker, disregarding the probability that if they were quiet, they would learn more information from the rest of the speech.

The lady was Larange Greenly. She had taken over, or perhaps had always been in charge of Lysent - at least this region. She was the one who had announced that the train system was now functional and would run its route to deliver mail and goods to the townships. She was the one who had announced that the rations for the townships had increased, decreased, then increased again. Greenly raised a hand and lowered it to signal she wanted to continue, then waited. The two hundred people quieted.

"All the townships have been sent letters to this same effect. We already know the infected are not dead. We know this because we have seen that the infected can die - sometimes of natural causes. They are sick with a virus that can be eradicated from the body. Once given a series of injections we've developed, the body returns to its normal oxygenation levels and higher brain function comes out of dormancy. The body regenerates only to the degree that the human ever could. Missing limbs will not grow back. Skin grafts may be possible in select cases.

"At this point, I would like to note, we will not be able to wake up everybody immediately.

"We barely have enough resources in the town as it is. We cannot have the entire population at our doorstep demanding food, water, and shelter. Many of those people out there are not your family. You do not know them."

Even before the speech's end, the crowd polarized in sounds of dissent and praise. Some were unhappy with the rations and space available now. They did not want others. A few were already encouraging an obligation that everyone should be awakened whatever their connection or lack thereof.

It was clear where Lysent stood.

"They do not know any better remaining how they are. And, to that effect, I'd like to explain the policy that has been put in place, balancing bringing back our loved ones into our lives, and not toppling us into famine and despair.

"You will be able to list the loved ones you are searching for who you would like cured and placed into your household. I would like to stress this first point. The people you list, if found, will be in your household and you will be financially responsible for them. You will have to care for them as they heal and transition into our new world. They will live with you. Do not wake up all the people in your old suburb. Wake up your daughter. Wake up your partner.

"Secondly, once the person is found, we will wake them up for a negotiated fee. This will demonstrate that you have the means to care for your loved ones. You will not create burdens on our society. Instead, you will help your returned ones grow in health, wealth, and contribution. This will effectively limit how many people you can wake up. Also to note, this fee does not include any medical bills for skin grafts, rehabilitation, or hospitalization.

"We are currently not taking any collaterals or payment plans. Our first phase will be cash only. After the first phase, we will match our new consensus data with projected crops. We will analyze the population data and determine if more can be cured. We will then consider other payment options.

"The only payment option that will be in effect besides cash will be a work-for-awaken plan in which a dedicated worker may be able to earn enough cash to awaken their loved one. This worker would be out in the field, finding others' loved ones who are incapable of finding them themselves. It would be dangerous work, but generously rewarded by having a loved one awakened when otherwise it would be financially infeasible."

Audra refused to live within the fences of the town, instead just entering to trade. But today she clung onto the fence, just within listening range. This was her answer and her mind reeled with the possibilities.

*　*　*

Dwyn, who seemed thankful that he was not "Wilfred," learned quickly. Audra first helped him whittle down his pack weight since he couldn't run any decent speed with it on. She removed over half of his belongings much to Dwyn's balking. She put it in another bag and hid it in the brush.

"We can come back in two weeks and you can get anything you want from it," she encouraged.

After two weeks he didn't even want to go look inside the bag. Audra was right.

And while she thought she would use him as bait for a couple two-person zombies and then send him on his way, he was showing promise as a partner. She taught him the basic strategies: Bait & Switch, Loop-de-loop, and Space Jam. They then moved onto more advanced two-person strategies like Leap Frog. Despite tagging nearly a dozen zombies, they didn't find anyone of worth.

They had been out there for three weeks, waiting on Randy's negotiations, but they finally had an answer. Audra considered the length of negotiation with a grim smile. Maybe the family did not have enough money. They were scrambling for more and trying to negotiate a lower price. But another likely scenario was that the family was rich and yes, they wanted to wake up Randy and a few other relatives, but they were not expecting to pay that much for Randy. It was amazing how many people did things out of obligation to someone that only knows "eat humans" on a daily basis. That would come out in the negotiation when they needed to put a price on their "loved" one. Most of the negotiation was the personal journey of the healthy person. A bunch of bullshit.

Audra made up the time lost in negotiations with her delivery speed. While others took multiple days to get in and out of the town, Audra was fast even with a zombie in tow. In her childhood school, she hadn't been a runner. It was a skill she learned and loved out here. Audra had met many people who hated running. It meant fear. It meant running for their lives. And Audra sort of got that, but she also knew she had always survived. She had always outrun her troubles. And that was something in her pocket. The people who did not want to run anymore stayed in their townships, got rations delivered by a fence-protected train, and negotiated with their loved ones' lives.

The trio ran along the ten-foot-high fence towards the main township. There were several townships now, all along the trade route. Following the track was the most direct and cleared path. It was also a great place to catch up on gossip from the other taggers as they came in and out of towns. Randy followed along behind them, occasionally getting caught along the chain links that tore at his clothes. It was a wonder he was in such good condition. Besides taggers, an occasional lone hiker returned from a resupply. Some people did not transition well from surviving in the wilderness back into the strict towns with measured rations and daily reports. Audra felt the same.

Even ten feet away on the opposite side of the fence, she felt the buzz of the electric track. Audra questioned if it actually made noise, but at the least, it vibrated and made her hair stand on end. She slowed to look back at the train. Randy tried to take a bite from her neck. She shook her head and returned to speed. The fifteen cars of a sleek silver train passed. It carried each week's rations, mail (subject to Lysent perusal), and trade goods. At times people used it to get from town to town, but it was an expensive endeavor for the sentimental. The train and its technology galvanized Lysent as the organization in charge after people began rebuilding.

No one could remember if Lysent had always owned the trains, but they owned a lot explicitly or under an umbrella in the world before. The train hadn't broken down with the rest of the modern world. Solar energy collected by the rails and train cars supplemented the electromagnetic rail system. It was self-sustained. They only needed two fences to keep zombies from piling up on the tracks, and a periodic patrol to clear it. At first, that meant killing the zombies. But now that everyone was aware the zombies were not dead, and instead, alive and recoverable, more humane ways were required to keep the zombies from being an inconvenience to the fastest trade route. Lysent built corrals out of sight to confine the zoms in the name of safety. Everyone was thankful for Lysent's reach and capabilities.

Audra understood that they would not have progressed at such a rapid rate without them, before or after the outbreak, but that did not mean they were worth the price of their autonomy and agency. They were too organized and too meddling. They left an awful taste in her mouth. But, here she was, working for them, like any government worker, just one who did not bathe often, and ran around chasing and running from zombies most of the day. Audra would drop off Randy, receive payment, and leave as quickly as possible. Their partnership was a necessity, but not one she needed to prolong.

Not even a couple miles in, a raunchy looking guy, thin and haggard, walked toward them from the opposite direction. He complimented their nice find, Randy's business suit dirty and flapping open.

"Watch out for Audra, though," he said toward Dwyn, "She'll leave you out to dry."

Dwyn made no comment but noticed Audra give Randy a little yank to increase his pace.

After an hour or so, Dwyn was forced to walk. He was not a conditioned runner like Audra. She kept going. It was part of the deal. He could tag along as long as he wanted and had the ability to do so. He knew where she was heading. Audra finished the thirty miles and camped not too far from the tracks. A couple hours later, after it was dark, he caught up with her. She had already eaten, her food tied up in the tree, and she was sleeping, hugging her pack in her tent.

Audra was up at dawn. She checked the cloudless sky and muddied her face and arms to protect her from the sun. She gave Dwyn a little kick, knowing he had come in late. He groaned but did not move.

"I'm heading out. I'll see you at the township."

"Mreh."

3 Safekeeping

Hands bound with neat twine and mouth covered with a red handkerchief, Belinda followed her sister obediently into the Lysent plaza. Audra had wiped the protective mud off their skin and combed their hair. The human bite on Belinda's right forearm had been cleaned and dressed. They both needed to look their best for the committee. But, no amount of preening could disguise Belinda's eyes - frozen wide, lifeless, and gray.

Against the plaza, behind a waist-high barrier, several people shouted angry words at them.

"Don't wake her up! It's against God's will!"

Audra knew there would be dissenters opposed to curing. They believed the infected had proven themselves incapable of surviving in this world. Reviving them would be a waste of resources. Audra walked past them without a word. She did not completely disagree with them.

The protesters were not allowed in the plaza and as the sisters approached the entrance to the main white building, the yelling faded. A sign posted on the door stated, "NO INFECTED THIS WAY".

Audra glanced around and found no one to help. She was sure she shouldn't leave her sister unsupervised outside. Lysent would not approve and she didn't trust the protesters just outside the barriers. Before she made a decision, a tall thin man in uniform robes met them at the bottom of the white porch. The man raised his eyebrows at the pair. Audra had thought she had cleaned them both up, but they remained a stark contrast to his crisp, clean glow. He waved them to the side of the building and Audra followed, no longer eager to step inside.

Beside the building stood a small metal outhouse. It was the perfect size for one person. Audra held back and Belinda bumped into her. Would they be separated? The thin man noticed the hesitation in her steps. He raised his bushy eyebrows once more, but his voice was friendly and assuring.

"What's her name?"

"Belinda."

"That's a lovely name. Belinda will be really grateful that you took such good care of her while she was sick. She looks great. It must have been hard to keep her in such good condition."

Audra gave a grateful smile. It had been hard to keep Belinda out of trouble. She was always wandering off toward any noise or movement in her peripheral. At first, Audra had kept her in her tent at night, but Belinda never tired. She was constantly shuffling. Eventually, she'd convinced herself that Belinda would be all right tied up outside the tent with a tarp draped loosely around her to keep off the rain. It was Audra's least favorite part of corralling Belinda, but Belinda didn't seem to care.

"Belinda will be safe inside while you meet with the Awakening Committee," he said as he opened the shed door.

Audra weighed her options. She had promised her mother she would keep Belinda safe. This could be the only way to revive her, but it could also be a trap. The thin man tested the ties as Belinda shuffled in, and an image of an alive, kicking, and screaming Belinda protesting her confinement forced its way into Audra's mind as the door clicked shut.

Audra felt small and childlike following the tall man back to the main entrance. She was not sure if she was supposed to be this small, or if she hadn't gotten enough nutrition during her puberty and adolescence. Belinda was still much taller than her, despite her slowed metabolism in the last year.

The yells kicked up again as they turned the corner.

"Keep them dead!"

Audra expected her escort to dismiss the protests conversationally, given her purpose and his business, but he did not. He only motioned her inside when they reached the door. The front lobby had a tall ceiling and matching windows to let the light in. It was a nice feature. Given that electricity was rationed, the sun was preferable. Audra felt more and more inadequate as her muddy feet left marks on the white marble and she saw the clean and bright lady behind the desk. Would they give her the time of day?

"Hi Clyde, someone looking for their parents?" the lady behind the front desk asked.

Her dark curly hair bounced as her fingers flitted from one stack of paper to the next on her desk. Audra was reminded of the doctor's office of her childhood, or the few times she had visited her mom at work. She hadn't realized people still had office jobs.

"No, she brought her own. Would like to see the committee, I imagine."

He looked at Audra, who nodded approvingly.

"OK, well, answer this questionnaire, sweetie, and we'll get you in as soon as possible."

She guided Audra to one of the chairs. As she handed her a clipboard and pen, she whispered into her ear.

"Do you know how to read and write, sweetie?"

"Yes ma'am," Audra said automatically.

That was the truth, but she had not done so in the last three years. Her eyes were trained to follow movement and as she looked at the paper, the letters swam around. She took a deep breath and willed the first word to stop moving. After a few slow, stumbling sentences, she improved.

The questionnaire was blunt and clinical. It asked her name, age, previous occupation, and current living arrangements. It asked her how long she had known the infected, and what she intended to do with the infected once awakened. The final questions stung.

"Do you have at least 1 million credits to awaken the infected person?" No.

"If yes, will the transaction be cash or through the bank?"

"If no, are you willing to discuss a payment plan?" Yes.

Audra returned the paperwork. Initially impressed by her literacy, the receptionist glanced at the bottom of the form to confirm her suspicion. Audra had no money.

"You can wait back at your seat. The committee will review your application and meet with you in the next hour or so. They have lunch right now."

Wait? What people had the luxury of waiting anymore? She thought of her low food rations. She thought of checking on her sister. Perhaps she could come back later? She decided not to be a difficult person. She waited.

Eventually, the lady at the front desk escorted her down the hall. She roughly whispered quick advice to her as if she had just decided to help.

"There's a big group but you only have to convince the one."

Before Audra could ask which one, the receptionist swung open a pair of doors. There sat seven men and women in robes behind a long desk. A single chair faced them. Audra sat and nodded. A soft jab in her shoulder told her she should stand back up. After a few awkward moments, the lady in the center gave a small smile and told their rude guest she could be seated. Audra recognized her gray slicked back hair and small dark eyes. It was Larange Greenly, the woman who made all decisions impacting the towns and delivered the news - good or bad - on the plaza front.

"The infected is your sister?" she asked, her voice's pitch rising in amusement.

Audra opened her mouth to answer, but Greenly did not wait.

"Why do you want to awaken her?"

"She is my sister and I love her."

Her response was met with snickers and patronizing looks. Audra swallowed her anger. She needed them to be on her side.

A man to Greenly's left with a full white beard cleared his throat.

"We understand you do not have the full payment yet. How much do you have?"

He sat back ready to do calculations in his head.

"Well, sir, I have no credits to my name."

He sat back up and leaned toward her.

"Then why are you wasting our time?"

It was easy for them to sit in these meetings, making assessments and dictating people's lives behind their table and walls. They did not understand what lay beyond the fences. Their undeserved power could not be overturned, though. Audra realized she was losing their patience and possibly her chance.

"I'm not wasting your time. I'm a good runner, sir. I can run a 7-minute mile in the woods. I can run twenty-five miles one day, and thirty the next. I've been out there for three years. I would be a good tagger.

"Let me tag zombies for you in exchange for waking up my sister."

Audra looked at each committee person. Most seemed unconvinced, but Greenly's mild amusement had grown into a sly smile.

"Let's hope your abilities match the grit we see here," she said, not missing Audra's simmering attitude.

"An ambitious girl. She may be one to watch. Give her a contract. Committee dismissed," announced Greenly.

"Wait, that's it?" she asked as the receptionist ushered her to the lobby.

"Yes, I'll give you the contract to look over. It says as a tagger, you get ten percent of the negotiated price of an awakened zombie. You can get that money in cash or put it toward awakening your sister. Your sister stays here and you pay rent each month, pulled from your account. If more than two months pass without communication, Lysent reserves the right to put down your sister."

"How many people do I need to catch and bring in to awaken my sister?"

"If you brought them all in tomorrow and everyone, including your sister, went for the average price, ten people would do. Unfortunately, rent and indenture fees add up quickly."

"Rent and indenture fees? Aren't those the same thing?"

"No, unfortunately, they are not."

"So, practically, how many people will I need?"

"If you're good at it, maybe fifty?"

"What if I keep Belinda somewhere else and don't pay rent?"

"It is part of the deal. She is collateral for the biometric reader we are lending you. We guarantee she stays in her current condition, barring death. If she stays somewhere else, she may degrade. You will be out running and won't be able to care for her. Did you have a secondary place in mind?"

"No."

Audra considered how much care her sister required, especially the hunting. Belinda couldn't eat anything farmed or gathered. She looked over the contract. Even with a lack of formal education, she surmised it was not in her favor. It was a piling of debt she might never repay.

She thought of her sister, outside in the dark closet. It had seemed a fool's errand to keep her body for so long. She sat and shed a tear for every time she considered ending her sister's existence. Would it have been for her own selfish desires? Did she really think a person needed to pass on from this world to be complete? Audra had her answer, a promise to her mother and promise of a cure. Settling in a town, Belinda would thrive behind walls, under roofs, and behind fences. They would learn occupations. Belinda would be a seamstress. Audra would do labor and mail runs for extra money. It would be the life that Belinda deserved.

She signed the paper.

*　*　*

Audra realized the committee agreed to make her a tagger because there was nothing to lose on their end. Someone would bring in her biometric reader for a small reward fee when she died trying to tag her first zom. And then, they would destroy Belinda. But she proved them wrong with every tag and return.

Audra tugged Randy. Her quads twinged with each footfall and her back ached, but she could handle more speed for a few more moments. Even if Dwyn had not slept in, he would not have been able to keep up with her. Randy matched her speed without complaint. She would be rid of him soon and tomorrow he would wake up under the watchful eyes of scientists.

The dissenters outside the plaza had changed their chants in the last two years.

"Don't add to the rich!"

"Lysent owns us!"

With every awakening, another was added to the corporation's community who required food, energy, and clothes. They argued that their job never matched their burden on the community. No one ever woke up and became a farmer. They were part of the elite, part of the rich. Audra did not disagree with them, but she rolled her eyes at them all the same. These protesters who yelled at her went home just a few hundred feet away from Lysent, cozy within their fences. They hassled her as if she had a choice.

It was old routine now. Audra ran Randy over to the metal closet without an escort. It was unoccupied. She secured him and sauntered into the lobby. She greeted Rosie who was sitting at the desk, shuffling through paperwork strewn all over.

"I've brought Randy… I mean, Randolph… Ludington?"

"Ludington, Ludington… Audra…" Rosie said as she shuffled through yet another set of papers and folders behind her. She found a blue folder and pulled it out and placed it on top of all the other papers on her desk, the easy cause of her clutter. She gave some of the papers in the folder to Audra.

"Audra! You got me another winner?!" called out Clyde as he entered the lobby. Audra just smiled politely and started her paperwork without banter. Clyde and Rosie exchanged knowing glances. Audra would withdraw against her Finder's Fee today.

Clyde returned from his review, assessment in hand. He compared his notes with Audra's form. Their rating on body condition differed.

"That bite is bad, Audra."

The sullen expression on Audra's face erupted into an amiable grin. Her laughter reflected their years of friendship.

"C'mon man! He has been out there for years, and he looks amazing. That bite is not my fault. That's how he… y'know got infected."

"He does look great, besides the bite," Clyde said with pride in his voice as if he had anything to do with it.

"You'll graft it, it'll make a good scar for his story. The men like that, right?"

"Yeah, I guess so. I'll knock mine back a grade."

"Thanks, Clyde. I owe you one."

"You bring in the best bodies, Audra. You're great out there."

"I hope I don't have to be out there much longer."

"Speaking of, do you want your payment, minus rent, in Belinda's deposit? It's a nice one."

"No, I'll take half with me."

"Well, progress is progress, I guess, Audra," he half scolded her.

Audra did not reply, but her face fell and she lost her twinkle.

They finished the transaction and Audra tucked the several credits in a pouch near her breast. Clyde was already outside prepping Randy for his inspection by the Awakening Committee. Audra turned before she walked out the door.

"Oh, if a guy comes in here looking for me in say… two hours?"

"I'll let him know where to find you," said Rosie with a pained face.

"Thanks," she said, refusing to acknowledge Rosie's concern.

* * *

Still in the tree she'd scrambled up to escape the herd, Audra concluded that days would pass before there would be a passerby. And chances were a passerby would avoid her group of twenty-one zombies at all costs. The surrounding trees were not large enough or close enough for her to reach. So there she sat, perched on the first weight-bearing branch, midway up the tree. She would have to get out of this herself. And the only way was down, now, before she became dehydrated and exhausted.

Audra tied up her hair and with a deep breath, she pulled out her dagger. When her family had abandoned the car and walked into the forest, her mother had given her a dagger for safety. Now, Audra always had at least two, one to use and one to lose. Belinda used hers to whittle small figurines.

Audra positioned herself upside down, her legs wrapped around the rough bark of the tree. Looking straight down she did not see people, at least not salvageable people, just death in multitude, enthusiastic about her approach.

The clearance between the crown of her head and her zombie friends was minimal once she got close enough to leverage her weapon. The sun had not been kind to those in the field. The first corpse, weathered and shredded, reached its lanky upper limbs toward her. Audra held fast to the dagger and stabbed squarely in the crown of the head and yanked back. It became inanimate but did not fall down. Other bodies braced against it and began to climb. Audra repositioned and looked to the zombie closest to her weapon. Possibly a woman. Her dry teeth made a clicking noise which Audra ended. She crossed the dagger across her body and moved it into a third.

With those dead, Audra retreated up the tree to gain a little space and rest. The inverted warrior looked upon the battlefield. The trio had now fallen. Others stood on them, gaining a few inches of height. Audra shuffled back down. She was determined to get five more before she climbed back up to a branch to let the blood rush back to her legs and away from her head.

She pierced another and received a face full of blood. Her supporting hand reached in a panic. She slipped inches downward before her legs caught her fall. Squinting her eyes and pursing her lips, she willed it not to go up her nose. Her stomach turned and her mouth gaped as she gagged. But it did not matter in the next moments as another lunged. She swung shallowly toward the nasal cavity, slowing it down and getting her dagger stuck.

She yanked back hard and popped herself in the face with the handle when it released. The blood from her nose mingled with the blood from her kill and tickled all her senses and those of her friends. She took a moment to wipe the blood off her face and into her hair. The bugs were already collecting around her, attracted to the smell. Dreaded gnats flying into the fluids and into her eyes. Despite the hole in his face, her pursuer still needed a final blow.

The stupidity and heaviness of what she was undertaking sank in. Tears washed her eyes clean. Audra took a deep, gasping breath and reached for her injured target, splattered with bloodstained tears.

*   *   *

The burly man on the other side of the bar nodded to the door. Audra did not have to move from her draped position over the bar's surface to know Dwyn had arrived. He approached her peripheral, cautious in this new environment. The barkeep pointed to the vat of foul smelling moonshine behind him.

"Looks like she has had enough for both of us," Dwyn declined.

Audra rolled her eyes in his full view.

"Did you turn in Randy?" he asked.

"Mm-hm."

"Did you get the money?"

"Mh-hm."

"Did you give it all to this guy?"

Audra peeled her face off the wood to glare and curse. Her intensity smelled of anger and moonshine.

Dwyn tipped his chin at the bartender and walked out.

4 Against

Audra tried to find the sun through the trees and clouds. She judged she had about an hour of daylight left to pull Debbie Lancer. She ignored the temptation to set up camp early. While most of Audra's life was already well-practiced in camping, staying out of sight, and finding food and water, escorting a zombie to Lysent was still new to her skill set. She tugged on her leashed zom. A sack on Debbie's head gave a small amount of protection to Audra's backside, but it blocked Debbie's sight, and that led to many falls, sometimes atop Audra. Audra settled for a longer lead and constantly checked the distance between her and the unsecured face of Debbie.

With a few tags to her name, Audra noticed the underlying theme. The families were rich and the zoms were gorgeous. Even in death and weathered exposure, Debbie had kept her figure, face symmetry, and thick hair. The rich and pretty ruled this new world, too.

Audra managed to not get eaten for one more hour as they trudged closer to the corporation for her payout. With a sigh, Audra settled in front of her perfectly crafted fire. At least she could do that well. She planned to move only if the smoke drifted her way for too long. She let darkness engulf her. With a few moments of peace and no immediate problems, the thoughts flooded in.

It was her fault.

No, she never should have been put in that situation.

Still, it was her fault.

The thoughts churned and Audra's eyes welled. She stared deep into the fire but it did not register. All she saw was red. A wall of red and it warmed her head until she felt she was on fire. And then the air escaped her. An inhale did not follow. How could she sit here while her sister rotted within herself? She would give anything to make the pain leave, to have her sister here and well. Heaviness and impossibility sank in.

A large, triumphant growl filled her ear. She snapped around to find Debbie inches from her face. Audra pushed her away and assessed the bodily damage. Debbie had been bound at the edge of the campsite. She had pulled her wrists loose of her ropes and the majority of her flesh in the process. Skin and muscle flapped around as she pulled herself to Audra. No one would be able to sew her up and Lysent would not wake a double hand amputee. Someone had loved Debbie and Audra had destroyed her. It was her fault. Audra yelled out and in an instant had pulled out her knife from her boot and launched herself at the crawling remains.

The two wrestled on the ground for a few moments. With each glancing blow from the floppy hands or attack from the jaws, Audra got a renewed sense of strength, a strength drained by this world. Then she stabbed her.

Again. And again.

Until Debbie was no longer Debbie.

Audra saw a different shade of red, but her thoughts were quieted in the blood and stench. She passed out next to the corpse before the cyclic thoughts roared again.

*　*　*

Audra emerged a few days later from the hole. She took inventory of her pack. She had no money. She rummaged to find her cooking pot, hickory nuts, and a couple of worn photographs of her family from when the world was normal. It could have been worse. Sometimes it was worse. Audra would need to take a job to get a few more supplies before she returned to the wilderness to tag. She stepped out of the town, past the fences to keep out the dead, and found a familiar creek. She rinsed her face, switched out to a clean shirt, and headed back into the market. There she would find the jobs she needed.

As she searched for the unofficial post, a voice called out behind her.

"Do you always fall out like that?" Dwyn asked casually.

"Not always," she said shortly, trying to hide her shame behind impatience.

She did not have to prove anything to Dwyn. The world had gone to shit. She could too, occasionally. It didn't seem to stop him from following her.

Once she remembered which town she was in, she found the unofficial post. The fastest way to mail a letter from town to town was the train. But the train only ran once a week and all mail was subject to review. Lysent didn't allow correspondence that disrespected the company or promoted outside governments or groups. They explained that this was their right because they had invested so much in rebuilding. If you wanted to create another system of government, go somewhere else and create your own infrastructure.

If you wanted to send a letter during the week or under the nose of the governing body, you needed to send it with a traveler. A tagger's ability and constant need for a quick buck made them excellent unofficial mail-keeps. Audra had earned a reputation for being one of the fastest mail servicers when she was available. Without a body in tow, Audra promised same-day delivery.

They entered the house to find a gruff looking man. His wide grin competed with his large frizzy beard in magnitude.

"I heard you were in town," he said motioning to Audra. His smile wavered as he looked to Dwyn with suspicion.

"He's with me," she answered his unasked question. "You got any mail for me?"

"Of course, I started gathering it this morning. Told them it'd be a few hours before you'd be ready," he said hunting for the hidden folder of mail. He found it and she tucked it into her bag.

"Money on receipt," he said as he disappeared into the back room.

Audra rolled her eyes and headed out.

"I just need to grab my pack," said Dwyn as he ran around the corner.

Audra considered running off without him but decided against it. She needed to eat. Under the shade of oak trees outside the fences, she opened hickory nuts while she examined the destinations on the envelopes. There were three different townships, seven envelopes in total. She could get this done in a day, no problem. She'd buy supplies, sleep near the last town, then head out to tag another zombie in the morning. Audra tucked the envelopes back into her bag and focused on pulling the last of the nut meat from its shells as Dwyn approached with his pack in tow.

"I thought you left without me again," he said, out of breath.

"Thought about it."

Audra and Dwyn started with a steady pace toward the first township, using the train tracks as their easy guide. It was not two miles later when Audra keeled over and vomited her hickory nuts into a bush.

"I brought you extra water," Dwyn offered.

Audra took it in silence. She drank the whole bottle and sat there for ten minutes. Ten minutes was another mile they could have covered. Dwyn offered to help steady her as she stood, but she refused. She ran another half mile and vomited off to the side. She did not stop this time but kept running.

For once, Dwyn could keep up.

The sun had set well before Audra and Dwyn made it to the last township. Audra held out her left hand and ran it along the chain link fence to keep the correct trajectory. Dwyn ran staggered to her right, keeping an ear out for zombies. They heard them in the distance, mildly interested in the light "chink, chink" the fence made against Audra's hand. When they neared the township, a large floodlight flashed and blinded them. A bow and arrow hid behind the light. She waved to signal their vitality. As they approached the gate, a stern eye greeted them.

"Why are you coming in so late?"

"We got held up. We're sorry. Can we stay for the night?"

He said nothing but motioned to someone below and the gate opened.

"Thanks. Do you need any water?" Audra offered.

She wanted to stay on the good side of the guards. You never knew when your ass would be in trouble and you'd need a speedy gate opening. He smiled his thanks but waved them on.

Audra and Dwyn walked into the dark center of town. It was the smallest township and everyone had already retreated to their homes. Audra found the location that served as the underground post office and gave it a small knock. Inside, she heard rustling. Dwyn looked reluctant.

"Maybe we could leave it to morning?" Dwyn mumbled.

A woman opened the door. She wore a night robe and a face twisted in confusion and annoyance.

"Mail," Audra stated.

The lady opened the door wider and removed herself from the doorway to let them pass. Inside with the door closed, Audra let one of her arms out of the pack straps and let the pack fall to her side. She pulled out the mail and handed it over. The lady received it and shuffled to a hutch to retrieve their money.

Their eyes met as she gave Audra the credits.

"I've been told to ask you to stay at your camp in the morning. There is someone who would like to speak with you."

Audra nodded but was not impressed. Lots of people wanted to use her skill set. They often couldn't pay more than what Lysent offered.

The runners left as quickly as they had arrived.

Rather than annoy the gatekeeper once more, Audra and Dwyn climbed over the fence that protected the township. They landed with a thump on the other side, tired and ready for sleep. All the running, and in Audra's case - vomiting, had taken its toll. Despite her exhaustion, she couldn't miss Dwyn's anxious fidgeting.

"What's going on?" she asked, daring him to delay her bedtime.

"I don't know if we should stick around and meet that person."

"It's probably no one. I'm not staying for them - I'm staying for sleep and for the market tomorrow."

She kicked away sticks and rocks from what would be her tent's foundation. Out of the corner of her eye, she noticed Dwyn hadn't even begun his camp setup. He shuffled from foot to foot. He was still not telling her something. Audra stopped and looked him in the eye.

"Do you know this person, Dwyn?"

He returned her look and exhaled loudly. Then the words rushed out before he changed his mind.

"Yes. I was sent by them to recruit someone for the next step in the plan."

Audra's eyebrows rose. She took one step forward and punched him in the left eye. Dwyn staggered back from the force, grabbing his eye as he doubled over.

"See," he said. "We need someone tough. We don't have anyone tough."

And then he blurted out his worry.

"But I don't know if you should meet her because you're um… not that reliable. I don't know if you're the best person."

Tiredness and sickness overwhelmed what remained of Audra's anger. Dwyn's secrets were about to unravel and she found she didn't even care. She wanted to sleep.

"I'll punch you again in the morning," she said as she threw herself into her tent.

*   *   *

A shadow across her tent woke Audra to the bright morning. She didn't usually sleep in, but she didn't usually sleep in vomit-soaked clothes, either. Audra pulled her spare shirt out of her pack. She would scrub the other in the creek after breakfast. Outside, Dwyn's shadow stopped moving as she lifted her arms over her head. Audra could not stifle her sly smile. He was watching her silhouette undress. Dwyn was not unattractive, and he had gotten even fitter in the weeks they trained together. She put on her shirt, but then stretched her arms up again and leaned back to show off her figure behind the safety of the canvas tent.

She took a deep breath and asked herself what she was doing. This guy was recruiting her for a harebrained scheme. She rolled her eyes. She yanked her arms down and wrestled with her pack. Dwyn suddenly began moving as well, making too much noise to be convincing.

Like she did every morning, she rolled up her things and placed them in her pack, except her t-shirt. It was nasty, possibly worth replacing in the market. It was soft and worn though, perfect for running. Maybe she could salvage it after she scraped off the hickory nut meat. She threw the shirt out of her tent with her pack. Her quads ached from dehydration as she climbed out of the tent. Drinking all of Dwyn's treated water did little to mitigate her head's throbbing, incited by the day's brightness.

She had not even finished breaking down her tent when a woman approached their camp. A shawl protected her salt and pepper hair from the sun. Her age was difficult to determine. Even at a distance, her skin and eyes were clear and young. She carried herself upright, not yet fighting the gravity of age. She gathered elderberries as she walked, her excuse for being outside the township today. Audra continued to break down her tent. Instinct demanded she be ready to retreat, to run away, even from an innocent-looking lady with a bucket of berries.

Audra finished packing and stood to confront the newcomer. Audra was a head shorter, and she wondered once again if malnutrition or genetics had stunted her own height. The lady tipped half of her berry stock into Dwyn's empty bowl.

"I will need to come back with some," she said explaining her half-generosity.

"Thanks!" said Dwyn, thrusting his hand into the formerly empty tin bowl.

Audra ignored his trusting actions. She did not have time for him. She turned her eyes back to the woman.

"Hi, Audra. It is truly a pleasure to meet you. I'm Vesna. Dwyn sent word about you." She smiled but eyed Dwyn.

"So Dwyn's his real name, huh?"

Audra perched on a log and grabbed a handful of berries from Dwyn. She popped a couple in her mouth and dared Vesna to continue.

"Audra," Vesna repeated her name to garner rapport, "I heard you are an indentured tagger. You have a loved one infected?"

Audra stared into her eyes, not allowing her an answer or emotion. Vesna was trying to propose her idea in terms of Audra's desires. Audra knew the trick. She used that trick all the time. Vesna returned the silent stare and calculated her. She dropped her strategy and picked up another.

"I lead a small group that questions the current system of government. Lysent should not control who wakes up, or keep us from our loved ones. We want to change that."

"And how will you change that? Lysent is everything."

"Lysent works to limit resources and the population. We have a plan to cure many, all at once. It will topple the current economics on which the corporation gains their power."

Audra did not hear past "cure."

"You have antidotes?"

"We have a scientist who worked with the antidote. She is confident she can synthesize her own batch. We just need help to set up everything. We need someone to clear out this old laboratory…"

Audra's excitement faded. They did not have a cure. They had someone who talked. Vesna could tell she was losing her recruit. She once again changed tactics.

"You were young when it happened, but think about where you went when you got sick."

"The doctor?"

"Where was the doctor?"

"In the white corporation building."

"Lysent owned so many things. Medicine, technology, transportation, communication. They were tasked to fight the disease. The world was decimated and yet, they came out on top. How?"

Vesna's voice held an insinuation.

"You don't think they fought as hard as they could have?"

"More than that," Vesna answered with grimness. "They developed it."

Audra had met many conspiracy enthusiasts, but Vesna appeared to be in a category all her own.

"Lysent started the infection? Why?"

"To diminish the population and rebuild the world? I don't know. Maybe they didn't mean for it to go this far, but now they control everything. They're even reversing their work as they see fit. How else do you think they had the antidote?"

"Because they researched. You just said you had a scientist who was part of the research."

"No. There was no research. My scientist found out that there was just a stockpile of antidotes, a formula, and workers brewing up new doses."

Vesna's eyes were fervent that her potential recruit listen and understand.

Even if all this was true, Audra was not sure she cared. She had no positive feelings toward Lysent, but was this a fight she wanted?

"Sorry, lady. I'm not interested."

She pulled her pack onto her back to go to market. Vesna made noises of disagreement.

"Please, Audra."

"I'm not going to tell anyone about your pretty little plan. Just leave me out of it."

Vesna gathered her courage as Audra turned to leave.

"You're never going to awaken your sister through indentured tagging, especially if you drink away half your findings."

Audra ignored her and kept walking. She needed supplies.

5 Shelter

The family of four created their new home. It was a large tarp on sticks, a cleared area for a fire, a line to hang clothes, and a few logs to sit on, but it was more than they'd had in months. The parents argued over their decision to leave Atlanta, but with each passerby coming from there, it became evident they had left just in time. The city had become a stronghold of zombies. The family's chance of survival increased hidden in the woods, even if their camping experience was limited to a couple of poorly executed family vacations.

Dad, Audra, and Belinda headed for the lake to fish. Belinda complained that she was tired of fish. Why couldn't their dad catch a land animal or a bird? Audra kept her mouth shut and followed the almost familiar path to the water.

Halfway there, they heard rustling up ahead and a burst of noise as birds took off from a bush. Belinda screamed, turned tail, and ran back to camp to her mother. Audra and her father did not stop her. They could catch more fish without her.

The pond was big but maybe not large enough to be called a lake. Audra didn't know the size requirements for labeling bodies of water. They baited their hooks, both secretly wishing that Belinda had not run off with the third. The duo could have manned three. They sat in silent but comfortable camaraderie.

Audra and her father understood each other. Audra watched her father take care of his wife and his children. She modeled her care for Belinda on his - giving opportunities for growth while keeping her safe. Her dad was teaching them how to use different weapons. Her mom loved the machete for its big swing and power. Audra loved her dagger for she was quick and could anticipate the moves of her attacker. Their dad gave Belinda many weapons to try, but her constitution did not seem affected by any equipment provided.

Breaking the silence, as if they had both been discussing Belinda's difficulties without words, her dad surprised her.

"Audra-sweets, if something happens to your mom and me, which is likely given our situation… you need to know something."

Her father paused, trying to find the right words. He stared out into the pond as if the view was more thought-provoking than it was.

"Belinda… she will not make it in this world. And that will not be your fault. OK?"

Audra disagreed with her father's assessment of his older daughter, but she did not argue outright. Belinda was fearful, but Audra had been too when it all began. Belinda would come around. She just needed more time. Her family needed to support her, not give up. Belinda may not be the best fit for this new world, but that did not mean she did not deserve to be in it. The pair would make it through, together. She wished Belinda had ventured back to the pond, to prove their dad wrong, if only in this instance.

Audra knew she could help Belinda, but she nodded with obedience and respect. Then, she wished for more fish.

*　　*　　*

Dwyn caught up with her heated pace as she entered the market. Audra did not acknowledge his accompaniment as she purchased chicken jerky and oat bars for emergencies and en route convenience. She would get most of her food from the woods, where it was free.

Her interaction with Vesna reminded her why she did not want to dwell in the villages. The tenants had only been awake for an hour, but she had already grown tired of them. She detested their grumblings and protests when they did nothing to change it. Everyone had opinions but stayed safe within the confines of the fences. At least Dwyn had ventured out to find her. With her new food items tucked into the side pockets of her pack within easy reach, she ran out of the town with Dwyn at her heels.

That Dwyn had an ulterior motive did not surprise Audra. Everyone had one, including her. She'd taken in Dwyn to pull off a few two-person jobs, get tags she would not get otherwise, and though she would not admit it, have company once in a while. Since Belinda, she realized everyone had personal agendas. And now she knew Dwyn's.

"Hey, I'm sorry that I wasn't honest with you. My name is Dwyn. I was sent to find someone to help clear out a laboratory that no one uses anymore. We want to synthesize the antidote there and cure everyone we can. I don't understand why you're upset. Do you want to keep working for Lysent?"

Audra's face flushed. She did not want to keep working for Lysent. They were awful, but there was no way around it.

"No," she spat out, "but what can any of us do?"

"Well, I can't do much," he admitted, "but, maybe you can."

She hated the village's inhabitants for their compliance, but only because she saw the same in herself. Lysent was taking advantage of everyone, including the taggers. The system was tilted against her, but it was her only concrete choice now. No one else awakened people, just the corporation. What else was she going to do besides swallow the hypocrisy of it all for her sister and hope to catch a break that would set her ahead of Lysent's rotten curve?

Audra came to a halt. Dwyn was slow to react and circled back around. She didn't know why she needed him to understand. Maybe she felt guilty.

"This is my best option right now. You're not recruiting me."

Dwyn was not ready to give up.

"OK, what if we hire you? Give you a payout after you clear out the laboratory? You don't have to believe in us to accept our money."

Audra's eyes squinted. If she got ahead on Belinda's rent, she could make leeway into the awakening fee.

"I'll think about it," she said. "Are you still interested in tagging?"

"Why?"

"I want to travel I-16 toward the Savannah port, but tagging is a two-person deal there. Do you want to come, or are you, uh, done with whatever it is you're doing with me?"

Dwyn smiled, "Well, I've never been to Savannah."

Audra started her run again. Dwyn pulled up alongside her, instead of chasing. Audra was excited to pick through the many cars sitting on I-16. There would be easy tags along the evacuation route. Maybe they had families who'd survived.

There was one thing that kept bothering her.

"Are you actually bad at tagging and running or was that a ruse?"

"Wait, I'm not that bad, am I?"

Audra scoffed and kicked up her heels a little higher.

*　*　*

Today was the day. Audra packed their supplies in happy silence as Belinda, on this rare occasion, cooked breakfast over a fire she had crafted herself. It caught just enough to warm yesterday's leftovers with water poured over, but Audra was happy for the break. Audra was always the one gathering the wood, building the fires, and cooking the meals. Belinda stopped muttering to herself and looked up from her fussing to smile at Audra. Audra smiled back.

Yesterday while collecting firewood, Audra had discovered a zombie couple and their campground. There was no perpetrator in sight. One must have gotten bit and was too scared to tell the other. Or perhaps, they went down together. Whatever it was, the sisters didn't know or care. What they did care about was their available supplies, particularly their tent. A real tent! Not a patched tarp propped up by sticks, but a real, modern tent.

Neither dared to say it was their last night under the tarp as they finished the rabbit and frog stew. More substantial than berries and leaves, it would stick to their bones for the day. Ready to tackle the Zombie Couple, the two threw on their packs. Belinda did not even complain about its weight compared to its contents as they walked the few hundred yards to the Zombie Couple's camp.

Audra and Belinda eyed the scene. It was much like their own situation, but these two people had lost. Their fire had long died. A metal pot and other supplies were strewn about the ground. The camouflage green tent appeared in perfect condition except for a hole in the back that mice were using to transport things in and out. Mice meant more supplies hidden inside.

Had they both been capable, the sisters might have just waltzed into camp and killed the couple. However, Audra knew Belinda had a knack for freezing when life required her to stay in control of her body, and she could not handle the Zombie Couple by herself. The couple remained close together even in death. Audra could not kill one without being attacked by the other. She was much smaller than either of them and if she was bitten, who would care for Belinda? Audra decided Belinda would lure the pair into a slow moving single file. Audra would come from behind, kill the last in line, then kill the first before it had time to catch Belinda.

Near the perimeter of the camp, Belinda didn't dare shout to excite them. She just kicked about leaf debris to catch their attention. The man, in his flannel shirt and mussed thick-rimmed glasses, was closest. His heavy new work boots changed direction and headed for Belinda.

The woman with tied back blond hair full of leaves saw her husband change direction in her peripheral vision. She turned and followed him. Belinda walked to keep her distance. Audra could hear Belinda whimpering. Poor Belinda. It was one thing to be scared of these things; it was another to be constantly asked to be bait.

Audra tip-toed through the camp to approach the blond woman from behind. The woman's linen shirt and leggings were moth-eaten and inappropriate for the weather. Audra took her dagger and plunged it into the back of the woman's skull. She crumpled onto the dry leaves, signaling her husband. He turned to his love and saw Audra still standing over her, her breath held. Before anything could be decided, another fall in the woods interrupted them. This one was unintended. Belinda cried out about her ankle as Zombie Husband flipped his head around. Audra exhaled relief before realizing Belinda was still rolling around on the ground, making no effort to escape.

Zombie Husband had closed almost all the distance between injured Belinda and himself before Audra arrived. He was too tall for Audra to reach from the ground. She jumped on his back, but they were too close to Belinda. Belinda froze in fright as the duo fell on top of her.

Audra had wrapped her legs around the zom on the way down and now was pinned between the two bodies. She used both hands to grab as much of his head and hair as she could and ripped it away from Belinda. She felt vertebra resist and then crack as she dislocated Zombie Husband's head. His back wrenched underneath her. The zombie made large bites into the air, barely missing Audra's fingers, his head internally decapitated and at a ninety-degree angle from his body. Belinda fainted.

Audra's dagger was lost in the leaves during the scuffle. She held his head with one hand and found her second dagger with the other. She let it cut through his forehead and his motions ended. A dead blond lay in a heap behind them. An unconscious blond lay underneath the flannel-clad zom. Audra, still piggy-backed, collapsed with exhaustion, burying her face in the camper's neck.

The Zombie Husband's putrid scent renewed her energy. Audra pulled her head up and inhaled the fresh air deeply. She leaned to one side and pulled the opposite leg out from underneath the heavy body. Freeing her second leg, she momentarily left the corpse on top of Belinda, who still had not revived on her own. Audra rested her head on her forearms, which were perched on her bent knees. That was much harder than she'd intended. And it would make every next encounter that much worse for Belinda.

Audra turned toward her sister. She braced her feet and rolled Zombie Husband off of Belinda, putting a foot on his face to yank out her dagger. She cleaned it on his pants and checked his pockets before pulling off his flannel shirt. The shirt was large enough for either of the girls to wear as an outer layer as the weather got cooler. Audra rolled it up and put it in her pack. The corpse remained in his undershirt with his farmer's tan showing. Audra pulled Belinda to a sitting position and let her rest against a tree. She could try to revive her now, but her breathing was steady and it would be easier to go through the supplies without her.

The tent looked glorious.

As she did the final sorting and replacing of items, Belinda stirred. Audra came over and crouched by her. She stroked her face and brushed the hair from it. Belinda did not open her eyes, but gave a content smile and murmured sweet sounds like a child waking up from a happy dream. Audra sat hip to hip with her, leaning against both Belinda and the tree.

"Good morning Beebs," Audra whispered.

Belinda made a bubbly noise.

"We got a tent, Beebs," she said as she crossed her legs in front and twiddled her thumbs, waiting for her sister to wake.

*   *   *

It took two days of running to get to the city of Macon. From there, you could take I-16 to Savannah or go west to Atlanta. Some runners considered tagging on the outskirts of Atlanta, but the risks and costs were high. Finding a handful of requested bodies in a metropolitan area swarming with infected was not a good business or life plan, but Savannah was doable. Savannah was a port city, but still small. If they could get close enough, they could reach lots of supplies. And if not, there were plenty to tag whose last known location was "evacuating Savannah."

Audra knew most taggers had not been out this far. They stayed closer to town to minimize travel days, but finds were getting sparser and the search was becoming the largest expense in the tagging business.

I-16 had two lanes east and two lanes west. Westbound cars filled every lane and the median. People had remained in the unmoving traffic for days before they abandoned their cars looking for better opportunities. The cars had been long stripped of supplies, spare blankets, food, water, flashlights. All of that was gone. Audra and her family had been out here doing the looting once upon a time. But many of the cars did contain zombies. Were they people who had been bitten with the sense to isolate themselves? Or were they simply in denial that the traffic would clear and they would be on their way? Either way, a sprinkling of the cars had cooped up zombies without the fine motor skills to operate a door handle.

Easy pickings.

They approached a red sedan with an elderly lady lying on the back seat. Dwyn thought she was dead and started to the next car. Audra knew she just needed stimulation. Audra gave the car door a bump with the side of her hip. The little sedan jostled and the woman in her high-waisted khakis and knit sweater sprang up from the waist. Her eyes popped open and her face contorted as she realized food was about. She clawed at the window and Audra wondered why she had bothered. Grandma had already been abandoned once.

She was the first zombie in two days though. They had not seen a single one in the woods en route. Audra found it odd, but perhaps all the zoms in the area had followed people toward bigger cities or perhaps there was a corral. Lysent had hired "shepherds" to direct unwanted herds into contained areas to keep them from the towns.

With a tool from her pack, she popped the lock on the front passenger door like her mother had taught her. She nodded to Dwyn, who reached in and scraped Grandma's outstretched hand. DNA captured.

Name: Diana Lessing
Gender: Female
DOB: 2/2/1999
Status: No Inquiries

"Sorry, Grandma. Guess they should have just left you at the old folks' home."

Audra reached to place a yellow tag on Diana's ear. A pearl earring fell to the ground. Diana turned to bite in protest and Audra gave her a gentle punch, causing her dentures to fall. Audra had trouble placing the tag over her giggles. She locked the door behind her and hoped Grandma would calm down and return to her resting spot. At least her family would know her location if they ever inquired - in the red sedan where they had left her.

The second occupied car showed more promise. A teenage boy sat in the driver's seat wearing baggy jeans and a grungy t-shirt. In the emergency evacuation, he had found the time to style and gel his hair. He may have run away and was hiding out in cars when he was bitten. Maybe his family had thought of him after the cure was announced. He was worth a shot and good practice for Dwyn.

Audra munched on chicken jerky, trying to pass the time while Dwyn tried her tool on the lock. She coached him over a few steps but mostly let him flail about as she sat in the shade of the car. He put pressure on the window, trying to gain leverage. It cracked. Audra shook her head and laughed. Dwyn shrugged and used the tool to finish breaking the window.

Name: Link Culpepper
Gender: Male
DOB: 1/6/2063
Status: Inquired

"Audra, an inquiry!" said Dwyn, jumping up and down.

It was his first. He used Audra's reader per their agreement. Audra did not want to get her hopes up, though. An inquiry was far from credits in her pocket.

"OK, submit the find, tag him, and put him in here," she said as she stood up and popped the next car's lock in a fraction of Dwyn's time and effort. "We'll come back and get him if his parents want to pay up."

"Parents?"

"I doubt his high school sweetheart was dating him long enough to care, nor do I think she has cash. I'm betting on parents."

"Or, maybe a sibling?" Dwyn asked carefully.

"Yeah, maybe," Audra replied with a shortness that ended the conversation.

Dwyn unlocked the car door through the window and tempted Link outside. The teen's overenthusiastic desire for flesh and his poor processing skills tripped him over the car's door frame. He tumbled and scraped his face.

"Link, man, please remember to walk," requested Dwyn.

Audra's tendency to talk to the zombies had rubbed off on Dwyn. At first, Dwyn thought she was taunting them, but he admitted that her teasing respected their dangerous nature while still remembering that they were, somehow, still human.

Link pulled himself up and mumbled his distaste in his prey. He leaned forward too much, then over-corrected back. The drunk-looking teenager eventually made it over to the second car with Dwyn's luring.

This zombie could not chase people for a living. It was best if it stayed inside.

The door to the back seat was open and Audra stood on the other side of the car and banged on the window, trying to tempt Link with some girly flesh.

"I don't know if he's that discerning, Audra."

"Are you saying I'm lacking femininity?"

"Of course not."

Dwyn gave her a smile. His curly hair bounced with his movement and his blue eyes shone. He seemed to be enjoying their work. He pushed on the small of Link's back. Link landed in the car.

"Link, sweetie, you stay here. We're just going to run into the store," said Audra.

She was already looking for the next zombie. Who else was hiding in these cars? They could wrangle a tiny herd for a large payout worth their travel time. Audra looked to the endless line of cars. Maybe they would not have to travel the long miles to Savannah to find what they needed.

Ten cars down yielded the find Audra was looking for, a young girl. Jackpot. Audra did not wait to let Dwyn practice on the lock. The girl with plaited hair was a poster child for tagging. Families were looking for lost children and missing spouses (unless they had already picked up another). Audra almost stabbed her with the reader.

Name: Unknown

Gender: Female

DOB: Unknown

Status: DNA not in database, no similar matches

"What does that even mean?" asked Dwyn.

"Well… I've never seen it, but her DNA isn't registered."

"How is that possible?"

"Guess she wasn't born in a hospital. They did that stuff routinely. She's off the grid."

"How will her family find her?"

He watched her inside the car. She didn't show interest in them. She was starving and tired.

"Similar matches would have been a parent or sibling, but she doesn't have any. Her whole family might be off the grid. If that's the case, they probably don't trust the corporation to find their daughter, anyway."

"Maybe she ran off and hid here after she got bit. I hope they find her out here," said Dwyn.

He pulled his pack up tighter and looked toward the forest.

"I'm sure they will," Audra lied.

Audra decided not to tell Dwyn that no one was truly looking anymore. Sure, her job was based on finding loved ones, but it was a haphazard way to do things. Family members would toss in a request and if someone happened to find the person, then arrangements were made. No one was leaving the comforts of their new townships to search for lost loved ones. This little girl and thousands of others were discarded and forgotten. Dwyn's ferocious optimism made her wonder. Would he show up on the DNA reader? Had he forgotten or been forgotten?

They saw nobody else for the next half mile and climbed on top of a tractor trailer to eat lunch. Audra lay out with an oat bar lazily in her hand. She felt safe up high and the heat coming off the metal felt good on her tired bones. Still, she knew she would regret falling asleep on the hard surface. Dwyn watched her with another goofy smile on his face as she fought her falling eyelids.

Audra spent a little longer on top of the trailer than she intended. They decided to run to the Savannah outskirts and camp there for the night. They could check vehicles on their way back and pick up Link, who Audra imagined was brooding in the car. In another life, she would be doing the same, not chasing zombies.

For a zombie chaser, Dwyn was becoming a talented runner, keeping pace with Audra as they pushed down the middle of the two lanes. Only a jutting side view mirror or mis-angled car slowed them down. Audra enjoyed the terrain change of flat asphalt and lack of thorns and brush. She inhaled with another right step forward and thought the slight breeze was what made the day's running perfect. Dwyn led by a little more than a car length.

Her inhalation took a sharp and unintended escape as a car door kicked open with great momentum. Audra ran into it full force and it did not give despite its hinges. Her head lurched forward above the car door while her torso remained behind her. Her body and head fell backward onto the asphalt in unison. Her head took an extra bounce. She heard a voice which faded into darkness.

*   *   *

When Audra's mind emerged, she felt cramped and on something structured and soft. After a few more moments, she realized she was lying in the back seat of a car. She did not believe a lot of time had passed. It was still daylight. She did not sit up but remained as still as possible. She did not want to alert her attacker she was awake as she assessed her pained body. Nothing appeared broken. The sound and pressure of her own pulse overtook any awareness of the back of her head. Audra imagined a big knot forming.

She tried to remember what had happened.

Someone had swung open the car door in front of her. They had braced it so it would not shut when she hit it. They'd known she was coming and trapped her.

Dwyn was up ahead.

Did they get Dwyn, too?

They had to have seen Dwyn. That meant he either escaped, or they had captured him, or worse. Audra tried to replay the visual moment she hit the car door. Was Dwyn also being hit by a door? Was there more than one assailant? She couldn't remember if she had seen Dwyn being attacked.

Audra closed her eyes to focus on a sound beyond the pounding in her head. She made out voices, two voices. They were arguing in hushed tones. Neither was Dwyn. Audra willed her pulse to quiet as she struggled to hear.

"Look, you can't mess with her. Corp said — only steal her pack — this isn't a level two op."

Audra's eyes widened. What the hell were they talking about? The other guy mumbled something that Audra could not make out.

"Dude. I ain't got time for this shit. Grab the pack and let's go. We gotta be gone."

Audra heard cursing, more grumbling, and someone kicking cars and debris. Her heart sank. She expected to hear a scuffle next and then for someone to come for her. She wanted to run, to jump out of the car and sprint for it. Her body ached. Would adrenaline let her run into the woods or would her head double her over? She was in no shape to outrun anyone, but at least she had the element of surprise, awake in the car. Audra stayed slumped with her eyes closed, despite what all her instinct screamed.

The noises faded. Audra was not sure how much time she let pass before she dared to open her eyes. It was still light out. Had she passed out? Were they still here? She could detect her pulse in the distant part of her head, birds outside, and nothing else. Five minutes passed, then ten. Were they gone? There was nothing left to do but to sit up and gather more information.

Her body felt bruised and heavy, but responsive. She planted her hands and straightened her elbows to pull her torso and head up. As she strained her neck to the window, pain seared forward from the knot on the back of her head and bubbles of light filled her vision. To gather herself, she attempted a deep breath, but her ribs popped in pain. When the stars left her, I-16 materialized in the window - cars everywhere and no one in sight. She took her time to position her back against the seat. The car felt like it was moving, but it was not. She was alone.

Were they gone for good? If they planned to keep her, one would have gone out and the other would have stood guard. Instead, they had left her alone. Was Dwyn in another car? It was time to find out. Audra stumbled out of the sedan and into the road. A quick glance in both directions showed that her pack was nowhere to be found. She pursed her lips.

BANG BANG!

Audra's body dropped to the asphalt without her permission, her eyes spread wide. They had come back for her. She wasn't safe.

BANG BANG!

Audra came to her senses. The sound was coming from a car up ahead. She called out and recognized Dwyn's voice. She raced to the muffled sound and popped the trunk that hid it. Dwyn barely sat up before Audra fell into his arms.

"Thank God, you're alive," she said in between the tears that overcame her.

All the fear bubbled up and threw Audra over. It threw her and wrecked her, much to her surprise. In just a few short moments, she composed herself. She let Dwyn emerge from the car trunk where he knelt. He struggled to swing his legs over the side, perhaps in as much pain as Audra.

"Do you remember what happened?" she asked.

He leaned up against the bumper and looked at a distant spot on the ground, willing his memories to form.

"I heard you hit something… I turned around and saw the car door. I ran toward it and got pushed from behind."

"Yeah, there were two of them."

"We fought, but I was already on the ground. He must have knocked me out and shoved me in the trunk. Are you OK?" he asked, suddenly realizing that he did not know what happened after that point. Anything could have happened.

Audra nodded, "I'm fine. They shoved me in the car. Stole our packs."

"Do you know who they were?"

"I overheard one of them say they were from the corporation…" said Audra grimly, not providing all the information she heard. "They made it sound like it was a planned attack by Lysent. Would they do something like that?"

"You tell me, Audra. You're the one who works with them. Maybe they thought you were getting too far in your contract. You found Link pretty quickly after Randy."

Audra stayed silent. But how did they know where she was?

The reader. It sent her location every time she ran DNA. They knew she was running along I-16. She was predictable.

The two sat and leaned partially against the car's back tire and partially against each other. They looked up and down the road, surveying their predicament. A small sigh escaped Audra's lungs. That pack was her livelihood. Her tent, her food, the bit of money she had left, her spare clothes, her cooking pot, her photos of her family at Disney World and another one by the Christmas tree. Soon she would have to stand up and fight to survive, but for a moment she mourned for what she had lost.

The Christmas tree and the amusement park were gone. And now, their photographic evidence was gone, too. She stood as the last vessel that could recall those memories. And if Lysent prevented her from waking up her sister, they would fade forever.

Anger set in. And she stood up.

6 Found

Audra smiled over the simmering pot. She caught a rabbit and had stretched it over three meals supplementing it with mushrooms and wild onions. As she scooped it into their tin cups, Belinda did not thank her for once again providing for her. Audra noticed Belinda eat the vegetables around the meat.

"I'm going for a walk. I'll finish on the way." Belinda was never a good liar.

She had not eaten any of the rabbit in the last three days. Audra watched her walk into the woods in the dusky light, ignoring her temptation to follow her. How would Belinda grow if Audra was always right over her shoulder? She needed space.

And so did Audra. She appreciated the few moments alone. Belinda required constant comforting, not to mention help to stay alive and fed. She had trouble accepting her new life. When can we go back to the city? When can I sleep in a real bed? Belinda was not content with survival. She wanted more.

A cry broke through the woods.

Audra jumped over the fire and into the woods where she had seen her sister disappear. Belinda wailed again and Audra adjusted the trajectory of her sprint. Not knowing what she would find, she pulled out her dagger. The woods seemed to have become so much darker in the few minutes' gap between thinking it was OK for Belinda to wander and now fearing for her. She should have kept a better watch on her. This was her fault.

Audra spotted Belinda underneath a small outcropping and stopped when she realized that Belinda was not crying for help. Belinda knelt over a bloodied mass, crying over the animal she had been feeding. This was where Audra's rabbit had been going.

Belinda's back was to her and it felt, to their new world. Audra stood at a distance deciding whether she should leave Belinda to mourn or provide help. However, something else began to encroach.

"Belinda! Zombie!"

The animal blood mingled on his face and clothing. The zombie responsible for the death had returned. Audra ran toward them but stopped in her tracks as Belinda turned, reared up, and roared. Belinda grabbed her whittling knife from her belt and sprinted toward the shambler. Audra's surprise wore off, but she remained back to observe. Belinda needed to learn combat.

"You killed them!" she shouted, shaking with anger as she came down on it.

It was on the ground before it could understand what was happening. Belinda was on top, screaming, stabbing and stabbing. What she did not have in accuracy, she made up for in enthusiasm. Eventually, the zombie stopped moving and Belinda grew tired. She sat in the leaves with her legs in front of her, panting to catch her breath.

Perhaps Belinda would get the hang of this after all.

After a few minutes, Belinda went back to the mama dog and her dead pups. She mourned for them like she mourned for all lost life.

*   *   *

Audra and Dwyn kept to I-16. It was a direct path and cars were available for shelter anytime they needed it. But, foraging for food and keeping water was difficult, and even Audra was forced to slow down. From I-16, they reached the rail line and a week later, arrived on Vesna's doorstep with nothing to their names. Vesna fed them immediately. Despite Vesna's secondary agenda, Audra struggled to name another who would have been as generous. Maybe Rosie if they had ever had any dealings outside the corporation. Rosie tried to look out for her. Or so she thought. Did Rosie know what was planned for her? Was she letting it happen? There was obvious truth in Vesna's speech, but how much? Audra always felt uneasy about leaving her sister in their care, but now fear crept in. If they hired people to hurt their own contractors, how safe was her sister?

The next morning, she arrived in the second township that held Lysent and her sister. Lysent charged indentured taggers for family visits, citing transportation and safety concerns to justify the fees. She had last seen her sister in July - Belinda's birthday. She was in no position to confront Lysent, nor ready to reveal what she knew, but she needed to make sure her sister was all right.

Audra waved to Clyde, who was wheeling a body outside the township fences to be buried. With a shake of his head, he confirmed it wasn't a zom Audra had known, but it was a reminder that she was running out of time.

As always, Rosie greeted her from the desk. Audra tried to decipher whether there was a hint of surprise in the receptionist's eyes. She could not tell.

"I want to see my sister."

"Sure, the usual fee will apply. Did you… bring in a zombie?" Rosie asked, riffling through her paperwork for maybe a communication she had missed.

"No. My reader was stolen. I need a new one."

Rosie stopped rummaging through papers and looked up at her. Her eyebrows came together and wrinkled with worry. She looked back to her papers as if she thought better of whatever she might have said.

"Sure, the usual fee will apply…" as she rummaged through papers again.

Rosie located Audra's thick folder in the cabinet and matched it up against the pricing sheet she found on the desk. Her eyes furrowed when she saw some of the recent notes. Audra tried to catch a peek, but the papers were strategically positioned.

"You've already lost a reader. This one will cost double."

Audra gave a puzzled look.

"I've never lost a reader. Look again."

"Sorry Audra, it says you lost one last year. Serial number 23."

"I never had 23. Mine was 9."

The receptionist showed signs of impatience.

"Well, bring back your reader and we will read the number on it."

Audra glared at Rosie. They were typically cordial, but Rosie's trust in her sloppy paperwork annoyed Audra. And she wanted to know what was written in her chart that suddenly made her down two readers. Every step back she encountered with Lysent flashed through her mind. Had everything been perfectly balanced to leave her screwed without her realizing?

Audra sighed.

"What is my account at?"

"With the THIRD reader, the visit today, and the month's rent since you were last here… 1.8 million credits. 1.2 if you bring back the reader this time."

How could she be in worse shape than when she walked in with Belinda? She had been working for years. Rosie distracted herself by pushing paperwork around on her desk.

"Fine. Let me see my sister."

"Sure, give us an hour and we will be ready."

An hour later, Clyde escorted Audra farther onto the campus, which looked something in between a hospital and a prison. Clyde had aged more than the three years they had known each other. He had lost muscle mass, leaving him as thin as any other Lysent office worker. But Audra knew he was deceptively strong. If a zombie had crossed the front plaza, Clyde had manhandled it. He escorted both claimed and collateral zoms around the property. He wore his white robe which was not commensurate with his job, but with his status. Audra had never questioned it, but now she questioned everything. Why did they have time to be clean and sparkly? Where did they get such nice fabric when she only had the shirt on her back?

A man in a white lab coat was waiting for Clyde and Audra in the front lobby.

"This way," he said without greeting as he turned down the hall.

Audra waved her goodbye to Clyde as she followed, feeling like a kid in trouble at school. This was "the hotel" where zoms were stored and awakened. The windowed front rooms showed the rich their loved ones' accommodations. Zoms often occupied the rooms, "in holding" to be awakened. Audra swore she saw repeats though as if they were on rotation. Audra had ignored it, just as she had ignored the fact she had never met a success story from the indentured tagging program. She had overlooked a lot in the process of helping her sister.

Her escort opened the door to the visitation room. Audra looked farther down the hall before entering. She had once asked for a tour but was told it would stress out the "guests." They reported the scientists were trained to keep the guests perfectly calm and healthy. Audra wondered what it looked like back there. How many zoms? How much space did Belinda have?

"Just come out when you are ready," he prompted.

Floor to ceiling acrylic glass split the white sterile room in half. Drilled holes at the top and bottom of the glass equalized the air pressure. On her side, a white pine chair sat for her convenience. On the other side, stood an almost stranger in a white jumpsuit with thinning hair and a sallow complexion. She stared at one of the opaque side walls, unmoving. Audra noticed less and less movement from her sister with each visit. Was it because she was left in the dark between visits? Maybe the hour was to help her adjust to the light of the room.

Audra walked forward until her body leaned against the glass. She used her full palm to tap twice on the surface. Belinda's blond head turned slowly toward the noise. She stood for a moment looking at the frozen image of Audra. Belinda appeared intact but empty.

"Hi, Belinda."

Belinda's jaw dropped and her body pivoted. She walked with a small stagger, each step slow and shuffling. Audra remained still with her hand on the glass and watched as her sister came to meet her. She was the same height. They had the same cheekbones, but even in ruin, Belinda's beauty was undeniable. Belinda's mouth opened wide to capture Audra's. On close inspection, Audra noticed Belinda's skin drooped on her cheekbones.

"I'm sorry you're still in here."

Belinda's bare feet kept tapping the bottom of the wall as she continued her walk. Audra looked down at her feet. They were clean and unbruised. Were the baseboards in her room padded? Did she have a room at all? Audra had handed over Belinda to Lysent, burying herself in debt. She was not sure if they had started the epidemic, but they had started this lie. Audra wished she had never approached them.

Belinda followed Audra as she walked along the room to one corner. Audra knelt down and stuck her knife into one of the holes. Careful to avoid Belinda, she sawed at it to test its durability. It gave way, but slowly. Audra would need another tool to cut enough acrylic to access her sister, but at least it was an option.

Belinda dropped down to her level.

"I promise I'll make it right," Audra whispered.

Audra heard the door behind her swing open. Her fingertips guided her knife up her sleeve as she turned on her heels to look. She was shocked to see Larange Greenly standing there, two guards on either side. Had she set off a silent alarm? With no other option, she shot a surprised and annoyed look at the person interrupting family time.

"I am sorry to bother you, Miss Audra. I heard you were here, visiting your sister. How is she?"

Audra's anger simmered in her chest above her heart and threatened to overflow from her collarbone. In truth, Audra did not know how her sister was doing. They were on opposite sides of acrylic. And on this side, Audra wondered, for the first time, if she should incite change with her knife hidden in her sleeve and the leader at arm's reach. Audra imagined that was why she was escorted by guards even within her own walls.

"You should know how she's doing. You're the one in charge of this shin-dig."

Why was Greenly bothering her now? They had not met since she'd asked to be a tagger those years ago. Greenly had better things to do than to confront an indentured tagger, didn't she? The audacity overwhelmed her.

"In fact," Audra continued, "you've been in charge from the start, so I've heard, anyway. I was just a child when this virus broke out. Seems odd that such a big biomedical, communications, blah blah blah company dutied to fight the virus as it swept the nation could still land on top at the end."

Audra stared Greenly down as she spoke and saw her eyes dodge hers almost imperceptibly. Audra searched her face for the truth, but the flinch disappeared as Greenly retorted.

"From your current status, it seems, my dear, that you have no idea how to manage your own personal finances, much less know what big business is all about. I heard you've lost another of our readers. Those are very valuable. Something will have to be done if your account continues further in the red."

Greenly's eyes moved from Audra to the girl behind the glass, pointedly. Her face withered into disgust at the presence of her charge.

"I think I know exactly what this big business is about."

*　　*　　*

A few blocks away from the corporation campus, Dwyn approached her with two oat bars in his hand. He was anxious to feed her again. They had gotten quite weak during their time out. Audra waved him off as she picked up speed and ran out of the village. Lysent was watching her. And while they already knew Dwyn tagged with her, she didn't want them to know how close they had gotten. Audra didn't even like how close they had gotten. But she didn't have time to think about that. She needed to wrap her mind around meeting Greenly. A drink was tempting, but she had no money to her name. So instead, she went for a run. There was no better place to think than on a run.

The runner stayed on the well-traveled path. The soft pounding of her feet ushered her thoughts. It was clear the indentured path would never work. Greenly would never let her or her sister out of the contract. She was too valuable as a tagger and Belinda was her motivation. In a world of uncontrollable zombies, Greenly settled for power over individuals. Greenly had made that clear by arriving in person to the visitation room. She used Belinda, but Audra could use Belinda, too. Surviving the week to find her sister still alive, gave her a new sense of urgency. She had tagged for three years now. If she wanted their lives back, she was going to have to fight for it. Vesna's group was a new opportunity and for now, her best bet.

As if her decision dictated the run, she found herself back near the village gate. There, Dwyn waited. He hadn't waited to eat though.

"How is Belinda?" he asked as he handed Audra a half-eaten bar.

Out of sight of the village, they walked farther away from possible ears.

"She looked OK. You guys are right, though. That place is not what it seems."

She described her encounter to Dwyn.

"Why is Greenly suddenly interested in you?"

Audra shrugged her shoulders. Greenly had seemed amused when Audra had arrived a rail-thin girl accompanying her infected sister, asking to go on dangerous missions for the chance to wake her up. She had gone through the ranks of taggers, and now, as Audra saw it, often cut down by the corporation when her own failures did not see an end to it. Her stomach boiled with the revelation. She handed back the oat bar and they ran to Vesna's village. She needed to talk with her.

The open-air market housed many vendors, but Vesna ran a Lysent-sponsored supply shop which carried hard-to-find items. Rather than drag everything in and out of the market, Vesna ran her shop. Dwyn explained Vesna had to do paperwork on any unusual purchases, like laboratory equipment or big weapons, but otherwise, it put her in a great position to supply a rebellion.

They entered the little cottage on the main drag. Equipment for camping, farming, and hunting was stacked along the walls and on the shelves. Vesna was the only occupant.

"How is your sister?" Vesna asked as she popped her head out from under the front counter.

Dwyn's and Vesna's concern for her sister surprised Audra. Few in the world inquired about her and her sister's life. Audra answered, not mentioning Greenly's visit. Dwyn noticed but did not interrupt. Audra was not there to share but to gather information. Just because she was not on Lysent's side, did not mean she should default to Vesna's.

"Where are you from? What did you do before?" Audra asked.

If Vesna was taken aback by the personal question, she did not show it. Audra was showing interest in their group. It was a good thing. Vesna's face dimmed as she recalled her prior life.

"I was a mother and an attorney. I lived in what used to be North Carolina with my family. They are all gone now. Lysent recommended we burn all the bodies and the state government complied."

With every syllable addressing Lysent, her shoulders hunched more in anger.

"I've hated them from the start. I think they started all of this. As a lawyer, I was involved in a few suits against them. I know what they are about."

Audra recognized a strong ally with hatred coursing through her veins. While they had dissimilar goals, they had a common enemy and the same strong thread of motivation. They were both the last of their families. If all of Lysent fell, it would be the last of that "family" as well. She cut the interrogation short.

"I will help if you help retrieve my sister and cure her."

Vesna nodded, her face almost grim with seriousness. Her anger still intense. But Dwyn broke into a large grin.

"Hand over your reader. Let's open it up," commanded Vesna.

Audra jerked back. She had just gone down the hole another 0.6 million credits to get this damn reader. She didn't even have a backpack to put it in. Now her new leader wanted to break it open?

"I'll be careful. Readers send out your GPS signal when you submit a find, but we need to make sure they did not doctor this one to track your movements."

Audra sighed but gave her the device. Vesna pulled out a screwdriver and carefully pried it apart. Vesna looked it over and seemed satisfied.

"It's clean. It will only transmit your location when you read DNA and submit it."

"So, I still have to be careful where I submit DNA. They will know where I am and possibly guess where I'm going."

"Yes, that's correct, but we also can use that to our advantage. Eat up, and you can sleep here tonight. Dwyn will give you details of your first mission. You'll get supplies tomorrow."

"I'd rather sleep in a tent. Do you have a tent I could borrow?"

"If you want to sleep in a tent, you might as well resupply now. Take what you need." Vesna swept her hand to gesture at the entire store.

Audra looked over at the shelves of equipment. Working with Vesna was a good choice. She picked up the lightest pack she could find and layered it with a small tent, blanket, a light cooking pot, a canteen, and food. Audra had never collected so many things at once. She had worked hard for every piece of equipment in her pack, especially that tent. Audra tested the weight of the pack. Some of the things were heavier than she desired but necessary to have.

As Audra gave her thanks and started to leave, Vesna turned to Dwyn.

"Oh and see that she does not get into trouble."

Dwyn did not acknowledge the command. Audra let out a "humph" of disapproval but did not pick a fight, since she had an entire pack of gifts. It appeared her recruitment did little to soften Vesna's directions.

The pair walked out and into the late sunshine. Dwyn tilted his head to look at his partner, whose mind had already wandered to the nearest moonshiner's hideout, around the corner on a dusty road. The shiner's specialty was "blue moon corn," but Audra only cared about the alcohol content. Perhaps she could work for a few drinks?

Dwyn interrupted her thoughts without confronting their contents.

"Want to go for a test run with our new packs?"

7 Laboratory

It was not quite dawn when Dwyn stuck his head into Audra's tent.

"They are here."

"Have them be here later. It's not even light out."

"They're… an enthusiastic bunch."

Dwyn had spoken the truth. When Audra stumbled out, a hand thrust itself into her personal space as an engineer greeted the sleepy woman.

"It is such a pleasure to meet you! We've been waiting weeks to move onto the next phase in the development. I'm Ryder, by the way. We can't work in the village anymore without risking being detected," the young woman with spiked brown hair chattered on as Audra mustered the patience.

Ryder's two partners stood back. One gave a little wave, but neither looked keen to be outside the fences. Ryder introduced them. Ziv had long hair and a full beard that took over much of his thin frame. Satomi looked younger than Ryder if that was possible. Her dark hair shimmered in the sunlight as she brushed it out of her face nervously. Audra noticed Dwyn's grin was larger and goofier this morning.

Audra sighed when she looked past the trio to their four large wagons of stuff they would take to the laboratory.

"You can't transport all of this in one trip," Audra said with an air of impatience.

This trip would be a long one if she was going to pull somebody else's wagon of unneeded crap. Ryder smiled.

"Yes, I guess we have a lot of equipment, but…" Ryder said, pulling out a remote with joysticks on it, "all the wagons are solar powered and remote controlled. As long as we stay on the road, it shouldn't be too hard for the wagons to match our pace."

Audra's eyebrows rose as one of the carts picked up speed and traveled down the road.

"Impressive," said Audra.

Here she was with nothing to her name, and this girl was making solar powered motor vehicles.

"…I had some time while we were waiting for you guys," said Ryder with a shrug.

Audra stepped back and addressed the group.

"OK, listen up. Dwyn and I will take turns taking point, so we don't stumble into any herds or corrals. The other will stay close to the group to guard against lateral movements from zoms and to protect our backside. I don't know how much experience you have with zombies but stay away from the end that bites. They are attracted to loud sounds, bright visual stimuli, and human smells. Please avoid being those things."

"Yes," said Satomi, "those are all housed in the lower brain."

Knowing anatomy was not the same as being able to survive a zom attack, but Audra nodded. At least Satomi and Ryder were engaging in what she was saying. That was a good sign. Ziv just shuffled from foot to foot. Maybe he would get eaten.

Ryder thanked Audra, and they were soon on their way. Months ago, Dwyn had located the laboratory through old paperwork and maps. He had visited, but there were too many zombies for him to clear out on his own. The lab was thirty miles down the highway, and then ten miles off. Dwyn would explain the situation at the lab en route.

Boredom set in for the new explorers. Ziv was the loudest, complaining about blisters after just two hours. Audra was not sure how hard to push them. She did not want to stress them, but she also did not want to spend the rest of her life walking forty miles. Audra could do that in a day and a half, at leisure. This was painfully slower than leisurely pace and occasionally interrupted by a cart flipping and tossing all its contents. She tried to distance everyone from their displeasure, including her own, by learning more about the new team.

Ryder had worked with the antidote at Lysent. Her parents had been Lysent scientists, and she was recruited at a young age. No one at Lysent had been able to tell her how the antidote was developed. It just existed. When she'd learned that she was just replicating limited batches of doses without work to advance their knowledge or better help the country, she had looked for ways to leave.

Ziv had taught biochemistry at a local college but was quick to point out that he had little practical experience. He offered no information on what he had been doing since. Audra gathered it was not much. He was not pleasant to talk to, so Audra did not try.

Satomi was about as much of a medical student as people could be now. She had studied under a traditionally taught doctor and had pored over medical textbooks. More than the practical day-to-day, she learned epidemiology and immunology. Satomi was interested in how the virus spread and methods of eradication. How the corporation had not picked her up yet was a curiosity to Audra. Ryder reported the recruitment would have come shortly.

The group walked eight miles before they decided that a dinner break was in order. Audra suggested they set up camp and start back out in the morning. It would be best to keep the explorers rested. Perhaps renewed energy and enthusiasm would compensate for their lack of experience. Audra doubted it.

When Ziv's head emerged from his tent the next morning, his eyes darted left and right before he stepped out. He surveyed the woods despite everyone already being out and about. With no dangers in sight, he finished with a glare directed at Audra.

Audra raised her eyebrows in amusement.

"Yes?" she offered.

"This is ridiculous. You should have cleared the path, the lab, and then come to get us. You're unnecessarily risking our lives. We're very valuable. We're scientists."

His answer was quick, something he had been stewing on for most of the night.

Audra looked around to see if anyone agreed. Satomi seemed to become smaller, wishing to avoid the conflict. Ryder was about to dismiss him in her cheery, talkative way, but Audra interrupted.

"All lives are valuable, Ziv. The sooner we get you to the laboratory, the sooner you can help them… all."

Ziv huffed and retreated into his tent. This was the person she would be relying on to save her sister?

"I'm sorry," said Ryder, apologizing for him. "Of course we believe everyone is worth saving and that there is still a sense of urgency after all these years. We're just not used to being… out here. It's a little scary. I don't think Ziv has ever been outside the township. I just left my job at Lysent. We're just new to all of this."

Breakfast was silent after the outburst, except for Ryder's sporadic attempts to boost morale. She bounced around enthusiastically, but it didn't hide the fact they were all tired and sore.

They got a later start than Audra had imagined. Everything seemed to take disproportionately longer with scientists in tow. And Audra could only listen to their complaints so long. When she tired of them, she would charge ahead and Dwyn would stay with the crew, helping to balance things on the cart, encouraging tired and blistered feet, and making sure nobody got lost.

It took seven days to get to the laboratory. Seven long days. Thankfully it did not rain. Audra thought that would have been the end of the scientists' morale. All of their water repellent gear would have been used to cover the sensitive equipment, leaving the group to soak in the rain. The scientific trio cheered when they reached the industrial park, surrounded by tall chain-link fences topped with barbed wire. Audra and Dwyn motioned for them to be quiet. They still had to clear out the place and it would not help to get the zombies riled up before they could establish a plan.

*   *   *

Dwyn and Audra escorted the scientists out of visual sight of the park and had them set up camp. They were getting much better at it. At least scientists were fast learners. Dwyn and Audra walked a large perimeter around the camp to verify that the crew would be safe before scouting out the park. Dwyn repeated the information he had gleaned from his last trip, words he had recited to her many times already. Audra did not quiet him; she knew he was nervous. He had seen almost a dozen within the fences, outside the buildings. The laboratory was along the east side of the industrial park, close to the fence. Looking through the windows, he had seen several zombies moving around inside, but did not have an exact count. It was too much for one person, especially with Dwyn's skill set when he last came.

They circled around the park until they found the entrance with just a traffic arm bar across the threshold. A quick inspection showed a chain-link fence that could be pulled closed. They would leave it open for now, in case they needed a speedy escape. The dusty road that led to it must lead to the highway, the opposite direction from town.

They both had daggers in their hands and spare ones in their boots. Dwyn's right leg shook in nervous excitement like it wanted to tap the ground, but it did not for fear of making noise. Audra's leg shook too from lack of cash and moonshine as of late. She was glad to reach the pinnacle of their mission. Vesna had agreed to pay her afterward.

"Ready?" asked Dwyn.

Audra just gave a grin, ducked under the arm, and ran to the first building. Dwyn gave chase to get ahead. They wrapped around the building and Dwyn turned the corner to look. He motioned that there were two within view. Audra took the right one. Dwyn took the left. Quick motion with their knives let two fall.

The front side of the park was now clear. Now to pick a building to be their zombie pen. A quick peek inside the front office showed four in there. The front office it was. They would corral them all in there for a pool of experimental subjects.

Audra moved to the next building and tested the door. It was unlocked. A woman wearing a long dress, fake pearls, and an administrative-appropriate hairstyle greeted her at the door.

Audra apologized for not having an appointment.

She baited her outside and into the front office. Dwyn pushed her farther in and closed the door with a smile on his face. While he had less experience killing, he had learned great handling skills.

Not all were as demure as the assistant. Some zombies were faster and required the two to run and even sometimes sprint. It was difficult to tell who would be fast. Audra knew if she was ever bitten, she would be damn fast. By midday, they reached the laboratory. A quick peek inside the door showed more occupants than in the other buildings combined. There were at least twenty. What was this isolated group doing? Audra and Dwyn both needed more energy to tackle the group. They would come back after lunch.

With no screams heard from the camp, Audra did not worry. They were met with a roaring fire, treated water, and a rotating nap schedule in the pop up tents. The scientists had taken up guard to watch for biters. They did well although the fire was a little large. Audra gave them a pass - this part of the country seemed abandoned, the road unkempt and the laboratory forgotten.

"How many subjects will you need?" asked Audra.

She used her jaw to tear off a particularly tough piece of jerky.

"It really depends, but we'd like to keep them all alive. Why? Are there a lot in the industrial park?" asked Ryder.

"We've corralled about twenty, but the laboratory has at least that many."

Audra looked Ryder straight in the eye, letting her jerky hand fall to her hip.

"I need to ask you something," Audra said.

"Yes?"

"How did you know this laboratory was here? Why is it full of people?"

No answer from Ryder. Satomi, who usually leaned toward silence, spoke up for Ryder.

"Ziv worked with a group in there, studying the infected. It went bad."

She walked to her tent, knowing the rest of the conversation did not need her. Everyone turned to Ziv.

"I had just started there. None of that was under my control," Ziv retorted.

"You were experimenting with… people?" asked Dwyn.

Ziv's head hung low and his long hair covered his quiet face. What Audra had already realized, suddenly came to Dwyn.

"Did everyone get infected but you?" asked Dwyn with some innocence left in his voice, but gradually doing the math in his head.

Ziv was slow to answer. Audra rolled her eyes. She did not want to listen to the sad story he was about to draw up. She was instead concerned about more pertinent information that he had kept from them.

"How many are there?"

"Fifteen scientists, three original infected. Eighteen total."

"How many rooms are there? Is anybody locked up? Are the doors locked? Are there other exits?" Audra spouted off questions.

Ziv seemed relieved that some of his secrets had been revealed. He answered her questions as well as he could. Audra tried to hide her anger. If they had not come back for lunch, they would have been clearing the laboratory without this information, information that could save their lives.

After she gleaned what she needed, she and Dwyn headed back. A look inside the lab showed sallow men and women in white lab coats splattered with blood, but otherwise clean. Besides some knocked over beakers and Erlenmeyer flasks and liquid on the floor, the laboratory was in fairly good shape, too.

They approached the front door, which would open into the lobby. It was locked, just as Ziv shared. Although Audra had pulled a lot of information from Ziv, she still did not fully trust it. The infected group, one survivor, and one locked door revealed his character. She needed to trust her own instincts.

And here, her first chance performed a hip-heavy walk toward her, clad in a white lab coat with a large blood stain on the hanging sleeve as if her arm had retreated farther into the lab coat for protection. Audra grabbed the hanging sleeve and pulled on the other to tie it into a faux strait-jacket. Dwyn caught sight of Audra's doing as the zom ping-ponged through the door frame. He rolled his eyes. Dwyn bear hugged it from behind, securing the arms low on the hips, and shuffled to the front building. He called back to Audra to close the door and wait for him, but Audra had already slipped inside.

The dark wood panels on the wall gave a distinctly dated and untouched vibe. Paneling like that was long gone, often used as firewood or reinforcement. On the front desk, a phone sat with many lines unblinking and papers strewn, or thoughtfully organized if you consulted Rosie. A couch, soon to be fought over, shared its space with fading magazines - fodder for future sleepless nights. The rest of the room was empty. Audra opened the interior door and the warm colors of the front gave way to the more classic white tile and counter tops of a lab. Geeky zombies bounced from counter to counter, no longer able to perform their research.

Audra considered the knowledge lost in the minds here; knowledge seemed in short supply now. They should be saved if she could help it. One came running to her and grabbed at her neck. She sunk her dagger into it. Well, if they had such great minds, they wouldn't have gotten infected.

Dwyn joined her outside the doorway, saw the downed zombie, and scolded Audra playfully with his eyes. Audra smiled slyly, which received a joking push in return. It was then she realized he was close enough for her to feel his breath on her ear, moving the wisps of hair along her neck. Her lack of movement signaled Dwyn. He backed off, but a second adrenaline pulsed through her body as they entered the laboratory.

Audra and Dwyn returned late into the evening. The campfire had been calmed down a great deal more, despite Audra's silence on the matter. With the darkness of the night and their protectors busy on the other side of the fence, they did little to draw attention to themselves. Audra and Dwyn leaned up against a log, kicked off their boots, and breathed. They had done well. As their reward, the scientists gifted the two with freeze-dried meals. The reconstituted hash browns and chicken gave blessed variety from the jerky and oat bars that filled their lives.

Her feast was interrupted by the scientists' chatter about their future endeavors. Their casual talk of human experimentation frightened Audra. It seemed foreign and cold. Ryder noticed Audra's trepidation and stepped outside her scientific circle to comfort.

"We get that they are real people and what we're doing is of consequence, but it's better for the process if we coldly analyze. And honestly, burying ourselves in our work allows us to distance ourselves from the event and from dwelling on how it has personally impacted us. It's our way of coping and hopefully it also eventually helps others."

Audra could understand. Her escape was not science - it was running. The comfort of the repetition, the skill, it let her forget that the world was crumbling down around them.

With a full belly and a greater understanding, Audra leaned against Dwyn's shoulder and stared into the fire's sparks. Even if she now went back to tagging in the morning, she did feel secretly accomplished for helping this group under Lysent's nose. And she was actually enjoying their company. They weren't like the other villagers, content in their shell of existence. They and Belinda had that in common. And if they figured out how to create an antidote, Audra's Belinda would be the first in line.

The next morning, the scientists were up bright and early to move into their new laboratory. Audra showed them how to operate the front gate and gave them some tips on how to avoid being seen by people passing on the road. They had trouble listening. Even Ziv was excited to restock the laboratory and go back to their happy science lives. After a quick inventory, Audra was handed a letter for Vesna requesting additional supplies.

Audra was six miles out before her body and her mind realized she was running. Away from the chatter of the scientists, she sensed the solitude even with Dwyn on her tail. Just the rustling of the debris beneath her, the scratching on her pant legs by the brush, and the speckling of the sun on her face. Running seemed to be her natural pace. Her body which seemed awkward and small when near others, felt most natural in movement, running in the woods.

While Dwyn had much improved, Audra still outran him in the longest distances, but Audra did seem exceptional in that regard. Dwyn slowed to walk after twenty miles. Audra scolded him for not eating enough to get through the four-hour mark. Dwyn rolled his eyes.

"I'll meet you up there," he conceded.

Audra ran the forty miles back to the township. It was late in the evening, but Vesna was there to receive her. She perused the letter as Audra unpacked items she did not need. Vesna reluctantly counted out the money she'd promised Audra.

"Are you sure you don't want to stay here for the night?" asked Vesna.

Audra heard the judgment in her voice. She did not know Vesna well enough to wait for Dwyn in her company. With her payout in her pocket, she said her good night.

Audra stepped out into the cool air. She was proud of her work. Food and sleep could be enough after the long run. Maybe she wouldn't drink tonight.

A drink, just one, would be nice.

She shouldn't.

An odd but distinct odor wafted to her. Yelling broke out into the night. She turned the corner toward the commotion and saw a small stable on fire within the confines of the township. There were people running to help. Audra ran to help too, but then the flames licked up. She froze.

8 Rest

Belinda jumped up and down, clapping her hands. Her eyes squinted with her large smile. Audra had just given her the all-clear after searching the tiny wood cabin and finding no zombies or humans within. Zoms were easy, humans were not. Audra kept them clear of people, much to Belinda's loneliness. There was only so much protection Audra could provide and people were unpredictable. But the horizontal surfaces of the cabin had a short layer of dust, everything creaked, and there was no food to be found. Audra almost jumped off the stoop to get out of Belinda's way as she stormed the place. Belinda ran circles around the small cabin, stomping inside.

"It's like Christmas, Audra! Do you think it's Christmas time?"

Audra looked out the grimy window for reference, but could not see much. It had been cold for about a month. There was no snow in southern Georgia. Could be Christmas, for all they knew.

They would possibly find a well outside, but the kitchen had been destroyed. The sink had fallen through the cabinets, all the cabinet doors were off their hinges as if someone had opened them in search of food, and they had rotted off their hinges by their own weight from being open for so long. The place was full of mildew and cobwebs. As awful as it was, it had been Belinda's dream for months. Tears of joy found the corners of Audra's eyes. This place was dangerous. Had she been on her own, she would not stay here. It was safer to camp in non-permanent structures, moving from place to place. But she'd risk it for Belinda. Belinda needed this rotting two-room cabin.

A scream from the other room pierced Audra's heart with fear. She followed Belinda's earlier march, pulling out her dagger. She recalled all the spaces in the bedroom. What had Belinda uncovered?

A bed.

Belinda fell backward onto the mattress and spread out her arms and legs. It fit her entire body. Belinda had not seen a bed since they'd evacuated their homes and gone to the community "safe" house where she and Audra had shared a cot. Belinda hated it then, but she had since stated she missed it when the uneven earth poked at her sore body.

"Come on, Audra! Come sleep with me!"

That night, they curled up together in the bed. It emanated funk, but it was so soft and so big. Belinda nuzzled up against Audra's neck. So many years ago this bed would have been in their nightmares, little mouse holes from their nesting and removal of stuffing, cockroach eggs, and proof of other vermin. But none of those things could worsen their condition now. They slept with mice and bugs in warehouses and even in cars. At least now this thing was soft and actually meant to be a bed. Audra pulled the surrounding blankets tighter and fell asleep with her sister in her arms.

She woke up without Belinda by her side. The spot next to her felt cool to the touch. Audra reveled in being in a real bed, stretching her arms above her head and her legs below. The grime in the window was lighter than before. The sun must be up. Audra's socked feet touched the dusty floor. As she stood up, the floor gave a little creak.

"Belinda?" Audra asked toward the other room.

It was odd not to have her by her side.

"Come in here!" said Belinda cheerfully.

Audra felt surprised to hear sleepy-head Belinda so energetic in the morning. She shuffled into the front room to find Belinda holding up a small three-foot fir tree. It leaned dangerously far as Belinda had not neatened the cut edge on the bottom. Underneath it lay a basket of winter berries and a small wooden cardinal that Belinda had been whittling during their long hours in the woods.

Tasked with keeping her prize upright, Belinda did not approach Audra, but she shouted a "Merry Christmas!"

Audra ran to Belinda and gave her a big squeeze around the waist. She whispered in her ear, "Merry Christmas" in return.

The two girls lived a fairy tale for a couple of weeks. The cabin made a great home base where Audra could hunt and Belinda could gather. Audra was always on the look-out for how it would end. She would search the woods for signs of other humans, for signs of zombies. They got zombies, but Audra would bait them into going the other direction. She would run away from them and then lose them. The zombies would continue until something else caught their eye.

But then one night Audra awoke to a crackling laughter in the pitch dark. She looked toward the entrance and saw that the whole front room was ablaze. The long flames shot this way and that, with the most heavily invested flames on the front door itself. The top half of the room's air was already filling with dark heavy smoke. Audra pushed on Belinda until she fell off the bed. Belinda groaned as her body hit the floor with a large thunk.

"Wake up, Belinda! Wake up!" Audra shouted.

Audra jumped over her sister and grabbed the rickety chair that neither of the girls was brave enough to use. She rammed the chair into the small glass window in the bedroom. Both the chair and the window broke. Audra used a leg of the chair to finish breaking out the glass. Belinda sat up but had pulled her legs close to her and wrapped her arms around them to create a small ball of a person.

"Belinda, you have to get up. Climb out this window. We have to go."

She could hear yelling outside. Audra pulled on Belinda, but she did not move. This was not the time to freeze. Audra slapped her hard in the face.

"GET UP NOW!"

Belinda, still in a daze, was at least now in a moving daze. She uncurled herself and Audra helped her crouched figure toward the window. She gave her a push and with some squeezing, Belinda was out the other side. Audra felt the heat invading the room. The mattress had gathered sparks and was about to catch. Audra grabbed her full pack, which she packed every night, and shoved it out the window. She followed behind it, landing on it before slinging it on. She grabbed whimpering Belinda by the arm and they ran.

"Is that them?" shouted a voice from the front of the cabin.

Audra grabbed Belinda's arm tighter and forced her at a speed that was not owned by Belinda. They kept tripping and falling all over the woods, smashing into trees, the scent of smoke still on their clothes. Belinda was sobbing, but Audra would not let her stop. Audra would never let her stop.

After the adrenaline had faded, fear still clung to their brains.

They ran all night.

*　　*　　*

Dwyn arrived almost midday to the township, finding Audra passed out up against the border fence. He suspected there was a moonshiner not far from her current location. He threw a blanket on her, making his way to Vesna. An hour later, he returned to her body, which had not moved from its awkward position.

"Let me rest," she muttered, "I ran forty miles and beat your ass here."

Even hung-over, she still had a quick wit. Dwyn rolled his eyes before leaving her and returning to their last camping spot. Setting his things down, he pulled off his boots and climbed into the river. Dwyn took off one article at a time, scrubbing and wringing them out, leaving them on the bank to dry in the sun. Audra appeared unexpectedly. She sat on the bank and watched carefully, much to Dwyn's embarrassment and pleasure.

"Did you get in before the fire, last night?" asked Dwyn, standing deep in the water.

A pained look swept her face. Without a word, she stood up, grabbed his clothes and walked off. She dropped them several meters into the woods.

After a few days of errand running and zombie tagging, Audra and Dwyn were happy to bring the scientists their requested supplies. The gate was closed when the duo arrived. Audra was pleased to see that the place still looked abandoned. There were even a couple zombies surreptitiously tied up front to give the impression that the place was still overrun. Audra called out and Ryder emerged from the laboratory. She let out an excited squeal and gave them both a hug after she opened the gate. She barely allowed them to walk into the lab before she tore into the new supplies like a child on Christmas day. Audra was amazed to look around and see the lights on.

"Ryder got the solar panels working again," said a proud Satomi.

Ryder blushed.

"Well, Satomi has been managing this lab better than Lysent!" she said in a joke only the two of them seemed to understand.

The girls exchanged playful pushes until Ryder spotted a new device.

"Oh my! We've been dying without a centrifuge," Ryder said.

She forgot her modesty and jokes to rush a machine box over to the counter. Ziv tinkered with its settings, frowning at its features. Audra nodded and pretended she knew what a centrifuge was. She looked over the counters, covered in notebooks, beakers, and other science stuff. It looked like they had been busy.

"So, tell me more about what you're doing out here," said Audra.

Satomi smiled.

"So, as you know, the virus is only transferred by bodily fluids - typically from a bite. The virus shuts down the complex parts of the brain that make us who we are. The only things that run OK are the primal portions lower down, close to the spinal cord. That's the brain stem and the cerebellum."

"How does the virus know the difference?"

"It doesn't, actually. The virus only attacks a specific type of neurotransmitter whose primary role is communication in the more complex parts of the brain. The primal parts also use them, but not as extensively. Somehow the brain adapts to keep the primal parts functioning, but the rest of the brain cannot communicate. So the lungs keep breathing. The heart keeps beating. Gross motor function remains. The hunger response is there, too. The virus evolved to stimulate hunger in the presence of potential hosts so it could continue to replicate."

Satomi's answers made sense to Audra, so she dared to ask another question.

"Then, how do you cure it?"

"We introduce antiviral molecules with special tags into the bloodstream. Instead of attaching to the neurotransmitters, the virus attaches to them. This neutralizes them and then the body removes them through natural processes. The neurotransmitters slowly replenish and wake up the rest of the brain."

"Wow. How fast can you develop the antiviral?"

"Well, it will be slow if we have to develop it ourselves. We can do it. We're working on it. Replication would be much easier."

"So, if you had a sample of the cure, you'd have a head start?"

"A big head start."

Audra pondered over that for a moment. She couldn't help with all the science, but maybe she could help in other ways. The sooner they developed the cure, the better.

"Ryder, did you ever see where they keep the antidote?"

Ryder paused before answering.

"You want to steal us some?"

"Can it be done?"

Ryder thought about it.

"No, you always get escorted around, right? You'll never be able to get back to the secured area."

"Any time they are not in the secured area?" Audra prodded.

"No… well, I guess for transport to another township. The other townships hold their own infected and they like to keep it available for outbreaks."

There was only one way Lysent transported items from town to town. They were so damn proud of it.

"Do they use the train?"

"Yeah, they do," said Ryder seeing where Audra was going with this.

The antidotes would be most vulnerable en route on the train through the forest. If they could get a few samples, then they would be that much closer to replicating the cure. And Audra thought, even if it did not work out, she could steal one for Belinda. Perhaps this group was worth something after all.

"Train heist!" yelled out Dwyn.

Ziv contributed nothing to the conversation. He shook his head in disapproval. Everyone avoided asking for his opinion.

9 Heist

"I'm just so tired of it all," reported Belinda. "I'm tired of surviving, tired of death, tired of life."

"We have to keep going, Belinda. We have to take care of each other."

"Why?"

The question stung. Audra tried not to take it personally, but Belinda questioning both of their lives hurt. Belinda sat on the forest floor next to her first zombie kill. Her anger which had brought on the violence had turned to sadness. She had swung one way and was now the other. Audra imagined the statement pained her because of the truth within it. Belinda did look tired… of everything. Audra pulled a rag from her pocket and knelt down next to Belinda. She cleaned the splatter from her face. Belinda did not respond. She stared down at the blood-soaked animal corpse and the remains of the pups.

"They were my friends," said Belinda.

"I'm so sorry."

Audra was sorry, but there was no way they could have fed themselves, a mama dog, and her litter of pups. Audra wondered how much Belinda had eaten in the past few days. A lot of the meat had gone to the dogs.

"I don't know why we keep doing this."

"Well, what do you want to do?"

Silence. Her eyes unwavering from the masses on the ground.

"If we weren't worried about surviving each day, what would you like to do?"

Belinda thought for a few moments. Audra herself had a difficult time conjuring a dream without an invading zombie.

"What would you like to see?" She prodded again.

Belinda's streams of tears faded as she spoke.

"Well, remember when we went on vacation and saw that waterfall?"

"Yes, I do. Mom and Dad made us walk up all those steps, but it was beautiful."

Belinda paused at the mention of their parents. Audra thought of the purple scarf their mom had worn that day. The wind kept sweeping it off her head. She remembered their dad walking up the steps behind her, pulling on the scarf to add to the trouble.

"I'd like to go there again," Belinda offered.

"Deal," said Audra without hesitation.

"What do you mean?"

"I mean, let's go. We're wandering anyway. Might as well go some place pretty, right? Let's go."

Belinda wiped her face with her sleeves. She gave the bloody dog one last look.

*　*　*

Ziv stood with the dissenters outside the plaza. His sign displayed disapproval of the corporate policy of waking the dead. The chants were easy to learn.

"Less dead means less food!"

"Keep them dead!"

In reality, he was watching Lysent move goods to the train depot to see if any antidotes were being transported today. Last week, it was nothing but food stores. Today, a small cart with a cooler on top, made its way from the laboratory to the convoy heading to the train station. Ziv cheered one more protest with the group then dismissed himself to signal Satomi. Audra noticed that he'd chosen the role farthest from the train. He didn't want to be associated with the theft. His survival instincts were strong.

For as fancy as the train technology was, the station was not - a loading dock and a passenger area. Several people mingled around, including cool and collected Satomi. As she walked by, she marked one of the round corners of a silver car with charcoal, the car which had a cooler from Lysent Laboratories in it. She hoped the scribble would stay for the swift train ride. Lysent cleared the railway of non-passengers and the rail buzzed to life. The train took off fast, too fast to jump on or off.

The train sped along until its computers alerted for an emergency stop. A fallen tree had smashed through both fences and lay on the rail. The buzzing noise of the lines faded as power was cut until the debris could be cleared. A young girl hiding in the brush watched the front car for a crew member to step out and investigate. It was not unusual for the trains to be unmanned. Seeing no one, she ran down the rail along the train, looking for the small charcoal mark. She had to hurry. Workers would be out soon. They weren't far from a station; the location of dying pines dictated their unfortunate proximity.

Audra then saw the mark. She rubbed it off the sleek metal with her sleeve before she slipped into the car. The shiny metal of the cooler was easy to spot among the wooden crates. She separated it from the others and examined it. It did not have a lock, but the black case surrounded by ice within it did. Audra did not dare take the whole container. GPS units were plentiful in the Lysent company. Plus, she hoped by only taking one vial that the theft might not be pinpointed to the train and the pine tree. Perhaps Lysent would think the antidote was stolen when packed or received. Audra listened outside for the crew to arrive or for the passengers to grow restless. She heard nothing. They still would have to remove the tree - she had time.

Audra set the black box on top of the closed cooler and pulled out a small metal tool set to pick the lock. It only took a moment to realize it was a hybrid, part mechanical and part electronic. She fished the electronic lighter provided by Vesna from her pocket. Did she have time? She pulled out its battery and some of the wires, stripped them with her knife and stuck them into the lock. The lock blew out when it made contact. She picked the mechanical part and opened the lid. There in insulation were thirty small vials labeled "Zombie Anti-Viral". She grabbed two, sticking one in each pocket. She closed the lid. The mechanical portion of the lock clicked, but Audra was sure the electronics were fried. She put it back into the cooler and pushed it back where she'd found it.

Audra glanced out of the car. She heard voices, but no one was in view. A crew worked on the tree in the front, talking to each other about how unlucky it was that it had fallen on the tracks instead of any other way. She slipped down and underneath the train. It was a stupid place to be. At any point, they could clear the debris and turn the rail back on, electrocuting her. She crawled six cars down. Emerging from underneath, she walked down the track for a bit, hidden by the train. She could hear them chopping at the tree. When she had gotten some distance, she got off the track and found where the fence had been snipped in a few places for her to peel up and slide through. Dwyn had suggested she climb over, but the concertina wire at the top was not something Audra wanted to fight.

"Hey!" yelled a worker who happened to be by the fence, supervising the tree work.

Audra's face swung toward the voice out of reflex before she slipped through. The fence edges scratched her escaping body. Would they recognize the tree as sabotage? Maybe she was just an opportunistic thief scouting the train.

"It has come to my attention that someone has stolen antidote vials off the transport train. This is NOT how we do things. We cannot just wake up people without due process. As punishment, there will be no awakenings for the next six months. If you think things work better in your hands, we will keep ours off," Greenly announced to the crowd.

Audra hung back and listened. She heard the cries and frustration. Another half a year without their loved ones. Her job would be impacted, too. Negotiations would be different. If she found someone tomorrow, the family may decline to make a deposit. Why pay six months' rent? They might need that cash during the unpredictable winter. Tag them and come back later when it was more convenient to all parties involved, minus the tagger.

Audra herself would struggle to pay rent for another six months with low wages. Her only out was the second antidote.

Audra had considered keeping the second antidote secret. She questioned Satomi, who explained the antidote was unstable and sensitive to temperature changes. Audra did not want to risk ruining the dose. She needed the scientists' help. She disclosed her theft of two vials.

"No, our foremost concern is getting the antidotes out of Lysent's village and to the laboratory," Vesna stated, matching the determination in Audra's eyes.

Audra had ventured to ask Vesna for help to retrieve her sister. She feared the six-month probation. Lysent had quickly tied the antidote thefts to those interested in waking up loved ones. They had effective hostages under their roof and it would be easy for them to retaliate further. She needed to get Belinda out and they would not hand her over willingly.

Vesna packed the solar-powered cooler with the vials. The scientists were ecstatic to have real samples. Once they could replicate it, they could begin experiments on delivery systems. Audra had been told about Vesna's plan and knew the risks. They did not want to just wake up a bunch of people and hope those people would be on their side.

They would wake up everyone.

A large population increase would overwhelm the corporate systems and cause them to fail. It would destroy the economy as it stood. Then, the people would be forced to rely on themselves, on their own systems. And the corporation would lose their power. If Lysent wanted to limit the resources and population artificially, Vesna's group would do the opposite. They would aerosolize the cure, treating zombies at a distance en masse.

Audra had her doubts. A lot of the people enjoyed the corporation's care. Would they be able to rely on their own resources? Yes, the plan destroyed the corporation, but what was best for the current and future population? Audra stayed silent on the matter. She now had access to cure vials. Anything more than that, she did not care.

"Then Dwyn can escort the scientists back to the lab with the antidotes and I'll stay here and get my sister by myself. I think I have done more than my part, already."

Dwyn shot her a look that declared he did not like that idea at all. Audra knew he was determined to accompany her into Lysent.

"Vesna, Audra is a part of your group now - do you at least see her concerns?" asked Dwyn.

"I do, but having her sister roaming around my store and Lysent chasing after her isn't going to help our replication process!"

The outburst relayed to Audra that Vesna would not see it her way. Audra sighed.

"OK, let me run the antidotes by myself. I'll get them there in record time. Then will I have permission to come back here and figure out my sister?"

Vesna sighed and closed her eyes to think. Something had to give.

"You can run one antidote. Dwyn will take the other and the scientists behind you. When you both come back, we can TALK about what to do with your sister. Your sister's life isn't the only one at stake here."

Audra left in a huff. She would grab a few drinks while the crew got the antidotes ready for transport. At least she had control of that, despite what Dwyn and Vesna thought.

Audra returned a little less argumentative. She examined the new addition to her pack that Ryder had built. It was a small engineered cooler that used refrigerant from an old appliance and a small solar panel that attached to the top of Audra's pack. Dwyn thought it was the coolest thing. Ziv suggested that she run in sunny areas. Audra winced at the idea. The sun was rough on her fair skin, and being out in the open was less than ideal. He showed her how to read the efficiency of the small panel and the meter of the battery. She would only have to change course if the battery got too low. Audra hoped for a few well-timed sunny hours that would keep the battery full. Barring battery issues, it would only take a day and a half to get to the lab.

Audra set out on her run. Her head felt warm with her buzz. Only three miles in and the only thing she could think about was the antidote nestled in her bag. She could break out her sister and cure her. She had never had an opportunity like this. And now it was within her grasp. The scientists did not even have a plan for her sister. They wanted to wake up everyone that was roaming free, not just the ones with known loved ones on the other side. To appease her, they suggested the stored infected would be released when the corporation became disorganized and when villagers took over, but they did not know for sure. They did not know that at all. All the zoms in Lysent's possession could be destroyed as punishment. Enacting the six-month probation was a demonstration of that power.

Lysent's plaza and her sister were in the other direction, but she was now far enough away that she could turn around and sidestep the township which contained Vesna and the others. Audra would wake up her sister and they would run off together. Dwyn would understand. They had the backup sample, anyway. She had trained Dwyn well. He would provide the backup and make sure that the group's efforts were not in vain. She would not be hurting anyone, just slowing them down for a few days while they waited for Audra's return. It was their fault, anyway. Why would they entrust Audra with the antidote when she was the only one with a sick loved one? Or, was she? Did the others have loved ones they cared about in waiting? Audra had never thought to ask. Their common goal was the dismantling of the corporation. Audra had not looked further than that.

No, it didn't matter. She did not care if Lysent stood or fell, if the scientists had people they cared for or not, she needed to make things right.

Audra turned around and went southwest. She would run far around the township and then make a beeline to the corporation. Audra would have plenty of time to consider a plan. She had hoped breaking out her sister would be a two-person job, but she couldn't trust Dwyn to understand her subterfuge. He would try to change her mind. Her duty was to her sister, not to him or any others.

Her footsteps matched her heartbeat in both cadence and determination. Each was a march, not just a step away from the laboratory and all it meant, but a step forward to her sister.

10 Chances

The mugginess of the morning amplified the sun's heat and made Audra stir. Without opening her eyes, she could tell she was alone in the tent. Belinda's presence was a strong force. You always knew when she was near.

With Belinda starting a fire and gathering breakfast, Audra rested her aching bones in the still quiet. Quiet was something missing from Audra's life, even in the woods when most of the population had been rendered speechless. Audra spent most of her days comforting and loving on her sister, encouraging her, and listening to her problems. She had to be there for her, and the sun-speckled morning before Belinda woke was sometimes the only peaceful moment Audra experienced during the day. Audra decided to laze for a few moments more.

They were seven days into their journey. In just a few more, Audra expected to hear the sound of rushing water. They could camp near the bridge closest to the edge. Audra wished the falls would conjure to life something in Belinda she had not seen in a while - hope.

As the warmth filtered onto her face, a shuffling threatened to upend her peace. Soon it was closer. A figure leaned up against the tent, clawing haphazardly at the canvas, trying to get inside. Audra sighed. So much for a quiet morning. Belinda must be out gathering wood or water, for she had not screamed out. A zom was out there, threatening to damage their hard-won tent. Audra slipped on a long shirt and hat and pulled out her dagger. With the zom still focused on one of the side walls, Audra unzipped the front of the tent and stepped out.

The zom was much taller than her, but with a quick jump, she sliced into his softened temple. His curly red hair tinged with darkness as he crumpled onto the tent, much to Audra's dismay. She pushed him off. She knew she should drag his stench away from the campsite, but it was just so early in the morning. They would leave soon, anyway. She compromised by pulling him behind the tent and let him be, with his arms above his head and his legs dragged straight. While this was not how she had wanted to start her morning, she imagined this was not how he had wanted to spend his, either.

The humidity found in the tent was not present outside, and the warmth gave way to the still chilly morning. Knowing Belinda would have veered off if she spotted the zombie, Audra readied herself to go seek her out. Entering the tent to add another layer of clothes, she noticed Belinda's pack, neatly disassembled as if she was taking inventory. Audra wondered why she had not woken up for that activity. She glanced over the items. Belinda had left anything needed to carry water, and her usual bundling material to gather sticks also remained inside the tent. Where had Belinda gone? Audra pushed back the disturbed feeling settling in her heart as she stepped out to decipher her sister's last movements in the campsite.

She did not have to look far to find the note sitting by the remains of last night's fire. The little bird statue Audra had received at Christmas weighed down the small paper. At once, her mother's voice sprung forward and echoed in her head.

"Take care of your sister. You are all she has left."

Audra rushed in the direction of the falls without even thinking to grab her own pack. She ran, realizing that all she had left was her sister.

*　　*　　*

Audra ran, lost in the nuances of stealing a person from a corporation's prison. Thoughts in stationary positions seemed just that, stationary. With motion, she encouraged and pushed her thoughts forward. Each step gave a new view, a new perspective, both physically and mentally. Audra focused on the problem at hand as she worked through the brush. The leaves crunched underneath her. She stayed off the path. She wanted no one to know where she was going and at what time.

Audra needed supplies - something to cut the clear acrylic that kept her from her sister, a suction cup to pull the plastic toward her so she could lower it to the ground, and perhaps a firearm to make their escape. Could she fight her way out? Would she?

She could inject her sister through one of the air holes. How long would the wake-up process take? Besides the bite on her forearm, she was a perfect specimen. Would Belinda be able to recognize her after the injection? Would she be able to help in her escape? Audra realized that Lysent had kept the whole process hidden for a reason. It was doubtful that the antidote was fast-acting. But what if she took the escape out of the equation? She could administer the cure using the air holes near the floor. Belinda would wake up, eventually.

Lysent would know who stole their antidote, but she would be long gone. She would never show her face in the townships again. She would lose Belinda. Belinda would curse her name, saying she abandoned her, but she would be safe and healthy. She would find friends and a life in the township. And as much as Audra longed to see her smile of recognition, she also knew it would be OK to just make things right.

It was settled. She would visit Belinda, give her the antidote, and then run far from here.

Audra ran past the township where Vesna and the others waited for word that the cure had made it to the laboratory. Instead, she arrived on the outskirts of the township housing Lysent and her beloved Belinda. She slowed to a walk to gather herself and automatically pulled out a snack. If it all worked out, she would soon run again, faster than ever for a long time. Audra considered camping and resting for the night. Rest could do good before Lysent's goons were on her tail. But, a glance at the battery meter shaded her with doubt, and the scientists would grow nervous concerning Audra's absence. No, she would have to summon the strength to save herself when the time came.

With the corporation in her sights, it was time to prepare. What would she need for her long journey into the wilderness? How light would she need to keep her pack to outrun Lysent's horses? How long would they chase her? What else was out there? Audra didn't know, and she didn't care. She only hoped they would release her sister when she rose.

Audra set aside the solar panel. An indentured tagger would not have such high technology and gear. Her fingers gently pulled the antidote out of the cooler. As she knelt to hide the panel and cooler in the brush, she heard a crunch, crunch, crunch.

THUMP!

With a well-placed tackle, Audra found herself on her side on the ground. It was not long before she found out who was on top of her.

"WHAT THE HELL ARE YOU DOING, AUDRA?!" yelled out Dwyn, his face in hers.

Despite his anger and her surprise, her body involuntarily responded to his warm frame on top of hers. The reaction confused her, and she did not respond. Dwyn also looked uncomfortable. He pulled off of her but did not help her up.

"You're taking the antidote to your sister, aren't you?" he said in a calmer voice.

Audra stayed silent, sitting on her rear. She pulled her knees close and brushed leaves off of her pants and arms. She couldn't be angry about the tackle. She had deceived him. Dwyn paced in front of her, panting from the chase and jump. He was also covered in debris, but that did not concern him.

"That isn't yours. You're stealing it," he tried to explain.

Audra bit her tongue. It was not his either. And she had already stolen it once. But she understood.

He crouched down close to her.

"Audra, I thought we were… friends. Why would you go behind my back?"

She looked down at the ground between her knees. She could not look at him. Audra could convince herself that she couldn't care less about the scientists, but Dwyn was another story. Dwyn's trust and camaraderie meant something to her. She wasn't sure what though. Sometimes it reminded her of her sister, but she dared to consider in a more complete or equal way. There was more give and take. And, she had just dared to take a lot.

"I had to, Dwyn, I'm sorry. I owe it to my sister. This is my best bet to make it right."

He grabbed her by the arms and gently shook until she met his gaze. He did not understand.

"Make what right?"

The gravity of leaving everything behind and embarking into the western wilderness away from not just Lysent, but Dwyn and Belinda, sank in. Her face did not change shape, but still, tears came steady, tracing the edges of her cheekbones and falling onto her collar.

A simple and convicted, "It's my fault," fell from her mouth.

It answered no questions, but he motioned to bring her closer and she fell into him, knocking him off balance and sending the pair backward. Pinning him underneath her, Audra cried until there were no more tears, which took much longer than either expected.

When the tears stopped, Audra found herself still buried in Dwyn's chest. He was warm and heavy. Audra rolled off of him and onto the ground next to him. They lay side by side with no words. Dwyn did not push her to explain. He was content for a moment to know Audra did not take pleasure in abandoning him or the others. They stared into the tree branches and the sky in between the leaves until Audra found her voice. She was surprised how composed and calm it was.

"It's my fault Belinda was bitten. I'm the only one looking out for her now. Sending the world into chaos by waking up everyone outside does not help her chances. She's inside."

"OK."

"OK? Okay - what?"

"We will get your sister out before we release the antidote. I'll convince Vesna. But let us work on the replication first, so we're ready. You can have the second dose if we accidentally destroy the first. You risked the most to get them. It should be your payment.

"You've waited three years. Can you wait another couple of months?"

Audra attempted to wipe her face, but she felt the wetness smear. She pushed it around as her thoughts cleared. Waiting on people and being part of a group was not her specialty. She would rather depend on herself and get things done. This required trust and patience. But, it also afforded an alternative to waking up her sister and disappearing off the face of the earth. In a perfect world, she could wake up her sister right before Lysent came tumbling down. Then things would be made right on all levels, and they would be together.

"Give us a chance, Audra. Don't run from us."

He sent his request into the sky but did not want to miss her response. He rolled onto his side, his elbow on the ground and his face on his hand. Dwyn took his flannel sleeve and wiped at her face. There was no helping it though.

Maybe she would give this a try if just for a while.

"I shouldn't have run..." she admitted.

Dwyn said nothing, but continued to touch her face with the cuff of his sleeve, then moved to his hand. Her skin felt cool with the tears evaporating from the surface. His hand felt rough and strong. Audra closed her eyes to the touch and was jolted ever so slightly when she felt his lips touch hers. She leaned forward and felt his hand in her hair. He guided her back down with a hand at her hip.

11 Trials

"It is good you are here this time," said Satomi in her genuine way.

It was not meant as a jab, but it reminded Audra that she had been missing during the last two human trials to replicate the antidote. While she had consigned herself as part of the group now, she still felt out of her element in the confines of the laboratory. She spent days, near weeks, at a time occupying herself by tagging in the woods as the scientists worked.

Vesna had not been surprised when Dwyn told her of Audra's transgression. There was a reason Audra had only been given one vial. Vesna had expected Audra would act out of dire need, but hoped she would also figure out she needed the group, and the group needed her. Vesna stated she would not tell the others of Audra's excursion. They could all work together a while longer, even if their goals were different.

The first two attempts to replicate the antiviral had failed and killed its subjects. Ryder understood there would be failures before success, and tolerated the deaths. Satomi, more in the medical field where it was "first do no harm," had the most trouble accepting that harm was inevitable. After many weeks, the group was ready to test their new version of the reproduced antidote.

Satomi, Ryder, and Ziv hung back as Audra and Dwyn looked in the front window of the building that served as their miniature corral. It was rumored among the taggers that Lysent regularly rounded up the unwanted zoms with yellow tags. Lysent kept high-traffic areas like the townships and the railway clear, by creating large outdoor corrals to keep the sick out of sight. But unlike a Lysent corral, Ziv knew many of the people in his place of work. Satomi pleaded with him not to share any information, but just let them pick one at random. It felt unethical to make an informed choice on whom to wake up. It felt even more unethical this early in the trials when it was more likely to kill the subject than cure her.

"We've just been opening the door and letting one slip out," said Satomi.

"Well, that's not going to work this time," Audra replied.

Zombies swarmed the front door and window, drawn by the previous activity. Scientists peeking into the windows during the day had not helped either. The windows needed to be covered before the zombies tore each other apart. Audra sent Dwyn for a window cover as she circled the building. The next window showed a separate room, closed off, and empty. They would use Satomi's strategy, but with another door. Audra finagled the lock on the window and slipped inside. The room seemed to serve as a second office and storage area; a desk sat in the center, but cleaning and extra office supplies also shared the space. Audra hid behind the interior door to the zoms as she opened it halfway. She resisted the urge to show her face to the zoms and instead allowed Ryder and Satomi to relay the information to her.

"Three maybe," shouted Ryder.

"Oh, there are more!" called out Satomi.

She was not surprised to hear others were coming. They may not have seen the door, but they saw their comrades change directions and followed their lead. Just as Audra was growing impatient, one cleared the doorway. It met Audra's boot at once then hit the floor. She shut the door on the others.

The door did not close but bounced off more flesh.

A forearm poked through.

The floored zombie spiked with energy, feeding off the smell of life coexisting in the room. It both tried to pivot on the ground to eye its prey and stand up to charge, resulting in a half-crouched spin. Audra still had a few moments while it gained control of its stubborn body. She returned her focus to the door through which it had come. Audra held pressure on it with her body as she tried to return the arm to its owner on the other side. She had to avoid its claw while being careful not to slip her arm into its face.

She had gotten all but the hand through when she noticed added pressure on the door. A third zombie had arrived and was adding its weight. Audra gave a glance at the first zombie, who had settled on crawling toward her feet. She could ask for help. Dwyn would come help. But it seemed silly to ask for help for one on the floor and two against the door. That was child's play. But to Audra's surprise, it was not Dwyn that pulled himself through the window. With Audra's smiles of encouragement, Satomi walked behind the infected on the floor and gingerly pulled it away by its ankles. Her job completed, she moved as far away as possible from it, while Audra untangled the doorway of limbs and confirmed the firm click of the door mechanism.

Their subject was a male, mid-thirties when he turned. His face was strong and angular, his glasses skewed but not broken on his face. He was lucky to have them still. There were few places to get prescription lenses currently. No one was making them as far as Audra knew, only collecting them. The township had a glasses library. You would try on pairs until you found one that improved your vision, but it was better to have just kept up with yours.

His hair had continued to grow in his state, but it was apparent it was previously short and neat, even gelled conservatively. It was easy to see he was a strong fellow despite the recent atrophy of his muscles. He had found his feet and was doing a Frankenstein's monster walk toward them in his mussed lab coat.

Ryder stuck her head through the window to see their progress.

"Oh, he is big! I wonder if the antidote is mass dependent..." she said as she dropped back out to discuss the scenario with Ziv.

Audra pinched the bridge of her nose and squeezed her eyes shut to summon patience from the front of her face. Even without a degree in science and having grown up basically in the wild, it still sounded like something they should have figured out before asking her to retrieve someone. She realized she might have created a mass-dependent problem of her own. The exit window was small. Satomi, who had sneaked behind Audra for safety, appeared to be thinking the same thing.

"Erm, maybe we should tie the subject up before we attempt this window."

Audra nodded in agreement and Satomi poked her head outside to ask Ziv for some rope.

A small smile drew on Audra's lips as she realized she had come into the building to wrangle a zombie, not even bothering to bring a rope. She was becoming overconfident, cocky even. Ziv's small hand gripping rope appeared in the room through the window.

For a sheltered scientist, Satomi seemed willing to help out when it came to the infected. Audra saw her approach was respectful, almost religious, like a person preparing someone for sacrifice. Audra pinned the zom's arms against his body. With the rope in hand, Satomi pulled his wrists together.

"Actually, nobody likes bondage scars. Let's do this instead," said Audra.

She directed the rope around his chest, wrapping his arms tight on each side. Satomi nodded and assisted.

"But for the record, there is, or at least was, a select demographic that like bondage scars."

Satomi's dry chide surprised Audra. She burst out in laughter as she looked at their scientific zombie. It was possible.

With the arms under control, Satomi managed the upper half of their standing zombie while Audra wrapped the rope around his legs. She tied it off with a surgeon's knot before she and Satomi switched places. With a warning to Ziv and the others outside the window, Satomi picked up the zombie's legs as Audra knocked him off balance. They headed with their cargo to the window. By this point, Audra ordinarily would have named the zombie, but this one was different. He would have a name soon. Or not. The thought weighed on Audra more than the body did.

They pushed him through the window until he reached a tipping point. He tilted at an angle and slid. They heard a thump and a crunch as the side of his face hit the ground.

His glasses.

"We'll just tell him that they were broken when we met him," Audra whispered to Satomi with a half smile.

Audra could tell that Satomi enjoyed being included on the secret. With the man's legs still in the window, Audra squeezed out. She pulled him away so Satomi could exit as ungracefully as needed. Her slim body slipped through with no problem, impressing Audra.

Dwyn pulled the zombie up on its bound feet. Audra pulled off the ropes from his legs. He was too heavy to carry around. She tied the rope around his waist as a leash of sorts. He liked her and it took little persuading to have him follow her toward the laboratory. Audra wondered if she should salvage his glasses. One lens was still intact, but he did not look willing to allow Audra to reach for them. Audra did not know if zoms needed vision correction. She left them on, just in case.

The odd procession made its way between two counters. Satomi had shown glimmers of lightheartedness, but back in the lab with her colleagues, it seemed responsibility lay heavy on her again. Audra could not decide if it was because she respected life, or because maybe she doubted their formula. Ziv barely entered the room. He leaned against the wall, looking rather bored. Audra's side glance accused him of wanting to be closest to the exit, but Ziv did not move closer.

The zombie seemed overstimulated with the surrounding crew, anyway. He gained energy and pulled at his restraints. He turned to Dwyn and teetered dangerously on his feet. Audra, who stood in front of him, gave a giant clap to bring his attention back to her. No one made mention he looked like he was fighting what was to come. Ryder's hand shook ever so gently as she readied the serum and handed it to Satomi, who approached the subject from behind.

"Subject Three, thank you for your service. It will change the world," she said with a whisper.

And with that, she leaned over with a syringe and injected him in the shoulder. Subject Three turned his head toward the stimulus. Dwyn used two hands to grab the sides of Subject Three's face with a firm grip to keep Satomi safe. She did not flinch as she finished injecting the serum. Ryder requested that Subject Three be escorted to the observation room. It was almost anticlimactic, Audra thought. She expected some immediate reaction, like convulsions or at least a yawn of the jaw. Instead, they left Subject Three in the small conference room, no different than before.

"I'll take first watch," offered Satomi.

"I'll stay, too," added the curious Audra.

Ryder fidgeted and then left to clean up the laboratory. Dwyn helped. Ziv continued his work on aerosolizing formulas with similar molecular weight. There had been an argument as to whether this was the best way to go, but Vesna was set on aerosolizing the antidote and waking up masses.

Audra and Satomi observed Subject Three walk circles around the conference room, which was empty besides the table. Previously, they'd used it as a space to eat meals. They took out the chairs, but the table proved more difficult to remove.

There was no big reaction. Nothing at all yet. Audra was not sure if that was a good thing or a bad thing. She didn't want to offend by asking. Twenty minutes passed and Audra considered moving onto other things, when Satomi broke the silence.

"What is different about him?" she asked.

Her head gave a slight tilt, indicating a thought process forming inside. Audra looked at Subject Three. He was still walking in circles around the table, like a slow hamster on a wheel. He maintained the same slouched posture as before. His mouth was slack-jawed.

Underneath his broken glasses, his eyes looked dead, blinking. Blinking. Audra watched his eyes. He blinked again.

"He is blinking," her tone pitched upwards, her excitement growing.

"Blinking is a parasympathetic response. Infected humans blink," Satomi dismissed.

"Yes, but not this often. This is... human often."

Satomi followed.

"It is unusual. Definitely a change in his behavior. Maybe his nociceptive neurons are firing."

Audra wasn't sure what that meant, but she had been observing zombies for years. She spotted them passing through terrain as she hid in fields or above in the trees. They all had a certain range of motion and behavior. There was something different about the one in their conference room. Someone was inside, stuck inside that sick body. Audra's thoughts turned to her sister. Belinda was in there, imprisoned in her body, in her cell, in that wretched corporation. And Audra had put her there. It was her fault. All of it.

That thought in the back of her head came slowly burning to the front. She needed out, away from others, away from herself. Without another word to Satomi or mention of the developments to the others, Audra walked out. Satomi could tell the others. Even if the process was successful, it would be slow. He was just blinking now. If it was unsuccessful, it would be slower. She had time. Without knowing where she was going, Audra walked from the laboratory door to the entrance of the small plaza. She let herself through the gate. Her knees and feet picked up higher as she found speed. She did not bother to tell herself it was a scout run, a supply run, or a perimeter check. It was not any of those things. She was running because she needed to run.

Audra kept all her senses open and alert, but the meditative motion of her cycling legs left her mind churning. She did not find relief. Her emotions bubbled up, unknown sudden emotions not safely tied to specific thoughts. As she wondered if she would burst, the feelings would subside as if she had made distance from them by running faster than they could keep up. Then a new surge of feelings. It came like waves, rolling in and out. Audra did not cling to anything for fear it would consume her. It was not safe to run like this, but it seemed even less safe to be alone, stagnant, and sitting in her thoughts.

From behind a tree, someone walked across her path. Audra almost collided into her. She skidded to a stop and only years of suppressing instinct prevented her yelp of surprise. But it didn't stop her trembling or falling backward. The infected woman turned to look at her, her blond hair stuck to the sides of her face, her blue eyes huge and hungry. Young, alone, and lost, she reached her arms out and Audra thought for a moment to reach back. The vicious, teeth-filled snarl forced Audra to roll off to the side, tears in her eyes. Emotions she could not handle or name flooded her, her vision, her discernment, and what felt like her identity.

Just run.

It came to the forefront of her mind. Audra could almost see the words in her vision, blurring the zombie approaching her. She picked herself off the damp, leaf-littered ground and obeyed. Audra would run away, just like she had run away all those other times. Just like she had run away by throwing her sister into that corporation.

She had not done enough. Her sister had been trapped for years while she was out here. Why did she deserve to survive over her sister? What made her so special? Her anger pushed her legs to work harder and her chest expanded to keep up. Her arms did not flail in grief or fear but pumped, propelling her forward. She felt that fleeting pleasure of sprinting before her legs slowed. She stayed on that brink, back and forth between fast running and sprints.

She came upon a grassy field mowed short by animals. Audra made it halfway across when she flung herself onto the warm ground. She gasped for air. Her body was exhausted. For a moment, she focused on that. She focused on her breath, her expanding rib cage, the dizziness in her head. It grounded her. Putting her body in that catastrophic state allowed it to sync with her mind. Then placing that writhing body on the firm earth, she hoped to ground the abstract things behind her eyes.

If she could just identify what she was feeling, perhaps she could handle it. Why did she freak out over blasted blinking? Those first signs of life made her feel angry and resentful. Was she angry the virus had taken so much from her, or was she angry that she was about to get some of those things back? Though she was already flat-backed on the ground, that thought knocked her over.

She loved her sister. Her sister deserved life. But Audra had known this life and this purpose for so long. What was next for her? Audra avoided any more thoughts. It did not matter. Her obligation to her sister mattered. She had caught her breath. She pulled herself off the ground. The sun was making its journey to the other side of the earth.

She needed to get back to the laboratory and face what was happening there. Audra sucked in her lips at the thought, took a deep breath, and brushed herself off. She was sweaty from her run, the grass and straw stuck to her body and dried, her face covered in dried tears she did not remember spilling. Despite the physical mess, she realized she could return to the laboratory. Countless times she had run straight to a moonshiner. She would get herself trashed and become incapacitated for hours. It provided relief, but here was some relief too. It was not as perfect and absolute as alcohol could achieve, but it had become bearable. Dwyn would be surprised at her same-day return.

Audra began her walk back. Her muscles stiffened from their strain and sudden stop. She worked them as she walked and soon they loosened. Everywhere the grass touched, her wet skin itched. Audra rubbed her hands along her arms until she found her way to the creek. She could follow it to familiar territory and the lab. Before moving on, she took off her clothes and boots and slipped into the cool water to rinse. She imagined all the emotions she had been carrying floating away as debris. It felt good to be clean. She climbed onto a small rock outcropping that was smooth and wonderfully warm from the sun. She lay there, eyes closed, finding peace.

Audra heard a rustle. Having spent years in the isolated wood, her instinct was no longer to cover up in modesty. It was all too often an animal or a nonjudgmental zombie. She felt safe on the outcropping. She looked to her right over the water to her clothes draped over rocks. There was movement in the woods. Audra squinted her eyes adjusting to the sun as the woman emerged.

It was the blond she had run into earlier in her run. Now in a calmer place, she considered tagging the zombie or at least securing it to increase the safety of the woods. No feeling was worse than finding yourself in a precarious situation with a zombie you dismissed earlier. The woman was drawn to the raw scent on the clothes, but could not find Audra. She wandered the bank, searching the ground. Her hair hung and covered her face. Audra could not stop watching. It felt like watching Belinda on those days when she looked lost in the world, confused over where she was and why. Those times, Audra would hold her hand in silence and hope she would come back to her.

Could the antiviral bring her back and then some? Audra imagined a Belinda more self-aware, confident, and steady. Her eyes returned to the lost zom. Either way, that could be home again.

The woman wandered away, having never found motion connected to the scent. Audra slid off the rock and waded to her clothes. She was going to go home. It was a long journey, not to the laboratory, but to finding her sister inside her sister. Belinda would be home. And if Belinda was home, Audra was home.

Audra walked on.

12 Pain

Audra returned to the laboratory and ignored Dwyn's surprised look. Both Satomi and Ziv were working. Ziv peered up from his work and eyed her wet hair.

"How is Subject Three?" she asked.

Ziv set down the pair of beakers and continued to stare her down. "Where were you?"

"I had to deal with some things," she said, shrugging off her misadventure.

He squinted his eyes to analyze her answer.

"Did you tell someone what we were doing?"

"Stop," she said with tiredness in her voice rather than anger or defense, "I'm not a spy."

"Then why did Dwyn have to go get you when you were moving the antidote?"

"I ran into trouble. There is trouble out there if you didn't notice. Now, how is Subject Three?"

Satomi broke in.

"Ryder is watching him. He is continuing to exhibit aberrant behavior, atypical from the classic locomotive traits of those of his condition normalized for size."

Audra looked around for help.

"He rubbed his face," Dwyn offered.

Audra glanced around the room. No one had spoken up for her when Ziv accused her, but no one looked like they agreed either. She did not worry about him. He did not seem capable of much more than dissenting speeches and weaseling out of his chores. Before Audra decided whether to further address the topic, Ryder stuck her head into the main portion of the laboratory.

"You should come see," was all she said before her head disappeared again to watch her keep.

Everyone assumed you to be the plural 'you' and walked the paces to the observation area. Subject Three had slumped over the table, twitching and threatening to fall off. No one knew if this was part of the process or if he was dying.

"This might get worse," stated Audra.

She looked around for some bindings. Dwyn was right behind her, preparing to open the conference room door. Satomi stood guard as the two entered the room. They hoisted the man fully onto the table, his face sliding on the slick table. Audra and Dwyn log-rolled him supine. His jaw hung open but wagged at the sight of Audra. Then his eyes faded and the reaching of his chin lessened. Either his innate desire to eat humans had subsided or he was no longer aware of his surroundings. Audra tried to be gentle with the tired body, wrapping the long length of rope around his body, arms, and table, avoiding the spread-eagle look. He would be secure, safe, and accessible to the scientists.

Satomi took advantage of that access immediately. She examined with a comfortableness that Audra found refreshing if not worrisome. She tested his pupils with a flashlight, checking dilation and eye movement. She took his temperature from his armpit, avoiding his mouth, and left the room without giving voice to any of her thoughts.

Audra watched the patient on the table. She remembered the time her sister got sick and stayed in the hospital when hospitals were still big corporations, light switches worked, and her family existed. She remembered looking down at her sister, hoping the medicines worked so they could go play again. Now, she looked down at this guy, not knowing his life, and wished the same. She hoped the medicines worked, so she and her sister could go play again.

Her soak in the creek had refreshed her, but she had not replenished all her energy. A wave of tiredness washed over her as the adrenaline, emotions, and nervous energy dissipated. With the sun still up, she wanted a nap. She would need her rest to cover her shift later. Audra gave Dwyn a small touch on the shoulder to signal her upcoming disappearance. They both exited the conference room and Audra found her way to an office that served as her room for the nights she stayed in the industrial park.

The brightness from the windows showed the contents of the converted office. There were papers and books shoved in the corner, the remnants of the previous tenant. She would have left them where they were, but they were stacked precariously on all the horizontal surfaces. She did not want them to topple in her sleep or during a quick exit. To slip on a pool of loose paper was not her idea of an efficient escape plan. Messes like these were rare. No one had this amount of stuff anymore.

She dry-brushed her teeth before fluffing the blankets and soft things she had collected. She considered pulling another blanket from her pack, but that would be a blanket she would not have if vultures forced her out. Sleeping inside was still difficult despite having done it for the last week. The ceiling seemed so far away as compared to her tent. She lay her head underneath the desk for some protection. From what, she did not appreciate. She slipped into a fitful sleep.

Audra woke up to a dark room. Was it time for her shift? She hoped no one had peeked to find her tucked under the desk. She wandered out into the main area. No one was out and about. The silence was heavy. Perhaps they had retired to their rooms. But as she reached the observation area, she discovered the entire crew, having pulled all manners of seats together to watch.

"We considered waking you, but there isn't much to see," whispered Dwyn.

Despite his claim, his eyes did not veer from the subject. The others barely acknowledged her. Audra looked through the window frame and understood. Inside was not quite human and not quite zombie.

"Did he untie himself?"

"He did."

Zombies did not have the fine motor skills to untie knots or even the problem-solving skills to realize they were tied up. They gave constant force to whatever was in their way. Some things moved, and some things did not. But, despite Subject Three's ability to untie himself, he still did not seem aware of his surroundings. He did not examine the door or attempt escape; however, Audra noticed a chair was propped underneath the doorknob on their side as a new fortification. The subject shuffled around and around the conference table. He directed his eyes downward, which was not uncommon for zombie or human alike, but he also occasionally brushed his left hand on his shirt, as if he was pressing out wrinkles. A nervous habit from his previous life, for sure.

"Have you made any attempts to communicate?" Audra asked.

"Not yet," said Satomi. "He doesn't appear to be in any distress, so we don't want to stimulate him and activate any lower portions of his brain based on survival or hunger. We don't want to slow his progress."

"If he looks distressed, we'll try to talk to him," added Ryder.

Every time someone considered retiring for the evening, or even just spending time elsewhere in the laboratory, Subject Three would perform some new subtle task that would leave everyone talking about its meaning, his progression, and what they thought his next steps would be. Satomi believed functions would return in order of importance to survival based on the structure and hierarchy of the brain. Ziv based his theory on biochemistry. As the levels of neurotransmitters increased, the brain would wake up as a whole, but slowly. Ryder with no complete medical knowledge still thought a good theory was that he would be like a stroke victim, with damage and healing unique to the patient.

Then, Subject Three did what no zombie would do.

He sat down.

Zombies sat up, stood up, walked and ran all the time, but they did not sit down. It was an unforeseen milestone. They cheered and hugged. Subject Three was still in a mental fog, but he had the modern human tendency to sit when given the opportunity. Ziv offered everyone high-fives and went to work on creating the aerosol version for this antidote version. Even if the antidote formula needed tweaking, his work would not be completely off. He hurried away, excited and patting himself on the back for his part. Ryder disappeared and reappeared with a sheepish shrug and a bottle of champagne. She smiled and reported laboratories usually had a bottle hiding around for that special breakthrough.

"It's not time yet," she said with a sly smile, "but soon."

"Maybe he can drink it with us," said Satomi with honor and pride seeping through her words and into her smile.

They all nodded and Ryder slipped out of the room to tuck away the bottle until the proper time.

Dwyn and Satomi retired for the evening. Having just taken a nap, Audra was not ready for bed, and stayed up with the enthusiastic Ziv and dedicated Ryder. Audra tried to balance learning with not getting in the way. Ryder loved to teach and explain. She showed her how she was using cell cultures to create the antiviral proteins she desired. Audra had to stay a safe distance away to avoid contaminating the cultures under the sterile hood. It was easy to accidentally introduce bacteria that would kill or overwhelm the colony. It amazed Audra that these microscopic cells contained the answers to their big world problem.

Ziv huffed and grunted as he moved objects around his counter. Audra did not bother him. His efforts appeared to be more trial and error, so the process was not fun to explain. He was attempting to add air to protein solutions of similar weight as the antidote. Ryder explained there were a lot of big questions about the process. Could they aerosolize it without denaturing the protein? Would the method of inhalation work? What would be an effective dose? What was the ratio of dispersed versus delivered? Most would be lost to the environment, the patients' clothes, the ground, their face. Would it have to be inhaled or could it be absorbed through other mucous membranes - eyes, nose, tongue? Why did zombies have to breathe so shallowly? Ziv had a lot on his plate.

Audra didn't have to understand it all to realize it was a complicated undertaking. In the back of her mind, she considered a Plan B. If they provided a supply of antidotes to the villagers, the villagers would seek and demand their families. It would be a different structure of a rebellion and maybe safer for her sister. Audra said nothing for now. The scientists seemed hell bent on doing things for the greater good, not for individuals, not for themselves. They would take convincing.

Audra's mind and body were tired. She did not realize how long difficult days and nights could be. They were usually shortened by a strong concoction which let her mind swim in soporific numbness. Choosing to stay sober was not just one decision, but many. It was much easier to say 'yes' the first time than to say 'no' one million times. Tired of the process, Audra made motions she would try to sleep again. Ryder looked over her shoulder.

"You look wiped. It's been a long day for everyone. Have you eaten?"

Audra shook her head and wandered to their collective food store for something she might find appetizing. She did not know why she bothered. If you were not excited about food blocks or other dried food, you were long lost for something to strike your fancy. Audra chose a food block that appeared to have more oats than the protein substance Audra found chalky.

When the food bar was finished, Audra wished them both a good night. Ryder gave a small smile over her shoulder. Ziv made a humph noise that Audra assumed meant that he was upset she would go to bed when he was working on something important. But Audra could not help him with his important thing, so there was not much to do.

Subject Three was still sitting on the floor against the wall, slumped with his eyes closed. For a moment, her heart crept to her throat as she watched for breath. Was he dead? No, he appeared to be sleeping, another impossibility of the zoms that moved unceasingly. Audra wondered how much longer the process would take. Sleep healed, but she imagined that an awakening brain did not produce a dreamless sleep. He twitched, confirming Audra's thoughts. She wished him and herself a still night. Audra did not want her thoughts to devolve into dreams, but she already knew they would.

The next morning, she pulled herself out from under the desk and wiped the cold sweat from her brow. Last night's clothes hung over the wooden chair to freshen. It was not the same as rinsing them in the creek and letting them dry in the wooded sunshine, but at least they were spending time away from her body. Audra slipped them on over her base layer. She always left some semblance of clothes on, just in case. Most of her life was about just in case, because many times, it was the case.

As she slipped into the hall, sleepiness muffled her hearing, but she recognized conversations in the laboratory. One voice was strange. Without another moment passing, she was awake, alert, and her knife had made its way from her waist to her hand. She crept down the hall searching for signs of distress. The voices sounded neither happy nor strained. Audra stood just on the other side of the doorway, out of sight and listened.

It was Subject Three.

It must be Subject Three.

They were questioning him. And he was answering them.

Audra stepped into the doorway and saw that the conference room converted into an observation room for Subject Three had now become a conference room once more. Subject Three sat upright in a hard-backed chair. He almost looked to be interviewing for a job, except one lens of his glasses was broken, which was not acceptable interview attire. The man looked pale and nervous, but otherwise trying to give a good impression. He shifted nervously in his chair, and Audra wondered if they had offered him necessities such as the bathroom, food, and water, prior to his inquisition.

Dwyn stood up from his seat and smiled at Audra.

"Audra. Meet Gordon. He was a scientist here before the infection. Gordon, this is Audra. She is a warrior."

Audra's eyes narrowed a bit at this description of her occupation. It brought up images of warring people attacking each other with blades like she had seen glimmers of in the movies and television. Her parents had tried to keep her away from that stuff when she was young, to protect her from violence. Little good that did. She judged it against her reality, which was battling zombies, suffering under Lysent goons, and fighting the elements outside. Maybe she was a warrior, but it was because she was a runner.

"I'm a runner. How are you feeling?"

This man was a walking corpse just yesterday. These scientists had replicated the antidote and now he was sitting with them, aware and alive. She needed to understand how he was doing as it related to how Belinda might do under the same circumstances.

"A little disconcerted," he replied, his strong face drawn into an honest worried look.

"Well, you remember the word 'disconcerted' so that's good," she replied wryly.

Audra abstained from showing her excitement, but her heart was pounding. It took all that was in her not to run out and into the corporation to demand her sister.

She almost forgot, too.

"Do you need anything?"

"I don't know. You'd think I'd be hungry, right?" he asked, confused about his body's continued contentment.

"Yes, you should eat something," chimed in Satomi. "Your body needs it whether your brain has caught up or not."

Ryder stepped out and retrieved a protein bar. She handed it to him with a grimace on her face.

"This is all we have," she said, wishing she could offer him something more special for his first meal back.

"Thank you," he said genuinely.

Audra remembered that he had not been eating the bars for years like they had. It was new to him. Hell, eating was new to him.

Gordon seemed to notice Ryder's hesitation, though.

"Is it bad out there?" he asked. "It was just getting started. We didn't realize what trouble we were putting ourselves into by bringing one of them in for studies. We thought we could help. I'm betting many people did the same."

Ryder and Dwyn shared how things were terrible at the start, but now everyone was rebuilding. Gordon was not surprised that the corporation was a key part in that. It made sense. They were so big before the world ended.

"So, is this outpost one of the last few to be treated?" he asked, confused.

"No. Unfortunately, Lysent does not want to cure all the infected," said Satomi.

Gordon's face buried in on itself in confusion while Dwyn explained Lysent's role, reasoning, and the process and payment system behind waking people up.

"They've commercialized a public health crisis?"

His half-eaten protein bar hung forgotten in his hand.

"Haven't they always?" asked Ziv.

"I recognize you." Gordon blurted as if Ziv's snark had woken up that memory.

"Yes, I had just started working here. That's why we're at this lab – because I knew of its existence. I, um, survived when everything fell apart here, while we were trying to figure it all out."

"Thank you for coming back," said Gordon.

Ziv just gave a small nod, not going on about a rescue like Audra expected. While Ziv was typically a pain in the ass, maybe there was more to him than sarcasm and a keen sense of survival.

"So, if Lysent doesn't want to cure people… Why am I awake?"

"We woke you up illegally," Ryder said carefully.

They hoped Gordon would understand and appreciate. They did not know him. He might sympathize with the corporation. Gordon could need something from Lysent, like a family member, and turn them all in. He did not understand this world, but they woke him up hoping he would be a good and helpful person as they set this world on a different path.

"We stole a dose of antidote and have been working to replicate it. You were a trial subject given the replicated dose. As far as we know, you are the first unregulated awakening."

Gordon's eyebrows rose. He absentmindedly raised the protein bar to his mouth and chewed for a moment.

"Well, I always wanted to be part of a scientific breakthrough that changed how the world worked," he said, gesturing to the lab. "I never thought I'd BE the breakthrough."

Ryder and Satomi smiled. As part of the science and engineering fields, they understood. They too were excited about making scientific history. As an added bonus, their work had produced another of their kind.

"So, no one knows I'm alive?"

The entire group stole glances at each other.

"How do I know about my family? Are they alive? Where are they?"

Gordon seemed to remember his life outside the laboratory. It had taken awhile. This place must have meant a lot to him. What had become of the rest of his life?

"I have a daughter, Eliza. And, I guess, an ex-wife."

Audra weighed the pros and cons in her head. She had her biometric reader. She could sample Gordon's DNA and process it through the system. They could find out if his ex-wife or others had inquired about his status. But, a lack of inquiry could weigh heavy on someone's mind. Likewise, using her reader would tie her and this GPS location to the illegal awakening.

If Gordon wandered into a Lysent-sponsored village and asked about his family, there would be questions after so many years. Travelers were not welcome. He would be brought forth in front of a committee and questioned about his previous whereabouts. Lysent worried about others. They feared something much like themselves, large, organized, and predatory. Gordon would not be able to answer the questions satisfactorily, even with help.

"We will give Vesna, our leader, your family's names. She will get the word out, see if they are still in the area. She will help you," said Audra.

"I remember Vesna. Her husband?"

"No longer with us."

It seemed to sink in how different the world was. He did not push an urgency concerning his daughter. He had been ill for years. The world had and still did continue without him.

"Look, guys," Gordon said, looking each person in the eye before continuing. "I appreciate on a very personal level the efforts you all have taken here. I imagine this illegal process had risks, some of which you haven't even considered yet. If what you're saying about Lysent is true, and from my experiences I know it to be feasible, then I want to be an even bigger part of this. I want to help. You chose me because I looked like the scientist type, right? I am. Let me stay and let me help."

Audra was not sure if the speech was given because he felt conviction in his few hours of consciousness, or if he was playing his best card for survival. For all he knew, the world had not ended, and they were just experimenting with his body and brain. Audra felt all the suspicions she felt Gordon should have. The request was probably just his play at survival, to get on their good side - the provider of protein bars and information. Either Ziv seemed to share Audra's suspicions or he did not want another in the group. His face showed disdain. Dwyn and Satomi were not readable. Ryder seemed convinced. She grinned and nodded her head. She went to say something and Audra cut her eyes at her. Ryder changed what she was going to say.

"We will have to talk about it and decide. To be honest, we were not getting our hopes up that this trial would work. Sorry." Ryder said nervously.

She did not realize the others were not behind her.

"You'll, of course, want to get to know us before you join our group anyway," said Audra in a more diplomatic way. "We will not kick you out to the curb. Don't worry about that."

Audra tried to change the subject.

"You're probably a good fit if you know Vesna. How do you know her?"

"Her husband was a scientist here, but he went home to his family. I hoped he had made it."

This was news to Audra. Ziv wasn't their only connection to this lab. Audra recalled that Vesna had yet to visit the outpost.

"He left to care for his family. We weren't even trying to find a cure. I figured lots of facilities were working on it. We were trying to determine if the work Lysent paid us to do had played a role in the epidemic."

"What do you mean? What work were you doing here?" Satomi asked.

She glanced around at the equipment already in place and tried to imagine what could have been done.

"We had our own independent work through grants, but often we did Lysent contracts to keep the place afloat. The contracts would only be small pieces of a broader project. That way individual private labs could not figure out what the end product was."

"Standards of compartmentalization," piped in Ryder, familiar with the concept.

"We had handled RNA sequences a couple of times for Lysent. They always had viral applications, but not for any of the viruses we had. We figured out how to add a little tail of information to the RNA that was nonfunctional but served as an identification marker. It became protocol, but we didn't mention it to anyone and only used it on Lysent projects."

"Damn, you thought you'd find your work somewhere you didn't want it to be? Like… in the virus?"

Audra had never heard Satomi curse. Tagging RNA must have been an extreme measure, the procedure likely flying over Audra's head, but the implication did not. Could there be proof that Lysent caused the world's downfall?

Ziv's voice was cold.

"And that's why you brought an infected person in here and killed everyone. I told you it was a bad idea," he announced.

"Yes, we were trying to retrieve a sample of the viral infection, isolate it, and then find out if our tag was in the RNA material of the virus."

Despite the heaviness of the room, Audra hid a giggle. She remembered the words Satomi had shared with her at lunch. She joked that Ziv had not been eager to bring an infected person into the laboratory, "especially if it would be smarter and more useful than himself."

"What does it matter if it is there? Their plan succeeded," said Ziv, his snark back.

"Not everyone believes that Lysent is behind this, in fact, few believe it. They trust the corporation will get us out of this mess with rationing and governance. If we have evidence they were behind all of it, we would have a lot of leverage against them," spoke Ryder.

"Leverage to do what?" asked Satomi.

"To know and be with our loved ones. To get fair food rations and shelter. To not have the corporation hands all over everything."

"Do you guys have a cell line going?"

"No phones," said Dwyn, happy to know more than someone in the room.

"No, no… a cell culture line we can use to isolate the virus."

Dwyn's body seemed to retreat into itself in embarrassment.

"I've been trying to immortalize a cell line," said Satomi.

Turning to Dwyn she explained, "Cells don't replicate indefinitely. But you need them to in order to do experiments like isolate a virus."

Satomi gave a sweet smile and Dwyn pulled his chest back out and nodded in understanding. Audra was not sure what to make of the interaction.

Gordon agreed to help Satomi in creating a medium to grow and isolate the virus. When they were ready, they would need a saliva sample from another infected subject.

Gordon's eyes hung heavy. He had been able to converse, maintain body posture, and be a real person, but it seemed to take a great energy expenditure. He was still recovering, no matter if he could think of and say words like 'disconcerting.' Dwyn offered to share his room as it would be comfier than the conference table that Gordon had slept on the night before in his half-zombie state.

Audra's eyes squinted a little at the offer. A surprising amount of envy and anger washed over her. She took a moment to place it. Then, she recognized Gordon's charmed life. Here, he had played around with a zombie at the start and gotten bit. Perhaps the laboratory was a gory scene, but it was a single scene he'd endured. He did not see his family get ripped apart or spend months in the woods hiding and hoping that the world would not end. He would not be unable to sleep because the office ceiling was too high. Audra fought hard and he waited in a lab.

"How are you feeling?" asked the ever medical-assessing Satomi before Gordon left the room.

"At first, I didn't know. But now I can place it. It's not pain. I've just spent the last… how many years again, did you say?… in pain. My joints and muscles - they were on fire. I felt like I was on fire," whispered Gordon.

Audra ran from the room.

Belinda could feel. And all she could feel was fire, a burning pain. Audra's mind rushed to the cabin in the woods. Belinda had had night terrors from that day on. And all of Audra now sank into the thought that Belinda was living it. She had been living it all these years.

Did Lysent know? Of course, Lysent knew! If they had awoken anyone, they knew. Lysent hid this from its people and continued to treat loved ones like currency despite their pain and suffering.

13 Negotiation

The group worked long hours on the three projects, isolating the virus to identify the marker, replicating the antidote, and aerosolizing it for an effective delivery system. Audra and Dwyn felt useless in most regards in the laboratory, but they supported and protected the scientists on all other fronts. They foraged for food, kept morale up, settled minor disputes (always involving Ziv), and retrieved supplies. Audra and Dwyn also took turns tagging zoms far from the laboratory, never circling it. As expected, no one had put down a deposit on a six-month rent. It didn't matter. Herders could come corral her tags for all she cared. Audra just wanted Lysent to believe this was her only choice.

More than a month passed before they sequenced the virus's genetic material, but the truth came out. Gordon's RNA marker was found in the virus's genetic material. With some paperwork and data, it was possible to show that Lysent had employed people and contracted out work to develop the virus. Breakthroughs usually led to rejoicing, but this one didn't.

For the scientists, one question remained. Why? Why would a successful company worth billions of dollars effectively destroy their customer base?

Audra would deliver their findings to Vesna. They gave her a full briefing and verbal tests afterward to make sure she knew and understood their case, front to back. Audra had learned more about RNA than she ever cared to know. She learned more about virus life cycles than she knew existed. Despite the microbiology, the premise of the proof was simple and undeniable. While the scientists wondered why, Audra wondered how. How could their group use this information for their benefit? With documents in her pack and Dwyn by her side, she ran to Vesna in hopes she would act. Was Vesna made of guts or talk?

"How did you and Vesna meet?" Audra asked Dwyn during their run.

"Vesna was my first stop when I became a tagger. She saw I was kinda lost and offered to let me stay and work for her until I was ready to set out on my own. When she saw how much I hated the system, she explained her role in the resistance network."

"Is there a leader?"

"Over Vesna? I don't think they're that organized yet, despite what Vesna would tell you. She puts on a show to protect. If we're small, we're easy to wipe out. A pervasive and large network is better. She may share this information with other towns. She may not. I hope she does."

Tears streamed down Vesna's face when she realized the gift Audra and the scientists handed to her.

"Ziv was right. Gary was right," she muttered to herself.

Gary. Gary must be her husband's name.

"Explain it again," she said to Audra.

Audra disseminated the information to Vesna in lay terms then with science to support it. She was proud of herself and her elementary school education. Sure, she might not be perfect in her explanation, but if she could understand it, others could, too.

Vesna stopped muttering to herself to give orders.

"Dwyn, you go back and help the others with the antiviral. Audra and I will take this to the corporation to get more food rations for the villagers and get the six-month hold taken off."

This is what Audra was waiting for. She could hardly believe her ears that Vesna was including the ban without her prodding.

"Why those things?" Audra dared to ask.

"It's a good starting point. We will also ask them to release the prisoners of the indentured taggers. Let the indentured decide if they want to continue their contracts. We will get concessions. In return, they can stay in charge. Then, we topple them with the antidote."

Audra's jaw dropped.

"Thank you," was all Audra could muster.

She had tried to take off with the antidote. And yet, Vesna was ignoring the betrayal and even rewarding her. But, the fire in Vesna's eyes told Audra that she had little to do with it. Vesna was after Lysent. Even she had grown impatient. She was ready to strike.

"Dwyn, please head back to the lab and help the scientists. That is the next part of the plan," requested Vesna.

Dwyn's face wrinkled. Doubt shadowed his face, but no one sought his opinion.

"OK, but at least let me help you plan out the negotiation before I go."

*   *   *

Vesna threw up her hands after stumbling again through the explanation.

"School was never my strong suit. Gary was the smart one," she admitted.

They both felt it was important that Vesna present the science during the negotiation. Audra tried again to trace the connections in the material for Vesna, the same as Satomi had for her. At the end, Audra glanced to Vesna, who met her with deep set worry. Eyes that did not show concern when she sent scientists out into the wilderness or predicted that Audra would join their ranks, showed a past life of under-confidence resurfacing. Audra gave her a small squeeze around the shoulders to reassure. She set aside the paper and made her own illustrations as she talked it over once more in simpler words and fewer presumptions.

Vesna's eyes brightened up three-fourths through this new presentation and Audra could see the ideas click together in her brain. Vesna then explained it back to her, even connecting ideas mentioned in previous lectures. With a second round, she was ready to explain this to a layperson like Larange, because she herself learned it that way. It was time.

Audra wrapped a light fabric scarf around her head and face and tucked it in tight. It would not be unusual and would disguise her identity from all but the most familiar of faces. Vesna may be willing to show her hand to Lysent, but Audra was not.

Audra and Vesna walked through the plaza and up the steps to the large building. Inside Rosie sat in front as always.

"We would like an audience with Larange Greenly, please," Vesna requested.

Rosie gave a questioning look to first Vesna then Audra.

"No, that won't be possible."

"We have something of the corporation's interest. Give us the highest person you can and we will start from there," said Vesna undeterred.

"Actually," said Audra, "give us a scientist."

With some amusement, Rosie picked up the phone and pushed buttons.

"Dr. Lambert, do you have time to see a couple walk-ins?"

"Your names?" she directed toward the women.

"Ashley Williams and Veronica Peters."

Rosie recited the names through the phone, staring at Audra pointedly. Rosie had helped Audra every time she'd visited, and had seen her grow in the past 3 years like she was her own child coming back from play. She recognized her but kept her secret for now.

Rosie nodded, even though Dr. Lambert could not see, and hung up the phone.

"He will be with you shortly."

Dr. Lambert was a tall, skinny man with glasses and graying wavy hair. He smiled when he arrived at the front lobby. Without greeting, Vesna shoved the papers into his chest. His eyes squinted in confusion. He looked through the stack of papers, reading each title page and scanning its contents. After he finished his first scan, he offered nothing to Vesna or Audra. He walked over to the front desk and spoke in hushed words to Rosie.

"It's probably a good time to tell you that this is not the only copy and we have people waiting for us," Vesna said.

She spoke disproportionately smoother and cooler than Audra's rapid heartbeat suggested.

Rosie ushered them into a conference room. Audra sat down and Vesna paced back and forth. Dr. Lambert had not followed them.

"Just sit down, V. They will make us wait uncomfortably long. You might as well settle," she said motioning to a chair next to her.

Truthfully, Vesna's pacing was making her nervous. Audra did not know how the corporation would handle this. They were probably somewhere on the other side of the door trying to figure it out as well.

Vesna agreed and just as her bottom was about to reach the chair, she jumped back up as the conference doors swung open and there stood Larange Greenly, her small petite frame dwarfed by the large entrance. It was difficult to picture her plotting the end of the world. Audra looked at her graying hair and weak frame. She could not help but wonder if they were wrong. Larange sharply turned her face and Audra saw a spark of both fire and darkness in her eyes. Her heart dropped into her stomach.

Two guards were behind Greenly, the same size and shape of the two when she'd announced the cure to the crowds. Dr. Lambert and a few others followed behind them. Audra assumed them to be officials for Greenly. Two of them were rather portly, an unusual sight considering.

Vesna did not want to give away that she jumped in fright, so she reached over the table to shake Greenly's hand. Audra was not about to stand up and offer her hand to this evil woman. She gave a small nod, instead.

"Why are we here?" asked Greenly, her voice noncommittal, proper, and with an accent Audra couldn't place.

"These two have an interesting theory. It's a new stab of propaganda. Their theory is that the corporation started the virus. That is… what this concludes, correct?" He looked at Vesna.

"It's proof."

"And where did you get such 'proof'?" asked Greenly.

She spat the last word as if it tasted foul. Her lips cringed upward on a sour face.

"It only matters that we have it," answered Vesna weakly.

Neither Greenly nor her cohorts had sat down, as if they were uninterested in staying. They pretended they had the upper hand, even if that was not the case, and Vesna was already floundering. Vesna did not sit down either but seemed undecided about both that decision and the conversation's direction.

"We will figure out where you cobbled together this incorrect information. A nearby lab, no doubt," reported Dr. Lambert.

Audra's mind went to Dwyn and the others. If her eyes flashed fear, she reeled it back in. They needed to change the direction of this meeting now. Being the only one sitting, Audra stood up with the others.

"Look. You can do that, but it's too late. We've already got the documentation and sent it to others. You can't cover this up. Everyone will know.

"However, we are willing to work with you," Audra said.

Greenly's stance did not change. Her expression did not change. But she did not leave or open her mouth, so Audra continued.

"We think it's great you're in power. No one can do a better job. To be honest, we know the people are better off not knowing the truth about this epidemic. We just want a few changes for them."

Vesna seemed to collect herself by this point. She stood with her arms crossed, mirroring Greenly.

"We want to even out the food rations between those in the corporation and those doing meaningful jobs in the village. And everyone has a meaningful job in the village," Vesna noted.

She continued.

"We also want you to remove the six-month awakening ban and give the indentured taggers an opportunity to find different accommodations for their loved ones outside the villages. They will still owe you, but they will be able to stop the insurmountable growth of their debt.

"We think this would be best for you, too. It's better for long term stability if the worker ants are happy and busy."

"You do not want control?" she asked, her eyes shifting back and forth between the two. She even seemed to almost imperceptibly exhale.

"No, you would stay in control."

Greenly motioned with her hand and the papers were delivered upon them. She scanned through the documents, her eyebrows almost coming together, perhaps due to concentration but maybe emotion. Greenly knew something. Audra had always assumed that Greenly was an opportunistic manager of a Georgia Lysent branch, but was that all of her story? She didn't seem surprised by their accusations.

After scanning the papers, she looked up and assessed her confronters. Audra felt that same discerning gaze that had given her a reader and a contract years ago. Then, in a flash of anger, Greenly closed the distance between them. Her guards followed with a delay, taken aback.

"If I hear any rumor of this," shaking the papers in their faces, "then I'll cut rations in half and shut down the awakening project altogether. You don't realize how difficult it is to keep balance in this village. You think you are suffering, but you don't know the half of it. Without my determination to do what's right to keep things going around here, we'd all be hurting. Take your stupid zombies, but you won't get rations until the debt is paid. Wake up whoever has cash. What do I care? I'm just trying to hold this HELL HOLE together."

"We appreciate your um, cooperation, considering. How do we know you will keep your word?" Vesna asked.

"I will make an announcement now," said Greenly.

She turned to her assistants and barked, "Gather the people."

"No gratefulness to the leaders…" she muttered as she spun on her heel to leave.

*   *   *

"I am pleased to announce that due to some great successes in farming, we are able to increase the food rations. This will mean less scavenging and trading. With this added abundance, I have rethought the six-month re-awakening ban. We will go back to a case-by-case basis. I realized what a strain it was for everyone, especially the taggers who do such good work for us.

"Whoever stole the antidotes," she looked at Audra and Vesna, "shouldn't ruin it for everyone."

Another official, one of the portly women who accompanied Greenly during negotiation, took over the speech as Greenly walked away from the large noises of the crowd. She explained that taggers could come in the next week to fill out paperwork to pull out their person if they no longer wanted Lysent to render care.

"We want no one to feel stuck."

Audra smirked at the statement. That was exactly what the indentured tagging program was. The woman made clear that money would be owed with interest compounding, but they would not use humans as collateral, only giving the option of care. Other fees would apply. After out-processing, they would be available at the end of the week.

Audra waited a few days before arriving with her paperwork. She presented it to Rosie with a big smile on her face. Rosie gave a timid smile back. Audra hadn't shown Rosie any appreciation for not revealing her identity, even if it ended up not mattering. She softened her smile and mouthed, "thank you." Rosie nodded and accepted her paperwork. It landed in a large pile on her desk. Audra knew better than to argue. Rosie wouldn't mess up something so important.

Audra refrained from asking how many applications had been dropped off. She knew several taggers who were on the verge of giving up and some who had, leaving the township system entirely. Audra knew she would owe near a million credits, but she would have her sister. She would wake her up with a replicated antidote. And if they could incite Lysent's fall, this system of debt and her debt would be no more. Audra knew a lot had to go right, but it was the same as signing on as a tagger had been. For that, nothing had gone right. At least this time, she had more control.

Audra stepped outside to renewed protests. No longer on a six-month break, it seemed they were just as upset over removing the infected from the village as they were with waking them up. Releasing zombies near the towns, allowing people to keep them in their homes? They didn't care that the announcement stated that the infected could not stay in the township. Too many dead, unsafe and worthless, they argued, ignoring that others saw them as loved, curable, and important.

The infected were people. They deserved a chance, no matter how hard the community struggled. Or in Audra's case, how much she personally struggled. She couldn't imagine the possibility of her sister awake and talking by this time next week. Audra disappeared more than a few times. The moonshiners' spots were calling her name. She shook and paced in front, but she needed to stay upright to take care of her sister. Instead, she marched out of the town and went for runs, down easy roads, up harsh terrain, and coasted on rolling hills.

The next week, Audra arrived in the crowd, unsure if she was supposed to receive her sister at a specific location. Perhaps the infected would be escorted out of the town. Vesna was invited to stand with Greenly on stage as an act of good faith and collaboration. Vesna stood somber, realizing this was a business transaction, not a victory. Guards herded ten infected out into the plaza with linen sacks over their heads, all loosely bound together by their upper and lower extremities so they could walk on their own.

Audra heard the protesters gasp and squeal.

"What if they get out of control?" they whispered.

Even with Belinda in the mix, Audra let out a giggle at the thought of a mass of tangled zombies wreaking havoc on this stupid little town and its stupid little protesters. Audra tried to figure out which one was Belinda. There were a few the correct height and skin tone, but the formless white uniforms and linen sacks covering face and hair revealed little else.

Looking through the crowd, Audra spotted a few taggers here to receive or possibly just observe. No one tried to approach the chained. Taggers were a cautious bunch, and it wasn't zombies they feared. Greenly stepped up to the podium with Vesna on her left side, and even the protesters observed their place in society by falling silent for their leader.

"Welcome. You all have been doing a wonderful job building our community and making sure there is food for all. Your successes have brought us increased rations. You did that. Now we can all be that much more productive.

"There is one of our own. Perhaps you know her. This is Vesna. Vesna runs a little shop for the corporation. You have probably bought from her before. Vesna approached me and requested that I end the six-month waiting period and release any zombies whose loved ones did not wish to be part of the program anymore. And just last week I did that."

Greenly and Vesna looked a lot alike, petite women with graying hair. Both seemed weathered from the infection that swept the nation, but one of them was responsible for it.

"But, the six-month waiting period was imposed because an individual stole from us. One person hurt many because he or she demanded something for themselves. And the indentured tagging program exists because you must help others before you can help yourself - whether that is by giving money to further our lives here or by helping to wake up others. You cannot demand for just yourself anymore."

Audra's eyes widened and she hoped to make eye contact with Vesna. Vesna shifted on her feet and looked to the side of the stage. Doubt and panic filled both of their bodies. Vesna made a footstep to stage left, but two guards stepped forward and sandwiched her. Something was wrong. Audra worked her way around the crowd and to the stage.

"This woman is demanding for herself. She is not trying to help us. She is trying to hurt us."

Greenly gave a small nod and one of the large arms of a guard grabbed Vesna. Her arms were pinched to her sides, but she struggled all the same. He pulled out his gun and with a quick move to the temple, he executed Vesna. Vesna slumped to the ground in the midst of gasps and cries. This was unlike anything Lysent had ever done in public view. What positive public opinion her speech had garnered was lost in the display of violence. With no thoughts clearing her mind, Audra doubled over in shock and a measure of less oxygen.

Then, another smatter of noise. This time, multiple weapons.

Audra looked up to all ten in linen collapsing to the ground.

"We will no longer bow to the individual!" Greenly shouted.

And with that, the crowd was on her side once again. Cheers erupted.

Audra did not hear them as she too fell to the ground. Her ears rang with death. She screamed out with no release. Soon, she was forced to suck in, but she received only dust into her lungs. She rubbed her face on the ground as she attempted another yell out. What had she done?

Audra felt a warm hand grab her shoulder. She turned to push away the intruder but saw a familiar face she could not place. The soft face came down to her and her lips brushed her hair and ear as she whispered.

"I didn't put in your paperwork. Your sister is safe inside."

It was Rosie.

Audra froze on the ground, eyes wide, trying to process the information.

"Get up," Rosie ordered with a hoarse whisper. "Your laboratory is in danger. She knows where it is. They're going to destroy all evidence of whatever it is you brought, of you, of anyone who knows."

"How?" she choked.

"They're sending a herd."

Her sister was OK. She was not here in the mass of white and red? But Dwyn and the others? Vesna. Vesna gone. Her mind refused to wrap around to connect all the thoughts, but she reached a conclusion all the same. She pulled herself off the ground and without a word, a look back, or a brushing off of the smeared agony on her body, she ran.

14 Warning

The paths were empty. Everyone was still gathered in Lysent's plaza, not yet dismissed. Audra raced to their small outpost in this town. There, Audra and Vesna had packed bags in case something went wrong. And something had.

Audra would not be able to tote both bags. She opened Vesna's, retrieving a few things. As she did, a shadow came into the room. Someone was here. She whipped out her knife. Only Vesna knew this spot. And Vesna… she was gone. She rushed the shadow's origin.

"No no no, it's me," came Dwyn's voice.

She slacked her knife arm and fell into him. Her emotions smashed into his. He knew. He had just arrived, but he had seen. Then, he had chased her here. She buried herself in him and spoke into his chest.

"She, she, my sister... She wasn't in the group," she breathed.

Was that true? Dwyn wasn't sure. Maybe that was just shock or denial. It didn't matter in this moment. He needed to get Audra out of here. If Lysent identified her, she'd be dead.

"And, Rosie. An attack, an attack on the lab. A herd."

That. That made perfect sense to Dwyn.

"OK, we need weapons then."

Now they could bring both bags. Audra moved to reveal their contents - traps, knives, flares, noisemakers, all manners of self-defense. With emotions still churning, they took off with their loot while the rest of the town still reeled in the square.

"The laboratory is this way," Dwyn said, attempting to guide Audra.

"We're not going there yet."

"What do you mean?" he asked but followed her all the same. Her head seemed to clear now that she was in the forest and on her feet.

"We're going to the corral."

Dwyn had never seen one. Even with his extra gear, he picked up his pace in anticipation.

Vesna's goal had been to wake up the surrounding corrals. Lysent's goal was now to weaponize them by releasing them to kill people. Why not? Lysent controlled food, construction, and now were making public displays of murder. The villagers didn't care as long as it was in the name of safety and security. Vesna had seen how urgently Lysent needed to be stopped. She had prioritized accountability, which made even more special, her forgiveness of Audra's detour.

Audra's heart ached with the memory.

Dwyn interrupted her thoughts with something that had been weighing on his mind.

"Your sister? You think she is still alive?"

His timidity in speech gave away that he still didn't believe.

"That's what Rosie said," she replied with a harshness that ended the conversation.

Audra wasn't sure she believed it either, but she couldn't let go of the prospect. She had to hold onto Rosie's words. If they weren't true, Audra would fall apart and more people would die. And she couldn't let that happen. Her family was more than just Belinda now. It was the entire group. She wasn't going to lose anyone else.

But the guilt of Vesna's death covered, like paint, every thought she had. Every possible blame and future scenario flooded Audra's head as she stomped through the brush.

She distracted herself with endless pace calculations. The corral was ten miles east. The shepherds on horses would arrive in the morning to release and direct the zoms. They would move more slowly than Audra and Dwyn, but would not rest at night. Still, it would take two full days at least. They would possibly arrive in time for a nightfall attack.

Audra picked up the pace to give everyone more time to prepare.

The soft intermittent sirens told Audra they were close, and they slowed to a walk. It was not a good idea to rile up a herd. As they crested the hill, they caught sight of the corral, an expansive pen with close to five hundred zoms. Even from this distance, Audra's trained tagging eye could assess their condition. Exposed to weather and to each other, their skin sagged, muscles shredded, and bones stuck this way and that. They had torn and gnawed on each other. Flaps of skin and tufts of hair clung to the chain-link fences, pulled from their hosts.

Audra knew Belinda did not have the accommodations Lysent boasted, but at least she hadn't been left to this.

Dwyn let out a low whistle and then a curse.

"They're all coming to us?" asked Dwyn.

Audra looked at the five hundred as a mass. She imagined them destroying the forest as they came like an unstoppable ocean wave.

"No, no, not for our little place. They wouldn't. It would be unsafe to have all these zoms running around after they plowed through our laboratory," scrambled Audra, half convincing herself.

The scientists would be frightened beyond belief. Dwyn looked scared, too.

"Why do they look like that?"

"Lysent packed them all in together and left them."

"These are just chain-link fences. How have they not...I don't know… stampeded out?"

"Listen. Hear that siren? In a few minutes, it'll stop and another one will replace it coming from a different direction. They keep them going in circles, so they don't weigh on the fence."

"So, they direct them?"

"Sorta."

"And now they're going to direct them right into our lab?"

"Not all of them. Maybe fifty. A hundred?" Audra tried to estimate.

"I think we can handle fifty. Much more and we'd get overrun."

"That's why we're here."

"We set them loose?"

"Yes."

Releasing the corral prematurely might call off the attack. All hands would be needed to round up the zombies. Or, maybe not. Maybe hundreds more would be directed toward them, simply because they were available.

Despite her affirmation, neither made a move toward the corral. By ripping open select fences, they could split the herd and choose their general trajectories. It mitigated the risk to others but promised nothing. Zombies would stumble into the townships, onto people's paths, and increase the ill favor that the infected garnered.

They sat waiting for an answer to manifest. The bodies were walking corpses. Only the virus's grip on their metabolisms kept them alive. Without it, they would pass from their injuries. Death would be more merciful, but they did not have time. There were hundreds and Lysent was purposely keeping them alive.

"Vesna would release them," Dwyn concluded.

She would. Given her way, she would have brought them to Lysent's fences and she would have mass-cured them. She would let them all writhe and die in front of those who swore to protect and care.

"We're not Vesna."

Audra pulled away from their hiding place and headed toward the lab, corral untouched. They did not bother to cover their tracks. A giant herd would be on the way soon.

Audra pulled more food from her pack and encouraged Dwyn to do the same. It was crucial to stay ahead of the energy expenditure. Accessible food energy allowed you to run. Without it, your body had to convert fat stores. In twenty miles, you'd be forced to walk. Their pace might still be unsustainable. She hoped that adrenaline and salty snacks would see them through.

Her legs felt like concrete and she felt a snapping pain on her hip with each step. She reminded herself that the sooner she reached the laboratory, the longer she would have to rest. And even if she arrived useless and spent, the scientists would have warning. For now, they had no idea.

Dwyn and Audra ran by moonlight to reach the gate of the facility. After fifty miles, Audra's priority was still telling the others about the impending attack, but a disproportionate second priority was raiding their food supply. With just fifty yards left, their bodies demanded they walk.

The scientists jumped at the sight of their runners. Dwyn had left them just last night to support Audra and Vesna.

Good news never traveled this fast.

"What happened?"

Audra opened her mouth to speak, but no words came out. In the day of running, she had not considered how she would share the news, that she had been wrong, that Vesna had been wrong, that Vesna was dead. Soon, she found words, but they were not graceful or soothing. Confusion and sadness mingled in their wake.

What would they do without their leader? Leave? Surrender?

And they had lost a friend.

"I told you they would figure it out," came Ziv's smug brag.

Despite her complete bodily exhaustion, Audra still had to hold herself back from socking him in the jaw. Audra contented herself knowing that he was in the same path of harm despite his condescending mouth.

"What do we do?" asked Ryder.

Ryder, the one full of answers and ideas, had been confronted with a problem that overwhelmed her. She looked panicked. They all looked panicked.

"I know this attack is scary, but we have notice and time to figure something out. You guys need to finish any time-sensitive stuff. Then we'll buckle down and get ready for a siege, of sorts."

"About that 'time-sensitive stuff'…" said Satomi.

She motioned to the conference room window to reveal an infected man circling the table.

"Subject Four is our first aerosolized delivery," Gordon reported.

"Gordon and Ziv are working on that. Satomi and I are systematizing antiviral production," explained Ryder.

Audra had only thought of the human occupants of the laboratory when she rushed over, but now she realized all of their work was in jeopardy, too. Without the lab, Belinda would remain where she was, how she was. Lysent was sending a herd to destroy old evidence and any chance for her sister. With the fog of the corporation's promises lifted, Audra knew she would never get her sister through tagging.

The crew had stopped talking. Audra looked up and realized they were waiting for her approval.

"That's great," muttered Audra.

"How did you get him in there?" Dwyn asked, pointing to Subject Four.

"It was Gordon," said Satomi.

She gave Gordon a sweet smile, and he blushed in return.

The zombie was clad in a jumpsuit, perhaps a member of the maintenance crew. Audra wondered if he would wake in time to help them in the attack, but she did not voice the hope.

"Not much you can do about him. Let's first put away anything sensitive or fragile," suggested Audra.

She looked around at the various glassware and equipment strewn about the laboratory. Perhaps there was a method to their madness, but it looked like a herd had already passed through. Ziv wandered away, muttering about having to stop his experiment. Something about incubation time and additional variables. Audra looked over to Ryder to see how serious this was. Ryder just shook her head. Ziv was just creating drama, unaware of the drama unfolding around him.

Audra's body needed rest, but she did not want to abandon the scientists. She settled for water, food, and stretching out on the tile floor. The scientists were full of questions as they worked to clean up the lab. How far was the herd? How fast did a herd move? How many shepherds? Audra offered answers as she could and speculated on the rest.

Damn her calves were tight.

She tried to get everyone to bed early. The herd would be another two days, but sleep deprivation would hurt them sooner.

In the morning, Audra tested her body. Her legs felt shredded and her step tendered by blisters, but there was no joint pain, no dehydration headache. She counted her current recovery path as successful and grabbed a protein bar to repair her muscles.

She glanced in on Subject Four. Unlike Gordon who had paced, he stood motionless. The badge on his jumper had been torn and neither Ziv nor Gordon could recall a name. Audra asked if the process would be slower, given the delivery method. They all shrugged their shoulders. Doubt shadowed Ryder's face. Gordon joked that he himself was exceptional, but everyone agreed it was possible that Subject Four had not gotten an effective dose.

Audra was shocked to find the sun was two hours old. Daylight was lost by sleeping indoors, but the sleep had done her good. Without her, the scientists had eaten breakfast and finished storing away crucial supplies for their experiments. Audra hoped the zombies would not breach this room at all, but the precautions were necessary. Their work needed to be kept safe.

Audra set up some desks as fortification inside the laboratory. If zombies or people came in, they would have a choke point and fortifications to defend their space.

"I understand keeping the equipment safe, but shouldn't we clear out of here before they come?" asked Dwyn.

Audra shook her head.

"A few tents will not protect us from a passing herd. We need to protect our home and the research. We can't find a new lab or steal more antidote. That won't work again," said Audra.

They were safer inside, even if that was where their enemies wanted them to be. Audra sent the scientists to gather what they wanted from their sleeping quarters. They would stay and protect the lab only. It could be a week or more after the initial attack before they could move freely. Gordon took inventory and stockpiled food in the cabinet. Ziv was tasked with gathering as much water as possible. He stopped up the defunct sinks and filled them with water for drinking. Any clean container was filled.

Audra and Dwyn found two cars and positioned them on either side of the gate to block it when ready. Audra wished they had lined up vehicles along the facility's perimeter as soon as they had moved in, but it would have given away their presence. Now that they were found, they didn't have time. Dwyn cut the barbed wire off the top of the back fence and laid it in front of the gate as the others created more snares. Audra and Satomi cut down small saplings with hatchets and sharpened each end, one to bury into the ground and the other to stick out and skewer the zombies. If they could snare a good portion, Dwyn and Audra could kill the rest. Ziv placed the sapling spears into the ground. He complained that they were not using his brain to its full potential, and instead were having him do hard labor. Audra asked him to think of other fortifications they could build with their limited time and resources as he worked. He seemed content with that responsibility, and came up with approximately zero ideas as he dug.

Satomi had a unique job. After the attack, the shepherds would come on their horses and assess the damage. Audra wanted the place to appear destroyed, defeated, and overrun. Satomi opened the windows of all the other buildings, marking the exterior walls near the door frames and windows with ash to resemble burned-out buildings. She scattered debris from the buildings into the yard to distract the assessors. Satomi pulled even more sick ones from storage to plant around the plaza. Their movement might rile the herd but would discourage the riders from coming too near.

Ryder was given most of the noisemakers Dwyn and Audra had brought. She strung them together electronically and set them to a radio frequency to remotely control them. Dwyn and Ryder ran a mile west to set them up. Gordon gave great praise of Ryder's engineering, praise which she did not notice.

Two days of work and this evening's dinner didn't fill the time left to wait for the mass of deteriorating people. Nightfall might bring their arrival, but Audra imagined it would be closer to dawn before they caught sight of their attackers. Audra attempted to prepare the scientists for what they were about to face. These infected were real people but largely destroyed. Even if they had antidotes to give, the zoms would wake up in tremendous amounts of pain. They had lost skin, faces, and limbs. They would not survive as humans again. Their lives as scientists were more important. They said they understood and Audra hoped when the time came they would depersonalize the sick, and not get swept up by the horror they faced. Nervous composure filled the lab. Gordon offered to take first watch.

It was well past midnight when Satomi pushed on Audra's shoulder. Audra's eyes popped open, but Satomi was already heading to her bed. Her lack of a report said everything. Audra removed herself from all but one blanket. She pulled it along with her, also grabbing her jacket. Once she had navigated around the sleepers, she stretched from head-to-toe before slipping on her jacket and draping the blanket over her shoulders. In the front office, she settled into the chair pushed close to the window, which had been boarded up except for a small slit. She looked into the courtyard. Their tethered zombies rocked, but otherwise remained motionless, a sort of zombie sleep. The darkness and lack of visual stimuli allowed rest for them. Past them, the moonlight bounced off the chain-link fence. Audra cracked the front door open and was met with the sound of frogs and the breeze through the trees. The cicadas had quieted since the weather had cooled. The draft hit the back of her neck and Audra retreated further into the blanket. Nothing moved past the fences. Audra waited as part of the night.

An hour and a little more passed with nothing to be seen. Audra walked back into the laboratory and woke Ziv. He only had 45 minutes left in his shift. He could pay it forward or wake up the next person if he was tired.

"Thank you" came the whisper, surprising Audra.

Ziv had slept in his jacket, so it was already warm. He, too, dragged a blanket behind him. Audra returned to her confined space, sandwiched between a counter and Dwyn. She pulled blankets over her head to create a tent. She may have drifted off, but she was undecided on that point when Ziv came in with rushed whispers. He could see things moving out there.

Ryder threw off her blankets and jumped up. The others were fast behind her. Audra moved deliberately slowly and encouraged everyone to do the same. Rushing around would not help anything. They did not want to draw attention to their building or swell into a panic inside. She directed Satomi to roll up the bedding and place it in the corner. No one would sleep now, even if it was a false alarm. She asked Ryder to check that everyone had two knives, one to use and one to lose. With her requests in place, she followed Ziv to confirm his sighting.

The front room was dark except for the moonlight through the boards. Audra looked past the fence. Yes, there was movement. Ziv was correct. Someone, a lot of someones, moved through the forest toward them. Audra wished it was not so dark. She could not count how many bodies were heading their way, just that they were coming.

She called for Dwyn and Ryder to judge their location relative to the noisemakers. Sounding off the noisemakers at the optimal time would distract a good number of them away from the facility. Soon they were all in the front room, waiting. Once Ryder determined it was time, Dwyn sent the radio signal.

A tornado siren blared in the west accompanied by three successive flares into the sky. Ryder did a few silent fist pumps as the noise pierced the night. It was impossible to tell how many were leaving and how many were still heading for them. The motion of the trees highlighted by the moon was their only reference, but there was no way all the zoms were still heading their way with the lure in place. Everyone gave Ryder a pat on the back. With the siren blaring a mile away and the anticipation of the zoms hitting the first snares of barbed wire and tin cans, Audra knew requesting that the others sleep was a futile effort. They sat and rested, but no one dozed.

15 Leading

In lieu of sleep, Audra ordered everyone to eat at sunrise. When the sirens stopped during breakfast, Ryder could not confirm if they had run their course or if someone had shut them off. The new quiet soon gave way as the first zombies tripped over the knee-high tin can and barbed wire contraption in front of the plaza. It would stop the ones on the front line, but not the rest. A large herd would fill up the barbed wire with bodies and others would climb over.

As the sun rose and more arrived, it became clear the herd was massive. Near a hundred zoms approached, crawling over those caught. Some tangled in the wire did not stay, leaving clothes and skin behind. They hit the stakes next, of which there were not enough. Audra watched as a burly zom levered the spear that bored into him. He now approached with a skewer lodged in his chest. Some worked as planned, the stick going straight through their chest cavity and out the other side. Struggling just pushed them farther onto the skewer, leaving room on the other side for another.

The mass of dead kept coming, past the spikes, up against the cars and fence. The crew watched the drove of torn bodies, jagged limbs, and hanging gray flesh. Their laboratory zoms pulled at their tethers toward the visitors, making wide arm motions. Visitors, two layers deep, leaned on the fences. The chain-links bent and bowed.

"Should we go protect the fence?" asked Gordon.

"I think we should leave," muttered Ziv.

Ziv pointed to pockets of denser numbers creating weak points in the fence. The gate was pulling open from the pressure on either side. No one had managed through, but it was only a matter of time. The fence would fall. The gate would tear open.

Audra looked but feared more intelligent enemies, who might use the zoms as a distraction for a bigger plan. Would they have firearms or explosives? Audra imagined a grenade attack would make short work of the laboratory. Although there were so many infected and riled, it did not matter. No ammunition needed. This place would be torn down.

"If we leave, we'll lose the antidotes," explained Satomi for the third time.

Audra broke the news.

"We can't go out and kill them. The fence will come down before we get them all."

"What do we do?" asked Ryder.

Audra wasn't sure. She examined the situation. Lysent had gathered a sick population and left them in the elements to rot. Then, instead of killing them, they used them to kill others. Their consideration for humanity was vitriolic. Maybe Belinda was right about this new world. Audra shook the thought from her head. Looking past the philosophy, their group could also use the zombies to intimidate and destroy. They just needed to redirect them.

"We will move them."

Dwyn looked at her to assess her seriousness.

"We send them to the township," she said.

"Audra…" Dwyn hesitated.

"We've caught a good many. Lysent will handle them well before they wreak havoc on the town's walls. If not, maybe people will wake up to what is happening."

"It's a good idea in theory, but how are we," he motioned to the group who already looked scared at the prospect of doing anything more than killing a handful through the fence, "how are we going to move them? And possibly under the nose of herders?"

"We jump over the back fence. We get behind the zoms, start up some noisemakers, and run toward the township."

"I could run awhile," said Satomi timidly. "I ran track in high school. I could get a mile."

Gordon nodded, signaling he would help.

"I'm not leaving here. That is truly a stupid idea," said Ziv.

He crossed his arms, not averting his eyes from the horror that Audra was asking him to engage.

Ryder looked at the others, trying to decide.

"Do we need all of us to do the run? Could we do it if Ziv refused to go?" she asked.

Ziv looked offended that they would continue without him. He meant to squash the whole plan, not be the only one in the safety of the lab.

"Sure. Dwyn and I would run the inside lanes. Gordon will be just out from us. You and Satomi would be the perimeter runners," she replied, and knowing Ziv's approval would sway the others, she added, "Ziv, you could deal with any zombies that clung to the fence after."

Ziv seemed to like that idea and did not press his first opinion.

"I think Vesna would agree to this plan," shared Dwyn.

Audra wasn't sure if that was an encouragement or a deterrent. Ryder watched the fence sway, her mind doing engineering calculations.

"Well, let's get to it then," she confirmed.

They would be within chain-shouting distance of one another, but still, Audra hastily equipped everyone with a flare and a small pack along with their noisemakers. The pack would not hinder their running but would give them enough supplies to last a couple of days if they got separated.

"Only use the flare tomorrow morning if you get lost. Then head east where the sun rose. The flare will attract the zoms," she warned.

"I might not be able to take care of all the infected on the fence. There will be plenty not drawn away," discussed Ziv, not even giving others time to ask questions about their riskier roles.

Audra and Dwyn climbed over the empty back fence where Dwyn had removed the barbed wire. They helped the other three down.

"Good luck," called Ziv on the other side.

He seemed scared on all fronts - too scared to go with them and too scared to be alone. Ryder gave one last look to Satomi, blinking but trying to stay focused before Audra escorted Satomi and Gordon around one side of the plaza and Ryder went with Dwyn to the other.

Audra led her two a good deal away from the compound. They would need to get around the crowd without being seen prematurely. Audra continued to listen for sounds of herders, and watched for signs of their presence. She saw none and hoped that Dwyn found the same lack of signs. Perhaps the herders had gone home to rest their horses and themselves before coming back to assess the damage. Everyone who worked under the corporation desired shelter and safety. Audra never saw a corporation worker out in the field for long unless they were indentured. The group could use their dependency on comfort to their advantage.

Near a thousand meters away from the laboratory, Audra saw Dwyn and Ryder again. She had left Satomi at a similar distance on the edge and Gordon between them. Satomi and Gordon would both be in the rough brush but would have less distance to sweep when it came time to break away. Audra could see that Dwyn had pulled out his noisemaker. It was time. The others would know soon enough. On the noisemakers went.

The sound emitted from Audra's device settled on a pitch between a tornado siren and a rescue whistle, but screeched like an alarm clock. In between the pauses, she heard Dwyn's more soothing chop-chop helicopter noise. The others joined in, but fainter. They were already running. Audra and Dwyn waved the devices over their heads, the sound swinging from ear to ear. They jumped up and down. More than just a novel noise, they wanted to be bait. The zoms turned from the fence and toward the runners. Audra and Dwyn smiled at each other and pulled away. The noisemakers had enough battery power for about half an hour. When the last one turned off, they would know to run to their respective sides and out of sight.

Audra's turned off shortly after Dwyn's. She set it down and then returned to it, second guessing for the ringing in her ears. Eventually, all the noise was just a faint echo in her head. Audra looked back to the zoms careening toward her. The long run to the lab was two days ago and though she could still feel it in her quads, she was ready to run again. Quick stepping around roots gave her a rhythm that nothing else did. She ran farther and faster until she was out of sight. She then veered east to get around them. She caught up with Gordon. Despite his previous zombie state, he had an innate strength he had shown several times already. This run was no exception, although his recovery would be slow. Together, they found Satomi and ran back, having escaped the herd. Satomi was both pleased with her running performance and her sense of direction. Audra shared that she would make a good tagger with conditioning. Satomi smiled under her bangs and they walked and ran in intervals back to the facility. They hoped Dwyn and Ryder were doing the same on the other side.

Audra was pleased to see that the place was still standing. There was activity, but just of the sick on spikes, on the ground, trying to gain footing once more. The sick wandered this way and that, their attention being drawn in too many directions. Their clothing and skin hung in equal proportions off the bone. While it was chaos, it was slow chaos and easy to see that there were no shiny new corpses amongst the army.

She smiled when she saw the front gate was still crowded. They would find Ziv inside and comfortable with some excuse. They got to the back fence and threw their packs over. It looked like they had beaten Ryder and Dwyn.

Satomi was already talking about how hungry she was. Running had that effect on people. Audra smiled. They would go eat with Ziv and talk strategy on how to clear the fence. She also wanted to suggest a move. Lysent might continue to monitor this location. It was best to take their equipment and settle elsewhere. Her sister was another subject to discuss. Surely the scientists would understand the danger she was in now that they had experienced it for themselves.

From the front lobby, Satomi and Gordon entered the lab ahead of Audra. As they crossed the threshold, a flash of color filled up the doorway and pushed the two out of sight. Someone had blindsided them both. Audra sidestepped and braced herself against the wall. Her knife found her hand.

Why the hell was she so stupid? There was a reason Ziv was nowhere to be found, not just because he was lazy.

"Come on in here. We have your friends now. Nothing you can do but get one of them killed if you don't show your face," said an unknown voice from within the lab.

"What do you want?" she asked buying time.

"We're just going to take you to headquarters. We have a nicer lab, less zombies."

The voice moved something inside Audra, but she did not know what. Did she know him?

"Are the three of you all right in there?" Audra asked, seeking more information.

"The three of us are fine. These two haven't hurt us yet."

So, there were just two in there. Audra scraped the number "2" into the wood panel as quietly as possible. She pushed her knife in between the panels to punctuate it, hoping Dwyn would see it in time. She then raised her arms above her head and pivoted around so she was in front of the lab entrance.

"OK, I'm coming in."

"Good job, now sit down there and keep your arms up."

The spindly cowboy held Gordon with one arm, the other hand wielding a switchblade. He motioned to a chair for Audra before tying Gordon up and leaving him seated on the floor, several feet away from the whimpering, half-leaning Ziv. The man sauntered up to Audra. He looked at her face and his expression changed. Audra did not recognize him, but he appeared to recognize her. His grin got wide and his eyes sparkled.

"Shit, Lars. We've met this one before."

He grabbed her outstretched wrists and zip-tied them together behind her chair. He pivoted the chair on its back legs, presenting Audra. Audra imagined that if they still had football teams, Lars would be on one. He was wide, strong, and without a neck. He was an overwhelming presence in the room.

"Geez, we have!" he said.

Hearing their voices together reignited Audra's memories, too. These were the voices she heard after she'd been knocked out by the car door on I-16.

"Is this level 2 now?" asked the large guy anxiously. He hugged Satomi with one large arm over her arms and breasts and the other around her waist, but he looked at Audra greedily.

Gordon jumped up and charged into the man that had secured Audra. They both ended up on the floor in the struggle, but Gordon was at a disadvantage. A few hard punches into the side of his jaw left him slack.

"Thanks for the help, Lars," the man snarled.

He pulled himself off the floor, favoring his left knee.

"Aw, you had it, Lindon," Lars said with his arms still around Satomi.

Lindon tied Gordon's feet and dragged the unconscious body into the closet.

They returned to their conversation.

"Well, I guess since this is our second meeting, by default, it IS level 2, Lars."

He tied each of Audra's ankles to one of the chair legs. Out of desperation, Audra considered biting the top of his head but did not think that would help. The two looked strong, and Satomi was the only one not tied up. They would have to buy time until Dwyn and Ryder arrived to change their odds.

Large motion caught her eye. She looked over at the conference room. Subject Four was writhing in front of the window, foaming at the mouth. The duo looked to see what Audra was watching.

"Why you got this one?" asked Lars.

He looked around the room for a volunteer, but no one offered an answer. Had he been told why he was sent here? The terms they used like 'Level 1 and 2 encounters' led Audra to believe they were privy to nothing. Lars squinted his eyes as he came to his own conclusion.

"Well, you're scientists. That looks like an experiment," he said.

He tapped on the window. Subject Four did not respond, yet he seemed overstimulated, perhaps even having a seizure. His eyes closed, and he slid down to the floor.

"Wow, you guys are sick."

He walked away from the window and turned his attention to Ziv, who had found his rear and was sitting up against the wall.

"Do you want to watch?" he asked Ziv.

"Psh, we should make him join in. I bet he'd be enthusiastic after a while," said Lindon.

Ziv stared down into his lap, afraid to ask what he would be watching. Nobody said anything. Satomi now lay hogtied on her side on the floor. Audra shot glares at the closet door that hid Gordon. He had disadvantaged himself so much. He made no noise in the closet. He was either still knocked out or he had realized his mistake.

Despite the discussion, it seemed to be just idle talk for now. Audra was not sure why the men waited. Were they waiting for Dwyn and Ryder or more from their own team? The two men perched themselves on the laboratory counters. Lindon kept alert, hands on each side of his hips ready to spring up into action. His dark eyes read the room, and he swung his greasy hair out of his face. Lars pulled his legs up onto the counter and jammed himself into a corner. He barely kept his eyes off Audra, who sat spread on the chair.

Dwyn and Ryder would arrive soon. Would they heed the warning signs? Audra tried to glance nonchalantly out the window looking for any hint that the duo was out there and making a plan.

"Looking for your friends?"

Audra's eyes shot to the speaker too quickly.

"That chick and your boy? Must have found something fun to do in the woods…" he trailed off as he made a crude gesture.

He must have watched them jump the fence and let them move the zombies. Why? And were they being taken to Lysent or were they going to be executed here? Audra imagined that even if a trip to Lysent was on the horizon, a trial and execution would also be.

Shouting came from outside and disturbed the pair on the counters. Lindon and Lars jumped down. Lindon walked to the front room to investigate. Lars remained behind to watch the prisoners. He pulled out his knife and traced it high along Satomi's thigh. Satomi whimpered and pulled away, her face hidden by the fall of her black hair. Audra listened hard to the noises outside.

It was Dwyn.

"Audra! Audra! It's Ryder! Oh god, we got overrun! She's gone! My leg… I think it's broken."

"So you're the only one left. Come inside before I kill the others."

"Argh, we've got a runner," Lindon yelled into the lab. "Come help, Lars! I ain't running after him myself."

Lars cursed under his breath.

"Did you threaten to kill his loved ones?"

"Guess he don't love them much," called out Lindon.

Lars chuckled at the crew and headed out the door. It was the first time they were left by themselves, but it wouldn't do much good. Audra pulled on her bindings, but they only pinched tight on her skin. Was Dwyn providing a distraction or had something horrible really happened to Ryder? Satomi was crying.

A head peeked from the doorway - Ryder.

"Me first!" cried Audra, her tone somewhere in the broad spectrum of a fierce command and a pathetic cry. Ryder obeyed and snipped the hard plastic zip ties that constrained Audra before rushing to Satomi and holding her. Audra jumped up as soon as she felt the freedom gather around her wrists and ankles. Without a word to the others, she made a direct line to the door to chase the men chasing Dwyn. Dwyn's actions had freed her, but she would not let him fight them alone. She crashed through the front lobby, turning to jerk her knife from the wall. She had enough. She didn't want to know what a level 3 encounter was, but she did want them to regret pushing that door into her months ago. She launched through the front door, readying her sprint to Dwyn.

BAM!

Audra hit something hard. A human arm was braced in front of the door in anticipation for someone Audra's size to come barreling through. Audra felt the back of her head smack the floor and stars floated through her vision. The owner of the clothesline maneuver, Lars, filled up the doorway, solid and angry. He must have assumed subterfuge and had doubled back. Despite the fog in her brain, she did not lose her determination to leave. She rolled away and pulled herself up. She thought for a moment about attacking Lars, but she remembered that was ill-advised. He was at least twice Audra's size. Audra was no match, no matter her enthusiasm. He was an employed goon, paid to be a fighter. Audra was paid to run.

Lars took his time entering the lobby, pleased with his power and in no hurry to run after Dwyn.

"You think I'm that dumb? I'm taking you all back for my payday."

"I get that, but didn't you ever stop to think about why Lysent wants us? We're trying to create antivirals here, but Lysent wants to keep control."

She backed up into the laboratory.

"Let them have control. I like it here."

Audra looked around. The second door had been barred shut, a poor decision on their part. The only other escape routes were the windows. Audra grabbed the centrifuge, much to Satomi's disagreement, and threw it through the window and followed it, cutting her arms and legs in the process.

It was not until she was a hundred yards away when she realized she had left the scientists on their own. Would Lars follow her? Everything in her wanted to find Dwyn. The predicament was resolved when Lars emerged from the building and began his chase. Perhaps he had taken the time to secure his prisoners. Now he would be on her tail.

Having someone chase her almost felt natural to running. Sure, this person was more intelligent than her typical pursuers, but this one could tire. Audra's mind forgot someone was behind her, more encouraged by the possibility of what was in front of her. She knew what general direction Dwyn would head, to their more familiar and favorite running grounds. They would treat them as zombies and pull one of their tricks. Audra would bet anything that Dwyn was setting up for a Bait & Switch, but he might not know Lars was behind her. The configuration required Leap Frog. Would Dwyn figure it out?

Audra was ready to see this end. There was no way she would let them get the best of her again. They handled the zombies. They would handle these two thugs. Her mistakes reeled in her head – giving up Belinda, getting attacked by these two on I-16, letting Vesna be killed by Greenly's men, it had to stop. It would stop. She had given Lars a chance and he had refused to listen. The only way it would end was if Audra ran fast.

With Lars at her tail, she picked up speed, but not a sprint. The thugs were built to bully on even ground, but this was challenging terrain. She decided to catch up to Lindon and veer left. Her closeness would be too tempting for him, and he would go after her. This would allow Dwyn some distraction while he doubled back to come up from behind. That is, if Dwyn knew to do that.

It wasn't long before she caught up to Lindon.

"Hey! I'm about to pass you!" she jeered as loudly as she could.

She could see movement in the brush, of someone just out of sight. That must be Dwyn. He would be able to hear her. He would know her plan without a word of confirmation.

Lindon let out a slew of curse words, already tired from his current chase. He looked up ahead at his target who was getting away, then looked sideways to Audra. Her tease was just too much. He would make her pay for all of this inconvenience. Jobs were not supposed to be this hard. He changed directions.

"Oh, you think you'll get me? I'd like to see you try," Audra flirted.

She was flirting with danger though. It would only take one misstep in the root bundles to twist her ankle and have both men on top of her. She was playing with fire.

With the change in direction, Lars met up with Lindon and they ran as a pair.

"Where are you even going?!" shouted Lars. "There isn't a sanctuary in this whole world. We will get you."

Audra was impressed he could form full sentences behind her. She took a glance back. They didn't even have their weapons out. They were just going to manhandle her to the ground once they caught her. Audra knew it was perfect. She ran north, then northeast, before heading back around. She ran right under an outcropping of rock and felt a little dust and pebbles hit her shoulder, signaling he was in position. As the two thugs ran past the outcropping, Dwyn launched himself from above and fell on both.

As soon as she heard the thumps and crash, Audra turned around and sprinted back. Her knife in her hand, she was ready to come down on one of the two and end their lives at first physical touch. Audra arrived to see all three struggling. Even in the tussle, Audra could tell that Dwyn was not ready to take anyone's life. His moves were defensive and his cuts shallow and toward extremities. Audra reached in and kicked a head. It just made it angry.

Lars had managed his knife. He was close to Dwyn's neck while the other punched Dwyn hard. Audra launched herself and her knife sank into Lars's ribcage. He cried out in pain as Audra yanked it out and slashed for his partner. Lindon pulled back, but into Dwyn's arms.

It was Dwyn who cried out as he made the gash along Lindon's neck, ending his life in a violent, pulsing gush.

Holding his side, Lars lunged again for Audra. Audra held out her knife in front and Lars stumbled onto it. Audra was not sure if he was disoriented or if the move was purposeful. He gasped a few breaths, whispered sorry to no one, and slipped away.

Dwyn shook. His whole body trembled in the excitement, the heaviness, and the distress. Audra cleaned her knife and put it away. She then took Dwyn's and cleaned his too. She put it in his side holster before pushing her arms underneath his to wrap him in a hug. He stood limply for a moment before draping his arms around her. She kept close contact for several minutes, trying to get his body to settle. When Audra thought it safe to proceed, she took him by the hand and they walked wordlessly toward the laboratory. They needed to make it there before dark and preferably before Dwyn went into shock. They had nothing out here and they had run quite a distance.

16 Gone

"They made it back! They're safe!" yelled out Ryder.

She was keeping watch from the front. Gordon came from the back of the property. The others rushed from the laboratory with crying and smiling and hugs all around.

"Where are the men?" asked Gordon.

"They weren't men. They were goons, and they refused to be anything else," addressed Audra.

"We had to... we..." tried Dwyn, who shook again.

"We killed them."

Satomi gave her a hug and whispered, "I'm sorry, thank you."

"They deserved it," sneered Ziv, "they killed Vesna."

No one agreed, and no one disagreed. It wasn't the outcome they had wanted, but it seemed to be the only acceptable one. They were alive. They had survived. A solemn calm washed over them. Ryder pushed the group inside. Satomi gave them food and turned on the kettle for some foraged tea of mostly dandelion. The entire team was wordless for the entire night. No one ventured to their rooms, but instead, they shared the lab again as their sleeping space. Eventually, bodies shut down despite brains reeling, and sleep overtook them.

Ryder was first to broach the topic in the morning.

"What will happen when the goons don't return to Lysent?"

"I don't imagine that the corporation will care where they are and why they haven't collected payment. But, they will send someone to check on the status of the laboratory. If we're still here, they will attack again. This time with trained people, not shamblers," said Audra.

It was important that they understand that the corporation was not going to forget about them.

Dwyn suggested options for the crew.

"The safest course of action would be to close up shop and move elsewhere. Otherwise, we tear up the place to make it look abandoned and hide out until the coast is clear. We could even hide a spot for you guys to do limited work while we wait for the checkup."

Ryder sat in silence. Her brain worked through the options, trying many simulations and perspectives. She then reported her findings.

"We can't move the things necessary. Some are fragile. The thermostat-controlled fridges are impossible to find replacements for, and too bulky to move. We need this place. We will have to convince the corporation it is destroyed, so when they arrive they do not set it on fire or smash it up more, but just go on their way."

"Who will stay?" she asked her friends.

Satomi said nothing but grabbed Ryder's hand to affirm.

"Of course I'm in," said Gordon.

He had nowhere else to go.

"I was here for Vesna," explained Ziv, "now she's gone…"

Audra expected to hear his opt out, but wasn't sure what his alternatives were.

"I guess I must carry on for her memory."

They all nodded in agreement. No one had any time to process that Vesna was gone, murdered, but they would keep going for her and to stop Lysent.

"We will have to break down the fence, burn down some of the buildings, and have zombies marching around. And we have to do it quick. When will the corporation expect Lars and company?" asked Dwyn.

"Lars and Lindon would have finished up yesterday, set up camp overnight, then made sure the stragglers wandered the opposite direction of the villages. They wouldn't push their horses to cover the ride back in one day. That would take them two. And then the corporation would give them at least one extra day before sending another couple of riders to check on us. I imagine they'll just take a day to get out here on fresh horses."

"Four days," said Gordon. "That should give us enough time to hide the valuables and destroy this place."

"After breakfast," claimed Ziv.

They worked together in glorious fashion destroying the laboratory. Gordon noted that everyone else had an eye for it. Satomi suggested it was all the destruction they had witnessed. When you realized what was essential, everything else faded away or in this case, could be smashed. Dwyn suggested that it was that Gordon may still be attached to things.

"I was still caught up on 'things' when others weren't. I was amazed at how little they survived with," Dwyn said as he dropped two Erlenmeyer flasks.

With the fence torn down, Audra and Dwyn gathered all the nearby zombies and placed them in the plaza area to roam around and make inspection difficult. It gave them a chance to speak alone.

"Hey, I want you to understand, I talked with Lars. They liked their jobs. They liked hurting us," Audra said.

"But did you talk to the one I…"

"These were the same thugs that hit us on I-16. They've been doing this for a while. You only did what you had to do," she said half convincing him and half convincing herself.

Dwyn had done what was necessary. He was always protecting the group. He had shown up at Lysent's plaza because he recognized their negotiations were too good to be true. Audra knew it too, but she hadn't discouraged Vesna. She'd cheered her on because it had a chance of benefiting her. Audra felt she had taken advantage of the group. And now Dwyn had to deal with the predicament her choices had caused.

Audra refocused her efforts on destruction. In a particularly brilliant move, Audra staged zombies poking out each building's windows, just itching to get out. That would create a sense of urgency. No one would want to be around when they broke free. They had fun burning an unused building, too. Anything to distract the coming scouts and themselves.

They minimized the number of temperature-controlled refrigerators and hid them away. If the lookout signaled someone was coming, they would cut the power to them. Audra hoped that the scouts would not scavenge their solar panels, but at least they could not carry them off same-day with the sheer number of zoms in the plaza.

With the place a mess, they packed up their supplies and left. Audra hoped they got the timeline correct and would not be out in the woods for long.

"It feels so sad to leave the place looking like this. It's like we were never here," said Satomi.

"That's the point," said Ziv gruffly.

The scientists longed for impact like Audra longed for Belinda. It was a worthier cause.

"You were – because I'm here," said Gordon, leaving the plaza for one of the first few times in several years.

They set up their tents a good distance away from the laboratory, and someone ventured back to keep watch. They used their tents from their travels to the laboratory, and now they had gotten to know each other more and were enjoying the time together in camp. It also left time for the scientists to consider what went wrong with Subject Four. At worst, nothing should have happened. Instead, the antiviral had killed the man. Ziv, who had created most of the process, was more defensive than helpful.

During a quiet moment during dinner, Audra broached their next decision.

"We need a new leader."

She still was not sure if she meant 'we' or 'you', but she knew the group would function better with a leading voice. They were all specialized, and someone needed to look up and make sure they were going in the right direction.

Ziv sat up taller. Audra rolled her eyes. He wanted leadership so he could order others into danger and stay out of it himself.

Satomi hesitated but then offered, "I nominate Dwyn. He is fair and doesn't seem to have a personal agenda."

Dwyn smiled at Satomi's compliment. "I fear I don't have enough experience," he said glancing at Ryder, "knowledge," glancing at Satomi and Gordon, "or skill," glancing at Audra, "to be your leader."

He continued.

"I nominate Ryder. She was the first person Vesna recruited. She has engineering and science knowledge, and she also has shown great leadership here at the laboratory."

"I'm just thankful to be along for the ride," said Gordon munching on his oat bar.

"That should be your election slogan: Take the Ryde," giggled Satomi.

They all let out a little noise before grief settled upon them again. The lightness seemed to remind them all they were choosing a new leader because theirs had fallen.

"Maybe you should hear what I think before you elect me. I don't agree with Vesna's plans. Greenly is murderous and Lysent has to go, but did you see those zombies?"

Audra had never heard that word come from any of the scientists' mouths. It was always infected, sick, or subjects. Never zombie.

"Those are the infected that Vesna wanted to awaken. Can you imagine their pain? They were in pieces."

Silence remained over the group. It was true. They were not viable people.

"Yes, it would topple the corporation, but at what cost? I think we should forget the aerosolization project. It's not working and I don't think it's what we want to do. We can talk about it, but none of us seemed as dedicated to that part of the plan as Vesna. We will still honor her, but we need to decide how we will continue our work."

*　　*　　*

Audra was on lookout duty, up high and tucked away, when they came. She heard the crunching and clomping of horses and saw the movement in the woods on the other side of the laboratory. She pushed a button on the remote rigged by Ryder. It stopped the generator from turning on and alerting the riders that electricity still flowed. Audra used another relay device, built by their bored engineer, to alert the campsite crew.

Before the intruders reached the plaza fence, Dwyn had crawled up next to Audra. He did not want to wait at the campsite for news. They watched the two on horseback circle the plaza, gathering three or four zombies behind them. One horse kicked at a zom that got close to its rear. The commotion attracted more. Audra smiled. The more zombies they gathered, the more rushed their inspection would be. One rider gave the other his reins, and as they passed near a tree, the rider jumped off, out of sight. The zombies continued their path of following the horses. Dwyn gave her a little jab with his elbow, expressing that he was impressed with their moves. She was, too.

Once the tiny herd turned the corner, the dismounted rider approached the downed fence and stepped inside. Audra stifled a giggle as the man encountered a zom behind every door he opened. The man glanced into the laboratory and saw smashed flasks and things upturned. Another building was burned out. The man spent all of five minutes there before hightailing it out of the plaza with two zombies chasing him. He escaped when they got caught in the fence opening and tore at each other. At the sound of his whistle, his partner sped up in his lap around the plaza to meet him with his horse. The rider had lost all but one zombie. Audra was not even sure how. The man mounted up, and they left the way they had come.

Dwyn squeezed Audra's hand in celebration. Audra looked over with a warm smile before realizing they were sharing the same space. No longer in lookout mode, she could sense the warmth radiating off his body. Their faces close, Audra could see the curls of his hair sticking to his forehead.

Audra rolled out and left to notify the others.

*　　*　　*

"I knew Vesna before… all of this happened."

Ziv stood next to Vesna's memorial while everyone exchanged glances. Ziv always seemed so detached or at least reserved. It surprised them that he was speaking of her.

"Her husband, he got me this job at the laboratory, just a few weeks before all this happened.

"After, I didn't have much in terms of family around here, so Vesna took me in. She let me be a part of this. And even though I don't always agree with the way you all do things, I wish I could have given more to her. And I will stay here and find the courage to fight because she believed in me… in all of us."

With quiet tears, the rest shared their piece. And when there were no words left, the scientists returned to their laboratory and their work, leaving Audra and Dwyn in place. Dwyn gave her a light touch on the arm which seemed more for him than her. Despite having access to an antiviral, death seemed closer to them than ever before. He needed to know and touch life, to make sure it still existed. Audra did not respond. She did not want the touch to lead to a hug, to being wrapped in his arms. There was only one she was obliged to - and she was so far away.

The group was safe and doing well. She was proud of their pivot concerning the aerosolization. Audra's stubbornness and determination had sided with Vesna's direct confrontations, but she had seen where that had led them. And her desires isolated her from the others, no matter how much she cared for them. As her foot tapped the ground, her knife in its holster weighed heavy. It had been there for years, years she had been working for Lysent just like Lars. She needed to stop helping Lysent and instead, take care of her own.

That was what Vesna had done, even when her own took off with antivirals. The death hung close to Audra like a heavy tapestry she was trying to hold up. She was not sure how to help the group and help her sister. She needed to choose.

Dwyn was still at her side.

"You're thinking about leaving, aren't you?"

Audra wanted to say no. In truth, she wasn't sure, but in action, she had hidden her pack in the woods before the ceremony.

"I need to know she's alive, Dwyn."

Audra could not be sure of Rosie's words.

"And, I have to get her out of there by myself," she continued.

"Don't you understand that you are a part of this group? We can all work together to save your sister. You don't need to do it alone."

He was trying to persuade, but it confirmed her ideas. He was right. She was a part of this group. But she had one last thing to do, and it pressed on her heart.

"You can't help. None of you can," she said.

She marched to her bag and slung it onto her back before breaking into a jog. She could hear the thuds of Dwyn's feet on the ground, following her. For once, he caught her. He touched her arm, and she pulled away. He grabbed it more forcibly.

"Just stop, Audra!"

She punched him in the face. Hard.

"What the hell!" he said and then noticed that the girl was already in tears.

"I can't let you. I can't bring more thugs here. I can't risk you all - you're doing something good. And I'm - I'm doing something worthless but at great cost."

Dwyn's face screwed in confusion.

It was time to confess. It was time to give it up.

"She doesn't want to be saved… she never did," she spat out, remembering the last words.

Audra reached into the side pocket of her bag and handed Dwyn the ever-accessible letter. It had been in her pocket when Lars attacked months ago. She still had it to remind her, a letter her sister had written years ago. She walked off, disgusted that she would risk his life, Vesna's life, the scientists' lives for hers.

Audra,

I cannot do this anymore. I cannot walk around the woods, surrounded by the dead, hoping not to join their ranks. I cannot continue to rely on you, slow you down, and make you stumble. I do not want you to save me. I never did.

Take my supplies. I will not need them.

The falls are not far. Do you remember how much fun we had there? How our family was together? Laughing. Enjoying. Living.

Do not go there. I will be there, hanging from the uppermost bridge.

I want to spend my last moments where I have wanted to spend all my moments.
With love,
Belinda

With every rescue, Belinda had grown colder, angrier, and less grateful. Audra had believed if she took care of her a little longer, saved her another time, Belinda would get a handle on it and thrive. She just needed more time than others.

Dwyn read it over and for the second time, caught up with her.

"But, she got bit?" he asked, confused.

"She either got bit on the way there, got lost, or decided against hanging herself. She tied herself to a tree, not realizing there would be a cure. That she was not ending the burden, but increasing it with her infection.

"I just wanted her to be happy."

"Sounds like she couldn't be. And that's not your fault. That was never your fault."

The words cut into Audra. She had dared to repeat similar words to herself once or twice, but he spoke them with such certainty. For a years-old happenstance, it stung like a raw hurt. She retrieved the worn letter from his hand.

"I should have seen it coming. I protected her from death every day. We were surrounded by it and I didn't see it in her eyes. Death got to her anyway.

"Death is everywhere. I wanted to take this back from it. I will not let it keep taking from me.

"Vesna is gone! But YOU, YOU will stay safe! Satomi will stay safe. Ryder will stay safe. Because I'm leaving to finish this. You can't help me with this one. I need to do it on my own."

Audra took off on a run again. Dwyn tried to keep pace, but even without a pack, he could not keep up for the third time. He let her go.

17 Decisions

She saw it up ahead.

A glimmer of blue.

Not from the sky, but at eye level.

Audra drew closer, afraid of what she might see.

Blue flannel.

Her sister's shirt.

And there was her sister.

Her face washed and her lips stained with berries. Belinda's effort toward beauty was her signature, one lost at the end of the world. No one had time for beauty, art, or music over shelter, food, and survival. Well, that was not true. Belinda had time for them. Her blond hair was always combed and straight, occasionally oily when water was scarce. She whittled her figurines - robins and blue jays, a squirrel with a fluffy tail, once a whale with a waterspout. And when Belinda was not fearful, angry, or sad, she hummed throughout the campsite.

Her eyes were no longer blue.

They were gray.

Her skin was soft.

But it was gray.

Audra touched her skin and looked into her eyes and saw hauntingly nothing.

Belinda opened her mouth and reached toward Audra. And for a moment, Audra considered letting her.

She was all her sister had. And her sister was all she had. She had nothing now, but a broken promise to her mother. She dismissed her father's voice settling in the back of her mind. Belinda did not deserve this, no matter what her father said.

With a firm but gentle touch to not bruise her, Audra held each of Belinda's arms against her sides. She locked her elbows to keep distance. Belinda struggled a bit against her captor but remained calm. In these transformative hours, did Belinda still have some cognition to her? Would she be able to understand anything Audra was doing or saying?

"I'm sorry," Audra whispered.

Audra noticed Belinda's rope tied around her waist and looped around the thin pine they were standing underneath. Belinda had taken the time to restrain herself so she could not hurt others. With the rope secure, Audra backed off. Belinda remained calm, but still opened her jaw whenever her sister dared to move. Her groans frightened Audra. She hid behind another pine tree, her back against it. Audra stared into the woods. What was she going to do?

*   *   *

An unexpected visceral response accompanied her proximity to the Lysent plaza. The last time she was here Vesna was murdered, and Belinda almost died. At least, Audra was told she had escaped death. She had to be sure. A deep inhale and exhale lowered Audra's stressed shoulders away from her ears. She stepped onto company property.

"Hi Rosie," said Audra presenting herself to the receptionist.

"Audra!"

Rosie's eyes welled up and a smile Audra recognized from her mother warmed the woman's face. Audra knew it was true then. Rosie had saved Belinda from her stupidity and naivety. Audra opened her mouth to thank her but found no words.

"It's good to see you. You know we're under a six-month ban, right? You're often out for a while. I wasn't sure if you heard the news."

"Yes, I found out when I got back in town. Nasty business going on with a villager, right? I'd like to visit my sister, let her know it will be awhile longer before I earn enough."

Rosie smiled graciously and shuffled through paperwork. No one seemed perturbed by Audra's presence. They must not have known the identity of Vesna's companion.

"Just give me an hour to set it up. There aren't a lot of visits today."

Audra was escorted into a room like so many times before. She would sit on the pristine white pine chair and watch her sister until they asked her to leave. She had watched her for years, but now she understood. She was in pain, on fire, trapped in that body.

Belinda moved to the acrylic glass at the sight of her sister. Audra lured her out of sight of the door, to a section of acrylic with air holes drilled near the bottom.

"I'm sorry," she said for the millionth time.

It didn't begin to cover it, but she said it anyway.

She pulled out a syringe that Satomi had synthesized for this moment. Audra had made her promise to not tell anybody although she was sure she had told Ryder. Audra lay on her stomach and reached the syringe through the air hole, seeking the space between Belinda's toes. She injected slowly as to not excite Belinda and so it would not bruise. Belinda did not react at all. Her physical sensation seemed dulled by her illness and isolation.

Audra stood up and put her hand against the glass and apologized once more to her sister. She wished her sister would match her hand. She would soon if all went well, but for now, her gray eyes remained lost. Audra knocked on the door. Clyde came by and escorted her out.

"She was looking a little sallow. Could you have her checked out?"

"Of course, for a fee... since she's not scheduled for a checkup. We'll have Rosie set it up," he said.

"Thanks, and of course. It's like us going to the doctor... costs money."

"Yes, ma'am. There's Rosie. Enjoy your day."

"I'll come by tomorrow. I'm sure it's nothing, just want to be sure."

A few hours later, Audra watched two workers pull a cart out of the plaza and then outside fences. The body was buried, and the cart dragged unceremoniously back into Lysent.

Once they were gone, Audra began the furious but careful digging. She pulled out her sister, threw in some forest debris, and replaced the dirt so no one would notice. Audra put the body on a blanket and used it as a sled to pull her farther into the woods. She would wake up soon. Well, she would return from her coma state back into her zombie state, anyway.

Audra got her farther into the woods and set up her tent. She put Belinda inside with nothing for her to destroy when she came to. She made herself dinner and plans to run with Belinda in the morning, almost forgetting she would need to show face at Lysent to learn of her sister's fate. Would they believe her?

When Belinda emerged from unconsciousness, she did so with a frenzy. She thrashed about and yelled out as her senses were overwhelmed by uneven ground, warm temperatures, and concurrent sounds. She was no longer in her controlled environment and whatever old arrangement they had was lost. Audra gently gagged Belinda, laid her on her side, and bound her limbs. She covered her with blankets to dull her senses. It was not how she had imagined her sister's return. She left her writhing and took a long walk in the woods.

"Hi, Rosie. How did the doctor's appointment go for Belinda?" she asked.

Her nerves rattled underneath her skin, but her skin kept still and did not betray her.

"Dear, dear, come sit down in here. The doctor will come talk to you."

Audra was led into a side room. She put on a look of small concern and waited impatiently for the doctor. Just as Audra felt sure she'd been found out, an older female entered the room. She wore a white lab coat and small glasses. Audra stood up and shook her hand.

"Hi, Audra. I treated your sister yesterday. She fell in her room. You were right. She was sick. We do not know with what. She died."

Audra did not say a word for a few moments, but sat back down in feigned shock. The doctor gave her a pat on her shoulder.

"Where is she?" Audra asked, her voice empty.

"We destroyed her body. I'm sorry. With the illness, we can't be sure it won't spread."

Audra gave a confused look at the lie. She recovered and mumbled understanding. She stared at her hands in her lap.

"Did her caretakers note any signs before then? When I saw her I knew right away. If only I had awakened her sooner..." she said half to herself.

"No, ma'am. Unfortunately, any signs she was ill were within normal limits in our observation notes. You must have a sister's intuition. There was nothing we could have done."

"I understand," she said.

She hesitated before her next question.

"What about my indenture contract? What happens now?"

"Front desk can answer those questions."

And with that opportunity, the woman excused herself and Rosie returned. She gave Audra a couple pats on the back before sitting down next to her.

"I'm so sorry dear. I remember when you first came here. You were too small and young to be a tagger, but you did it anyway. I'm sorry it didn't work out."

Rosie's eyes had questions. Had Audra killed her sister? Audra couldn't answer her here. She touched her hand in appreciation. Maybe one day.

"I understand you have questions about your indentured service?"

"Yes ma'am," she sniffled.

"Well, while you were in here, I was doing the math. The one million credits you need to awaken are, of course, not necessary anymore. Unfortunately, you still owe for rent, the two readers lost, and then, of course, the return of your current reader or the money equivalent.

"And also, we are charging rent for the six months no one can be awakened. Everyone is getting charged that to be fair."

"But Belinda is not here. You could put anyone in her cell. I mean, room."

"It's unlikely we will find another tenant until the ban is over. It's a fine everyone is receiving."

Audra could point out the flaws in that justification. She could argue that she had never lost a second reader. But, it was all academic. No matter what, it was more than she would ever see, much less afford. She just wanted to know the total.

"The total you owe the corporation is 1.2 million credits. 1.6 million if you can't bring back the reader."

Before Audra could react, Rosie continued.

"And since it's now all due, you will earn interest on the total as well."

Audra no longer had to fake her shock and despair. It didn't matter that they didn't have her loved one. They still had her in a financial vice grip and they did not expect her to leave the tagging program anytime soon. Rosie gave her a quick squeeze and told her to take her time as she exited the room.

Before Audra had time to wipe away her tears and collect herself, she heard someone enter the room from a different door.

"Ahem," came a throat-clear. Audra turned around to find Larange Greenly in the room. Audra stood up, not in deference, but to stand her ground. Greenly's guards stood menacingly large. She refused to acknowledge Greenly's desire to speak, but Greenly spoke anyway.

"I know you were in on that ridiculous negotiation with the traitor Vesna. You got her killed."

Greenly's eyes narrowed and she continued.

"And I know you killed your own sister, just to get out of helping Lysent and the villages. You think I'm the awful human being here? I've fed hundreds for hundreds of days. You've never done the same."

She devolved into yelling.

"Get out. Get out now! Don't you ever show your face in this township again."

It was a bonus that Audra's stunt had angered Greenly. Greenly was awful, so was Lars. The whole damned corporation was sour. Audra was happy to oblige the command for now. She gave Greenly a glare, turned heel, and retreated. But she would be back. One day, she would bring Greenly and Lysent to their knees.

18 Falls

Audra couldn't stand to untie her sister's last surgeon's knot. Instead, she brought the camp to her. In her trek, she saw no signs of the infected responsible for her sister's fate. All of their supplies lay undisturbed and yet Audra felt as if she had nothing as she returned to her sister. And as darkness threatened to fall, Audra realized they had spent their first day in their new life.

Audra built a fire. Belinda reached for the visual and sensory stimuli without thought of self-preservation. The transformation was complete. Belinda was gone. Audra cooked and ate dinner in a daze. She periodically chided herself that she needed to figure what to do, but otherwise did not think about it at all. Audra set up her tent as close as possible, just out of Belinda's reach. She wanted to protect her from anything that might disturb her.

Audra awoke cold and reached for her sister before it all came flooding back. She ate out of habit, but little from lack of appetite. Her food supply was now plentiful. She found a good walking stick and rounded off the edges. She packed up her things and loosened Belinda's knot. She secured her sister's lead to her waist and guided her with the stick. They needed to remain on the move until they found something better. Belinda had always hated this plan, but now she followed without protest. Audra spun often to keep them from tangling on the brush. Belinda always gave a slow chase.

They walked an hour back to their earlier camp. When they arrived, Audra realized it was not where she wanted to be. She understood practicality would eventually win out over her grief. She would need a safe place to keep her sister or find the courage to put her down. But for now, she was moved to turn around. Her sister had wanted to visit the falls. And while that was where she had wanted to end her life, it was still a place of importance. She should see it one more time. Audra needed to see it one more time. She turned around and pulled out her compass.

The wooden signs marking the rules of the park stood tall but rotting. No one needed their warning anymore. A metal plaque gave information on the history of the falls. Probably important when the world came back to life, but survival now ruled. They approached the bottom of the falls and surprised someone bathing. He ran out and into the woods. By default, Audra hoped he was not part of a larger group that would return to change her plans. In truth, someone else controlling her destiny would have been welcomed. She would be free of choice, maybe even free of Belinda. She didn't dare think more.

Audra began the walk up the stairs she remembered from their vacation. Belinda could not coordinate the required movements. Every step tripped her up and put her on her shins and knees. Her face smashed into the stair edges. She tried to crawl, but still, it was too complicated for the diluted brain.

There were hundreds of steps.

Audra thought a moment and walked Belinda back to the signs. And yes, one marked an access road. Up the access road they went. It was covered in a couple years of leaves and fallen branches, but asphalted, so not overgrown.

When they reached the top, Audra tied Belinda to the bridge that went right over the falls. The moving water enticed Belinda, but the rope and railings kept her safe. Audra sat with her feet hanging over the edge and looked out. It was just a waterfall. Audra supposed it had been beautiful in a different lifetime. Not in this one. If she thought she would get closure here, she could not. She waited but found nothing. She still had a zombie sister tied to a rope, too many camp supplies, and nowhere to go. One of those issues was easily solved.

She pulled everything out onto the bridge and selected the things she needed. She left the rest in a pack for someone else to use. Then, they headed back down the access road. Audra had a fleeting thought of putting her pack on Belinda but changed her mind. Belinda was never good at carrying a pack. Why would she be now? Audra smiled for just a moment and continued their journey.

* * *

Even if she wanted to, they couldn't go back to the laboratory. Greenly had connected her to Vesna and the lab. The last she wanted to do was lead her back to the scientists' work. The first week of marching north was tough. It became clear that Belinda had been kept in tight confinement. Her muscles had atrophied and her motor skills had deteriorated. The stumbles were hard, but eventually, they fell back into old rhythm, just like the years when Audra had guided her after and before the bite.

Could Belinda survive in this world with just a little more time? With a little more help? Audra had not known how to help Belinda then, and she did not pretend to know now. But she had promised her mother. And she wanted to prove her father wrong. She was the last one hanging onto this rope. She had retrieved her sister and had hurt no one while doing so. And yet, peace still escaped her. It would come. Wouldn't it?

In the meantime, they would march. They would march for weeks. Audra wanted to take Belinda to a familiar place, even if she was sure that Belinda would not understand.

They took the access road up like they had done before. It was almost dark when they reached the top. And someone was already camped there.

"Finally beat you somewhere," came the familiar voice.

Audra said nothing as she busied herself tying Belinda to a sturdy tree. She was surprised that he had surmised her destination, annoyed he was there bothering her and her sister, and happy because she had missed him. She hated that he was there and yet, was glad to not be alone. The latter won out and after she finished her knot, she buried herself into a warm hug. She looked up into his face.

"It is good to see you, but I have other obligations."

She wanted to be clear that his appearance would not persuade her to rejoin the group.

"I came to give you this," he said as he offered a syringe from his bag.

An antidote.

Audra's eyes filled with questions. Dwyn answered them.

"A temperature-stable antidote. Turns out it's a lot easier to make them temperature-stable than to aerosolize them. At least, for Georgia's spring weather. Summer? Not so much, yet...

"I ran it here for you, and for her."

Audra fingered the syringe in her hand. Audra had worked hard, but all progress had been gained by her friends. Vesna had died trying to help a girl she never knew for a girl who had stolen from her. Satomi had made that syringe that had mimicked Belinda's death. And with another milestone achieved, a temperature-stable antidote, their first action had been to run a hundred miles to give it to someone who had abandoned them, to someone who after she received it, would have no reason to help them ever again.

"Thank you," was not enough, but the hug she slipped into and held was a start. She felt home. Dwyn gave his big, goofy smile and then settled into the hug. After a few long moments, she took his hand.

"I want you to meet someone…"

The river and falls below them seemed in perfect harmony with the insect noises around them. It was too late to give Belinda the antidote tonight. Audra slipped it into her bag, safely tucked away in towels. Dwyn had already eaten. Audra nibbled on a protein bar before she climbed into Dwyn's tent. She slept in her own bedding but curled up against Dwyn, who said nothing of the arrangement but rested his chin on the top of her head. They listened to the sound of the water and the slight shuffle of Belinda until they fell asleep.

The next morning, they woke up at the same time and left the tent together. Audra smiled at their spot near the river and walked with Dwyn over the footbridge to watch the falls.

"Something here lends itself to change, to rituals, to an awakening. It's magical," he murmured.

Audra gave a small smile as she hung her feet over the footbridge. Speaking of changes, she wanted to know what was going on with the group.

"We're scaling up our replication of the antidote. We've cured several other scientists, and they have been helping."

Dwyn hesitated before sharing the next part.

"They verified that there is pain during the infection."

Audra thought of Belinda at the campsite. She was in pain, and not just after the bite but before. Audra felt sure that waking her up to a world that was safe and civilized would relieve her pain, but maybe that wasn't true. And the world was not safe yet, anyway.

"We're going to undermine Lysent. We need help running, recruiting. I thought that the taggers who lost their loved ones would be interested in helping. Besides, if we succeed, many families will be looking for their loved ones. Tagging will be back in full force."

It sounded like a difficult world, but one she could help. It would get worse before it got better. Audra stood up and returned to camp. In the time that Belinda was gone, Audra had been angry, drunk, depressed. She had bargained her life in the process of making things right, but they were not hers to make right. Some things were out of her control. Some part of Audra knew that, but not the deep-down part.

When Audra turned the corner, she saw Belinda had pulled the blindfold off. She shifted her weight from one foot to the other in her excitement to see humans. Now whenever Audra saw the gray of Belinda's eyes, she saw the pain. She saw the suffering she had refused to acknowledge was so deep in Belinda. Belinda had made her choice to end her misery. She just had not known her torment would not end with a bite. Belinda was now helpless to the agony. Would waking her up end the pain? Or was Audra just refusing, year after year, to accept?

Audra turned her eyes away from her sister and toward the campsite and breakfast. After her meal, Audra sat for a long time staring at the fire, pleasantly warm in the cool morning. Dwyn did not ask her when she would inject her sister. He knew she would do it in her own time. She watched the fire die, from flames to embers, to no glow at all, just gray.

Audra picked up her pack and approached her sister's tree. She touched her face. Belinda pulled back and tried to bite the hand. Audra did not flinch. She reached into her bag for the antidote.

She arrived with something else.

"I love you," she whispered as she drove and withdrew the blade from her sister's temple with uninterrupted motion.

She reached out and caught the remainder as she crumpled, guiding her to the ground. She held her body and closed her gray eyes with a pass of her hand.

While a gasp may have escaped Dwyn, he did not say a word. He had come uninvited. He needed not invade anymore. With all his questions unanswered, he stepped away. Audra lay next to the body and caressed its face without attack until the sun began to sink opposite where it had arrived.

In that time Dwyn prepared a final spot in the woods aligned with the falls. After the silent burial at sunset, Audra sat by the grave and gazed out to the ever-moving water and the sun glimmering through the leaves until it was no more. She stayed for days and she mourned in a way she had never allowed herself. And Dwyn let her be.

When she opened her mouth to speak, she murmured partly to Dwyn and partly to the hushed noises of the waterfall.

"I feel like I've been running all of my life... away from zombies, away from death, away from accepting and mourning my sister's life and decisions. Belinda doesn't have to be in pain anymore. And neither do I."

And with that, she picked up her things and packed them away. They broke down camp and slung on their packs. It was time to move forward, to no longer meander through the woods focused on a dying mirage. Audra ran toward her group, to deliver antidotes, and to stop Lysent. She ran to awaken someone with the treasured vial stowed in her bag, toward a new life for the villages and for her. She ran toward herself.

>>><<<

BOOK TWO

CHASING REDEMPTION

R.M. HAMRICK

1 One goal

Audra swept the stray auburn hairs away from her face and ear as she paused on the half-cleared trail. She had been tracking it for a while, but now she could hear its shuffling. The speed of the walk told her it had no purpose to its wandering, but was lost and unfocused. She could relate, but not today.

Today she had one goal. To find one and save its life.

When Audra was a child she wasn't trying to save their lives; she was running from them in these same Georgia woods. Now zombies - zoms - seemed fewer and farther. Audra wondered if Lysent Corp was collecting them ahead of her to protect their business model. Lysent connected rich families with their wandering loved ones - and received a healthy cash sum in return. Audra had stolen their antidote to cure the zoms. Her group replicated and gave it freely, chiseling away at Lysent's corporate bullshit as they could.

And today they could. Today she had one goal.

She heard its snapping of twigs, the rustling of leaves. The fresh litter dusted the ground of years of pine straw. She could even guess it was male - larger feet, heavier legs dragging. She reverted to breathing through her mouth as soon as she got the first whiff. Male or female smelled the same - putrid. The summer drought hadn't allowed many to be rinsed off in afternoon storms, so the products of any bodily functions stuck to the zombies, wounds festered, and odors lingered on their remaining garments.

Soon she spotted her prize, although he hadn't caught a hint of her. Zoms were first and foremost provoked by sight, and she remained behind him. Would this zom voraciously attack when he discovered her or would he be too weak? The chase hadn't been much of a chase lately. It seemed last winter had weakened them and lessened their enthusiasm as hunters. Like most animals, the longer it had gone without eating, the more likely it wasn't going to eat.

Tired of following, she took a chance and let out a sharp whistle. Audra watched him stop before pivoting. She whistled again as he finished his one hundred and eighty degree turn with a wretched stagger and his gray, hollowed face came into view. She waved her hand in a joke greeting. The hair - no, the scalp - had fallen off to the side, revealing a thin layer of dermis over the skull. Otherwise he was intact, skin upon frail bones - disgusting, but salvageable. Clothes hung off his body, gray and indiscernible from his pallor. His rail-thin arms bore deep scratches where he had gotten caught on branches and pulled hard. Audra avoided looking at his eyes with her green ones. They were all the same - dark gray - the same as Belinda's. Audra had already spent days staring into them, trying to find someone, any part of someone, inside.

He shuffled to her, but Audra would not call it a run. Starvation had taken its toll. Audra reached into her bag. In the past, she would have pulled out her biometric reader to determine whether Lysent was interested in the person. Now, it did not matter. Inquired, deposit paid, no family matches available, other people and their actions no longer gave value to your life. The fact that you were here gave you value. You were worth waking up. Audra made sure of it. She retrieved a thick band of cloth to use as rope.

She wouldn't need to pull some clever evasive maneuver at top running speed to take him down. She merely sidestepped his clumsy launch and let him fall. From there she grabbed one wrist and turned him on his back before grabbing the other, avoiding his long, jagged nails. His neck and upper body craned to bite at her. She restrained him with a boot to his chest, gently as not to remove skin from his sternum. She wrapped up his wrists, finishing with a surgeon's knot. He struggled for a moment, like a dying upturned cockroach. How the world must seem different from down there.

The zoms were in pain. That much she and her team knew. Their first non-regulated awakening, Gordon had told them it was as if he had caught fire. Relief was unknown. As they woke up others, they heard similar stories. Did these zoms wander and search for food to ease their constant suffering? The virus tore away will, everything but their most basic desires - to be without pain, to have food, to spread. Audra cocked her head and wondered if she and the zoms were so different. The same virus had torn her from her family. She constantly searched for relief, food, and shelter. They had both lost to the virus. One had just turned gray. Audra wondered if she too would fade away, like this dying specter in the woods. Audra stopped, closed her eyes, and reminded herself who was to blame.

Lysent.

Lysent had created this virus. For what reason, she still did not understand, but she would make sure that it ultimately hurt them in the same way. They would be torn apart, searching for relief, food, and shelter. And then they would fade away into the grayness until it was just a dim spot in their history.

Audra stepped off the zom and twisted him up to kneeling before helping him to his feet. She was caught off guard and off balance as a yank pulled her in. Looking up into a wide-open mouth, she fought to keep her eyes from rolling back in response to the emanating smell. She regained her balance and swung forward and away before he could master his depth perception.

Audra shook the funk off and increased the clearance between her and her captive. If she found any mint leaves on their way back, she'd be sure to shove them into his face.

Minty decay.

Finding a rhythm, they started to the laboratory. One upsetting point about not using her biometric reader was that she didn't get to know a name for their journey. Walking through the forest with a zom with no name was not as exciting as it sounded. Names and the nicknames she derived from them made the zoms seem more personable and her days less lonely. She looked at his opposite combover. She was surprised he hadn't lost it. Should she, uh, put it back? Another gasping growl of foul stench told her he'd be OK for another day.

Audra wished she could remember the name of someone in past culture with a combover. That's the name he'd get, but it seemed all her childhood memories of television were fading. One day they'd get back to that, at least re-watching those shows as classics. Maybe they'd eventually make their own again. Audra couldn't imagine a town with resources plentiful enough to support a sitcom. Whatever. Not in her lifetime.

With a few miles under their belt, Audra felt a change in her zom's gait. She could tell a lot by the tautness of the rope, the sway of it, the fetor and noise. Something was different. She turned around then immediately diverted her eyes. She spotted a split tree and led her fellow to it. Pulling his arms through the opening, she wrapped her rope back around the tree and behind him. With his arms secure, he couldn't turn his body. Audra pulled up his pants and tried to tighten his belt, which crumbled in her hands. She pulled out a rope from her bag and tied them up. She didn't have to put up with that view the entire run.

Beyond her bodily-fluid soaked zom, she noticed another smell - the distinct smell of burning rubber. Curiosity got the better of her, and since - damn, why couldn't she think of any combover names? - was secure in more ways than one, she investigated. Audra shimmied up a thin pine, the bark scraping her hands. Not the highest view, but she could verify that the scent on the breeze was from miles away. The thick, dark plume rose in the distance, near the highway, probably on the highway.

A car fire? Audra tried to rack her brain for a reason an abandoned car would catch fire on its own, but she knew there had to be a person behind it. Staying hidden was usually a layer of protection against others; whatever their reason for the blaze, they were giving up their location and didn't care.

Audra wasn't too worried about them wandering off the highway and finding her community. Most people who left the highway followed the well-maintained train tracks. It was a golden road to civilization, and it led them to Lysent Corp's string of townships. Her community was hidden deep in the woods.

Her community.

It still felt weird to say that.

But that's what it was. What was first just a laboratory attacked by Lysent had now become a home. They had even named it. If by naming it, you meant they started calling it by the name on the industrial park sign. Osprey Point. Audra had never seen an osprey there, but whatever; it beat calling it "the lab that's now a community." It was a survivor's refuge with one weird exception. Most of these survivors were not initially survivors. They were infected, cured by the scientists at Osprey Point. She looked down at her bound prize. Curly here would be their newest member.

Audra came down and grabbed a handful of acorns from the neighboring tree. They weren't her favorite, but others liked them. They made good flour for bread, but the "coffee" was particularly disgusting. She put them in her bag along with the other found food. That wasn't her mission out here, but any amount helped.

The sun was no longer climbing. They would not make it back before dark. That was fine. They'd stop to eat and camp. She'd have to trap something moving for him - a small mouse or a squirrel would do the trick. Audra appreciated her timing; they'd arrive at Osprey Point in the morning. She'd be able to drop off, resupply, and head back out. With a day's worth of sunlight, Dwyn or the scientists wouldn't have a reason to keep her.

Audra figured the less involved she appeared at Osprey Point, the less likely it was that Lysent would hurt the community to reach her. Larange Greenly, CEO of Lysent, hated what Audra was doing and what she knew, but she didn't appear willing to wage war over her yet, despite her continued stunts.

To appease her friends, she left some things there and claimed a bed-thing. She regularly returned. But still she spent more nights out in the woods in her pop-up tent than in the confines of the fences, and ate most of her meals by a small grate over a fire rather than in the mess hall. Although often out of its range, the radio they shoved into her bag reminded her she hadn't traded much when she got rid of Lysent. She was still out in the woods, capturing zoms, just for a different community. At least this one didn't dangle her sister's life in front of her like a carrot on a stick.

She stayed to keep an eye on Lysent and wait for her chance to destroy them. Once Lysent was shut down with no chance of resurrection, and Greenly was dead for all the things she had done, then Audra would leave. She'd see what else was out there. She'd bring the antidote farther north or west and see more than live oaks and pines and damn mosquitoes.

She slapped at one. She and her zom together emitted that much more carbon dioxide to draw the buggers. And they preferred her fresh blood over the zom's once they arrived. Audra pulled on a long-sleeve shirt and wrapped a cloth around her neck, despite the warm late summer. One bit the high of her cheek. They were insatiable today. She muddied her face. She felt uncomfortable, but at least she was no longer getting chewed up. Not getting destroyed by insects was one thing she missed about modern civilization. She hoped bored survivors would fix that before reviving sitcoms.

With her coverings in place, she looked back - her new friend was now receiving the brunt of the attack. The thought of applying mud to his body made her sick; she decided against it. His kind had spent years trying to bite humans, infecting them. He could get a taste of his own medicine for the evening. When they stopped for the night, they'd get a good smoky fire going and get a breather from the bugs. A good fire, maybe a mouse for her, a rabbit for her friend, a nice sleep. Then they'd be on their way in the sunshine with renewed energy. Maybe he could even run. They'd get there in half the time. Today she'd had one goal. And now, it'd be a good night. Audra smiled and pulled along her new friend. He pulled up closer. Oh yeah, some mint... that'd make it better.

2 Osprey Point

Little creatures scurried in their wake as Audra and Curly ran for most of the morning. Only her zombie anchor slowed her pace in the soft sunshine and cool breeze that swept through the colored leaves. Before Audra was ready, she caught sight of the gray chain link fences surrounding Osprey Point, and the two guards who stood above the front gate in the scaffolding Ryder had built for them. Someone was on watch twenty-four hours a day. The gate was reinforced with metal paneling, something they hoped to eventually do with the rest of their perimeter. For now, they lined the interior of the fence with old vehicles. It shrank their livable space, but also helped to prevent the fence from bowing if a horde were to come through. The two men equipped with bows, arrows and baseball caps waved to Audra, grimaced at the sight of her find, and then covertly rock-paper-scissored to see who would climb down and escort their guest.

Audra thanked the loser, Branson. His blue eyes twinkled with humor at being caught. He fingered his long brown hair behind his ears before falling in behind the duo. Audra began her hero's walk inside the industrial park, which had taken on new life. Every building was in use - for food, sleeping, living. Real living. They had awakened everyone they could in the business park, finding scientists, maintenance workers, office workers - those who previously worked at Osprey Point were now citizens of Osprey Point. She got lots of smiles and greetings from faces she barely recognized now. Satomi did an excellent job patching people up. And with color to their skin, hair regrowing, and a smile on their lips, it was impossible to recall each of them. Audra returned the smiles, then laughed when they caught sight of her prize and gagged.

The industrial park's asphalt was dusty and dry, weeds cracked through, but the one-story buildings that scattered and connected were built well. The roofs were lined with solar panels, although their ability to store power was limited. The power was mostly used for group work

- medical, scientific, and cooking purposes. It wasn't perfect, but it was home for many survivors.

The center held a small plaza with a defunct fountain, the mess hall, the laboratory, and the medical office. Audra turned toward the medical office. The windows were curtained from the inside for privacy. Audra opened the door to its high-traffic carpet and front lobby, which had been stripped of anything comfortable to sit on. All the furniture had been moved into private residences. She peeked her head into the other half of the office. More carpet and three empty stretchers lay in a row with office cubicle partitions to separate the treatment areas. The other side of the room had a long counter with a sink, and shelves stocked full of odds and ends. At the end of the room stood a large metal table, used for office work or surgeries, depending on the day.

She pulled her keep into the office and found Satomi with her head in a cabinet, organizing her supplies.

*   *   *

Satomi pulled her head out of the cabinet when she heard the door creak open. She'd thought she had another box of adhesive tape hidden in there, but no luck. Satomi brightened at the sight of Audra - it was curing day. Audra pulled on her leash. Satomi cringed at the thought of a person on a leash but didn't know how else Audra would manage. She cringed again when she saw her patient.

That amount of skin grafting would not be easy.

"Oh, the poor man. Did you recover his scalp?"

"What? Oh, it's on this side," said Audra, maneuvering the patient. "It's flopped over a bit."

Having the headpiece would make the procedure much simpler. No skin graft needed. "I'll clean and stitch that up before he comes to. Will you find me some volunteers?"

"Yeah, sure. Probably a good idea," she said as she tied the patient's leash to a safety railing by the metal table. Audra left to find some able hands. Satomi cleared the table of her notes and the depleted supply of Lidocaine from this morning's tooth extraction. She pulled her long jet-black hair into a tall bun to keep it out of the way.

Eager to treat both virus and injuries, Satomi didn't waste any time, but rather gave the patient a visual exam as she waited. She then tried to take a pulse, but he swung his head toward her and she decided to wait for others. Still, she was happy it was curing day, another person to awaken and give a brand-new life. If it was up to her, she'd cure everyone as quickly as possible, but she understood the balance between having enough resources for those already in their community and adding more mouths to feed.

Before administration of the antiviral, she needed to clean and stitch his scalp. The procedure would be quite extensive and any trapped infection would kill him, so anesthetic antibiotics were a must. If she felt his prognosis was acceptable then she'd give him the antiviral to awaken him. In a process Satomi didn't quite understand, the virus protected the brains and bodies. Things that would kill uninfected humans somehow had less impact on infected individuals. Satomi had once treated a long-ago burst appendix in a patient, clearing out the debris and stitching him up. He was fine; the uninfected would not have survived so long. Satomi made sure to give each infected a thorough examination, and treat any possible issues before the awakening process removed the protective nature of the virus. Otherwise, the bodies would quickly succumb to whatever ailed them - mostly infections from injuries. It's like the bodies were on ice - everything slowed, including impending deaths.

Gordon and Dwyn arrived together with heavy leather chaps and jackets to assist with patient positioning.

"EW!" called out Dwyn when he saw the patient's flapping headpiece. His dimples, bright eyes, and constant commentary never hid his emotions. He was taller than Gordon but didn't add grace to his height. Gordon was more professional and made no comment, much to Satomi's appreciation. Although his time infected had slowed his aging, Gordon was still older than she was. He had strong angular features which dwarfed the thin-framed woman's glasses on his face.

The two approached the patient. Gordon bear-hugged him from behind, trying his best to not get a face full of head injury. Dwyn pulled the patient's arms out straight toward Satomi. Satomi set to work quickly, knowing that their hold could be temporary. She didn't have any inhalational anesthetics in her office's supply, so anesthesia would have to be given intravenously, which required finding a vein on patients who were not only dehydrated and sick, but also wouldn't stay still. She put a tourniquet on the bicep and cleaned the lower arm with alcohol and a rag, removing much of the grime to get a better view. Satomi saw her potential target. She slapped at it deftly with her hand before warning her friends of the impending sharp near them. Satomi stuck the patient and the vein rolled a bit (along with the entire arm), but Satomi was used to hitting a moving target. She stuck her tongue out just a bit between her teeth as she navigated around.

A spot of blood appeared within the plastic. Bingo. She secured it with tape as quickly as she could, balancing conservation of supplies and really not wanting to do another IV because this one was pulled out. She grabbed her precious bottle of Propofol they had found in their last supply run of the hospital and, eyeing his weight, gave him a hopefully appropriate dose. At one point, her office had made use of a bathroom scale. It had informed them all the residents were medically underweight, then it was broken shortly thereafter in a scuffle between infected and handler. She had put the replacement low on her wish list.

Her patient slowly stopped fighting, and then Dwyn and Gordon were trying to keep him up rather than keeping him from escaping. They pulled him onto the table as Satomi readied the flexible plastic intubation tube. She tried not to think about its prior uses. Previous single-use items were now used until failure. She had cleaned it out, and technically, it wasn't supposed to be sterile, but it still felt wrong. She got above the patient, still avoiding the wound, and tilted the patient's chin back. First the blade of the laryngoscope, then the tube followed. With the tube's cuff inflated to keep it in place and Dwyn using the self-inflating bag to control the patient's breathing, Satomi scrubbed her hands and began as quickly as possible. She could give him more Propofol in smaller doses to keep him under, but the faster she performed the procedure, the more anesthetic they would have for someone else.

"What did Audra name him?" asked Dwyn, ever curious about Audra as he counted to six under his breath before giving the bag another slow squeeze.

"Curly."

"She's not been very creative lately," he admitted.

"I'd name him Homer, after that old cartoon," said Gordon, before putting the stethoscope up to his ears and pumping up the blood pressure cuff. Satomi surmised Gordon was connecting the infected's injury with the combover of that character. But it wasn't their place to name him. He was a person. He always had been.

If the two men had continued their chatter, Satomi didn't notice. She became lost in her work. She cleared the wound with loads of homemade normal saline and another formerly-disposable bulb syringe. With her sterile tools, she pulled the scalp back into place and began her stitching.

Satomi remembered too late that she should have brought in one of her assistants to watch and learn. Gordon and Dwyn were part of the core team, and she had gotten used to their help. But if some of the new citizens could take on some of these duties, then perhaps she could return to the laboratory. She hadn't even entered the lab in the last couple of weeks. It seemed having a community meant needing a full-time medical doctor - although she hated to admit it. From sprained ankles to toothaches, it was all on her. When she wasn't treating, she was preventing. Illnesses could sweep quickly through their tight quarters and decimate their antibiotic supply. Now, she used a lot of herbal remedies to supplement or to curb sickness before it required traditional drugs. She wasn't sure whether she was a modern doctor or an apothecary at times. Perhaps they were one and the same.

It didn't take but a couple of smaller boluses of Propofol to keep him settled for the duration of the procedure. Gordon had managed to push an entire bag of IV fluid. The patient's skin was already beginning to look less gray, and the veins on his face receded a bit in the returning color of his cheeks. She'd try to give him another half bag of fluid before he woke up and pulled out the IV. Then if all looked all right, he'd get a dose of the antiviral. Often it took a series of doses, but eventually normal brain function would return.

Together they transferred the patient onto the third stretcher from the door. Gordon and Dwyn secured him with wrist and ankle restraints. Satomi continued using the bag to oxygenate him until he woke, then she deflated the cuff and pulled the intubation tube. She'd check its integrity and wash it again. Eventually he'd really awaken and tell them his name.

Satomi would bet a bag of prepared normal saline that it wasn't Curly.

3 Audra's Secret

Audra was on her way to the mess hall for a second breakfast when a young woman with spiky brown hair bounced over to her. She had a bright speck that decorated her tiny nose. Earrings lined one ear. The jewelry and her bright eyes just accentuated her fairy-like qualities, petite but tough. Her bright smile took over half of her face, and Audra couldn't help but be pulled into her office for a talk. It was always good to see Ryder.

They shared a long hug before Ryder pulled around to the other side of her desk which was covered with a bunch of schematics, measurements, and sketches. They were scattered in a mess that Audra couldn't decipher. More papers had crept their way onto the walls, secured this way and that. Not by tape. Tape was in short supply. While Audra had never thought much of the rundown business park, Ryder's vision, keen engineering mindset, and wicked hard work had created a sanctuary. And, as much as this office didn't look it - it was the office of the mayor.

"I want to do a council meeting tomorrow, since you're in town," she said, pulling herself onto her desk, sitting cross-legged on the mess. She looked down at a sketch that looked like a silo, frowned, and grabbed a pencil and scribbled a couple of numbers.

"Can't we do it today? I'd like to not stay," muttered Audra, not really wanting to elaborate. Audra didn't agree with the added complication of council meetings, much less them actually meeting. She had often voiced that concern in the council meetings, much to everyone's frustration.

Ryder glanced up, her eyebrows also rising.

"Satomi is going to want to monitor her patient... About the meeting, I want to nominate you as mayor during the meeting."

"Hell no." She crossed her arms over her chest.

"Look, I'm great at the town-building stuff. It's the rest of this leadership thing - I've no idea what I'm doing. I'm an engineer, not a mayor," Ryder confided in her.

Audra disagreed. Ryder was doing an amazing job creating a workable infrastructure with a population that was only growing. She had set up a water filtration system and was even trying her hand at designing the farms for efficiency. It made Audra's head spin - the way she balanced immediate needs with what was best for the future. She understood Ryder's desire to slough away the politics, but what she was actually asking, Audra wanted no part of.

"Audra, I don't think anyone's more capable than you. And it wouldn't be just you - the others are a big help. I'd be a big help."

"I wouldn't make a good leader. All I want is to wake up the sick and tear down Greenly. That's not much of a plan or a future. You need me out there pulling in more people. You can glean leaders from the cured."

It was hard to argue with it, but it was also just a really good excuse to not be a part of civilization. They were lucky she didn't run off in the first place, that she returned here as a home base.

Hell, maybe this was Ryder's and the council's secret plan to root her. It wouldn't be their first.

They were interrupted by someone coming in with a question about the storage silo. Nobody knew what they were doing except Ryder, and even she just went by principles she had learned in engineering, not because she had ever built a silo before. Ryder recited the new number she had written down in anticipation of their question, and they headed out. Audra didn't even know the person's name. Marla, maybe? And that's why they needed Ryder. Ryder connected with everyone. Even when they were first journeying to Osprey Point, she'd kept up morale and confidence despite not knowing what they would find there. Audra did not have the affability or patience for such tasks.

"I wish you'd think on it more. I don't feel comfortable here. I was happy to lead us - not an entire community. If not you, then someone."

Perhaps she was serious. Maybe she'd talk to Satomi and get her feel for it. Satomi, now regulated to full-time medical doctor (although Audra didn't dare tell her that) was Ryder's best friend. She'd know better what Ryder really wanted. Audra made a note to do that in the next couple of days.

Until then, to appease Ryder, she replied, "Yes, I'll think about who else could lead, but, you'll have to give us some time. You're doing great."

*　　*　　*

After a second breakfast in the mess hall, Audra raced to the refitted office building to find her room in the maze of hallways. Audra imagined from the amount of paperwork they cleared from there, it had been an insurance office, but she also never bothered to look at the legal-ese to confirm. She was given a small room toward the front - easy escape.

She began swapping out things in her bag. The morning had gotten away from her and she wasn't sure if she'd be fast enough.

She wasn't fast enough.

"Where are you going now?" asked Dwyn, his curly-haired head popping through the doorway of her little room. Damn, she should have shut the door. Were they really done with Curly already?

"Back out. I have the rest of the day to find someone else. How is Curly?" she asked, trying to keep the topic on zoms and not her or him, or worse, her and him.

"He is resting. You could also rest," he suggested as he did so against her door frame. His shoulders had gotten even broader, she thought. She dismissed the thought.

"I rested last night nearby." Not addressing the real point. "I'll check the snares before I head out."

"You're coming back tonight, though, right?"

"Why?" She slung her bag onto her shoulder.

"The council meeting tomorrow."

Shit. Ryder had already told him.

"When you're back, can we hang out?" he asked with some trepidation, then proceeded to slip off the door frame. Audra gave a giggle, much to her aggravation.

She enjoyed his friendship, but things had gotten complicated. The kiss. Then, she had been rather unguarded and emotional at the falls when he'd arrived and helped her bury her sister, but she couldn't stay that person. And besides, what was the point of owning an anchor? She'd be leaving here soon enough. It was easier to just... not.

"No, I don't think so."

His eyes darkened a bit at the invitation's decline.

"Give yourself permission to be here, Audra," he said as he walked away.

He could take a hike. She didn't owe him her company. Audra stomped through the maze of office halls to find the stockpile of clothes that people could pull from. She needed some new socks to compensate for the fact that she needed new shoes. What did he know? Her thoughts raced. Becoming permanent residents and setting down roots in a town was a dream for her and her sister. Belinda craved people and attention and gave love freely. She needed a town. To live here without her... Audra wasn't sure she wanted to.

With a quick nod from her to the guard, the gate wheeled to let her out. She ran out into the golden hues and burnt coppers of fall without looking back at the dusty overcrowded community. To live there and love there was for Dwyn, for Belinda. She didn't need it.

*   *   *

The crunching of the leaves underneath her feet reminded her they were running out of time to make provisions and preparations for winter. It could come fast. It could also leave again for another scorching summer-like day. The south was weird like that. Audra didn't know how those up north survived their intense winters, but at least winter was assured.

The oak trees were dropping their green acorns. Most of them had sunk into soft ground and she padded her way through. Occasionally one would catch underneath her feet and threatened to roll her onto hard dirt and roots. She laughed and stepped with fast short beats.

Audra ran past the stretch of planted mulberry trees, which had given all they had to offer weeks ago. Rumor had it that some of the fruit might reappear as wine in a couple of months. One could only hope. Audra observed that the hickory nut trees also needed a rest from hungry fingers. If she thought a single runner needed obscene amounts of food, it was nothing compared to a hungry settlement. Audra recalled Larange Greenly's rants about the difficulties of keeping her towns fed, despite their resources and stockpiles. Ryder had many systems in place for their community as well. Still, Audra wondered what they would do when things got scarce. If things got really bad.

The bleating and commotion filled her ears before she met the third snare. When she arrived to leaves flying, her excitement faded into a bit of sadness as she could almost taste the young doe's fear. Small. She could handle it herself. Audra pulled the magic out of her bag - a concoction in darts - a joint project by medical Satomi and engineering Ryder. Audra was careful not to touch the end. She was no match for something that could take out a deer. Rather than take aim at the flailing, she sat down and waited. The deer's coat was splotched in transition from summer to winter coat. It panted and writhed, but she knew it would eventually pause in its frantic motion to look at her. She'd already have aim and be ready to shoot. It would take a couple of good hits, but it was worth it.

Pop.

Got her.

And one more.

She took a few moments to let the sedation settle before unhooking the deer from the snare and setting ropes upon it. The doe was a heavy thing, but Audra was a stubborn thing. She braced her feet and found the starting momentum to get her onto the wrinkled patched tarp, and the tarp moving. Occasionally, the doe gathered enough strength to attempt another self-rescue. Its limbs kicked and bucked and more than once Audra had to let go of the rope. She'd rather pull zombies. They were a much more cooperative field partner.

A sense of uneasiness settled over the space between her heart and her stomach. Audra swiveled her head to look while still trying to maintain forward momentum. It was difficult to sense another presence in the woods with the deer so close. Maybe Dwyn had suspected she'd found something in the snares and had come to help. But he'd be coming up the path, which Audra had just reached, and there was no one in sight. On the worn single track, she dug her feet into the dirt and they picked up additional speed. She told herself that it would build strength in her legs. Maybe she should have let such a young doe go, but she needed it. Not to feed her people, but to feed her next people. Their turn.

Audra wasn't sure if she kept the corral of uncured a secret because of the surrounding politics or because she was ashamed of it. Osprey Point was founded on a cure for all. No payment. No indentured servitude. You were cured and that was it. End of story. However, it turned out it wasn't that simple.

Each person they awakened from their zombie state had only the rags on her back, heartbreaking confusion, and a disturbing absence of survival skills. A "catch and release" program would prove lethal, or at least counterproductive in terms of reinfection. By some degree, they were responsible for each life recovered. They taught each one to forage for edibles, how to hunt, and how to keep sheltered and warm - Audra recalled Dwyn's dismal attempts to build a fire prior to her teaching him. How Dwyn had survived without that skill boggled Audra's mind. Where had he been? But she didn't dare ask when she refused to share anything of her own.

Despite skills taught, everyone remained firmly within the fences, content to stay in Osprey Point. And a community filling to the brim meant a backlog of people to awaken. A backlog just in this small part of a Southern state alone. Audra hated Lysent, but they were right about one thing. You can't wake them all up at once. You need infrastructure. You need a system. And until then, you need a corral.

Dwyn and Ryder were the only other two who knew about the corral. Even among three, it remained a point of contention. It was too close. It was insecure. It was an accidental herd waiting to happen. Yes, yes, yes, it was all those things. A corral did nothing good for the zombies within or the humans nearby. After much debate, it was decided they would funnel any secured materials or time into expanding the community working toward eliminating the corrals once and for all.

The deer had given up its noise by the time they pulled up to the corral. Her head and neck rested sadly on the tarp. A rusted trailer, long emptied of its goods, stood in a cleared field - someone's loot a long-time past. Audra could hear them shuffling inside. She tied the deer's legs and hoisted it up with the pulley system that Ryder had built. After tying it off, she climbed up to meet it. The zoms could smell the fear and the meat. Their scuffling rolled into a frenzy. She dragged the deer to the rusted portion of the roof that had been peeled open with great manual labor. In one last attempt to save its life, the doe flopped and threw Audra dangerously off balance. The metal near the edge bent with her weight but did not give this time. Audra sat on her rear and scooted away before pushing the deer into the groaning darkness below.

Audra lay back and settled onto the warm metal of the corral. Her body vibrated with the activity therein. She listened to the scream and ripping of flesh. What sort of life was this? She'd give herself permission to live when the world was worth living in. She rolled off the corral and headed back toward Osprey Point.

4 The Stranger

When Audra came out of the woods and onto the asphalt, her stride opened up into a sprint to the front gate. Ziv jumped down and managed to slide the gate open just in time as Audra came bounding through. She skidded to a stop with a smile.

Two scientists manned the gates, the easy shift that ended with the fading light. Ziv, with his long straggly beard that overtook his thin frame, was one of them.

"Who's next on shift?" she asked. She hoped she had timed it perfectly to avoid another awkward encounter with Dwyn.

"Marcos and Gordon," Ziv reported.

Audra gave him a pat on the shoulder as thanks as she began to slow her breathing. She'd look for them in the mess hall. They were probably preparing for their shift, and if not, Audra could use a snack. She jumped onto the short walls of the fountain and skipped along its border.

Previously the mess hall was the designated corral in the industrial park. Now, the front room served as a place to gather and eat if one so desired. And one mostly did, since their rooms were isolated and boring. The back room served as a food pantry and limited kitchen.

Their diet was primarily a mixture of farmed, found, and hunted food. Late summer berries gave way to mulberry leaves and dandelion greens. These were supplemented with what meat they might have on hand, typically made into a stew to make it go further. They also traded for Lysent food blocks with some townships that were willing to keep it on the down low.

Audra entered the mess hall, which had a collection of eclectic tables and chairs, including the large conference table from the laboratory. She spotted Marcos first. His head was bowed, leaving his dark hair swinging low and covering his face. He was lining up his berries in size order on his plate, or maybe it was in order of ripeness - Audra couldn't tell.

"Yo Marcos," she said swinging her leg over the bench across from him. She grabbed a handful of berries from the bowl on the table as well.

Marcos looked over at her haphazard way of eating berries. She dared to put more than one into her mouth at a time. He disapproved by saying nothing in return. While amusing, she knew that his orderliness balanced the other scientists' absentminded messiness in the laboratory.

"Can I take your guard shift?" she asked.

"Uh, sure, but it's a double... I traded with Dwyn, something about he had plans."

Audra smiled at Dwyn's failed attempt. Her plan had become ironically perfect as long as Dwyn did not catch whiff of it. Then, she'd be stuck in awkward silence hoping for a zombie attack just to ease the tension.

"No worries. I got it."

Audra sat next to Gordon, whose thin-framed woman's glasses barely fit on his nose. Audra still had not mustered the courage to tell him what had happened to his original glasses. These did match his prescription, allowing him to work unimpeded in the laboratory and as guard, but they for sure didn't match his face.

They both sat cross-legged on the scaffolding and looked into the dark distance.

"How's the search going?" she asked.

Gordon had a daughter and an ex-wife he hadn't seen since before the outbreaks. She worked for Lysent; maybe they had survived. Eliza would be eight years old now.

Gordon scoffed. "I don't know. Still going, I guess." His voice broke at the end.

Audra wasn't sure what to say. She had known it was a long shot. She should never have scanned his DNA with her reader. She had told herself that there was no harm in trying, but there was harm in the false hope it had given him.

Audra had scraped the reader as lightly against his shoulder as she could, but the scientist had winced all the same. Audra had always wondered how much it hurt. It didn't bother most of her targets. Turns out, that was because their bodies were dealing with too much internal pain. Nothing external signaled as loudly, possibly why they kept going even when falling apart or torn apart by physical weapons. Nothing told them to stop.

BING

"What does it say? What does that mean?" Gordon had asked from his perch on the metal table in Satomi's office.

A single *BING*. Audra had known what that meant right away, but she'd pretended to read the display anyway. In her tagging life, almost no money had ever come from a single *BING*.

Inquired, but no deposit paid.

The logistics of finding the family, the family still wanting the individual and suddenly having the means to cover the expense? It always meant milling around until you gave up and found a better zom. Gordon had waited for her answer.

"It means 'Inquired'. At some point, someone asked about you."

"They're alive." His voice had rasped with all the possibilities. He'd jumped up as if he had somewhere to go.

"Gordon, it doesn't mean that at all," Audra had said, touching his arm to slow him. "It means at some point, someone looked you up. The tagging program has been running for nearly four years now. Your family could have checked and then moved on. And to be honest, I bet Greenly inquired for all the scientists in this laboratory once she realized its strategic importance."

"But if it was my family, they'll notify them now, right?"

"They're supposed to. But, I imagine all employees of this facility are marked. They're not going to help us."

"Then, I'll look on my own. This is hope."

Audra had kept to herself what the single *BING* meant to her.

"Do you think they'd head south or north?" she asked now, hating herself for encouraging him.

"North, definitely. She had family up there."

Audra nodded into the deep darkness. Gordon ran his hand through his hair and adjusted his glasses.

There wasn't much hope, but Audra knew she would search too if she were in his place. Besides, what else was there to do but look?

* * *

After a few hours of sleep and the promise she'd return in time for the meeting, Audra was back out with the coolness of the morning. She couldn't comprehend how anyone could stay cooped up in that industrial park. The padding of her feet and the soft dew greeted her like an old friend. Soon the dew dried, leaving the crunching rhythm of fall.

A rhythm that was being cut into.

Audra paused, but all of the crunching did not. She looked ahead toward the noise that approached and the figure that made it. Audra pulled out her knife and held it ready. Who was here so close to Osprey Point?

The figure did not change pace, so Audra stood and waited. It was a zombie. Or was it? Its feet shuffled but its back was straight as if the infection had started from the bottom and hadn't quite reached its way to the top. Even from this distance, she observed its drained color, that sandy gray that overtook flesh - a veil over humanity. It had no damage, no gouges, no weapons protruding from its torso. As much as it looked like a zom in excellent condition, Audra's mind refused to accept it.

Something was off.

Its movements weren't quite right. Its limbs moved with more coordination than what felt familiar. Audra swore it was making small corrections around obstacles. She watched its left foot rise slightly higher, avoiding a root.

As he got closer, Audra could see that he could have been a healthy survivor this morning. He was built. His muscles hadn't atrophied. His spine didn't droop in odd directions. He had all his hair, unlike scalped Curly.

He wore a loose burlap sack, not something people would choose for themselves. Audra remembered the dagger in her hand as her eyes searched the forest for the wardrobe designer. No one else around. None of this felt good or safe. He hadn't seen her yet, even though she was close to his direct trajectory.

"Hey you!" she dared call out.

He looked at her. Audra expected him to attack. She waited for him to spring, launch himself, and reach out with his strong arms. He was much taller than she was and she wondered how much his improved condition would be to her disadvantage. But he just looked at her, then turned his head ever so slightly back to its forward position as he continued his march.

"I'm talking to you! Are you OK?"

He did not answer.

A zombie that did not want to bite people? Or a trick, a man in disguise?

Audra wasn't sure how close to let him approach.

"Look, you can't go that way. I need you to go back where you came from. I've claimed all these woods. It's my hunting ground. You can't get to wherever you're going from here. You're going to have to go somewhere else and start from there."

No response. Not even a side-eye glance at her joke. Whether he knew it or not, he was making a beeline to Osprey Point. Maybe he'd keep walking right into one of their walls. Audra wasn't sure what the deal was, but she needed to redirect him like she'd redirected hundreds of zoms before.

He was almost to her and Audra could see the dark gray of his eyes. No one could fake that. He wasn't there. This wasn't a disguise; this was him. Whatever him was. Audra shoved his left arm. His right leg came out to stop him from falling. It was a reflex but usually not a successful one for his kind. He adjusted his trajectory ever so much to correct for her efforts.

If his instincts weren't strong enough to chase her on sight, then she'd have to become more enticing. What else drew zombies in?

Audra cringed. Blood. Blood drew zombies in. The smell, the sight, the crying that often accompanied it. She looked around, even though she knew it would do no good. There were no convenient animals or reservoirs of blood to grab on a whim. The only thing that had delicious blood was her. She looked down at her dagger, which she hoped she had cleaned more recently than she recalled. The zom brushed past her. She gave a little slice to her hand near her thumb before she could change her mind. He didn't immediately turn around so she recovered the distance. In a move that she considered only as she got there, she offered the knife with the blood on it rather than her bloodied hand. His head turned at the smell and his lip sneered upward. She had him with the scent of blood. But how much of him did she have? Not enough - something still drove him forward. He did not stay.

Audra pulled on his arm. When she refused to let go, a fist swung toward her. She let go before his fist followed through. Instead, she ran in front of him and dived for his legs. He did nothing to avoid her and fell over. She escaped him and he reoriented himself to his original direction, the direction to Osprey Point, before pulling himself up. She kicked him in the back, causing him to fall again. He just moved to get back up.

What was wrong with him? What was this?

She would not let him reach her community. He was a threat, an unknown infection. She pulled out the rope from her bag, the second time in two days, and swung it onto her shoulder. She'd kick him down again, but this time in a more opportune place.

She waited until he neared the right tree, then she drove her foot into the back of one of his knees. Down he went. Audra worked quickly but carefully. She wasn't sure what he would resort to when he realized he was being subdued. She dragged him close to the tree. So far so good. She tied the rope around him and then around the tree. Around and around it went. The zom began fighting at this point. Pulling, struggling, trying to get his hands free. He finally resorted to opening his mouth to bite.

Audra secured him with a knot and looked around to get her bearings. She would bring Satomi and the scientists here to examine him and treat him if they could.

She thought of the cure stashed away in her bag that Dwyn had given her. No. She didn't even know if it would work, or what he had. She would save hers for a rainy day. For that rainy day.

Audra started off in the same trajectory as the zom intended. Was it a coincidence that he was heading in the direction of Osprey Point, or something Audra shouldn't ignore? She was lucky to have found him. If they awakened him, would he be able to explain how he'd gotten sick and with what? He couldn't have cared less that she was there. Audra wondered how the virus spread if insatiable hunger didn't drive him. Maybe he was a one-off; Audra hoped he was a one-off.

Audra raced through the gates to Satomi's office. She'd oversee the treatment, possibly in the lab. The conference room hadn't been used for quarantine for so long.

Satomi was seeing someone on a stretcher behind one of the movable walls. Audra shifted from one foot to the other waiting impatiently. Yes, he was tied to a tree, but something felt off. Audra wanted to know what was going on. She knew zombies. Even if Satomi and the others refused to call them that, Satomi knew them too. This wasn't a zombie. This was something else. And the sooner they figured it out, the better.

Right as Audra was considering interrupting the office visit - probably some ingrown toenail or toothache - something interrupted her.

"HEY OOO!" called someone from outside the fences.

5 Jack & Jill

"We'd like to talk!" they said unnecessarily. Of course, they wanted to talk; otherwise they'd have attacked already. About what and on whose terms, was the concern. The infected in the woods quickly disappeared from her mind as she peered through the reinforced front gates to see an armored man and woman with a handful of support behind them.

"Invite them in?" asked a squeaky Ryder, sidling up to Audra. Lionel, one of the guards on duty, had found her.

"No. You don't want them to gain any easy knowledge about us. You want them to suspect that we are more powerful, more numerous, and more guarded than we are. You want them to doubt whatever moves they make," Audra said in hushed voices to her leader, her eyes glued to the group outside.

"Oh, right..." Ryder said. In a louder voice, she said, "let's meet them outside the gates where our guards can watch overhead."

By this point, Dwyn had emerged from the mess hall to join them. Others flooded from the community buildings and funneled into the residence quarters. At least they'd be out of the way.

As the gate opened, the doors further revealed the duo. The woman had long, blond hair that swept around her shoulders and into a braid that went down to her waist. She wore flexible leather armor tucked into her boots, and a sliver of skin showed that her suit was two pieces at the waist. Her wrists, hands, and neck – all popular and vulnerable spots for zombie bites – were covered and guarded. She stood of equal height to the man, whose blond hair was spiked with gel and styling. He wore heavy strips of leather on his forearms and on his shoulders. He carried a short, pointed sword and she carried a glimmering hand-axe. Their weapons showed that they liked close combat, and their being alive provided evidence of their ability.

The two looked similar, maybe siblings or just that weird thing where people start to look like each other when they are in relationships. Either way, it was obvious by their body posture that they were the power couple of the group: clean, pretty, and confident.

The others stood a few feet behind them, their hands on weapons as well.

"Hello!" said friendly Ryder, although her voice wavered just a bit at the end. "I'm Ryder. This is Audra and Dwyn."

The woman raised her eyebrows and the man made no gesture. For people who wanted to talk, they were not quick to do so. The pair sized up the crew visually before the man spoke.

"I'm Jack. She's Jill."

Ryder held out her hand to shake, but Jack and Jill made no movement to do the same.

"Where are you from?" asked Ryder as she lowered her unreceived hand.

"New Tennessee. We came to escape the winter. We like it warmer, although we imagine your zoms stay active year-round?"

"They slow down up there? We haven't really noticed a difference. Well, they get a bit smelly during the summer," remarked Dwyn.

Jill giggled, but it was a bit of a dark humor giggle. Audra didn't trust it or Jill.

"New Tennessee?" asked Audra.

"Yes. I guess it was Virginia? answered Jack. "But a group migrated up there from Tennessee and renamed it for their own."

So, there were more survivors, at least on this side of the Mississippi and south of the Mason-Dixon line.

"So, this place," Jack started. "Looks like it used to be an industrial park - offices and such."

Ryder nodded.

"Did you wake up anyone from here?" he asked casually.

"Yes, we sure did."

Were they trying to reunite with family?

"Any scientists?"

Ryder answered before Audra could signal her to shut up. "Oh yes!"

"Good. We want them. Doctors too."

"What?" choked Ryder at their demand.

Jack and Jill gave a cold stare. Their minions behind them tensed and seemed to grow larger.

"We won't give you people," Audra said, her patience thinning. Dwyn touched her wrist, a sign to be careful. Audra pulled her arm away. She was not going to be cajoled by him out here. Or anywhere. She shot him daggers and he backed off.

"We're stronger than you," said Jill simply.

"Then there must be more of you?" suggested Audra. "Because you're just five here and you don't look any stronger."

Jill laughed at her, like Audra had just told a joke.

"You'd be surprised," she murmured, "but yes, there are more. We could take over, but we might not want to. So, what do you have?"

"Audra's right, we don't deal in people. But if you're interested in scientists, we might be one step ahead of you." Audra closed her eyes and deeply inhaled as she listened to Ryder's mistake. "We have an antiviral for the pandemic. It works. We can trade it with you."

"So, you do have scientists. Good ones too. Bring them out to trade."

This wasn't working.

"We'll do no such thing," said Ryder, crossing her arms.

Jack and Jill turned heel and ominously walked away.

"Well good riddance," muttered Dwyn.

As the duo reached the forest line, Jill raised her arm. With the snap of her fingers, dark figures emerged from the brush in a long neat line. Audra flashed back to Greenly's attack with shredded and weathered zoms. These were not those. They walked purposefully rather than shuffling. Like the zom she'd met in the woods, these looked strong. It would be unlike anything they'd ever encountered before, and Audra suddenly wished they had done more to fortify their community.

Audra noticed the zoms all carried weapons, despite the assurance that they could not possibly use them. They were too clumsy and uncoordinated as zombies. Was it just a scare tactic?

She wouldn't believe it if she hadn't seen it with her own eyes. One of the zombies, a man with a rectangular face and a crew cut pulled a grenade from his belt, released the pin, and rolled the explosive along the ground ahead of their attack.

Audra and her friends scattered to avoid it.

"Is this real?" asked Ryder as the grenade came short of them and exploded into dust, sticks, and stones. It wasn't the best toss, but the fact that it could happen was amazing in itself.

And they were in danger.

The trio retreated back through the gates, which closed quickly on their tails, no request required. The guards, Marcos and Lionel, were seeing this too. Complex actions from zombies.

"I know you were ordered to come forward, but we don't mean you all any harm," called out Ryder through the gate. A shot in the dark. "We would like to trade. To learn. To understand."

No response. No reaction.

Ryder tried another tactic. "JACK! JILL! Stop this madness! Please, let's work together. Call off your soldiers."

But they did not. They were nowhere to be seen.

Twenty or so encroached. The car-lined chain link fence would hold against twenty zoms. Hell, it would hold against fifty or more, but what kind of attack were they about to meet?

Despite having seen one up close, Audra still didn't believe it. They must be humans posing as zombies to scare them, but Audra could see the purple veins webbing their gray faces. She saw the emptiness in their eyes. And she could see little issues with their stance, their swagger, their facial expressions. They might not be full-fledged zombies, but they weren't full-fledged healthy humans either. They were some hybrid.

Audra called out to Marcos, who had a bow and quiver of arrows. He made eye contact - his eyes were wild with fear and confusion. She motioned to her own shoulder then chose a zom - a half zom? The half zom's hair had been cut short - someone had given him a haircut - and he walked without concern for his wellbeing, as if he didn't understand the significance of enemy lines. Audra wanted Marcos to hit him, but not in the head. Would it slow or stop him? Would it rile the group? Marcos gave a nod and took aim.

The arrow came from above into his shoulder, blasting through his clavicle. His shoulder slumped as he was knocked off balance, but he didn't fall. Anyone would fall. Yet except for the long shaft emerging from his body, there was no other clue that the arrow had hit. She signaled again and another plunged into his chest, missing his heart. There was no evidence of pain, discomfort even, just a distraction - a slowdown. In the realm of weaponization they had all the benefits of zom and human - the ability to follow directions, perform complex movements, and the painlessness and fearlessness of zoms.

She gave permission to let arrows fly.

Regardless, the half zoms reached the fence and began to claw and climb. Audra grabbed several long spears stored near the fence for hordes. She passed them out to Dwyn and Ryder. The zoms moved fast but were not making perfect progress. Audra and her crew stood on the cars and started charging the spears through the fence. It was difficult to get an effective blow through their dense skulls, but strikes to the face or multiple jabs seemed to weaken their grip on the fences. They did not try to avoid the shots, as they were seemingly unaware of weapons, injury, or death. They climbed up and up then fell with the spears.

"Let's save one," whispered Ryder. Ryder was right; Satomi would want to study it. They would need to know if they could be cured. An awakened soldier might tell them what they were and where they were from. New Tennessee, my ass.

With just one remaining, Audra signaled to have the gate open. With the creak of the gate, the zom dropped from his position two-thirds up the fence. He hit the ground, planting both feet, his knees bent to soften the landing. It appeared his directive was to enter in the most efficient way possible. When it was easier to walk in, he stopped climbing.

Audra recognized him as he approached the fence. It was the one she had tied up in the woods. So, that was the way they had come. They had found it and untied it. He must have been a scout. Audra kicked herself for not having realized it, but since when were zombies scouts?

Audra and the two gave him a wide berth. She didn't spot any grenades on him, only a knife. He pulled it from its sleeve and stood in a defensive position without approaching them. Maybe he only had orders to enter? Maybe he was waiting for his comrades? Audra was not sure.

Ryder walked into his visual range.

"Hi. I'm sorry we had to hurt your friends. We can't suffer an attack here. Who are you? What is it you want?"

There was no answer, just a blank stare. Brainwashing? Was there a trigger?

"Look," said Dwyn, "we don't want to hurt you. Drop the knife and let's talk. You can be safe here."

Another blank stare. His dark gray eyes barely followed their movements. His mouth hung open slightly, revealing bloody teeth.

Audra sneaked behind in an attempt to disarm him, but as she approached, he swung around and hit her with a strong arm, knocking her off balance. She staggered. Audra realized she had little advantage here. He was a soldier, and Audra was small and used to chasing around dummies. But it didn't matter, this guy had to be taken down. She went in again, but someone pushed her to the side. It was Dwyn. He grabbed the half zom's knife hand and wrestled with it. Audra's eyes flashed with anger at his protective stunt. She pulled herself up and took the opportunity to punch the half zom in the jaw, releasing some of her frustration. The jaw did not give as she had hoped. He was not rotting; he just looked it.

Both Dwyn and the zom ended up on the ground. Audra's vexation melted into worry for Dwyn. Her mom's cut and seeping infection flashed in her mind's eye, making it difficult to see the situation now. Her eyes watered and her heart began to pound from her chest. She pushed forward to Dwyn, trying to distance herself from the memories. Together they pulled the knife from the zom's hand and subdued him.

Audra called for rope. He was a large man and they wouldn't be able to hold him for long. As she called, someone else called, too. Audra looked up at the noise coming from the woods. A snapping. A snapping of many fingers. Audra did not like the sound of this. A goodbye or a hello?

It was a hello.

Another forty zoms came sprinting from the woods. No longer walking, they took long, fast strides to the fences and gave a jumping start to reach the top. With Audra and Dwyn distracted, their prisoner punched free and ran back to the gate. He began climbing toward the guards who controlled the gate. Damn. Was this their plan all along?

Audra called for her own help. She wanted to hesitate. Her citizens were not fighters. They were just survivors. But they knew the dangers of living out here in the isolation. She stood in the plaza and yelled for others to come with weapons and to fight.

Audra took off to the gate, but the two above waved her off. They could handle this intruder. Arrows came flying into the plaza.

"No! Shoot the ones outside the fences. I'll get this one," Audra called out, pissed that she had fallen for their trap and had let this one in.

How she would handle him, she didn't know. He was bigger and stronger, but she did have his knife and she could run. She sprinted hard and fast and tackled his legs. She sliced into his Achilles tendon, causing his leg to buckle. She cut into the other then pulled high. Audra breathed a sigh of relief as he fell down, the knife landing in the small of his back. Another frantic move left it in his neck. Blood spouted and she rolled off.

But he rolled too. He yanked the knife from his neck and approached Audra with it. He at least swaggered with the blood loss.

Audra pulled out her own knife from her belt and hunkered into a protective stance. She watched the blood course. She only had to buy time before he fell again, but that same blood covered her too. Would it make her sick? He charged.

As he leapt, he fell at Audra's feet. Audra saw an arrow in his back from the guards above. She guessed Marcos hadn't believed she had it handled. She was thankful. Had that arrow done him in or just pushed him over? Audra drove her blade where his head and neck met, to be sure.

She found her abandoned spear and turned her attention to the fence. Lionel and Marcos were having little luck keeping all the zoms at bay. Audra stabbed two in the stomach. They gushed like stuck pigs but if the wounds and blood loss slowed them down, it was imperceptibly so. At least the blood made their feet slip on the links of the fence. Audra would have to wait for them to come down, on either side. The barbed wire at the top of the fence was curled to keep out humans but Audra knew it would only tear these zoms. They would be slippery and covered in infectious material when they landed in the plaza.

Audra heard yells from above. Lionel fell from his top spot, an arrow in his chest, and landed on the other side of the fence. Immediately two half zoms leapt upon him and began feasting. An instinct or a command? Numbness swept through Audra as he was torn to bits. Dwyn squeezed her shoulder. This was not the time to freeze.

She called out to Marcos to take cover - a useless command, as he had already done so. She looked behind her and saw a few men timidly coming with kitchen knives. There were only a few to be counted as warriors. Branson came out with a sharpened machete. Tess's white blond hair flashed in the sunlight. She grabbed a spear and began to attack those on the fences. Gordon emerged from the lab with his long knife. He sprinted to the fences and climbed up to meet the zoms at the top.

They were coming over the fences now. They landed firm-footed on the cars, leaving skin and clothes behind. One got caught by his belt and hung there. His head beat against the barbed wires as he tried to fight loose. Blood sprayed and bounced downward. Another approached Audra. This time she was ready. With her spear, she stabbed him in the eye, reaching into the brain. He stopped moving, then crumpled to the ground. Audra shook him loose and turned to find another.

"In the eye!" she yelled. She knew some of the others would not be as skilled, but it was better than stomach stabbing and jugular cuts that only doused everyone with infectious blood. Audra poked another from behind to get him to turn. His face was ripped open but Audra could still see his snarl. Into the eye she went, avoiding his knife swing, which was fairly accurate for his half blindness. Her spear sank farther in as he moved closer to her, jaw snapping as he died. He fell on top of Audra. His bloodied dead weight trapped her. The short spear dug into the ground, blocking one side. As she crawled her way out, she saw.

Ryder had lost her weapon and was frantically tripping backward in an attempt to gain some distance from a half zom about to overtake her. The zom's blade shone and flittered as he quick-stepped his way to her.

Audra pulled her legs out from underneath as she called to Dwyn, "Help Ryder!"

Ryder took a sidestepping dodge from the knife's jab. And another, and another.

Suddenly, Audra saw red and it was not the zom's. She called out. Audra pulled free and ran. She jumped onto the zom's back, anxious to change its direction, focus, target. Ryder held her side and cried, but her eyes remained glued to the scene from the ground. Her shouts brought out Satomi seeking her friend. It was the best thing for Ryder. A medic. Immediately. Audra yanked at the zom's chin, trying to break its neck but not having the leverage. Still, she knocked him off balance and down they went together. Her eyes searched for her spear.

Still in the other zom.

She grabbed a knife from her ankle boot. One to use, one to lose. She pursed her lips and squinted her eyes as tightly as she could without losing sight of her target, and came down on his neck. His jugular spouted, which was enough to distract him as Audra stabbed at his face. She guarded her eyes from the destruction, but she knew it would visit her dreams. Who was he? Audra's tears streamed down her face as he stopped moving. There had to be another way. A less sickening way.

She looked around. She wasn't the only one covered in blood. There were others. And everything was still. The few zoms on the other side of the fence retreated. Some of her comrades lay injured or torn. No sign of the dreaded Jack or Jill.

Satomi and Ryder had disappeared into the medical office but no one looked for Ryder.

They all looked to Audra, who sat atop a man whose face and life she had destroyed.

As the others combed through the bodies for friends and injured, she found a clean spot on her shirt and wiped her face of blood, being careful around her eyes. Infection was possible. And the cure may or may not help.

"Audra?" Dwyn called out from the far side of the fence. "This one is still alive."

6 Triage

Satomi couldn't do much in the battle; instead she gathered her triage supplies in the medical office. She sent away the mother and the child she was treating for a splinter. She cleared the area to make way for injuries and called in her volunteers. She'd help the fighters once they arrived here. Until then, she could only sit and watch at the window. And whom she watched most was Ryder.

Her volunteers, two young women, stood in the corner and fidgeted with supplies. Both with sandy brown hair and big blue eyes, looked positively terrified. They whispered to each other as Satomi ignored them. Their fear response was normal. Satomi knew they'd be worthless before they could be useful. It was the same when she had first started. This was a learning experience.

Satomi watched Ryder's spiked brown hair bob up and down as she dodged enemies. Satomi felt sick to her stomach. It was like watching a movie. She had no control. Her heart lurched forward, urging her to go help her friends. But she knew she could not. They needed fighters and she would not fight. In her medical studies she'd adopted an oath, Primum non nocere or "First, do no harm." And it went well past her medical practice. Besides, they needed her here. An injured or dead medic was no good.

Ryder's head went down. Satomi's face smashed involuntarily against the glass and her thin lips contorted in sympathetic fear and pain. She brushed her hair away from her face, and tried to get a better look by pressing even closer to the glass. Ryder was doubled over, holding her side. Was she bit? Stabbed? Satomi couldn't stand it anymore. Her hair swung as pendulums behind her as she threw open the door and ran headlong into the crowd.

When she arrived, she found Ryder's face scrunched in pain but it meant that she was conscious. Ryder's hands held her side. Blood flowed and bubbled. Air was entering her chest through her wound. She needed to be moved now. Satomi looked up to see Audra atop the back of the perpetrator and no one else available to help her move Ryder.

"Keep putting pressure on it. I'm going to get you out of here."

Ryder gave a small half smile, although it wrinkled through the wet tears. She gasped to gain air. Satomi didn't want to pull on Ryder's shoulders and interfere with the pressure Ryder was placing on the wound. She had to act fast. As Ryder grew weaker, her ability to hold pressure would lessen as well.

She grabbed Ryder by the ankles and told her to hang on. Satomi had never noticed how uneven the ground was or how many rocks were scattered about, but now she did as Ryder's head bounced up and down. Ryder groaned with each jostle. This was the best Satomi could do. Everyone was busy.

They finally made it into the office, where Mary and Jia waited. Satomi would talk to them about needing the courage to go into the midst of battle when the time was right, but for now she was worried about this injury. They helped her place Ryder on the cold metal table. Satomi cut Ryder's shirt to reveal the wound.

She didn't need to use a stethoscope on her friend's back to know what was happening. Her breathing was distressed and, away from the battlefield, she could see one side of her chest did not rise. She wiped blood from the wound and placed a plastic wrapper over it. She directed Jia to hold it tight, but to pull it away from the wound occasionally so pressure wouldn't build. Mary worked to establish an IV. Meanwhile, Satomi prepared the Lidocaine and necessary tubes.

"Ryder, your lung has collapsed. I have to place a chest tube."

Ryder nodded, not comfortable enough to speak. She would lose consciousness soon.

Satomi located the fourth and fifth ribs. She prepped the site and injected some Lidocaine. She'd need the rest for the deeper layers, which would only get more painful to the pleural, the potential space between the lungs and the chest wall that was no longer potential. She worked as quickly as the local anesthetic would allow. She didn't want to put Ryder into further distress. They had no oxygen tanks to supplement her and she also did not need her moving. Jia and Mary stole glances at the wound in silent horror as they performed their tasks.

Satomi probed with her finger to ensure she was in the proper location, making cooing noises to comfort her pained friend. She placed the tube, sutured it in place, then inserted the other end of the tube into a two-jar system she pulled from the cabinet. She watched the liquid inside the jars bubble as air came out of Ryder's chest cavity, unable to return to put pressure on the lung.

"They wanted medical scientists. They wanted you," muttered Ryder in between faints.

"It's OK. I'm here. I'm taking care of you. You're going to be fine," said the confident Satomi as she turned her attention to the offending wound, but guilt racked her. Should she have gone out there sooner? Her vow - had it allowed harm to come to Ryder?

Mary had gotten an IV in place. They both assisted her in cleaning and stitching the stab wound. With the worst of it over, Satomi gave Ryder another dose of their valuable pain medication to help her sleep. Ryder needed to sleep and heal.

Satomi treated the superficial wounds that crowded her office. Three men with defensive wounds. One with a sprained ankle. But her mind stayed focused on the frightening and intriguing manifestation of the infection. Those that attacked them had characteristics of both infected and non-infected. Had their experimenters somehow reduced the viral load of the infection, allowing some but not all of the brain structures that had gone dormant to spark and work? A sort of medical brainwashing?

She required that every patient be picked up by a non-combatant citizen and be watched for signs of infection. They waited on stretchers and chairs for their keepers. Was the attack today only physical or was it also biological? They had to take precautions. Satomi called for everyone who'd fought to come and be examined by her. Temperatures taken. Eyes examined for dilation. Satomi considered a quarantine but knew she didn't have enough evidence to remove freedoms. That was harm too.

Dwyn stuck his head into the office. Satomi took a moment to wipe her brow and sweep back her hair.

"Satomi, we have someone for you to see."

*　*　*

"He needs to be in the medical office. He needs to be treated!" argued Satomi. They could set up a quarantine area in the medical office. The laboratory was no place to treat a patient.

She looked into the conference room through the window at the simple brown tarp on the floor, and a man writhing on top of it. The conference table on which Gordon and their first few subjects had been secured had long since been requisitioned for dining purposes. This man's torso twisted and rocked. His arms were tied and his mouth was taped shut. His legs were unsecured, but lay in odd directions. Broken.

"Audra said to bring him here. You're not supposed to treat him. Just examine him. See what you can learn about our enemy," Dwyn tried to explain.

Enemy? That thought hadn't even crossed her mind. This man had injuries. He had an underlying illness. He needed to be quarantined to prevent an outbreak. Enemy had nothing to do with it.

"I'm treating him," she said as a statement. There was nothing to argue. She couldn't physically move him to the medical office, but that wouldn't stop her from providing treatment.

Dwyn shook his head, giving up, and left. She imagined he'd go get Audra to set her right. She'd set Audra right.

Satomi entered the room and closed the door behind her. The white walls held one white board whose markers had long ago dried out. Along the walls were stacked papers - white papers, lab reports, and journal articles from the previous staff and a previous life. Satomi approached her patient. He was built strong with wide shoulders and no muscle atrophy. His brown curly hair wrapped around his face and met his also-curly beard. He was covered in blood - his or others, Satomi had to determine. Underneath, his blue-gray skin had elasticity to it. His eyes were sleepy.

His legs would need to be set. He had a gash in his abdomen. Probably the inciting injury that had led to his fall and broken legs. It would be stitched.

"What have you learned?" asked Audra entering the room.

"Both of his legs are broken. They will need to be set. Superficial wounds to the stomach. I'll wash those out and close them. Shouldn't be a problem."

"Shouldn't be a problem? This is a big problem, Satomi. I need to know what's going on here. What is this?" she gestured to what she considered a creature in their building.

"It's a patient."

"It's not."

Satomi would continue her exam and hopefully also get Audra's information as well. She searched for an entry point for the infection.

He kicked at her with broken extremities. Scars were scattered across his body, but there was no fresh bite.

Audra stood in the corner, arms crossed, and exasperated. She had changed shirts, but she was still matted in blood.

Satomi pulled on the eyelids and revealed dilated eyes with a cloudy gray. Inside his mouth, his teeth were decaying. Satomi untied his shoes and pulled them off to reveal a decent stench and sores. It seemed he had been wearing those shoes and remnants of socks for days, weeks maybe. Potato sack tunic uniforms suggested a system in place.

The sickness was specific and the numbers revealed purpose, not accidents. Human survivor, z-virus, death -these were all distinct states at one point, but this specimen and what she had seen from her window, brought that all crumbling down. They had a permanent supply of these soldiers at their disposal. They created and took care of their army systematically, not haphazardly.

Audra didn't want her to treat him. Ryder's words rang in her ears. They wanted her. Why did they resort to fighting if they just wanted medical care?

7 Scouting

Audra stood near the mess hall atop the two-foot tall fountain wall with the bloodied fence as her backdrop. The bodies had been cleared, but crimson stained the broken concrete and gravel. The hidden families hadn't stayed hidden for long. Their timid heads poked out of windows and doorways. Women and men ushered the handful of children back into their rooms before flooding Audra with questions.

"We were attacked today," explained Audra. "The leaders called themselves Jack and Jill. They commanded zombies like I've never seen. They seemed half infected. They appeared to take commands, could climb fences and use knives, and they required a brain injury or excessive blood loss to die.

"I don't think this was their entire army. This was an expendable number meant to test and scare us. Which seems, based on your actions, you submit?"

She eyed the thirty or so who stared at their feet, kicking some of the blood-stained gravel around. To ask them to fight was a lot, but she didn't have anyone else.

"What choice do we have?" asked Ziv, his bushy beard flouncing around even after he asked his question. Audra noticed that Ziv had been conveniently missing these last couple of hours. Unsurprising. He had a history of cowardice, but Audra had seen him try. Disappointing today. Several nodded in agreement with him to add to her frustration.

"We don't have to sit here and wait for their next move. We can make our own. They haven't gone far. I recommend a scout group follow and find out what we are up against. Maybe we can figure out a weakness, or what they want, maybe even take out their leaders. We can become more trouble than we're worth. They'll move on. Would anyone be willing to join me?"

Audra realized that if they weren't willing to defend their homes, they probably weren't willing to venture outside of them. She waited in the shameful silence.

"You should stay here," said Dwyn. "This place needs its leader. It doesn't need you gone on a scouting trip."

Not only did no one volunteer, but Dwyn didn't even want her to go.

"I'm not your leader," she said, but even as she said it, she knew it wasn't true. She didn't see anyone else standing up. She knew the council and Ryder had wanted her leading even before all this. "Ryder is."

Noises of confusion and disagreement erupted. "Where is Ryder?"

Satomi gave a report. She was stable, but still had a road to recovery.

"Until Ryder is better, you're the leader," called out Tranter, who was here with his cured wife. Everyone nodded in agreement. Until then, it was all Audra. Audra accepted it, but she wasn't going to sit cozy while others scouted.

"Look, I'd love to stay," she lied, "but I've the most experience tracking zombies. And that's what we're going to be doing - tracking zombies. I have to go."

"I'll go too, then," said Dwyn. If he couldn't keep her here, apparently, he'd tag along.

"And I," called out Gordon.

"Not this time. You stay here," she replied to Gordon. She didn't want to leave Osprey Point defenseless if something went wrong. Gordon was surprised by this, but nodded.

"I will go," said Satomi, a quiet but clear voice. She stood resolutely with her hands behind her back.

"Don't you need to care for Ryder?" Audra questioned.

"No, yes, I mean, she's stable. She's going to be OK. I'll have Jia and Mary care for her for a few days. And she won't be OK if we don't figure this out. They wanted scientists, doctors, I heard. You need me to come so we can figure out WHY, what they want exactly."

She was right.

"What about your other patient?" Audra asked sarcastically.

"He is stable, stitched, and if we can keep him off his legs, they should heal properly."

"Have you tried the antidote on him?"

"Wait!" yelled out Tranter. "You have one of those here?"

"Yes, he's our prisoner," replied Audra calmly. She was not about to listen to their opinion on prisoners if they weren't going to be a part of any defense.

"The cure?" she asked again.

"No. I want him to heal before we do that."

Audra wasn't surprised. She needed answers and Satomi wanted a patient. She needed Satomi on her side, though. When they returned, she'd argue her point again. For now, she let it go.

"Ziv?" Audra asked for his company.

"Really? Do you need me?" His face contorted. His bushy eyebrows pressed together in concern. He pulled at his beard while he waited for an answer.

"Yes, I need your scientific expertise to help us figure out what we're up against." Audra didn't want him here, hiding.

"You're up against maniacs," he proposed.

She also didn't want him here, spreading lies and rumors to justify his fears.

"Maybe. That's why you're coming with. You'll help us understand." Audra wasn't going to take 'no' for an answer.

Ziv seemed to understand and conceded. Audra wasn't outright disagreeing with him. He would go along.

Thankfully, no one wanted to argue about the keeping of the prisoner, and they had their scouting group formed. Audra stepped down from the fountain, signaling they were dismissed. The men and women left to tend to their children and watch for signs of infection in those who had fought.

Audra and the others disappeared to gather their belongings, which were no longer neatly packed every morning, but daringly left out in their rooms with the promise that they would be back that same evening. It was a weird feeling, and now it was over. Audra knew they wouldn't be the only ones packing at Osprey Point. Everyone would be getting ready to bolt, packing their bug-out bags just in case Audra's crew came back with bad news or didn't come back at all.

Audra didn't blame them.

*   *   *

With the group packed, they trekked to where Audra had found the first half zom, then continued down one of Audra's forest trails. The dirt was soft and dry, and showed the traffic that had come through.

Once again, Ziv had packed too much. She watched him juggle his bag from left to right shoulder in attempts to stay comfortable. Satomi overtook him with her slim bag. Audra gave Ziv a small pat on his shoulder but did not stay for the complaint as she also passed him. As she did, she caught the metal scent of blood still on her. She had washed up, but certain movements still kicked up the scent and with her senses in overdrive, she noticed each time.

She pulled up alongside Satomi and touched her elbow. Satomi gave a weak smile with her bottom lip. The corners of her top lip were carried up rather than smiling themselves. In the women's last few interactions, Satomi had been a pain in Audra's backside, but she knew she had good intentions. She was glad and concerned Satomi had volunteered to come.

"Lay it on me, Satomi. Are you coming to seek revenge?"

"No... I can't as a doctor."

"Um, yes. You can." Audra didn't see what her profession had to do with her motives and actions. In fact, she could think of plenty of ways a doctor could get revenge.

"You see. I took an oath. 'First, do no harm'. I take it seriously. It's my mission statement, I guess."

Audra's eyebrows rose in doubt. "You can't just not do any harm. How do you protect the ones you love?" She thought of Ryder. Surely, Satomi would harm for her.

"I protect my loved ones by taking care of them, not by killing."

Audra wasn't sure if Satomi's mission statement could hold up. Someone had to fight to make things better. She had fought an army just an hour ago. Jack and Jill needed to be cut down. Larange Greenly needed to be cut down. That was how they protected their loved ones.

"Then why are you coming?"

"Their need for science work and medical care is going to be their undoing. It will be important for us to know."

At least they agreed on one thing.

Jack and Jill did seem to want something specific. Audra imagined they didn't need much of what else their small community had, but medical care and scientists were hard to come by.

Audra noticed the shuffling footprints had veered off the road, and pulled left away from Satomi. The zoms had gone off the path. Broken branches and kicked-up leaf litter met Audra's keen eyes. They either hadn't been taught or hadn't been commanded to hide their tracks. The others fell in behind her, trying to weed their way through the leafless woody plants that tangled and pulled.

Audra's heel was clipped a couple of times, but not by vines. Dwyn was tight on her heels, following like an overenthusiastic puppy. He asked her tons of questions about tracking - half of which she swore she had taught him before. Audra imagined he was happy to have a chance to talk to her. At least it wasn't romantic advances.

"Do you think Jack and Jill are a couple?"

Or, maybe it was.

"Why, do you want to date her or him?" shrugged off Audra, pretending she was focused on a particular muddy smudge.

"No... no... I don't think so. I just wondered. They seem to be some sort of pair." He paused behind her to check out what was so special about the smudge.

"They're at least a Jack & Jill."

"A who?" he asked, leaping to catch up to her.

Audra shook her head. She wasn't going to explain.

She heard a grunt from behind her. It sounded like a zom. She turned her head. No, it was just Ziv. At the back of the pack, trailing along, and of course, grumbling.

"Why don't you come up here as a mating call?" she called out over her shoulder.

"What?"

Audra shook her head. She wasn't going to explain.

In fact, she shouldn't have said either of those things. The snark was overflowing without much filter. And she knew why. Because she had failed them. And she'd rather point out their weaknesses than sit with her own.

Audra had known they were out there. Not Jack and Jill specifically, but that evil, wicked groups could march through and destroy everything they loved. She should have prepared them more. They were so focused on a cure, they had forgotten the uninfected could be the real problem now.

A small hand touched her shoulder. It was Satomi's. She didn't say anything. Audra appreciated the gesture, but felt crowded with the two, Dwyn and Satomi, on her heels.

"I'm going to run on ahead. Just a bit. Get a head start on this trail."

Audra was anxious to see what lay at the end of it. There had to be a reason they had gone off the easy track. Perhaps just the direct route. What did they care about some cuts and scrapes?

"I'll go with you," said the ever-present Dwyn.

"No, you stay here with these two. Practice the tracking I've taught you so far to track me. I won't be far. I'll double back if things get wacky."

She looked ahead where the sun glittered and the wind danced through the trees. She scanned the roots uncovered by low-clearance feet. And with that she kicked the two off her backside and wandered deeper into the woods.

Alone.

Where she belonged.

8 The Convoy

Audra continued to track the zombies through the woods, but she realized they were nearing I-16, the highway which emptied into Savannah. Audra had run miles and miles on these grounds, but hadn't realized they could be such a straight-shot from the highway. It wasn't exactly a marked exit.

She kept a steady pace, giving Dwyn markers to follow until she saw light from the clearing ahead. She attempted to pause at the forest line that delineated the highway, but found the line had blurred since she had last come through. The forest had crept and crawled onto the roads. Cars in the median had been swallowed up with weeds. Only vehicles firmly on the expressway were not being attacked by greenery. That wouldn't be the case in a few more years' time.

On the nearest side of the highway, the two lanes of cars had been cleared out of the way, haphazardly, but cleared nonetheless. Like a parting of the rusted sedan sea, the cars in both lanes angled outward as if someone had driven through the middle. Some were just pushed to the side, while others had wheels and axles broken. Glass and plastic scattered the cracked asphalt where weeds shot through and flourished. Audra dared to get behind a sedan and peeked her head down the line. The parting was far, but she could see something a mile or two down the road, something that was now taking up the middle spot. A convoy of sorts.

Jack and Jill had told the truth. They were not local. They were traveling, and thus, hopefully, not many in number. Numbers settled, made homes, farmed; small groups traveled, camped, and scavenged. Here their enemies were set up on I-16. Audra eyed the ragged forest line and the broken cars strewn in the ditches. There was plenty of cover for her to reach them and spy on their operations.

Audra turned and headed back to her scouting group. She shouldn't run off without them. If they found the highway, they might not be discreet in following the convoy. They'd need to do it together. At least this was something to give them, after her failure hours ago.

She had found their resting spot. They'd figure out how to stop them and Jack and Jill would die and rot on I-16, just like everything else, until the brush consumed them.

*   *   *

Audra was now happy to have the crew on her heels. She needed them to be nearby and quiet. Ziv pulled up close to her. He kept yanking on his beard nervously. Satomi and Dwyn walked in a pair behind him. Only the odd zombie in otherwise abandoned cars took notice of them. The zoms slammed up against gray smears on the windows, leaving further marks, their eyes dark and sometimes a yellow piece of plastic flashing from their ear. Tags. Tags from a bygone era when Audra thought that Lysent cared for the sick and would come scoop them up as soon as the cure became more abundant. How naive she had been.

Audra noticed Jack and Jill hadn't scooped them up either. Did they convert zombies into soldiers or did they start with healthy humans? The latter thought made Audra feel sick - which in turn, washed her with guilt. They were all humans. Their zombie status shouldn't make something more or less sad. It was all sad and it had to be stopped. Still, Audra feared for her comrades. Could they be recruited into the zombie army?

As the team got close to the convoy, they dived deeper into the forest. They did not want to be seen approaching, observing, or leaving. The journey was slow in the brush and everyone seemed to be deep in thought, worried about what they might soon find. When they reached the tail-end of the convoy, Audra signaled for Ziv and Satomi to fall back deeper into the forest. She and Dwyn would investigate first.

An RV marked the end of a line of over ten vehicles. RVs, passenger vans, eighteen wheelers. The fuel needed to move such things had long deteriorated in their region. Where had they found a reliable fuel source? Beyond the RV was a horse trailer. Arms stuck out and rested on the low bars. Eyes peered through dark shadows without a word - half zoms. It was hard to reconcile such human-like positions content in a trailer. The two held back gasps as they reached some sort of modified eighteen wheelers. The simple metal sheeting of the trailers had been replaced with transparent heavy acrylic. Within were many stalls, two stalls high. Holes for air flow lined the top and bottom, reminding Audra of the visitation room at Lysent. In each stall stood a person. Some wielded knives, some bows and arrows, some grenades. They were like toy soldiers packaged for any specific need. Through the stalls, Audra could make out a sort of hallway that allowed entry and egress. Then, another layer of stacked zoms. Many more than what had attacked Osprey Point.

Audra imagined the redesigned vehicles weren't highly durable, but they didn't need to be. Visible even from here, metal protruded from either side of the first truck in line, some kind of plow. They cleared vehicles off the road and these trailers followed.

A cleared highway with full access might have been convenient long ago, but now it was dangerous. Audra remembered being doored last time she was on this highway. Nothing good could come from it, just more enemies. The cars were worthless. Trunks had been pilfered of their blankets and snacks long ago. If Audra never had to sleep in a back seat of a musty car again, it would be too soon. She preferred almost anything makeshift in the woods over laying her head on rotting cushions.

"Where are they heading?" whispered Dwyn.

Audra shook her head. She didn't know. Wherever they wanted, she guessed, but it did seem to be a big production to just wander.

"Do you see anyone? Any place for medical care?" asked Dwyn.

Audra didn't see anything. They just seemed to be transport.

While they saw many, many zoms, they didn't see many humans. In fact, no humans yet. Dinner maybe? Audra counted the vehicles - there had to be at least that many drivers. Fifteen vehicles - five transparent trailers, a couple plain trailers, the truck, a couple of cars, the horse trailer, and several passenger vans. Depending on what was in the plain trailers, could be thirty humans, could be much more. Did it matter? Even if they could separate humans from zoms, thirty would be too many to handle.

Audra stopped calculating the number of zombies when she saw something moving in between the trailers. She ducked farther into the ditch. A man weaved in and out among the trailers. His dark hair moved side to side on his head as he looked around. He seemed to be on the lookout, but not for them. With a look behind him, he crept past the vehicles and headed toward the woods. Toward Audra and Dwyn.

There wasn't much time to react. The two started backtracking out of the ditch and back into the woods. Hopefully he just wanted to do some illicit task out of sight. Audra didn't intend to stay and find out.

They quietly fell back, slipping into the brush. The man was being quiet too, until he whispered.

"Hey, don't leave. Help me." Audra and Dwyn looked to each other. Why was he seeking help outside the group? Maybe it wasn't his group. "Please. They're going to turn me into... one of them."

Audra felt sick with the thought. The man crouched, searching for them. Why didn't he just run? Audra would be running, but then again, she was a runner.

"Please?" he whispered again as he walked blindly into the woods.

"Hey, I'm Dwyn!" Dwyn said as he stepped out. Of course he did. Without any discussion or even an apologetic look, he was out in the open. Audra shook her head. He was still as naive as when she'd first met him, and she still didn't believe it.

"Hey, hey, help me. Those crazy people fed me, helped me, but they're just fattening me up... like for the slaughter, but worse. They've got these crazy crawlers. They're like-"

"We've seen them," cut off Audra as she stepped out too. She glared at Dwyn, who was unscathed by it. Audra glared harder, but it did no good but trigger a sheepish grin and a shrug.

The man was just a kid, maybe late teens. His dark hair frazzled in waves over his fair skin. To his benefit, he did look scared or maybe his eyes were always that buggy. Bright blue. Green flecks.

"Where did they find you? How many are there? How do they convert them?" spouted off Audra.

"Whoa, dude, I'll tell you everything. You just gotta get me out of here first," he said, looking behind him once more.

"Of course," said Dwyn, approaching the kid and putting his arm around him. "Come on, we've got some supplies. Hungry at all?" Dwyn began to lead him to Satomi and Ziv. "What's your name?"

"Dennis."

There was no way in hell Dennis was coming back with them, but he could have just the information they needed. Audra allowed and followed behind them, one hand on her knife.

They found Ziv and Satomi sitting on a rotting log. They stood up and let Dennis sit down. Dwyn pulled out a food bar from his bag and offered it. Audra was not as impressed. She stood, watching out for any outside noise, with one eye on Dennis.

Dennis munched the oat bar. His eyes darted around as if the group might change their mind and take it back. He did seem hungry. It was easy to forget how hard life could still be. Osprey Point could be crowded and boring, but at least there was food and shelter.

"Cool beard, man," he said to Ziv, his mouth half full.

Ziv nodded but didn't say anything in return.

"Dennis," redirected Audra, "this group threated us with those... things. Do you know anything about them?"

"They're some sort of smart crawler. Jill told me that they found them like this. That these people were in the process of getting better. That's why they are more human than crawler.

"But, I get the feeling that they're... creating them. I mean, I've never seen anything like them in the woods or in the city. Have you guys?"

Audra shook her head. The half zoms were definitely being created, maybe by some bastard version of an antidote.

"I started thinking." Audra thought that was probably a strenuous task for the guy. "I started thinking, 'why do they have me around?' It's not like we were picking up every Sue and Sally. They were just feeding me. Not asking me to do any work, although I pitched in to help. I was pretty skinny when they found me." Audra thought he was skinny now. "Then I decided they were trying to get me healthy before they made me into one of them. Why else keep me around?"

The half zoms were strong because they transformed strong humans.

"Do they feed the zoms?"

"What? Yeah. Disgusting job. I kept throwing up, so they dismissed me from that task." So, raw, maybe still live flesh. "And there's more..." Dennis hesitated.

Audra and the others looked at him expectantly.

Instead of speaking, he swallowed the last of the oat bar with the slowness of someone who might not be fed again. He carefully moved his hand to his jacket. Audra responded with her blade.

"No, no, it's not like that." He moved even more slowly and pulled open his jacket to reveal a bright red spot on his shirt, stuck to his side.

"I feel fine for now," he assured the group. "I think it takes time to transition. I'm sorry I didn't tell you earlier. I just can't stay with that group. You wanted to know why I thought they wanted to transform me? It's because they did, or will, or have. I don't know. I don't know what will happen after this bite. But word is - you've got a cure? Do you think you can cure me?"

Audra put her knife back into its sheath, but did not let her hand go far. His eyes looked desperate. This was an infected man. Once he turned, he'd chase them tirelessly and attack them violently. At least that's what was supposed to happen. Audra admitted things had gotten weird lately.

"What bit you? A real zom or one of those half ones?" she asked.

"Half ones? What? No, this was a full-fledged crawler. But it must be the first part of my transition, right? I don't want to turn into one of them, any of them. You've got a doctor, right? Maybe he can fix me."

"I'm not a 'he', but I'll try my best," said Satomi beside him.

"It's you? You came out here?"

"Yes, can I see your wound?" She put her hand on his shoulder.

Audra's head tilted in concern. She interrupted the doctor's impromptu physical.

"Let me pat him down first."

"Is that OK?" Dwyn asked for permission.

Dennis nodded as Audra had already begun her search. He winced when she ran her hands along his ribcage that housed the infectious bite. No weapons, not even a knife. Still, she wouldn't underestimate him. He had survived this long somehow.

Audra gave a nod to Satomi to proceed, but remained close to their capture, rescue, whatever he was. Satomi had pulled out her first aid kit and lifted his shirt, and began dressing the wound.

"Have you always been a doctor?" he asked in an attempt to distract himself from the pain as she cleaned the wound with antiseptic.

"You mean before? No, I was too young before. I learned from a doctor. He tried to give me a broad education, not just stuff I would always see, but also stuff I might not. I think he wanted to impart the large knowledge base he received in medical school. He didn't want acupuncture or radiation treatments to disappear. Of course, I didn't have acupuncture needles to practice with. We used knitting needles in a man made of hay. I learned about chemotherapy, but don't have the supplies or even a way to detect cancer. I was a scientist too - gene therapy, biochem," she shared as she worked, mostly just to help distract him. Satomi was a good doctor.

Dennis pulled down his shirt and thanked her. He licked the crumbs off his lip.

"Do you - you think I can come back with y'all?" he asked. "If you give me one of your cures, I can work for y'all. I'm a hard worker."

"Of cour-" started Satomi, but Audra interrupted.

"I don't know about that."

It was one thing to give him an oat bar and some gauze in the woods. It was quite another to bring someone from Jack's and Jill's camp into their community.

"He can't come back with us," said Ziv, finally making his voice known.

"We can't leave him here!" cried out Satomi.

"What's the difference between curing a stranger and curing Dennis?" asked Dwyn.

"Cause Jack and Jill will be looking for Dennis, that's why," retorted Ziv.

Dennis looked furtively from one person to the other as they argued about his fate. Audra watched him. It worried her that she sided with Ziv. Wasn't he the one who had selfishly hidden? But as much as she hated to consider it - Dennis was a liability.

"Why are we even discussing this? He needs the antiviral and we have it. End of story." Satomi began packing her things to leave as if the matter was settled.

Audra considered the options as the others continued to argue. Leave Dennis here, he'd change, Jack and Jill would find him and add him to their collection. They'd be facing one more half zom. Take him with them and risk pissing off an enemy that outnumbered them. Audra didn't realize they were surrounded until it was too late.

Ten half zoms closed in with knives drawn, forming a circle. Their scouting group had been too loud or Dennis had been a trap. Audra looked to Dennis. He began to cower. Perhaps he hadn't known. Audra shook her head in anger - angry with herself for letting them get ambushed. They had stayed too long arguing.

"Dennis dear," said a syrupy voice weaving between the men. Jill emerged, a head shorter than her soldiers, and swept her blond plait off her shoulder. "Who patched you up?"

Dennis stared at the ground and mumbled, but did not give up the name of his physician. With the snap of her fingers, the circle grew smaller.

"It was me." Satomi stepped forward and looked Jill in the eye.

Jill pointed and Satomi was grabbed by two half zoms. Audra advanced, but two others moved into her path. Their large knives were held to attack.

"Anyone else educated here?" Jill asked.

Ziv. Ziv was a scientist, but no one gave up that information. And Ziv did not offer it as freely as Satomi had.

"Release her," Audra commanded. She tried not to let her voice waver. She pretended she had any say in the matter, that she had something of consequence behind her demand. She did not. She was wildly outnumbered.

Jill pretended to think about Audra's request for just a moment.

"...No. You will get her back when we are done with her. You had your chance to negotiate peacefully with us. Now we're just going to take what we need."

And with that, the zoms raised their blades at the remaining three. Audra went to move forward again, despite the threat. A hand grabbed her arm and held so tightly that she knew she would see bruises in the shape of Dwyn's fingers on her arm before the day was through. She could free herself, but the vice grip reminded her. There was nothing to free herself to, just death by blades or teeth. She was nothing, on the losing side. She bit her lip until it bled coppery juices into her mouth. She glared the daggers she wished she could unleash into Jill's body.

"LEAVE!" demanded Jill with an authority in her voice that Audra could only wish for. Audra spat shiny blood from her mouth. The metallic taste diminishing. She felt a dribble on her lip. With a snap of Jill's fingers, her crew holding Satomi and Dennis fell back toward the highway.

Audra had walked away before. She had left her sister in Lysent's hands, but now anger boiled to her very rim. Audra was going to get Satomi back. She would not lose another to a vicious bully.

She would not.

9 Captured

A thousand thoughts flashed through Satomi's mind as she was ushered out of the forest. Dennis. Was that a trick? No, the current fear in his eyes was real. The infected were directing his movements as much as hers. He needed treatment or he'd turn soon. Ryder. Someone would need to take out her chest tube in a couple of days. Would she be back in time? A jab in the back of her ribs to move her along discouraged that thought.

Dark smoke began to waft through the air - vinyl, rubber, plastic, and something salty-sweet. The doctor in Satomi winced at the fumes, followed by her stomach. It smelled awful. Satomi could feel her lungs gathering goop. What was the point of creating such poor conditions? The small fireball was now visible, a car up near the front. A circle of people gathered near. Gruff men walked alongside gruffer sick.

At the top of the circle stood two matching green and white striped lawn chairs. Jack, she presumed, sat in one and Jill took her spot next to him. Satomi was placed in the middle of the circle. Dennis was on his knees, whimpering and talking to himself.

"She's a doctor AND a scientist. How did we ever get so lucky?" asked Jill of Jack.

"I know a few things," lied Satomi.

"You know more than a few. We saw you in action. You were the one that pulled the leader into the medical office. And sounds like you're the one who treated Dennis," said Jack.

"I'm sorry I tried to run," cut in Dennis.

A laugh. "Didn't you think all of us gone was a bit convenient?" Jack suggested.

A setup. For her?

"'Fess up," Jill said turning back to her. "You came because you wanted to get a closer look at our... creations." She had a smile on her face, but it did not extend to her eyes. She flicked her long blond braid.

"They are presenting with some peculiar symptoms. Would you like me to treat them?" asked Satomi, impressing herself with her audacity.

The entire circle of people burst into laughter. Even the car seemed to spark a little more in response. The green paint melted and peeled along the edges. Thick billows of blackness escaped the broken windows and all the seams.

"No... we don't want you to treat them. They are quite excellent the way they are."

"So, you did it on purpose?"

"On purpose would be a little inaccurate."

"Were you trying to cure them?"

"Call it a byproduct. We did. Now we call them soldiers. You'll be making more of them. I guess we need your help, less as a doctor - more as a scientist."

Satomi said nothing. More than a doctor, she was a scientist. And they wanted her to make more of these sick people?

"But for now, please show our guest - uh, what's your name?"

"Satomi."

Jack and Jill and the rest of them looked at her with judgmental eyes. She imagined that they were considering her name hard to pronounce. Satomi didn't offer a shortened version, Americanized version, or a nickname. She didn't care what these fools called her.

"What?" she challenged.

"Nothing. Just the name of our last doctor. You all seem to be Chinese."

Satomi wasn't Chinese.

"What happened to the last doctor?"

"She stopped helping us," Jill said simply as she waved her hand and two guards came to Satomi's sides.

Satomi wasn't sure if another doctor was a scare tactic. Why would they get rid of a doctor if they didn't have a replacement yet? Then, the thought occurred to her that maybe they were getting rid of the first "Satomi" now. As if on cue, something made a bump noise. She looked to the car, where smashed to one of the few remaining windows was an infected and burning woman. Her black hair had incorporated into her face. Jack and Jill laughed at both of the women.

Satomi shuddered involuntarily as she was escorted away. It's just a scare tactic. It's just a scare tactic. She repeated to herself. Still they killed - or more accurately - didn't kill that woman to get to her. It was clear that they had not made the same vows she had. It was amazing that she could keep her cool with a scalpel in her hand, but now she trembled with each step away from Jack and Jill.

Her captors.

She was in trouble.

Her escort led Satomi to an old police car being pulled by a truck. She could make out that at one point it had read Wade County. To protect and to serve. She was put in the back, where there were no interior door handles and the seats were made of hard plastic. The windows had been replaced with rebar spikes. The door slammed with a distantly familiar sound.

A car door shutting, heard from the inside. It had been years since she had heard that sound. It was an odd thing to consider in her dangerous situation.

The escort stood over the car, a large, round man. Before she settled, he slipped her a water bottle through the rebar.

"Thank you."

"It's all you get today," he grunted before he stood a distance off and watched her with menacing eyes. Satomi figured she should be thankful that he wasn't trying to trade favors with her.

Maybe that would come later.

The replaced windows brought some air exchange into the car, but not enough and most of it smelled foully of burning vehicles. Satomi was glad it wasn't sticky hot, but she might be chilly tonight. Thick plastic separated her from the front of the car. The floor too was made of the hard plastic. Easy cleaning. No comfort. She curled up in one of the bucket-forms of the hard plastic. Waves of shivers came over her as her body suffered in her stress.

Where were the others? Were they trying to get her back? Audra hadn't wanted her to treat Dennis. She could tell. If she hadn't, maybe they wouldn't have been ambushed. Maybe she wouldn't have been captured. But wasn't their entire community built around giving the cure freely? Audra might be OK picking and choosing, but Satomi always extended her oath to the entirety of the universe, and that meant treating everyone placed in her path. She hoped she could continue that here.

A wave of tiredness crashed into her. A lot had happened and there was much more to come. She should rest if she could. But every time she closed her eyes she saw that woman, cooking, in that car. She imagined she could smell her, even now, over the burning tires. She hoped that she was dead by now, but in her heart, she knew she wasn't and at the same time, it felt like she was wishing herself dead.

10 Aftermath

Dark poisonous smoke filled the air and followed Audra, Ziv, and Dwyn back through the woods. It was all coming together. Jack and Jill were the ones who had set the fire yesterday. What did they care about visibility? They had an army of foot soldiers and cannon fodder to do their bidding. And now they had Satomi.

The march back was painfully slow. Ziv couldn't keep up with a run. And as much as Audra wanted to dash off to Osprey Point and fix this, she also could not leave the last two of her crew alone. No one else was disappearing under her watch. So instead of a run, they walked. Quietness roared, interrupted only by the crunches of brambles underneath their feet. Ziv, for once, didn't complain. Audra would've lost it if he had. She should have gone alone or at least should have stopped Satomi.

"We shouldn't have treated that Dennis piece of sh-" she muttered, half to herself. She kicked at a root before stepping over it.

"It's what we do. It's what Satomi does," Dwyn replied.

"Well we shouldn't. He probably agreed to that bite."

"Satomi wasn't wrong to help. No one would agree to being bitten. Pain takes over and you're trapped. You're trapped in your own body with no place to go. I'd never let anyone go through that if I could stop it. I can't tolerate seeing anyone in that state. I can feel it."

"You can feel it?" she asked, stopping and turning to look him in the eye.

"Well, not really," he backpedaled.

He hadn't said it directly, but Audra had heard it. She could hear the pain in his voice. It seeped through his words and imbued them with another layer of meaning. He remembered how it felt.

"You've been infected?" and before he could answer, "You knew about the pain."

Dwyn's eyes shifted, avoiding her gaze.

"I only knew of my pain. It wasn't until Gordon that I was able to confirm my experience. I didn't tell you, because I didn't want you barreling into Lysent and getting yourself killed." He was always trying to protect her. "And then, and then, I just didn't know how. I didn't think it mattered."

Didn't matter? Belinda had suffered for years because Audra couldn't let her go. If Dwyn had been a zombie, then someone had cured him.

"Who?! Who did you know in Lysent?" she rounded on him. He had never offered his connection.

"What? I don't know anyone at Lysent." Dwyn looked confused.

Ziv awkwardly shifted from one foot to the other.

"Well then you knew someone rich, who was she?" As soon as Audra said it, it was clear to her. It was a she. Vesna? Vesna didn't have the courage to tell her that she had just spent all her money curing this dimwit?

There was a stale pause in the air.

"Corette. Her name was Corette," Dwyn offered in a soft voice. "She was my fiancée. We got caught up by a couple biters. Early on. I tried to hold them off. A year or so ago, she cured me."

Jealousy, pain, and shame swirled in Audra. This Corette had succeeded where she had failed. But if she had cured Dwyn, why weren't they together?

"Where is she?"

"She's married to some rich guy. He gifted her a cure. She felt guilty I was infected and she wasn't. They pulled me out of the car she had left me in and I was cured a few days later."

"Must be nice." Audra's voice dripped with disgust. Cures as gifts.

Ziv pulled on some bark of a tree.

"Yes, it was, eventually... I woke up and thought everything was going to be the same. Nothing was the same. She wanted nothing to do with me. I had all the feelings I had for her then, but she had moved on in the time I had lost.

I was alone and cashless. I needed to find a way to survive quick. Vesna helped me, saved me again really. And then you were the best thing to enter my life, there in the woods."

There. That push. Over and over.

"Are you serious?!" she reeled on him. "You're constantly on me to share my feelings and to share my bed, and you don't bother to tell me you were infected!

You say you want me to lead our group but then you constantly push me out of the way or hold me back. 'Best things' require trust."

Dwyn's clinging was just the outcome of his sob story. Everyone had one and now she knew his. The front of her head burned with anger, but her eyes stung with tears. She jerked her head back ahead and stomped onward. The two men followed wordlessly.

11 Byproducts

A honeyed "Comfy?" invaded the vehicular enclosure. There weren't many women in the convoy.

Jill.

Satomi uncurled and separated her skin from the plastic divots. She refused to stretch in Jill's sight or comment on her accommodations. Instead, she sat up in one of the bucket seats and looked over to her as if they were passing on the highway. Her terror had transformed to numbness and she'd pass it off for confidence if she could.

Jill worked the handle and the car door creaked open. Satomi climbed out wordlessly but did give a look of curiosity. Was she about to find out what Jack and Jill wanted of a scientist? The sun was just starting to streak brightly at its fresh angle. It highlighted the dew on the reflective markers and the ambitious weeds that sprouted from the asphalt. Jill headed farther up the convoy, meaning for Satomi to follow. Last night's guard followed the pair. Vehicle after vehicle, until they reached their destination. An eighteen-wheel trailer with large graffitied metal doors. Maybe some ancient gangs. Satomi remembered a different world where people would smudge "Wash me" in the grime.

The guard managed the heavy latch, then Jill took one side and the guard took the other. The large metal doors were pulled open to reveal a mobile, scavenged laboratory. One wall was lined with large machines - refrigerators, freezers, a sterile hood, and digital ovens. The other side contained counters with rows of smaller equipment, microscopes, hot plates, a fancy centrifuge and an array of beakers and flasks on racks and stacked test tubes. Satomi had seen nothing like it as a mobile setup. The back had anchored tables with miscellaneous equipment and stacks of books and notebooks.

They seemed to have everything they needed except for staff. And Satomi guessed she was it. She tried not to show delight in her new prison. She at least stopped herself from climbing in without a word of instruction.

"The soldier serum is given to those infected with the z-virus. From there, their motor control and coordination improve. So does their ability to receive commands.

Dr. Bren developed the serum, but eventually she refused to keep making it for us."

"The woman in the car?" Satomi interrupted.

Jill gave a stern and satisfying nod. Satomi felt torn. Dr. Bren had created a horrible weapon, but then she'd had a change of heart? She stood her ground and was killed over it.

"So you can't make any more 'soldiers'?"

"Not right now. That's your job."

"How am I supposed to do that? I don't know the first thing about the soldier serum." All the equipment in the world didn't matter if she didn't have any foundational knowledge of the serum.

"Dr. Bren's notes will be available to you. In seven days, we will test your first batch and mark your progress."

"Human experiments?" Satomi squeaked. She hadn't even considered being here a week - or beyond. Suddenly life felt both long and sweeping by.

"I encourage you to get up to speed and make progress quickly. I also encourage you to accomplish the goal if you don't want to be replaced." Jill crossed her arms and nodded toward the entrance.

Satomi's guard gave her a hand up before heaving his body up the height as well. Jill laughed as she closed the large doors behind them, leaving Satomi at the laboratory's edge under the guard's watchful eye.

Away from Jill's coarse demeanor, Satomi let out a sigh. She felt her shoulders relax and she could breathe. She looked around the trailer. Large sun windows and strategic flood lights illuminated the space. She'd never imagined a laboratory with all its possibilities would be a prison. It was at least better than the cop car, and the scientific equipment elicited a certain peace. They intended these tools to destroy, but she could use them for good.

Satomi walked along the counter and fingered the small tools at her disposal. She turned to the man with a dark mane and a rare potbelly. It was the first time they were alone and isolated, but he didn't cast any dark shadows her way. She gave a small smile.

"I'm sorry. What's your name?" She was tired of her only anchor being nameless.

"Eli," he said. He stood with legs wide and arms behind his back at the trailer end as if she had anywhere to escape.

"Hi Eli. I'm Satomi. Will you tell me more about this serum I'm supposed to make?" She leaned against the counter, hoping to glean as much information as she could.

"What do you need to know?" His stance did not change, but he seemed willing to answer a few questions.

"Why did Dr. Bren develop it?"

"To protect her people."

"Why did she stop?"

"She changed." His voice faltered. He glanced downward.

"What do you mean?"

He straightened up to compose himself. "How is this supposed to help you make the serum?" he asked with his chin up.

"I'm not going to make the serum," she confessed. "I practice 'First, do no harm'."

"I don't know what that is, but if you don't make the serum, you're going to die like she did," said Eli. He didn't say it like a threat, just as if it was a matter of fact.

"I guess, I am," resigned Satomi. She opened the fridge to see what was inside.

Familiarizing herself with the lab, last touched by Dr. Bren, felt like her last rites.

"Where are Dr. Bren's notes?" she asked, looking around.

She could at least learn as much as she could about the soldier serum and how it interacted with the z-virus. Maybe even how to reverse it.

Eli pointed to the back of the room, where a work table with stacks of papers threatened to fall over. Notebooks of various age scattered the surface with notes hanging from all their edges. A disarray of information.

Of course.

"Why the car?" she asked out of her morbid curiosity as she walked gingerly over to the mess as if it might attack her.

"They burn the cars anyway. It smells awful. But Peter likes it."

"Who's Peter?"

"Their dad."

That was beyond disturbing, but she had learned something else. Jack and Jill were siblings. Next, she'd sort through some of these papers.

*　　*　　*

Sleep slipped away against the scraping reverberating through the plastic. It took more than a moment to remember where she was. Not in her soft bed pad, not in Ryder's room, not even at her desk having drifted off during late-night research. She was in a police car, captured by a group with an army of the sick. She wasn't allowed to sleep in the laboratory. 'It's only for working,' they said.

Satomi rose softly, trying not to alert Eli. A lantern bobbed, illuminating one man dragging another along the road - the source of the scraping noise. So many men here. The rest of the convoy was dark. Everyone had gone to bed.

"What's wrong with him?" she wondered under her breath.

"Sick. Has to be disposed of," said Eli, not missing a beat. He must have heard her stir.

"Can I help?" she said at volume. 'Sick' had many meanings here. Which one was this?

The man towing the sick stopped. Both he and Eli peered into her dark vehicle to see if she was serious.

"I'm here because you want more of them, right? Wouldn't treating this one keep your count high?"

The man on the road dropped his keep. "Get out," he said as he approached her abode. His blue-black hair was pulled back into a ponytail. As he got closer, Satomi could see he was darkened red by the sun and alcohol. Flecks of spit and other items ran through his beard. Satomi's stomach dropped. She backed away to the other side of the car.

"No, wait. Why?" she asked.

The door swung and bounced on its hinges. A large hand groped into the darkness of the interior and found her. She clawed at the smooth plastic but found no hold. He ripped her from the car and threw her on the ground at Eli's still feet. The asphalt felt cold and wet-smooth. Satomi pulled herself half up to look at her abuser.

"You want to help? Let's go then." He pulled her to her feet by her shirt collar. It cut into her neck, and the seams made popping noises but held.

Satomi found her feet, slipping at first, and his arm moved from shirt to arm. Eli fell in line behind them. He grabbed the sick man by the wrists and dragged him along. His body sounded heavy and thick with the ground's moisture.

Satomi tried not to think about where she might be going or the heavy hand on her arm. Instead, she focused on the reflective white dashes flashing in the light of the man's lantern. Tears pooled in her eyes and slipped into a stream down her cheeks, but she remained calm. She wished Eli was on her side. She could only hope she hadn't suggested leaving the safety of the car for... she didn't know.

Satomi looked up to see the lantern light reflecting oddly off of clouded eyes inside the acrylic cubicles. They remained passive in their captivity, not seeking the edges of their enclosures to reach them. Strong men built wide and no attempt to escape. At Osprey Point, Satomi had restrained the infected prior to recovery, but this was different. This was simply humans in cages. Satomi diverted her eyes. She focused on the highway markers again.

They passed the trailers. When they reached a plain container van, the man let go of her. Satomi smiled through her tears at the 'WASH ME' scribbled in the dust of the side panel, despite herself. The man disappeared in front of the van and Satomi dared to exhale since they appeared to have reached their destination, and it hadn't ended with her being pushed into the van - yet. He returned with a rolling stretcher of dark blue vinyl and metallic chrome, most assuredly taken from an ambulance at some point. Satomi disapproved. He hadn't bothered to use it for transport earlier, instead choosing to drag the sick by its arms. The two men heaved the sick onto the stretcher.

She heard his labored breathing and something within her clicked into action. She was here to help. While she still feared for herself, whatever happened afterward was not her concern at the moment. She walked assuredly to her patient and immediately saw the problem. His shin swelled and showed a red color that his gray could only sheen over. An infection.

"What happened to his leg?" she asked. She touched his forehead, forgetting she did not know a normal temperature.

"He cut it. We cleaned it up and stitched it up, but it's infected."

"It's more than infected. Something's in there. It'll have to be removed and the infectious material cleared before he has a chance."

"Don't tell us what needs to be done. Do it," said the man. He opened the back of the van to reveal an array of medical supplies. Satomi's eyes brushed over the inventory as the light allowed. At first glance, they had an abundance, but she realized amounts were sporadic and disproportionate to priority - the result of scavenging. How much would they be willing to part with?

She grabbed a blade, forceps, four by four gauze, a stitching kit, and a bottle of Betadine.

"Do you have any anesthetic?" she asked, looking over their shelves.

"They don't feel pain," the man said, arms crossed tightly.

Her patient's grimace said otherwise.

"The shock could kill him," Satomi tried.

"We don't waste anesthetic on the dead." He was unmoved.

The dead? Satomi rounded on the guard.

"HE'S NOT DEAD! If he was dead then having a doctor would be worthless!"

The man was not fazed. "Whatever. Either do something about it or don't."

Satomi looked back at the 'dead.'" They saw a disposable soldier. She saw sickness covering grief, pain, and confusion. She would help. Of course, she would help.

"These instruments need to be sterilized," she said as she set them down with the lantern on the foldout table Eli had positioned by the stretcher.

"They're clean," said the dark-haired man with a tone that said he didn't care, not that he knew.

Satomi shook her head and grunted her disapproval.

He added, "Do you see a hospital around here? This will have to do."

Eli had not contributed to either side of the argument.

"It doesn't have to do. At least get me a flame. We'll sterilize that way."

It was his turn to make noises of disagreement.

"Start another car fire for all I care," said Satomi. The woman flashed involuntarily in her mind's eye. "I'm not introducing more bacteria into this leg. While you do that, I'll prep the leg. Do you have any narcotics?"

"Not for the dead."

Satomi shook her head and began to prep the leg. The light was barely sufficient. It seemed the deep woods soaked it up. No narcotics. No anesthesia.

It was going to be a long night.

12 New Light

Audra had wanted to arrive at Osprey Point as quickly as possible, but with the cloistered community in her sight she hesitated. She had promiscd answers and instead she had lost their doctor and her friend. She had awakened them, brought them here, and now she was failing them. Would they stay and help her or would they scatter like cockroaches in the light of their new enemy?

They slid the gate just barely so Audra and her team could slip in, no longer generous with the opening into their community. The metal sheeting had been rinsed but small tufts of hair clung onto the edging. Dried blood had turned rusty brown in little crevices. Little indents marked the metal. The gate had seen battle.

Audra wasn't sure what system of communication had been put in place, but they seemed to assemble as soon as she stepped inside. No chance to put off what she didn't want to share. She walked up to the defunct fountain. A thin pyramid made up the height of the statue, atop which was a large ring and a swooping bird. For the first time, Audra realized that the eagle-looking bird with the impressive wingspan was probably an osprey. The empty pool underneath had muddy concrete and brass metal nozzles protruding from its surface. Audra sat on the smooth tan-orange limestone wall, tired from their fighting, scouting, and retreating.

A woman in a long ponytail offered her some water, but Audra waved her off. Yes, she did need food and water, but she would wait. This was more important.

"Where's Satomi? What happened?" asked Jia, the woman from the medical office. She pulled at her curls in worry. They straightened then sprang back up.

"We came across a man asking for help. He ended up being bait for an ambush. They took Satomi."

"Well, maybe they'll leave us alone now," suggested Tranter. "That's what they wanted, right?" The skin around his eyes wrinkled.

There were some nods of agreement from the crowd and only a few looks of concern. Audra balked. These saved survivors were so ready to give up on one another.

Audra stood up. She pulled her tired body onto the limestone wall to make her point. "I won't leave anyone to those people, least of all, Satomi. We need her here and she needs us."

"Maybe we can contact Lysent," said another, standing near the mess hall. "Make a deal with them and get under their protection."

Several more nods filled the community. Most of these survivors hadn't had personal experience with Lysent.

"Let's not get carried away," suggested Audra, who was ready to toss them all out on their asses. "Lysent kept the cure from you. They'd have you still wandering the woods to be captured by this Jack and Jill for their army. None of them care about your survival."

"And you do?" asked Tranter. "Honestly, I think your personal grudge against Greenly is keeping us from good food and security." Tranter was apparently the voice of bubbling dissent. He leaned against the laboratory front as if he was part of the assembled leadership.

"If you think I need to step down, I'm all damn for it. I don't want to lead a group that hides while their leader fights, and abandons the doctor that cares for their every need.

"Get the F out of here if you only care about your own skin. Trade your first born to Lysent or enlist as a half zom. Why should I -"

Audra felt Dwyn's hand on her arm. Tranter had struck a nerve. They were outnumbered, outgunned, and she'd just handed the enemy what he wanted. And maybe she did have a grudge. Audra sank at the thought that she did not have Osprey Point's best interest at heart. Didn't she?

She took a deep breath. "Let's just go over our options before we run to Lysent. The cost may be more than we've considered."

Could she swallow her pride and allow Greenly to be her solution to her Jack and Jill problem? Lysent could be the thorn they needed in Jack's and Jill's side.

Audra stepped down from the short wall and let the crowd disperse. She had no answers for them. Her shoulders pulled on her neck into a giant ball of tension in her chest. Audra made her way to the mess hall. She needed food in her belly, then to find her bed before she collapsed in the plaza.

"Audra?" came Ziv's voice.

It was only then she realized Ziv hadn't been the antagonizing voice in the crowd. The fact that he wanted to speak with her privately surprised her, but it didn't make his complaints less tiring. She missed his march back in fearful silence.

"I think we can neutralize the army," he offered quietly.

Immediately Audra was all ears. Hell yes. She looked around to see if anyone was listening. She didn't want their opinions at this point. She knew what they wanted - to run into the arms of anyone who promised safety.

"How? What's your new plan?" she asked, pulling him to the side by the laboratory. Its stucco walls held onto green grime and dirt.

"Actually, it's an old plan. Vesna's plan."

"Aerosolizing the cure? I thought that didn't work."

"We stopped trying when Vesna died. We're more familiar with modifying the cure now.

"I'm sorry, I know I've failed before. Vesna died, your sister died, because I couldn't figure it out."

"It's not your fault, Ziv." She placed a hand on his shoulder.

Ziv stared at the ground, evidently not comforted.

She tried again. "Aerosolizing wasn't the solution then. And the cure wasn't the solution for my sister. Redirects happen. They aren't failures."

Ziv met her eyes. Audra had never spoken to him about her sister's death. "Aerosolizing could be the solution to these half zoms, but what do you think Jack and Jill will do with the people afterwards?"

It was a moot point. Audra would set Lysent on Jack and Jill. Lysent would win, but wouldn't gain anything but a bunch of cured zoms. Ziv's plan was just what she needed.

"We can only give them the opportunity to fight back," she lied. "Can you start on this first thing tomorrow?"

"Sure. It shouldn't take me too long." He rubbed the back of his neck with his hand. "I only have to half-cure them, right?"

Audra leaned against the lab for support as she laughed through her exhaustion. He wandered off, letting her be.

With Ziv working on leveling the playing field, Audra just needed to find a way in, a reason to speak with - and distract - that king and queen pair.

13 Earl Grey

Time scrambled by as Satomi worked and came to a painful and frightening halt when her work was done. During the day, she studied Dr. Bren's notes and pretended to work on the serum. At first, she couldn't make heads or tails of Bren's lab notes, but when she accounted for the idea that these notes did not start post-outbreak, but instead began before, she was able to sort the years of notebooks.

Dr. Bren had worked for Lysent.

Not the Georgia division, but wherever she was from. Lysent was a global company, and to think that their branch was the only one who had been given cures for safekeeping was limited thinking indeed.

There were notes on the virus, modifications for the cure, the soldier serum, and some other serum. The formula for the soldier serum looked straightforward, but Satomi would not be following it. Satomi also couldn't figure out why Dr. Bren, who was possibly involved in the pandemic itself, had decided to stop cooperating and landed herself in that burning car.

Satomi was trying her best to stay out of the car herself. Jack and Jill realized the benefit of keeping their current 'stock' healthy, and the list of untreated injuries was long. She spent her nights treating the soldiers. In between her shifts, she was allowed a couple of hours' rest and a small meal of scavenged or stolen food, Satomi was not sure which.

On the second night, she had received a thin blanket. She was undecided whether it best served as a pillow, a buffer from the plastic, or as a layer of privacy as she rested. She ached. She ached so much. She didn't understand how Audra and the others had survived sleeping away from civilization for so long. Although she imagined that if they chose to sleep in cars, they did so in ones with upholstered seating. She refused to complain. Hostile interactions, bad sleep, and crappy food were on par for medical providers.

Finally, time to walk back to the laboratory. In just a few days, she had learned their routine, route, and the purpose of all but a few vehicles. The one they passed now, she assumed to be Jack's and Jill's residence. In the back, the metal doors had been sealed shut. Instead, a real wooden door, a window, and a stoop had been installed, like on a real house. Today, the curtains in the window fluttered and the door opened.

"Pleasure meeting you out here today!" said an older man as he stumbled on the height of the stairs. He straightened up and smoothed the wrinkles from his tartan shirt. "How are the children?"

He greeted them as if Eli and she were married and they were all old family friends. His haircut and beard were neatly trimmed and his clothes were clean and pressed. He was like a time traveler. Satomi just stared.

Eli left her side and went to usher the man back into the trailer. "Sir, sir, you really need to go back inside. It's probably time for tea. Did you leave the kettle on?"

"The kettle?" He glanced back at his home, but then rounded on Eli. "What's it to you!"

"Nothing to me, Peter. Nothing. I'm sorry," Eli apologized, obviously flustered. So, this was Peter, Jack's and Jill's father... and Eli was trying to keep him from her. Why?

"Hi!" Satomi said brightly, matching the man's greeting.

"Hello, dear..." The man searched her face as if trying to remember her name.

"Satomi. It's nice to meet you, Peter." She came over and her hand rose to shake his. She trusted that Eli would let her advances slide rather than escalate the scene further. Peter shook her hand.

"The tea!" he shouted and without letting go of her hand, he pulled her toward the door. She gave Eli a sly smile and followed in. Eli looked clearly exasperated, but Peter's comfort seemed to be the priority here, and she'd take advantage of it to learn more.

"Come in, come in. I'm sorry to say you're late. I already put the tea away. But no worries, I can bring it out again. Just next time call if you'll be late," he said, backing up so she could get through the doorway.

He continued. "Will your husband be joining us?"

Satomi looked at her gruff guard, who did not advance from the stoop.

"No, I think he has some errands to do."

"Oh ok," he said, but seemed to notice that 'the husband' made no movement to go do said errands.

Satomi smiled. "Can I help you put on the tea?"

That seemed to bring him out of it and he welcomed her farther into the home. Satomi let out a small gasp.

"I know it's a mess! I'm so sorry. I wasn't expecting company," he tittered as he wrung out his hands.

"No, it's pristine. It's so beautiful! What a lovely home!" She felt a pull to keep him happy too, even though she had just met him. But the truth was, it was pristine. The walls and ceiling were done in paneling, highlighted with exposed decorative beams, high windows, and skylights. A sitting area with a loveseat and table for four, a kitchenette, and a partitioned area of a presumed bedroom created a residence with anchored furniture. The whole place was decorated in white and pink roses. Embroidered pieces hung on the walls.

"White and pink. Laura's favorite colors. I don't care for them much, but I can't stand to get rid of them now. It's how I've lived, you know?"

"Of course."

"I wouldn't know what color to do it in. And the paint store is so confusing. I don't even know what my favorite color is. Just that Laura's were pink and white."

"I think it looks wonderful. She did a good job," Satomi whispered as she was led to the stove to help with tea.

Peter's gray hair was thinned, and his skin had the papery characteristic of age, but he moved with confidence and agility.

"Do you get to go to the paint store much?" she ventured.

"What? No! Do you work there? Why are you here?" he turned on her with an angry look. Another episode. Dementia? Alzheimer's? Satomi remained calm.

"Tea, remember? It's me - Satomi - here to have tea with you. OK?" she asked for permission.

"OK. But don't sell me any encyclopedias."

For a moment Satomi thought it was a continued lapse, but he had a sly grin on his face. It was a joke. At least that one was.

They sat down with their dandelion tea next to a framed photograph that featured a young and happy Jack and Jill. Besides their blond hair, their plaid shirts matched.

"Jack and Jill?" she asked, pointing to the photo.

"No, no - Peter and Evelyn. My babies. That's their senior photo. Inseparable those two are. You'd think they're twins."

She did think they were twins. They looked close in age. And it was both their senior photos?

"They graduated at the same time?"

"Yeah, Peter got held back a year. Although if you ask me, they just wanted to be together. Perfect grades ever since. They're in college now. Learning medical stuff. Doctors, I think. I'm so proud of them."

"I'm sure you are," Satomi whispered.

This pink and white home revealed a softer side to the siblings. After another few minutes, she ventured again.

"Do you know your house is on wheels?"

"I suspected as much. Otherwise there are a lot of earthquakes." He laughed.

Satomi laughed too.

"Do you know where you're going?"

"Everyone moves these days. We're just a-moving."

"Thank you for my tea. Dandelion is my favorite."

"Good for you. Mine is Earl Grey. Not available in the stores nowadays, I guess. Global warming or some shit."

"Something like that," she said. "If I find any Earl Grey, I'll bring it by for you. It's been a pleasure having tea with you. I'm Satomi. What's your name?" she tested him.

"You don't know my name? Why…it's…" his face crinkled. "What's it to you anyway?"

Unable to recall information on command, and anger to hide it, typical of Alzheimer's.

"It's OK," she said. "Thank you for the tea," she repeated.

"It's not OK. Get out of here!" he yelled with a large start, knocking over some silverware and upturning an empty cup. It chipped on the side.

"See what you made me do! Get out!" he yelled again.

Satomi did not need to hear it a third time. She had overstayed her welcome. Before she reached the door, his demeanor had changed again.

"Have you seen my wife?" he asked sweetly. "Please let her know to come back. I just need her to come back. It will all be OK as soon as she does. I just need her to come back." He muttered over and over.

Satomi's eyes watered, not sure if him thinking his wife left him was better or worse than the truth. Eli received her at the stoop.

"Happy?" he asked when the door closed, referring to her escapade.

"Is Jack's real name Peter?"

"Jack is Jack." The man huffed. He either did not know or was not going to tell her.

Eli continued escorting her to the laboratory. Satomi's mind reeled. Satomi was a doctor, and she had just figured out how to benefit Jack and Jill without breaking her oaths.

14 Proposals

The burned-out car broke Satomi's routine on the seventh day as she was brought to the meeting area. The gray and black smoldering of last night's fire pit marked the center and she stood just beside it. Two empty lawn chairs waited under the awning of a recreational vehicle. Before long another circle of men formed.

The man with the ponytail and beard brought in a z-virus patient on a leash and pole. The patient pulled and struggled against the device and all the outside stimulation. Satomi did not have to look hard to recognize the man with the now-ashen face and dark hair as Dennis. Her hand clammed and perspired around the syringe she was to inject him with.

Satomi knew she had taken a big risk not working on the soldier serum for the last four days. She had researched the notes heavily to inspire her newest route, but rabbit hole or not, she had been given orders by her captors and she had not fulfilled them.

And Dennis could die because of it.

She could die because of it.

Satomi stared numbly at the car, even though she knew she shouldn't. All the glass, plastic, and paint had given way. It was patched of black and ash white. If it was a scare tactic, it was a good one. Satomi imagined Ryder arriving to rescue her and being directed to the police car as Eli set it on fire. Would she ever see Ryder again?

The recreational vehicle's thin metal door opened with a clatter. Jack and Jill both tried to exit at the same time and fumbled over each other. Jack gave his sister a playful shove and came out first. Jill followed. The crowd laughed and cheered. Jack flounced down into his lawn chair, which creaked with the sudden weight. He flung his leg over the arm rest, which bent wide.

"Are you ready to show us your progress?" he asked.

"Perhaps she should thank us for her accommodations, first, Jack," said Jill, sitting down more gracefully. She played with her fishtail braid as she waited, staring at Satomi intently.

Satomi was hesitant to address them. "Um, yes. Thank you for keeping me safe so far. I appreciate the opportunity to work with the soldiers."

"Treating soldiers is worthless if we never get any more serum," said Jill dismissively, turning her eyes to her braid's end.

Satomi was very clear on their priorities.

"I understand you want to build an army, but I've thought of a better use for your resources and I think you'd agree."

A look of exasperation played on both the siblings' faces. How were they not twins? Ignoring Satomi's words, Jack tapped his fingers on the closest plastic arm rest.

"Get on with it," Jack said to Eli.

Eli grabbed Satomi roughly, which surprised her. He had never really touched her the entire week they had been together. He yanked the syringe from her hand, then moved toward Dennis, who had been forcibly pinned to the ground with the leash and pole.

"STOP!" Satomi shouted. "I think I can cure your father."

Eli froze with one hand on Dennis and the syringe in the other. He looked to Jack and Jill for direction. Jack raised his hand, and Eli let go and stepped back holding the full syringe.

"How do you know about our father?" asked Jill, arching back to relax into her chair.

"I met him, by accident," she replied, not wanting to get Eli in trouble. "He has some sort of early-onset neurodegenerative disease, right?"

"Uh something like that. What makes you think you can cure him?" asked Jack.

"The soldier serum," Satomi replied as if it explained everything.

"You are NOT going to infect him," said Jack firmly. Jill sat more upright in her chair with her disapproval as well.

"No, no, I'm not. It's just the soldier serum proves that you can modify the virus! You can keep some of the 'good' things about the virus and circumvent what's bad. Dr. Bren designed a serum that modified end-metabolism so that the infected could move better, but kept the end-neurotransmitter levels low so that higher brain functions remained damaged. Willpower and sense of self stayed lost."

"And what would you design?" asked Jack.

"The z-virus triggers an excellent cleaning system in the brain, destroying malfunctioning and dying cells. It also bolsters neuroprotective properties. I'd use that to heal your father. But, I'll prevent the virus from consuming neurotransmitters so all high brain functions will remain intact."

"We'd have our father back?"

"If I can make it work, yeah. But, you have to agree to not make any more soldiers."

Jack and Jill looked at each other. Satomi assumed they were doing that sibling non-verbal communication thing to discuss their options. Dennis struggled, but he and the soldier serum were quickly forgotten.

"Deal," said Jack. "What do you need?"

"I need to build a peptide. I have the right equipment, but I need a biopeptide anchor medium."

"All right..." puzzled Jill. "We'll take your word that's a real thing. Where can we get such an... anchor?"

"If anyone can find it, Audra can. She's your best bet."

"Your friend from your compound? She's your best bet. Remember what happens if this fails."

Satomi didn't need reminding but glanced at the sedan all the same. She knew what would happen. Death, one way or another. But she knew this was her best bet to keep her oaths, and herself alive. Eli handed her the syringe back, and Satomi pocketed the prepared saline with a hidden smile.

*　*　*

Audra sat munching on greens in the mess hall when the alarm sounded. It felt like confirmation to her nerves, which were already on high alert. She wasn't sure what she expected when she peeked through the reinforced slats on the gate, but her breath caught in her chest when she saw the long black hair of the half zom. It wasn't Satomi, but it was purposeful. The zom trudged forward. An arrow with a white flag fletching protruded from her chest. It secured a paper note, sealed in salvaged plastic.

Seeing no other signs of movement in the forest, Audra slipped through the gate and reached for the note. The zom made no motion to stop her. Upon closer inspection, the zom's body bloated and the glassy orbs of her eyes bulged. Audra pulled the note gingerly, avoiding the sticky masses of blood that clung to the wound and plastic.

Jack and Jill wanted an audience.

Audra's heart ached to see Satomi, and each step in their run drew them closer. She was happy that Gordon and Marcos had volunteered to come. She was still upset with Dwyn.

This time they spent no time in the forest line, but instead marched straight into the convoy. Two men escorted them to a central area where some of the vehicles had been circled around a campfire site. Even maniacs needed camaraderie and company, she guessed. The lawn chair thrones that held Jack and Jill were laughable, but Audra lost the thought when Satomi was brought to her. She gave her a giant hug. Her body felt thinner. Audra apologized that she hadn't been able to set her free yet.

"Are you OK?" Audra asked.

"I am. I really am." She exchanged hugs with Marcos and Gordon.

Audra pulled her close again and searched her eyes for the truth. She did, bodily, appear intact. No bruises. She looked tired. Her face was wrinkled in new places.

"How's Ryder?" Satomi asked as another fold climbed her face.

"She's great. We're fighting to keep her in bed."

Satomi giggled. Then, "her chest tube?"

"It stopped bubbling, whatever that means. Should we take it out?"

"Yes, but make sure to perform a Valsalva maneuver when you pull it. Then close it really well."

"- a what?"

"Have her hold her breath," Satomi explained.

"OK." Why didn't she just say that?

Jill cleared her throat. Satomi must have taken it as a hint.

"I need a biopeptide anchor."

Gordon nodded. He knew what it was. Audra didn't.

"For Jack and Jill? A what?"

"Yes, sort of. It's a medium used in peptide synthesis." This time the second explanation didn't help. "I wrote it down."

Thank God. Audra pocketed the folded-up paper.

"If you bring us what we need, we will return Satomi after this project," proposed Jack. He sat stiffly on his throne.

"What's it for?" Gordon asked.

"None of your business," replied Jill. Audra and Jill locked eyes. Jill was quickly climbing her hit list, right below Larange Greenly.

Satomi brought her back. "It's OK. Trust me."

It didn't really matter what Jack and Jill wanted in the interim. Audra was playing the long game.

"I'll get it for you." Another hug. "Hang in there, Satomi. I'm sorry you're still in here. I promise to make it right."

Away from the convoy, with the trees wrapped around them, the group breathed a little easier. Satomi was holding up well. She didn't seem abused. They seemed almost reasonable.

"So, what do they want?" asked Audra, confused.

"Satomi wants to make a peptide. Peptides are signals within the body," explained Gordon.

"And what will this one signal?"

"No idea."

He was of little help. Was this going to be used to make more soldiers? To create a new pandemic? The possibilities were endless.

Audra sighed. "OK, you two report back to Osprey Point. I'm going to go scout out this... whatever." She patted the pocket that held the note. She didn't tell the others, but she began getting her bearings for the most efficient route to Lysent from their location. Probably the rail line.

"Actually," started Gordon, "I was going to go out from here." Audra knew what 'out' meant.

"You got a lead?"

"Yes, someone told me a woman and her daughter go by their names in an outpost near Atlanta. It isn't Lysent-sponsored. It's another community. But if you need me here..."

"No, Marcos can get back by himself, right?"

Marcos shook his hair out of his face in agreement.

"She's married," Gordon confessed.

"Well, you guys were divorced, right?" she asked, not sure how that changed things.

"Yeah, yeah, we were." Gordon looked down, interested in the acorn he was pressing into the ground with his shoe. His small glasses fell a bit and he adjusted them.

"I'm sure they'd love to know you're alive. They probably think the worst."

"It was the worst," he said, finally looking up at her. "I didn't come home to them when things went south. I was too wrapped up in my work, intent on saving the world, instead of them."

"You did help. Go now."

*　*　*

"Well, well, well..." came a voice from the top of the well-manicured gate. Audra knew she wouldn't find tufts of hair on this one. It was taller and the crow's nest was more than a rickety scaffold.

"Hey Charlie," she said, approaching slowly.

"You know I'm supposed to shoot you, right?" He brushed the frizzy brown mop out of his face, but it quickly returned over his eyes. How he could stand watch like that boggled Audra.

"I know." Audra had hoped to have a plan by this point, but no revelation had revealed itself on the run. She settled for straightforward. "I have a proposal for Greenly. She'll benefit from it. I can't help who I am. There is no other way to get in touch... so I uh, came."

Charlie's eyebrows rose at her audacity. "I'll let Lysent know that you'd like to talk to the big boss."

"Thank you. I'll wait here."

"That's probably a good idea. You're not allowed out there, much less in here." He disappeared and another guard took his place immediately. Audra didn't recognize him, but he seemed to accept Charlie's instruction.

Just in case, she walked farther up the road and leaned against a pine tree. With her pack by her side, the bark felt rough against her skin and through her shirt. She rested on its solidness. At least trees were reliable. Everywhere else she was playing a game of fake trust and caution. She pulled a pine straw that stuck into her pants.

Audra dozed for a few minutes, not realizing how exhausted she was until she had settled into the pine straw. An hour passed and Audra was sure that Greenly had decided to completely ignore her request. But then sure enough, the gate opened and two of Greenly's henchmen waited to escort her in. Audra stood up and brushed off the things that stuck to her. A thought settled inside her - if she walked through those gates, there was a chance she'd never walk out again. Greenly could have her head. She took a deep sighing breath, pulled on her pack, and approached the gate.

With one hand by her waist and the other on the strap of her bag, Audra walked inside.

The town hadn't changed much. That didn't surprise her. Investments went into Lysent headquarters foremost, trickled into the township, then to the townships farther down the road. The trickle was... insignificant. Audra hadn't changed much either. She used to bring in tagged zombies here, trying to strike a deal for her sister.

Another deal.

Another sister.

Audra's escorts were two burly men who looked like they ate well. Must be a good gig in Lysent. They stopped her in the plaza outside Lysent's front building. Its tall windows glimmered with extravagance. Before Audra could wonder if it would take another hour to see progress, beady eyes emerged from the interior of the Lysent building. Her salt and pepper hair was pulled too tight into a bun. Her giant guards and her choice of all-black attire made her lithe body appear even more delicate. She walked with confidence and small steps down the white granite steps.

"I'm surprised. Quite surprised. You know I could have you hanged in the next few minutes?"

"I'm aware of that. You're also aware that I hate you. So between those two things, you know I'm here for a very important matter."

Greenly blinked slowly and tried to hide a smile. Audra swallowed hard and spoke before she could change her mind.

"There's a group with a formidable army that has entered our area."

"Is that so? How does that affect me?"

A motion caught Audra's eye. She looked over at the fountain. A bunch of dancing cherubs. Theirs worked. Water flitted from one arch to another. Audra turned back to Greenly.

"It's a big army. A hundred or so at least – well-built, strong zoms and people. I can take out their main strength, but it's still too large a group for us to handle. You have the numbers."

Greenly stared at her, her eyes darkening.

"We can't handle them without you?" she asked.

"If you could, I wouldn't be putting myself and others at risk. They're going to want your resources. And as much as I hate you - it's the devil I know. I know nothing about these strangers. I don't want them here and neither will you."

"And what do you need from me?"

"I need this biopeptide anchor thing that they want. That's how I'm going to get in and plant our sabotage. Then you'll come and sweep up the pieces."

Like Audra, Greenly didn't really seem to care what the biopeptide anchor was actually for. She didn't ask. They all had their own games to play. Greenly thought on it for a moment before adding her condition. "In return, I want your corral. Now."

"You're already getting all of the spoils of war," Audra countered. "Why do you want them?"

Greenly knew about her corral? Of course, she did. Maybe not for certain, but they had done the math. Somewhere, Audra had a backlog.

"Hm, more so, I don't want them. You don't seem to understand the strain you're putting on the area. And the safety risk." Greenly's arms crossed. One set of fingers gently tapped across her thin upper arm.

Could Audra give up the corral for Satomi? She wasn't really in a position to bargain. She needed Lysent's help.

Audra didn't think hard on it. It was a deal she was willing to make.

With the small insulated box housing the item Satomi requested in her jacket pocket, Audra was escorted by the men through the township back to the gate. Audra heard whispers from people who recognized her. She ignored their murmuring. At the gate, two men sat on horses waiting.

Shepherds.

"Hop on," said one, a man with red hair and a matching grizzled beard. He nodded toward the back of his saddle.

"Can't we run, instead?"

"Hell no. This is the deal. Do we need to talk things out with Greenly again?"

No, she didn't. Audra sized up her two escorts. She didn't recognize either of them. The redhead wore a cowboy hat and sat on a big, black mare. The other, a spindly guy with long, stringy blond hair sat on a smaller spotted horse. Audra looked up to see if Charlie was still on his perch. Maybe he could tell her if these guys were all right or not. Charlie was nowhere to be seen. The guards must have switched out.

Audra breathed a deep sigh. With one hand on her knife at her waist, she offered her other to the man. His giant, rough one swallowed hers and she was swung up into the saddle. Their hips connected. Audra's face wrinkled. He smelled of damp clothes and tobacco.

If Greenly wanted her dead, she would have done it herself, but that didn't mean that she wasn't in danger. The gates opened, and they headed down the road. Before the township was out of sight Audra felt the horse's momentum shift. Her nose filled with his scent and her breasts pressed against his back as she fell into the rider. Audra heard a laugh. He had done it on purpose.

Audra felt the knife's handle in her hand. She imagined digging it into his neck until arteries burst. She imagined him falling to the ground and his dead body being struck by the horse's hoofs as she left him behind. Instead, she just tried to lean back as much as she dared for fear of falling off.

She pulled a red hair from her. Her stomach boiled and threatened to heave over, but she held it down. No need to piss him off. The jostling of the horse didn't help. Audra wasn't used to traveling in a way that didn't use her feet. Her perspective made huge bouncing shifts while her stomach undulated in a lagging pattern.

Audra hadn't had much interaction with the shepherds. As a tagger, she had tagged individual zombies. Shepherds dealt with herds. Audra hoped she wouldn't be recognized for this trip. She and Dwyn had killed two shepherds - Lars and Lindon - who had been sent to move a herd through the laboratory. If things started going wrong, she could run into the thick woods where the horses couldn't go. That is, if she could get away.

Another jostle. Audra's face smashed into his shoulder, but she managed to arch her back away from him. He got nothing that time. The man readjusted in his seat, smashing between her legs. She heard a snicker.

Audra imagined slitting his throat and riding with his body until they reached a place she could string him up. He'd swing in the air like a toy.

"I don't get it, Manny," said the man on the other horse.

"What's that?"

"I don't get how this little girl got Lars. That man was honkin' huge."

They did know who she was and what she had done. Audra wasn't sure what that would mean for her, but in the moment, she felt a sense of accomplishment out of it.

Yeah, I took two of yours.

"That's a good point, Blue. I mean... Lindon, I get. Overconfident prick. Course, Lars wasn't the smartest."

Blue laughed. "He was a dumb SOB."

Manny laughed too.

Audra hated to, but pointed to a single-track off the road. They needed to go that way. Manny and she took the lead. Blue followed.

Manny let out a low gruff growl that only she could hear. "You can't do shepherds like that. You better watch yourself."

Audra glanced behind her to make sure Blue was still a distance away and not at her back. These two hadn't harmed her yet because Greenly wanted the location of the corral. Audra did not think her protection would extend far after that. Sure, she hadn't told Greenly where the army was located, but it wouldn't be that hard to figure out without her. She was in trouble.

She motioned to another trail, which Manny followed, but not without unnecessarily disturbing the horse to shift her again. After what felt like a lifetime, and not nearly long enough if this was the end of her life, they reached a clearing. Audra pointed to the rusty trailer needlessly.

"Shit, we never thought to look in there," said Manny.

As they approached, the zoms inside smelled the sweaty horses and sweaty people. They riled, grunted, and groaned.

"There's an opening at the top. We drop them in," explained Audra.

"Well, I'll be..." said Manny.

When they reached the trailer, Manny dismounted on the side Blue and his horse were on. Manny held the reins of the horse and looked at her expectantly.

Audra gave him a quick look before jumping off on the other side of the horse. She sprinted to the edge of the field. When she reached the cover of bushes and pine trees, she turned to check the shepherds. Neither of them had given chase. Manny was pulling something out of the saddlebags. Molotov cocktails. He climbed to the top of the metal trailer, lit them, and dropped them in.

The screams were primal. Audra dropped to her knees. The sounds of banging metal reverberated in her ears as the infected tried to escape their hell. Audra hadn't known them to know external pain, but being burned alive was too much for even their pain-numbed systems.

Tears poured from her eyes. Audra didn't care anymore that she might be in the two shepherds' reach. She deserved to die. She had collected all these people with the intent to save them. Instead, she had pooled them together for mass murder. How could she pretend she was doing good?

Sparks and smoke flew from the top of the trap. After what seemed an eternity, when the screams were still not quenched, the two men mounted their horses and turned them away from the wreckage. They were satisfied with the progress. They kept a good clearance from Audra as they entered the forest line again, but it didn't stop Manny from calling out.

"We'll get you. You can't get our own without paying the price."

Audra did not respond, but as soon as they were out of sight, she collapsed into a pool of regret.

This wasn't worth Satomi's life. This wasn't worth it.

*   *   *

"Can you really do what you say you can?" asked Eli from the door as she pored over more tomes inside the laboratory trailer.

Satomi wasn't sure if the question was triggered by skepticism or an honest concern for her wellbeing. She didn't look up to figure it out.

"No one's done it before, but the z-virus has laid all the groundwork, I'm just... modifying it."

She turned another coffee-stained page. Dr. Bren had never considered the potential expansions of her serum breakthrough. She had settled for mindless soldiers.

Eli wasn't satisfied. "I don't get it. How can you use the z-virus - something bad - for something good? There's good stuff in the virus?"

Eli was no longer by the door. Instead, he was looking over her shoulder, trying to glean clues from the notebooks she had open. He really was curious.

"The virus itself doesn't contain the 'good stuff'. It replicates inside us until it's consumed plenty of neurotransmitters, then it sends out peptide signals to boost the brain's natural defenses and repair functions. That's why the infected keep going, despite all their damage and the violence against them. If the brain and body live longer, so does the virus."

"Peptides? That's what you were talking about with Jack and Jill."

"Yes, I want to synthesize a peptide. They're just chains of amino acids... simply. It's difficult, but I can do it with the right starting supplies. I'll build the peptide that says to the z-virus that the attack is complete - the virus will skip ahead to the neuroprotective processes that we want for Peter."

"You trick the virus into thinking it's done the bad things, so it will do the good things?"

"Yes!" she cried out, raising her hands, proud of her friend for making the connection. "And that will be hopefully enough to overcome Peter's illness!"

She realized she had just considered Eli her friend. She turned back to the notebooks in silence, but with a shy smile on her face. As much as she trusted him, she knew she shouldn't. He had manhandled her when they met with Jack and Jill. Maybe he had just done it for show, but it scared her.

"Hey... I have a gift for you," he said suddenly. Satomi wasn't sure if he just remembered or if he had just mustered the courage to mention it. She turned on her stool to him out of curiosity. A gift? Better than a favor, she supposed.

"Well, I guess sort of a gift for you..." he said as he pulled two little paper satchels out of his pocket. "Earl Grey, for Peter."

"You heard us?"

"Uh, yeah, it's a trailer. I wasn't going to let you in there and not be able to hear what's going on."

"Oh." Satomi wasn't sure what to make of him.

His eyes watered as he continued to hold them out. And Satomi finally realized it was an apology.

"Thank you," she said. She smiled. He grinned back. "Would you like to go have tea with Peter?"

He pulled out one more satchel. "Yes!"

This time Satomi grinned. She began putting up some of the things she was working on.

"Where are you from, Eli?"

Eli shrugged. "From nowhere, really. Was a bit of a wanderer before wandering was the norm."

Satomi nodded as if she understood. She was reminded again of how traditionally she still lived, even in this world.

"Jack and Jill took me in. Feed me good." He smiled over his belly. "Guess it's better than wandering."

Satomi placed a small bookmark in the notebook and put it on the sorted shelf of books. Questions she had yet to answer still swam in her brain. If Dr. Bren had an inventory of antivirals, then why was there so much research on them and attempts to change the formula? Why had Dr. Bren refused to keep working? In the end, it didn't matter much. She'd use what research she needed and leave the rest. And she'd leave here. But what about Eli? They walked together to the trailer's doors.

"Where I'm from, we can use guards too, y'know... And you wouldn't have to care for hostages," she ventured. She didn't mean for it to be an accusation, but she saw Eli turn his head to avoid her anyway.

"I'm sorry," he whispered as he opened the door and let Satomi step out into the cool air.

"Earl Grey! My favorite!" called out Peter, wrapping Satomi in a hug. He smelled of sandalwood. Satomi glanced at Eli, who was happy to let her take the credit. They were both ushered to the table set with pink and white china. Eli struggled to get his girth into the chair, which was anchored a fixed distance from the table. He smiled all the same.

Peter wore a neat gray cardigan, penny loafers, and pressed slacks. However, his hair was uncombed. He turned on the water before sitting down with them. He happily chattered and rambled.

"Still not sure what color to paint the walls."

"Oh, I still like the pink," said Satomi, happy to see him happy. He was such a gentle soul. She nodded when appropriate. Most of his stories didn't make sense. Satomi poured them tea and Peter was delighted all over again by the Earl Grey. He seemed to be bouncing back and forth mentally a lot today. Satomi worried, but she couldn't make much progress without that medium.

Halfway through tea, Peter started to whimper then cry about how lonely he was. He said he couldn't remember the last time anyone had visited. Satomi was sure that Jack and Jill visited him multiple times a day, but that wasn't true for Peter in that moment. He sat in the chair, overwhelmed in his isolation.

Satomi patted his hand, but he pulled away. She might not be able to help him now, but she could help him. She'd create that biopeptide and put his brain into super-powered repair. He might not be completely cured, but he might be able to regain some function.

She just needed time.

Peter could not be comforted, try as they might. Eventually Eli led her out, her heart broken. Their Earl Grey tea sat cold and forgotten.

15 Mass Cure

It was long after the shepherds had left before Audra pulled herself off the ground. She couldn't find the energy within herself to run. Her legs and heart were heavy. Instead, she trudged through the forest. Sharp wisps of smoke spun around the trees, reminding her of the current death. Manny's scent clung to her front.

The adrenaline in her body fell cold and faded into regret. Once again, she dreaded going back to Osprey Point. If only she had the time and money to seek out an old moonshiner, she'd lose herself until penance had taken its course and her liver.

She took whatever solace the woods could provide, and came upon Osprey Point's fences before she was ready. She ignored any greetings she received from above as they opened the gate for her, but one message did catch her ear.

"You're needed in the medical office."

God, what had happened now?

Another whiff of Manny on her chest. Sickness rushed over her. She pushed it down with a loud utterance. Dropping her backpack right there, she ripped off her long-sleeve shirt. She threw it onto her pack and stomped off in her undershirt. It was the guards' turns to ignore.

She walked into the medical office. All the partitions between the stretchers had been set aside. Ryder lay on the farthest stretcher, but no one was rushing over to her. She seemed fine, distracted by the two men near the closet. The top and sides of the closet were sealed with white silk tape.

Ziv and Dwyn looked over to Audra. Ziv beamed. Good news. She needed good news.

"You got what we need, Ziv?" Audra asked.

Ziv grinned as he talked and made large energetic motions. "I think I do! It was difficult, but working from the temperature-stable antiviral actually made things a lot easier. It's just more stable in general. We had only tried to aerosolize that first edition of the cure. We never went back to it after, after -"

Vesna's murder.

"Are you ready to test it on the prisoner? Is the half zom in there?"

"Yeah. Look, I was thinking on it. Is this... ethical? Isn't he like a prisoner of war or something?" asked Ziv.

"Better him first than trying it on all of them, right?" encouraged Audra. She had just murdered an entire trailer of innocent people. She wasn't going to be stopped now by Ziv's cold feet for something that could ultimately be positive.

She could see the gears turning. He finally nodded and pushed the nozzle of the small tank under the door. Dwyn used another strip of tape to seal around it. Audra heard a click and the faint hiss of gas escaping.

"You look like hell, Audra," were the first words Dwyn chose to speak as they waited over the gassy closet. "Where have you been?"

She'd have to tell them. She didn't have to tell them all of it though.

"I went to Greenly to trade for that bio-pep-thing anchor."

"BY YOURSELF?" Dwyn's hackles rose.

"Yeah, I needed you all here. I used to handle Lysent by myself, all the time," she reminded him.

Dwyn shook his head. "It's different now." He leaned against the wall with arms crossed, pouting.

"How? Cause they don't have my sister to hold over me?"

"No. Because you have a family now."

Audra rolled her eyes. Belinda was family. She had a family then.

"What did you trade?" Dwyn asked.

Audra suddenly felt cold. Goosebumps prickled her arms. The words burned at the top of her chest, hurting to come out, hurting to stay in.

"The corral."

Dwyn slid down the wall into a slump. He didn't look at her, but she could see how wide his eyes were, trying to process it all.

"What corral?" asked Ziv.

Audra put her face into her hands. Rubbed off some of the shame and explained. Dwyn sat in silence. When she told them what the shepherds had done, Dwyn broke down in tears.

"What were you thinking, Audra?" came a voice from the corner. Audra had forgotten she was there.

"I was thinking that we need to get Satomi back," she turned to justify herself.

"Satomi would never have agreed to this." Ryder shook her head, tears in her eyes. Audra walked over to their disabled leader. The chest tube had been removed and her eyes were clearer - less painkillers at play.

"Satomi won't know. She didn't know we had one in the first place. Doesn't matter what she'd personally agree to. She's a hostage and I'm paying the ransom."

Ryder pulled herself up to sitting with her hands and an involuntary grunt.

"This whole place is built on caring for people. You've effectively allowed mass murder," Ryder accused.

Audra didn't need her to tell her this. She already knew.

After a moment's pause, Ryder choked out, "I'm not sure you belong here."

"What? You're just now figuring this out? Why do you think I don't stay more than eight hours at a time? I might not belong here, but you guys need me. You're not making it through this without some tough decisions and bloody hands. Vesna knew that. Just be happy you can be laid up in bed and hand me the reins."

Audra had never seen that glare from Ryder, usually happy-go-lucky. Her eyes slanted with sharp ends, matching her spiked hair.

Audra turned to Ziv, who waited quietly by the closet.

"Uhm, it will take some time," he said awkwardly about his experiment.

Audra stormed off.

Audra didn't have to be notified of the prisoner's change of status. His yelling from the closet could be heard throughout the plaza. In the meantime, she had retrieved her bag from the center of Osprey Point, washed up, and changed clothes. She returned fresh faced, but still reddened from her tears.

Dwyn and Ziv and one of the nurses, Mary, met her at the closet. Dwyn opened the door, tape peeling on all sides, and they looked inside the three-foot by three-foot pine paneled closet. There the man sat, his splinted legs anchoring him, and his arms flailing. His cries were incoherent, but it was clear he was cognizant and in pain.

Ziv watched in horror of his keep's anguish. Dwyn nudged Ziv into action and they both worked to get him onto the middle patient bed. Mary rushed to give him some painkillers through his IV, which she was thankful was still in place. Audra smiled over their success. These half zoms would be worthless.

"He wasn't ready to be cured. You should have waited for his body to heal," said Ryder. Her face wrinkled in tears.

"No time," said Audra, daring Ryder to argue.

The man whimpered as the narcotics took their course. He'd be OK. This was worth it.

Ryder grimaced and rolled over, no longer facing them. Audra turned back to Ziv. "What's next?"

"I need the trailer dimensions, number of infected, and size and number of exterior holes."

"You got it, Ziv." She turned to leave.

"Audra?" She turned back. "I don't know about the corral. But this - this cure - it's going to be a good thing."

Only because he didn't know the rest of her plan.

Audra nodded.

"I won't let you down," he assured her.

*　*　*

Satomi scribbled furiously the protocol she'd follow for the peptide synthesis. She sketched out the portions of the peptide she understood. This work table, mottled with indentations and stains, had become her table.

Eli approached her with caution and sat down next to her.

"What is it, Eli?" she asked. Was it sundown already? She wished she could work on this in perpetuity. The idea was brilliant, but the work was hard. She should have a team. Maybe she could work a deal to recruit Gordon and Ziv. Her mind reeled at the possibilities.

"I'm not sure you should experiment on Peter," he blurted out.

Eli had become a permanent fixture and occasional sounding board in her laboratory. They both really liked Peter. Was he worried about him?

Satomi set her pencil down and looked at him.

"You don't have to worry. I'll make sure the peptide works in vitro first... that is, outside the body. And, if it doesn't work inside Peter and he gets fully infected with the z-virus, then we have a cure."

"It's just, he's not -" started Eli, but he was interrupted by the door opening behind them.

Eli got up from his stool with a creak and scraping against the metal floor. He spoke with the other man in hushed voices. Satomi tried to remember which branch of the peptide she was working on.

"Satomi?" called out Eli.

"Mhhm?" she said, not willing to turn and lose her place quite yet.

"Your friends are here to meet with Jack and Jill."

"Oh!" She turned now, her finger on the spot she was checking. "Do they have the anchor?"

"I don't know, but you'll have to attend the meeting," he said.

Eli and Satomi walked to the meeting area, where Satomi was surprised to see the circle of men around the lawn chairs. Weren't Jack and Jill over this intimidation thing? The couple entered and could barely sit comfortably with all the extra armor they had donned. Satomi guessed not. The RV's awning had been pulled back and the sun bore down on the two, casting shadows on their demeanor.

Two familiar faces joined them in the circle. It took Satomi a moment to realize it was Marcos and Audra. It seemed like a lifetime ago, yet suddenly everything she was missing out on came flooding back. Ryder. Osprey Point. Audra did not seem to have any such lapse. Satomi found herself wrapped in a giant hug. It felt foreign.

"Ryder? Did you take the chest tube out?" asked Satomi.

"We did. She's good. Misses you. Are you OK?"

"I am."

Audra pulled her to arm's length again as if to examine her. Audra's face showed worry. I'm OK, really.

Marcos gave her a pat on the shoulder. His hand felt warm and heavy.

"Are you sure you're OK?" asked Audra as if seeking a different answer. Wasn't she OK? She pulled her close again. "I'm going to get you out of here," Audra whispered.

Satomi's face buried in Audra's auburn hair. It felt nice. She did feel isolated here, but she had decided her work was important. Something that needed to be done. Osprey Point could wait. Peter needed her here as a scientist.

Satomi heard Jack clear his throat. They didn't like being ignored. She looked to Jill. Jill glared.

"I've got what you've requested," Audra addressed the two. "But I can't give it to you until I understand what it's for." Marcos stood just behind her, arms crossed.

"I'm – " started Satomi, excited to tell her what she had learned, but Jill cut her off.

"I don't think you're in any position to question us." She crossed her legs and flicked her braid off her shoulder.

Satomi and Jack looked at each other with puzzled faces. It seemed Jack also didn't think there was harm in telling Audra what they were doing. It was actually for something good. But he followed his sister's lead and stayed silent.

Satomi looked to Jill. She was tense in her chair, her knuckles turning white against the white arm rests. Her paling lips were tight with determination. She was refusing to show any weakness, and in turn, no humanity. Satomi's heart broke for her.

"I think I am," argued Audra. "I have what you need and I don't fancy giving it to you if you're going to use it to make more soldiers or start another epidemic. We need some accountability here. I won't blindly give this to you when I'm not even going to get Satomi back right away."

Audra was rambling. Why was she rambling?

"You'll get Satomi when the project is finished. This supply is just part of an ongoing trade we have with you," stated Jill.

"A trade? Kidnapping my friend is a trade?" Audra rounded.

The trio argued. Why wouldn't they just tell Audra what they were doing here? Why this act? The car caught her eye. Was that an act? Satomi wasn't sure what to do, but felt she might be the only one who could prevent this fight.

*　*　*

Audra didn't really care why they wanted the supply. She just needed to buy time.

Dwyn and his four-person team waited off the highway. Dwyn tried to ignore the burrs digging into his arms from their hiding place. He had sent Gordon to scout it out and he reported only five men guarding the half zom trailers. The others must be farther down the convoy or meeting with Audra.

"Glad you're here, Gordon," he thanked the man crouched by his side.

Gordon nodded. "I wish I felt as comfortable approaching my family as I do this army."

Dwyn gave a wry smile. Gordon had made it to the outpost and watched from the woods as his daughter played with her new father. He confided in Dwyn that it felt good to know they were safe, but wanted to wait out this last mission before claiming his own survival.

Dwyn understood. This could easily go south. He pulled a thorn from his elbow.

He could hear Branson and Tess whispering behind him. With Ryder out and Audra and Marcos providing distraction, they'd had to bring rookies out to help. But Dwyn felt they had more than proven themselves when they came out of their homes to fight the half zoms. This was just follow-through.

Behind them, Ziv stood, guarding the tanks they had brought. The green and silver metal cylinders had once carried precious oxygen. Now they carried precious antiviral and propellant. They only had exactly enough, which meant they were probably short, but no one could find another tank in time. Tanks were valuable from the start, and many that had been stolen from their clean environments now lay rusted.

"Tess, come with me. Gordon with Branson. Hit from behind. Disable. Gag. Ziv, stay and keep the tanks safe. Pull out your knife. Have it ready. Everyone got it?" repeated Dwyn.

"What if I need to...?" Branson trailed off.

"Then do, but quietly. I'd love to do this without death, but this has to be done. If they unleash infected on us, a lot more lives will be lost," answered Dwyn.

Dwyn continued with his instructions: "Tess and Branson will work together to secure the exterior air holes and open the doors. As they do that, Ziv will place an antiviral tank and release the gas."

No one acknowledged him, but it was the fourth time he had said it since they had left Osprey Point. Dwyn surveyed the scene ahead of them and held back from repeating himself one more time.

Wooden bat in hand, Dwyn watched the guard turn the corner of the plexiglass trailer, then sprinted after the man with light steps. The flattened weeds from previous traffic presented little noise; so did the asphalt that crumbled to meet the weeds. Dwyn came up from behind and with a hollow pop, the man crumpled.

The half zoms within the cages watched passively. Did they understand what was happening? Dwyn moved to find his next target as Tess bound and gagged the first. He crouched down to check for feet. Far off, he could see two sets dragging a third. Gordon and Branson. He tried not to think about what they'd do next. What he might have to do next. He focused on the next set of feet.

Shit, they were coming toward him.

He rolled underneath the eighteen-wheeler, but it wasn't much cover. He pulled closer to the shadow. Better, but now he had no access to the man who after passing him would be catching up to Tess, or at least the secured guard. Their cover would be blown.

"Psst."

Dwyn turned his head to the other side of the truck and saw Tess, her blond ponytail swinging down, obscuring her face. She reached out for the bat and Dwyn gladly gave it to her. When the guard passed, Dwyn pulled himself out from under the trailer as quietly as he could.

Not quietly enough.

Dwyn watched the guard's head swivel to look at him, then his eyes went glassy and rolled as a bat plowed into the crown of his head with a sickening crack. The man fell to reveal a sheet-white Tess. Her eyes wide as dinner plates. Dwyn remembered his first kill. He pried the bat from her hands and pulled her into a hug, like Audra had done for him.

"We're doing this to protect our community," he reminded her. Dwyn noticed she had a swath of gray that barely stood out against her white-blond hair.

"Yes," she whispered as she shook her eyes away from the scene she had created. She looked at Dwyn with searching eyes. He hoped she was recalling her children whom she was keeping safe.

"I'll tie him up," Dwyn said gently pulling away, not wanting her to wonder if restraints were needed.

Gordon and Branson ran up to them.

"We got three," Gordon said in hoarse whispers.

They looked down at the mess.

"But not as good as you did," remarked Branson, his blue eyes twinkling.

"Hush," said Dwyn, cutting him off.

They worked together to block the air holes of the trailers with rags. Tess worked on her belly on top of the trailers to do the top rows. Rag after rag. Pop, pop, pop. It would be Ziv's turn soon. The men inside the plastic boxes did not seem to anticipate any sort of death or emancipation. They stood, all but lifeless, with deadened gray eyes. Their breaths suspensefully slow.

Dwyn looked back and forth, waiting for their enemy to appear and for hell to break loose. What if the meeting broke down and all the men were dismissed? Their team needed to work faster. Pop, pop, pop. He signaled to Ziv. He could start on the first.

Ziv came out carrying two of the refitted oxygen tanks. Branson and Gordon opened the back of the trailer and Dwyn climbed inside, pulling a tank with him. It made a scraping noise. Ziv grimaced and lifted it up higher with regret. He positioned it in the center of the trailer, fully opened the valve, and jumped out. Gordon and Branson closed the doors tight.

One down.
Four to go.

"Look, I didn't calculate for escaped air and the absorption of the rags," began Ziv's usual disclaimers. "I calculated based on complete air blockage from the exterior holes."

Dwyn nodded. It wasn't really time for such discussions.

16 Tanks

Ziv shook his head. An absentminded nod wasn't really what he wanted from Dwyn. He wanted him to realize that applying science to real-life scenarios was tricky and at the end of the day, involved some guessing. What if he had guessed wrong? You have to make assumptions and simplifications. There's a lot to get wrong.

Ziv took a deep breath. He didn't have to cure them all in one go. Any measurable blow would be helpful. He was confident he'd at least get most of them - the ones closest to the pressurized tank. 'Most' was just fine to cripple their army. It didn't have to be perfect.

Perfection was not needed in this instance.

He pulled himself up into the trailer. He didn't realize how tall they'd be, but no one else was asking for help climbing up and down. Tess was on the roof for Pete's sake. He scrambled in, surrounded by strong, ghostly men and women. The transparent walls made him feel surrounded and claustrophobic, even though he knew he was safe. The zoms passed their eyes over him, hardly interested. He set the tank in the center of the trailer. They would be awakened shortly. He twisted the orange plastic valve as wide as it would go and sprinted out as the tank wobbled with the propellant it was not meant to hold. He sprinted then turned around to gingerly climb out. Branson and Dwyn managed to swing the doors fast but then slow them just before they slammed, to keep their actions as quiet as possible.

Three to go.

Branson helped Tess with the last of the rags as Ziv ran back into the woods to grab more tanks. Dwyn followed. He quickly ran past Ziv and grabbed the two, leaving one for Ziv. Ziv's breathing was ragged. His chest burned. He kept telling himself that he'd work out - maybe go for a run with Audra or do push-ups with Gordon - so he'd be more equipped during these missions, but he never managed to bother. His mind was what was needed here. Strength belonged to others.

Great minds seemed to be important in this world, like Satomi's. Ziv wondered what Satomi needed the anchoring medium for as he slung the tank over his shoulder and headed back through the woods. It was obvious she was building a peptide, but what for? Ziv knew Satomi wouldn't create anything explicitly harmful, but she could be manipulated. If she was told it was for something good, she'd do it. She might not even think about how it could be used in a different manner.

He pulled out of his thoughts and looked around for the next trailer. Why couldn't he stay focused? He could never stay focused. Would he have survived if Jack and Jill had taken him instead? Would he stand and fight? The thoughts haunted him more than he cared to admit. He spotted Dwyn and Gordon and headed toward them.

Another deep breath to try to slow his heart. Lost focus was OK, he just needed to get this done. Perfection was not needed in this instance.

Third tank.
Two to go.

He was doing it. He was out here, helping to get Satomi back. He had feared so often that he'd get here and chicken out. Perfection of willpower was needed in this instance. He felt pulled by all these zoms. He was curing them. He watched them stagger inside their cubicles as the antiviral reached them. They were inhaling their freedom. He did that. Maybe he could be all that Vesna had said.

Fourth tank.
One to go.

Dwyn handed him the last tank, and he and Tess opened the trailer. Ziv climbed in, adjusted the valve and made his way out. He looked to his left and right at the zoms he'd be curing. They weren't looking at him. Their eyes focused behind him. Why?

A force smashed into him, throwing his body and momentum out of the truck. They both dove into the ground. Ziv ate dirt and saw out of the corner of his eye that Dwyn and Tess had abandoned the doors to help.

"NO! Close the trailer doors!" he yelled out.

He didn't want the cure to dissipate. He wanted to make sure the last twenty percent of the army was decimated. He tried to roll over, but a large body was on top of him. He sucked in air and dust as a fist pounded into his back.

Ziv clawed at the asphalt, his nails ripping. He slipped out from under the man's weight and rolled. Ziv noticed the knife flashed in the light despite its lack of sheen. It was an odd thing to consider. He raised his arms in defense. His attacker must have been in there the whole time, had seen the holes getting plugged in. Maybe heard a guard go down. He'd been standing in there with the zoms, waiting for his chance. Well, he got it, thought Ziv.

Dwyn and Tess struggled to regain their handle on the doors and get them closed. Ziv heard their slams. They'd done it. He'd done it. Tess held them shut as Dwyn came to his rescue. Ziv hadn't thought to pull out his knife. To him it was a tool, not a weapon. Hadn't Dwyn told him to pull out his knife? The man on top of him had wide eyes and a snarl. Drool fell from the corner of his lips. Ziv yelled out again.

The others - Audra and the others - would hear. It didn't matter now. Their army had been crushed. Just - had she gotten Satomi yet? He wished he knew as the knife found something soft of his. He felt Dwyn arrive, but he also knew it was too late. He felt gutted. But he had accomplished his and Vesna's dream. He'd made it happen.

*　　*　　*

Audra heard a yell, but before she could come to any conclusions, it was closely followed by Dwyn's high-pitched bird call. They had succeeded, somehow, someway. Jack and Jill had heard the yell too and waited for Audra to give them a hint. Now they just had to wait for - BOOM!

That had done it.

"What was that?!" cried out Jill, jumping from her seat, the lawn chair flying back and slamming against the aluminum RV.

"It wasn't us," said Audra honestly, shrugging her shoulders. It was Lysent.

Audra pulled her knife out all the same. She didn't raise it yet. Jack pulled a radio from his belt and asked for a status update.

Nothing.

That was us.

He motioned his men to go check on the armies. "Prepare them."

The man beside Satomi remained. Three against two now. They stared each other down, waiting to learn who had the advantage.

The radio crackled.

We have a situation here.

"What have you done!" Jill screamed out.

She charged at Audra, her ax in hand, her eyes afire and her mouth contorted with fierce anger. Satomi flung herself in between Jill and Audra, arms waving. Jill's momentum brought her and Satomi onto the asphalt. Ashes kicked up in the frenzied attack. Audra wasn't sure how to interfere.

"NOT NOW JILL!" yelled Jack, jumping up.

The pot-bellied man who stood with Satomi launched. Audra was sure it was to assist Jill, but instead his large hands pulled Satomi out of the fray. Satomi went stumbling out.

"You traitor!" screamed Jill as her wedged blade found his leg - high. He doubled over and Satomi scrambled to reach him. She lost her hands in the long, deep gash, but he had already bled out. Jack pulled Jill away.

"God, Jill, this was supposed to be for show," he shouted as he frantically tried to keep hold of her fighting armored body.

She roared again, but retreated. They both fell back to their trailers of armies, leaving Marcos and Audra with Satomi. Audra reached for Satomi, who sobbed over the dead man. Satomi wrenched away.

"What have you done?" Satomi yelled out.

"We have to go," said Audra calmly, even though her body was shaking and all she could hear was blood throbbing in her ears.

"You can't take me," Satomi said resignedly, still clutching the man. "Their army."

"No army," said Audra without explanation. "Do they have a way to make more? Where do they make those things?"

"My lab's over there, but we aren't infecting people. I don't understand. I thought you had a deal... " She had sat up, but still whimpered.

"I do. Just not with who you think. This whole place is coming down."

She gave Marcos a nod and he ran over to the trailer Satomi had pointed to. Looking inside, he gave another nod confirming its contents. He unstopped and lit a couple Molotovs before throwing them in.

"Noo," cried out Satomi, rushing forward. Audra grabbed her. Satomi was slick with blood and tears. Her arms flailed as she tried to gain traction and reach the trailer.

"Greenly's scientists won't have anything," explained Audra.

"Greenly?" Another large explosion at the front of the convoy sounded. Satomi's body went still. "You went to Greenly?"

"I told them there was an army on the road. I figured they wouldn't care for the threat. I'm taking care of things, like I promised. Now come with me. We have to go."

"To hell I'm coming with you! God, I have to go save Peter."

Satomi ripped herself away from Audra. Audra couldn't grab hold again of her slim limbs. Satomi took off down the road, heading toward Greenly's people. Audra gave one last look at the laboratory to make sure it was burning, then chased after her rescue. She had never imagined Satomi would be so uncooperative. Who was Peter? She had no option but to follow the dark-haired woman, who was making distance, fast.

Audra passed burning vans, the work of Greenly's men after they decided they had no use for them. She was glad Marcos had burned the laboratory. They would have spared that one. Audra turned to look behind her to see Marcos trying to keep up. Audra looked down to see familiar dark curly hair and the young man zombied and dead on the ground.

Dennis.

Satomi didn't notice. She sprinted until she skidded to a stop in front of a strange stoop attached to a trailer.

"Don't hurt him!" she warned as she knocked on the door. "He's innocent."

'Innocent' was a funny word. Was Dennis innocent? She didn't know.

There was muffled shuffling heard inside. Audra put her hand on her dagger despite Satomi's warning. Slowly the door opened and an older man poked his head out.

"Time for tea?" he asked.

"No, Peter. I need you to come with me," said Satomi, holding out her hand.

Peter looked around. The commotion was farther up the road but here it was quiet. He seemed to be left on his own.

"Peter, please?" she asked again.

He looked confused, but he put his hand in hers.

"Where are we going?"

"We're going into the woods to gather dandelion for the tea," Satomi offered.

His face perked up at her suggestion. Who the hell?

Audra shook her head and muttered, "We can't take him. Too slow."

Satomi wheeled around, his hand still in hers. "You might be bent on destruction, but I'm not. Do what you need to do. I'll take Peter home myself."

Audra glared at the person she had done all this for. Satomi seemed to have no appreciation for their current condition. The place was burning down around them.

"Get away from him!" someone shouted behind them.

Damn.

Jack. Peter let go of Satomi's hand and scrambled down the stoop, pushing both women out of the way.

"Thank God you're OK," said Jack, crying.

"Where's your sister?" asked Peter, comforting the younger man.

"I'm, I'm not sure. We got separated. There was an explosion..." Jack shook. They didn't let go of each other.

Maybe Satomi would be OK to leave this Peter with Jack. "Look we need to go," encouraged Audra.

The squealing of tires and a merciless laugh filled the air as a jeep came barreling down the road. They were too late. Audra and Jack steered Satomi and Peter off the road and toward the woods. Jack and Marcos started to follow, but noticed Audra wasn't leaving. Audra couldn't stand to let Greenly see her run.

She was surprised Greenly had left the safety of her fences.

"Audra. Pleasure seeing you here." Her eyes gleamed.

She stood up on the platform on the back of the jeep, one of her feet raised on something. Her guards stood near her. Two more men came around the jeep and lowered the tailgate.

There lay a body with a blond braid, Greenly's foot firmly on her head.

Jack cried out before falling to his knees. "No, no, no..." he pleaded.

"Glad we could work together," Greenly continued.

Jack was not too stricken to hear the words. He looked to Audra. "You brought this on us?"

Audra blinked. She had brought all of this down on all of them. How else would she keep her family alive? Smoke and the smell of fuel wrapped around the highway.

"Don't worry," comforted Greenly. "She's not working with you, or me. This girl murdered her own sister to get out of some debts. She's out just for herself."

She turned to Audra with a new nastiness. "I know you're destroying what we're trying to create."

"A world under your thumb?" she retorted. She glanced behind her to see if anyone was approaching from behind. Fighting could be heard off in the distance.

Greenly and her crow's feet smiled. "A stable world. Where no one is hungry. Where no one is threatened by others, sick or otherwise."

"They aren't threats. They're people. We work together, eat together, and fight together. We don't hide behind our corporate walls and milk the people."

"Sure, you just kill them instead," she referenced her lost corral. "I'm afraid you won't be doing much of anything anymore, either. You're wanted for breach of contract and crimes against Lysent. You'll be tried and punished," said Greenly.

They should have been long gone. Greenly's men encompassed them. Audra noticed Manny and Blue in the group. Manny winked at her. He licked his lips and left spittle on his mustache.

"Let them go," said Jack. "I own this army and I'll give them to you in return for us here."

"I'm sorry. I believe your army is already mine. I took out your sister. I can take out others," said Greenly dismissively.

Tears streamed down Jack's face.

"I'll tell my men to stand down. You'll lose no one else. Please just let me take them." His voice cracked.

"An army for you five?" Greenly nodded her casual agreement.

Jack immediately stuck his fingers into his mouth and gave a shrill whistle. The commotion died down as the men surrendered.

"Leave," she commanded.

Jack, Marcos, and Audra walked into the woods to meet Satomi and Peter. Audra kept her hand on her dagger. Had Jack sacrificed his entire community just to kill Audra with his bare hands? It didn't matter much. It was important to leave before Greenly realized how nearly worthless her spoils were.

"I'm not going to hurt you," he said before they got within earshot of the others.

"Why not?"

Tears streamed, kept streaming. He had lost his sister. The place he had called home.

"I'm not like that. We were never like that," he said simply. Audra was surprised that her heart believed him.

17 Outbreak

The sun hung high in the cloudless sky, but the tall pine trees provided cover. Spots of scattered light fell on the ground as they made their trek to Osprey Point. Audra's concern about Peter's speed was unfounded. Both Jack and Peter were strong hikers. They marched along without complaint.

"You didn't have to surrender for us," ventured Audra as she rounded her way around a rock outcropping. She'd have found a way out. It did seem like a peace offering, but Audra wondered why he wasn't more dedicated to his uninfected men.

"We had already lost. Whoever that lady was - she had our army. I just wanted to walk away with my dad. I'm sorry we ever picked this fight."

"That lady's Greenly and she doesn't have your army," shared Audra. "We cured them."

Jack didn't look to her. Instead he laughed and shook his head.

"What?" asked Audra.

"When we figured out the cure wasn't permanent, we decided to go a different route. That's how the soldier serum and the byproducts came about."

"Dr. Bren-?" said Peter, stopping. Satomi gently nudged him along. He didn't finish his question. Jack helped his father navigate the rocky terrain.

Jack continued, "The cure especially doesn't work on the soldiers. They'll be back to themselves in two days tops. That Greenly will figure it out. You handed her an army."

"The notes were true?" asked Satomi, looking to Jack as she put a supporting hand on Peter's shoulder to help him keep his balance.

"What notes?" asked Audra.

"Dr. Bren's notes," she said as if that explained things. "At first I thought your soldier serum was a detour in your attempts to cure people, but I realized you already had a cure."

"That's right. We had an antidote to the z-virus immediately. Things weren't too bad, but when people eventually reverted, all hell broke loose. That's when Dr. Bren created the soldiers to protect us."

"But their cure is different," stated Audra, attempting to understand.

"Formula-wise, they're the same," said Satomi. "Lysent stockpiles."

Jack helped his father over a large fallen log. "That thing we asked for - Satomi said she could help our father with it. I'm sorry we put on such a show. Jill's idea, but I followed along. It seemed the safest. I didn't think..."

Audra thought on Satomi's pleas to work with Jack and Jill. She thought of a family, not unlike her own, that did whatever they could to survive and protect themselves. Had she built up her real enemy at this family's expense?

*   *   *

They heard the shouts before they had even reached the fences of Osprey Point. Fear flashed in Audra's heart. She took off in a sprint down the gravelly road.

"What is happening here?!" Audra shouted as she waved to them to open the gates and to allow the others behind her to come in as well.

"An outbreak!" shouted the woman above.

An outbreak? How?

"Where is he? In the lab?"

"You mean 'they'. They're in the mess hall," the guard shouted at her back. Audra stopped to turn to see if she was serious. Her stomach sank. How did it get into the mess hall? That didn't make any sense.

"Is Dwyn back?" she shouted up to them.

"No, you're the first ones back."

Her heart sank. Dwyn and the others should have been back by now. She felt a sudden urge to run out and find them. Her crew appeared through the gate, breathless with their run. It brought her back to reality. She needed to deal with this, here.

"Satomi, clear the lab lobby now," she ordered. Satomi nodded.

Audra hesitantly pulled out her dagger for what seemed the hundredth time today. She couldn't help but look at the sun reaching its last arc - it was dinner time. The mess hall would be full. Jack came up beside her, his armor now looking much more appropriate. They stood on either side of the door.

"You don't have to," said Audra.

"I know."

With a nod, Audra opened the door wide enough to see inside. No one ran out. Were they all already...?

"Help!" someone called out. No. Some person was still in there.

Audra slipped through the door and entered with her back against the wall. Jack came up beside her and closed the door securely behind them. The tables and chairs had been turned and toppled over. Remnants of food joined blood splatter on the floor and walls. This couldn't be happening. Not here. Not now. Audra fought the urge to close her eyes and wish for a different world. She got a nudge from Jack. She took a deep breath.

Three, no, four zoms. Zoms. That's what they were. They weren't her friends, her new community. They were a threat. Two people cowered in the corner fending off one of the zoms with a chair. A second zom careened toward them. Another pair clawed at the kitchen door.

"I'll take the four." She motioned to the kitchen door. "That leads to the kitchen. I bet everyone is in there. Come out with me then slip back in. Subdue or kill any threat in there."

"I'll try to capture them."

"Thank you," Audra whispered, steeling herself to be bait and to encourage a chase.

"HEY Zs! Here Zs!" she yelled out, clapping her hands. The zom reaching for the two men behind the chair paid her no mind. This emboldened her. She picked up a leg of a broken white pine chair, jumped over a long thin table, and jabbed it into the zom's ribs. Blond hair whipped around. The face looked ragged with emotion and hunger.

Lisa.

Shit. Audra had stumbled upon her the day they cured Gordon. She was one of their first outside cures and she still reminded her of her sister. Audra took care not to slip on the red sauce or blood. She ignored the two's fearful faces as she drew Lisa toward her.

She shifted and found the wall opposite her exit, two clambering for her now. They tripped over chairs and dived after smacking into a table. She followed the wall until she reached the kitchen door with two zoms beating and scratching at the space where their prey had disappeared. How had they transitioned so quickly?

She swung and hit shoulders. They turned their heads at crooked angles in twin-like unison, veins spread from their cold eyes. Grayness tinged their skin except for the bright red spots on a forearm and a shoulder - a declaration of what had taken them over. Audra sighed relief at the sight of their clean mouths. Maybe this would be it.

Yells from the kitchen.

"Hush!" Audra called out. "I'm trying to lead them away!"

"It's Audra," she heard in hushed voices. "Oh thank heavens, it's Audra. It's going to be OK..."

Audra pulled away to let the twins join her other two. She now had her small herd.

"That's impressive," said Jack from the door.

"Clear out the plaza," she instructed him. It was a dumb and dangerous idea to lead a herd into the open air of their community, but she didn't want her community to think that if they got bit again, she'd just sink a dagger into their brains. They were over that, weren't they?

The command was unnecessary. The plaza was already empty. She appreciated everyone tucked away with their doors shut. This could be the end of the outbreak here. Jack waited on the wayside to reenter. The guards watched from above, no longer looking to the outside but to the creeping threat inside, the safety of the complex imploding. Audra saw the door to the lab lobby stood open. And she began to head that way.

Maybe their transition wasn't complete, but still the zoms' open mouths seemed unnaturally long, as if they could unhinge and swallow her whole. Saliva fell from their chins. Behind them, Jack slipped back into the mess hall to help those previously trapped in the kitchen.

"Oh my god!" cried someone from Audra's left. Shit. "Is that-?"

"Back inside and be quiet!" Audra shouted as her zoms found new trajectories.

The person scrambled to get back inside, but someone held the door shut on him, apparently having seen what lay outside.

"Holy hell! Let me in!" he cried. The door slammed open and shut in its frame, causing a racket. Audra raced to the four. They were no longer interested in her, no matter how loudly she yelled. She threw her baton at one of their heads; it did nothing but push them forward.

"Run to another door!" Audra called out. He turned at the command. Seeing the four scrambling toward him, he braced himself against the door and yelled out. His mouth and eyes were wide with fear.

"GO NOW!" barked Audra as she sprinted to get between them. The boy finally came to his senses and ran off toward another building. Feet kicking high. Audra scooted right behind him to create a visually large moving mass. Someone opened the door in the next building to receive them. He jumped onto the concrete stoop and raced inside.

"Not me," called out Audra as the boy's heels disappeared into the building.

Audra confirmed the door closed with a dry click before she trotted past it. Now they were back on her. Audra pulled away from the buildings and did a wide circle back to the lobby. The mess hall's door was closed, but people watched from the windows. Jack had pulled them out of the kitchen.

Audra ran straight through the front lobby of the lab, not stopping to admire the outdated panel wood walls. Satomi shut the door behind her as she scooted into the laboratory's main area. Audra sprinted through and out the back door to round the building. All four were in the lobby, scraping on the interior door.

Audra closed the exterior door and slid down against it. Her hand arrived at her brow to wipe the stinging salt from her eyes, but she found it covered in someone's blood. Down her arm was just as messy. She didn't get to clean up or rest. Satomi came around and gave her a hand up. She had tears in her eyes, but that wasn't surprising. She watched Satomi leave for the medical office to go see Ryder. For Audra, it was time to find out about the kitchen. Was anyone else bitten?

*   *   *

"Satomi, clear the lab lobby now!" Audra yelled to her as she and Jack ran off to the mess hall. Marcos climbed up to speak with the guards. Peter stood with her, dumbfounded. She felt the same.

Infected in the mess hall? The thought filled her with fear. She had done so much to take precautions. What had happened here?

Satomi nodded but she wasn't sure that Audra saw. They used to keep infected in the lobby before they established the medical office. The medical office - Satomi's mind flashed to Ryder, who would be in there, just a building away. She yearned to see her, just a glimpse of her form to make sure she was all right - that she was real. Both her time at Osprey Point and at Jack's and Jill's convoy seemed to blur. Which was her life? Satomi shook her head clear. There were higher priority tasks right now. And Peter was one of them.

She ushered Peter through the plaza. He stopped at the fountain.

"Why isn't it on?"

"Um, we turned it off in preparation for winter," she said to give him a simple answer.

He looked up to the sky as if he expected snow to fall. She nudged him along and he mumbled as he followed. They walked past the medical office and Satomi tried to steal a glance through the window, but they had been covered for privacy. Her idea.

Behind the medical office was a converted office for sleeping quarters. She opened the door and found no one in the front area. Here, Peter could be safe while she helped the others.

"Peter, please, I need you to go in here for just a moment."

Peter seemed to finally notice the doorway. He stopped in his tracks and stared in horror.

"I don't want to go in there," Peter refused. "I want to go home."

"Just for a moment," she pleaded. She needed to clear the lab lobby.

"You can't make me! I'M NOT A PRISONER!" he shouted. His eyes flew open.

"You're right. You're not a prisoner. This is Osprey Point. It's your new home but I need you to stay here until I come and get you. Is that OK?"

"It's not OK!" he shouted. He seemed really disturbed. He moved to step away. Satomi wasn't sure what to do. Burning car tires uselessly came to mind.

"I'm a prisoner!" he yelled.

"Why do you think that?" she asked in a quiet voice, hoping to reason with him.

"Because I did awful things," he replied, his voice lowering to match hers. Satomi went to put her hand on his arm. He pulled away and shrank into himself.

"No, you didn't. You're a good man, Peter," she cajoled.

"No, I'm not. I experimented!" He looked wildly around, not finding comfort from his strange environment.

"Experimented?" Was he gleaning new vocabulary and delusions from Satomi's chatter? She'd have to watch what she said around him from now on. She had frightened him. He started crying.

"You're going to experiment on me!"

"I'm not." She lied, a little. His treatment would be experimental, but she wasn't doing that right now. Right now, she just needed him safe.

"You're going to experiment on me like I did on the others."

"...the others?" she hesitated.

"Super Soldiers! We were going to make people better. It had to be done, right? The virus didn't have to be bad." Peter shook his head. His white hair danced on his head.

Satomi had never heard Peter say anything about the virus before. What did he know?

"I was going to be a hero. Make people better."

"How?" Satomi dared to ask. The hairs on her arms prickled.

"My serums! I made soldiers. My next round of experiments didn't go well... made me sick."

Satomi froze. This wasn't early-onset dementia or Alzheimer's disease? This was... self-inflicted? She tried her old test, but this time added another trigger.

"I'm Dr. Satomi Asai. Pleasure to meet you, Doctor...?"

He shook his head to clear it.

"Dr. Peter Bren," he said as he offered his hand.

That woman in the car wasn't Dr. Bren. He was.

She had risked her friends' lives to save the originator of the soldier serum.

And now, he was stopping her from helping. Tears slipped down her cheeks and the top of her head burned. Satomi pushed him into the building a little rougher than she intended. He fell to the ground. He glared at her betrayal. It didn't matter; she had friends to help. She slammed the door before he could get up.

"I'm sorry!" she said. She wasn't sure who that was directed towards, but she was.

*　*　*

Audra knocked on the mess hall door. It opened without ceremony with Jack just inside the entrance.

"Good running," he told her. Audra nodded and looked around. Twelve people inside. Some sat shaking on chairs, some busied themselves by cleaning up, others helped those who might be in shock.

"Are they OK?" asked a girl.

The zoms were still family.

Audra smiled a small smile. "They're fine. They're in the lobby of the laboratory. The scientists will prepare antidotes immediately. But first, I need to know what happened here."

"It was my girlfriend, Lisa," said a woman being comforted on a chair. Her shaking slowed as she spoke.

"When did she get bit?" asked Audra, kneeling down beside her. Although she imagined that her battle-torn look was not comforting.

"She... didn't."

The woman supporting her tapped her on the shoulder. "You don't get to say that. Now she got bit somewhere. Did you guys go out? Maybe to get some privacy?"

"No. That's what I'm telling you. We've been inside the fences. We've been together. Like hip to hip for the last three days. She wasn't bit."

"Then what happened?" Audra asked gently.

"She was just sick. Had a cold or something. I thought it was the season change. I offered to bring her food from the mess hall, but she said it'd help to move around." She pulled her arms around herself as if she was cold.

"What were her symptoms?"

"Fever. Chills. I'm sorry, I know she shouldn't have gone into the mess hall. She could have given everyone the flu."

"It wasn't the flu," corrected the woman at her shoulder.

"I know that now," she said flatly.

"It's OK. We'll get to the bottom of it. She was bit somewhere, somehow," encouraged Audra.

"Maybe she sneaked off," the standing woman offered.

That made the girl whimper and start shaking again.

The door swung open and Peter raced inside. His face opened with terror as he searched the faces in the room. He found the one he knew. Jack's.

"It's OK, Dad. It's OK," Jack comforted him.

Peter buried his face in his son's chest and cried. Jack held him fiercely. Audra felt a weird twinge for this broken family. They still had someone flesh and blood to hug and to hold. Audra would give anything for that. To belong. She understood why they had gone to such great lengths to stay together. Wouldn't she - hadn't she - done the same?

As the people in the mess hall quietly dispersed, a head of brown curls peeked through the doorway.

Dwyn.

She ran into his arms. They radiated warmth and safety through her body. She deposited her face into his neck and musk.

"What took you so long?" she murmured.

Maybe she did have a family. He felt like home.

"I... I had to carry Ziv's body back."

Ziv's body?

Audra pulled back and saw the tears filling Dwyn's perfect green eyes. He rubbed the back of his neck with his hand, staring down at his feet.

"I sent him in there..." said Audra. She felt her tears come on too.

Dwyn met her eyes. "No. He volunteered. Developed the mass cure and died making sure his plan succeeded."

The mass cure - which Jack said wouldn't even work. Jack. Jack's crew had done this. She turned in Dwyn's arms to reconcile what she knew about Jack. He had driven a half zom army, kidnapped Satomi. He had also stopped his sister, loved his father, and helped her twice today.

"I'm sorry about Ziv," said Jack. "I understand if you need me to leave, but I'd like to trade for some of Satomi's expertise if she's willing."

"I can't think about that now," said Audra in a short tone. "We have an incident to investigate and zoms to treat." She dismissed it for now.

"Investigate? What is there to investigate?" asked Dwyn.

"I don't know how she got infected. We need to find her bite and figure out what happened."

"She was infected before, right?" asked Jack.

"Yes, but that was a long time ago. We cured her."

"You cured her for a while, yes. She probably reverted."

Audra remembered what Jack and Satomi had discussed in the woods. Was it true?

"The cure... it doesn't work all the time," repeated Jack. "We thought it did at first, but it got slowly bad. People we've cured have gotten sick again. We haven't been able to permanently cure a soldier ever. Dr. Bren told us the virus either mutated or the cure was never perfect to begin with."

"We'll see. She probably wandered off," Audra borrowed from the unhelpful friend. "She'll have a bite."

18 Patient Zero

With the infected safely secured inside the front lobby and Audra safe, Satomi made a beeline to the medical office to see Ryder. She'd better be still in the medical ward. No way should she be discharged already. It had only been a week - or more? Satomi couldn't recall.

She needed to hug her friend and cry on her shoulder. Her failure was sinking in. She hadn't saved a family torn apart by illness. They had created it. She had tried to do no harm, but she had. The universe was much more complicated than she had given credit. Now she just needed something she knew was solid.

She opened the door to the office and could already hear odd sounds. Was Ryder in pain? She sprinted into the doorway, before staggering back. The soldier Satomi had treated with leg splints had been moved from the laboratory. But no one was here to watch him.

He had been restrained, but one hand was bloodied, broken, and free. His shoulder contorted with dislocation as he had pulled himself off the bed. He had torn down the partition and reached toward the next bed, where a figure shaped like Ryder was snoozing under the covers. Her back turned.

Satomi saw red. This thing was after her love. He would get to her and soon. Satomi raced to the counter across from the beds and ripped open a drawer to find her tool. A yell escaped her lips as she drove her scalpel into his craniocervical junction. He had no idea she was in the room before he was gone. His body crumpled.

Both of them slumped on the ground. Satomi's chest heaved high and low. She couldn't get air. The panic of everything hit her. Her home - Osprey Point - had been attacked. She had been kidnapped and forced to work for her captors. She'd slept in a crappy car and feared for her life. Her best friend had been inches from death.

She looked ahead at her medical supplies. They grounded her, reminded her that she was on the verge of hyperventilating. She slowed her breathing and tried to gain control.

First, do no harm.

She had broken her promise. She looked over to Ryder, who still slept. They must still be giving her narcotics. As she gazed on her friend, a sudden calmness overtook her. She was worth a promise broken. Satomi let the scalpel clatter to the ground beside her. Maybe the oath only applied to the world before. She went to her friend and gently hugged her awake.

She'd settle for doing what was right.

*　　*　　*

"I know this isn't the best time, but... this is important," Satomi heard Audra say as Satomi entered the back way into the lab. The stark white walls, small windows, and messy counters filled her sights and her heart. Oh, how she missed this place. Sure, the equipment was ancient, rusting, and cracked, but at least the building wasn't on wheels.

"Funny," Satomi interrupted. "I was going to say the same thing."

The occupants of the lab, Audra, Dwyn, and Gordon turned to look at her. They were dirty with battle and the blood of their enemies. So was Satomi.

"Oh my God. Is that blood?" Audra rushed over. She pulled Satomi onto a stool and began examining the doctor for wounds.

Satomi shivered. Gordon brought her a heavy blanket as she explained what had happened. He leaned up against the counter near her. Dwyn sat on the counter, kicking and dangling his feet, without much concern for the fragility of the equipment around him.

"Are you sure he's dead?" asked Audra. Yes, she was sure.

"Why was he moved anyway?" Satomi asked.

"Uh, because Ziv had cured him," said Gordon with a numbed tone.

A heavy silence filled the room at the mention of Ziv's name.

"So, all the soldiers?" Dwyn asked. He had stopped kicking.

Audra did not address Dwyn, but instead she turned to Satomi. "I need you to check our patient zero. We need to find out how she got sick again."

Satomi remembered Dr. Bren's notes. She nodded slowly, letting the scratchy blanket fall to the floor.

"What do you mean?" asked Gordon.

Audra stumbled, "Just check the body. Find the bite," she directed him.

Gordon nodded and cleared an area to receive their subject.

"Which one is patient zero?" asked Satomi.

"Lisa."

Dwyn left to dispose of the body in the medical ward. In just a few minutes, Audra and Gordon had bound Lisa and eased her onto the cleared laminate counter. Lisa writhed, arching and twisting her torso, and Satomi struggled to examine her. Her hands still shook with the adrenaline of before, but felt warmer with a medical duty to perform.

"We don't waste anesthetic on the dead," she whispered before she realized she was speaking. No one asked her what she meant, thankfully.

Satomi's gloved hands and observant eyes looked over all the likely spots, then the less likely spots, then the entirety of the body. Lisa's body was perfect; none of her skin was broken. A scar prickled at her ankle, a bodily reminder of her first bite, but otherwise Lisa's skin was flawless.

"There is no bite," Satomi reported.

"Maybe it healed?" asked Audra hopefully.

"Her first bite has healed. But I don't see anything else."

"What does that mean?" asked Gordon.

"Possibly she came in contact with infectious bodily fluids, blood, saliva, sexual fluids," said Satomi, not wanting to jump to conclusions, just because she had seen it written in a mad doctor's books.

"Or?" pushed Audra.

Lisa was just one case, Satomi told herself. And the soldier with the broken legs was given the antiviral via an experimental delivery system. He couldn't be counted.

"When was she cured?" Satomi asked.

"Near our start," replied Audra, looking down at the woman's large, foggy eyes and tangled hair.

Satomi looked down and saw the same. Of course, Lisa. Satomi wondered why she hadn't recognized her. Their faces seemed to distort in their sickness.

"It's possible," Satomi confessed. "I would think it would have happened a lot sooner, though. The virus could live in small dormant quantities. If something upended the chemistry of the brain or the virus found a way to adapt, then it could take back over." Dr. Bren had studied it for years and hadn't figured it out in his part of the country. Would she be able to figure it out?

Satomi continued, "I can test her viral load for any abnormalities. If it's mutated, we won't know if it's because she was exposed to a mutated virus or if it mutated within her – "

"Not now. It can wait," Audra interrupted. "We all need rest. You, especially."

Satomi didn't continue her ramble and didn't argue. She could barely keep upright over Lisa. Her body was shutting down. She watched Gordon and Audra move Lisa back to the lobby. Then Gordon escorted Satomi to her bed. Her real bed.

*   *   *

"Do you really think the cure isn't working?" asked Gordon quietly as he helped Audra return Lisa to the front room.

"I don't know," Audra replied, knowing she was speaking to someone who had been cured. Almost everyone here had been. Were they all at risk for reverting to their mindless, violent, shuffling selves? No, it couldn't be. The cure was permanent.

It had to be.

Otherwise, what were they fighting for? Audra couldn't imagine this hell without hope.

"You'll remain healthy for your girl. Don't worry," assured Audra.

19 Memorial

It wasn't long before Gordon and Satomi had news for Audra. After interviews, an investigation, and further testing, it was concluded that Lisa was only infected now because she had been previously infected. She had reverted somehow. Their first case of the antidote failing.

Audra stared at an empty beaker on the drying rack by the sink, as if it would give her the answers she needed.

"We need to let Greenly know," said Audra to no one really.

"Know what?" asked Gordon.

"About this isolated case. They can look out for their own potential issues. An outbreak in their townships could wipe us out."

Yelling in the plaza interrupted them.

The trio, almost forgetting to go the back way, walked out to see what the commotion was. They had postponed treating the group from the mess hall outbreak, much to the rest of the residents' disapproval.

A man lay on the fountain wall, his chest rising unusually tall. Audra knew him, a runner - a protege for sure. He had probably plowed through the plaza, almost being clipped by the gate. He stood up and wobbled a little with the blood rush.

He still had a lot to learn.

"When they got them... They... They were healthy, but some were not," he started.

"The army?" Audra asked.

He nodded. His hands held his sides - either to keep his rib cage at bay or to tell his lungs that yes, indeed, he was trying to breathe.

He tried again, "Over the next few days, they went back to being brainwashed soldiers. All of them. She has all of them." He gasped and tilted forward on his hips.

Audra took a hand and pulled his chest upright.

"You'll get more air this way if you aren't nauseous," she recommended as she fought her own nausea. Greenly with a half zom army made her stomach churn.

As if corporate power was not enough, Greenly had now been delivered a formidable offense. Audra had all but giftwrapped them. She felt herself turn green. What had she created? What would they face now?

"You wanted to talk to Greenly?" said the skeptical voice of Gordon.

Audra nodded dumbly.

"How are you going to get close with her new army?" he asked.

Good question.

She didn't have an answer for that - or any of it, for that matter.

*　　*　　*

In all the chaos, Dwyn and Gordon had buried Ziv. Audra had made trips to the river for large, smooth, speckled stones to stack and mark his grave. Their community, still in shock with the news of the reversion and never having enjoyed Ziv's brusque personality, had paid little attention. His heroic feat to save them all had been relegated to a futile effort. Another failure on their list.

Audra became familiar with the experience. The people of Osprey Point had liked the idea of her out in the woods, bringing people in - most people owed their lives to her - but this past week had shown them she was no hero. She had possibly wakened them, just for them to fall back into madness and pain.

They gathered at his grave to pay their respects. Satomi kept her arm around Ryder, who used a crutch to hold herself steady due to her injury or Satomi's tight connection, Audra wasn't sure. Gordon and Dwyn stood nearby. Audra looked down to Ziv. He was where he'd want to be. Right next to Vesna.

"When I first met you all, I didn't understand why Ziv was out here," started Audra. "He didn't seem to want to be out here, and he didn't have any qualms about letting us know."

Some giggles in the tiny audience. Then, a sniffle.

"But the thing about doing the right thing - is that you don't have to do it enthusiastically. You just have to do it. And when forced into situations, Ziv did the right thing.

"Ziv was loyal. He held onto Vesna's ideals and friendship long after she passed. He died making Vesna's plan to aerosolize the antidote finally a reality.

"Though they reverted, it gave us the time we needed to save Satomi. He did that. Sometimes it might feel like all we do is for naught. That's how this world is now. Most of what we do, try to do, see done - is futile. But it's still important to do.

"When Ziv stood here as we watched over and spoke over Vesna's memorial, he said that he wanted to be strong. He wanted to be here for us. And he was. And that says a lot about a person. A promise of change kept.

"He did both no harm and harm when needed. Rather than doggedly stick to old principles, he assessed and did what was correct. We can only hope to perform such a task as we go on about our days with both these two showing us the way. They've died to make sure that we're OK in the end. And we will be OK in the end, because of them."

Dwyn went to hug her and to hold her. And despite being in sight of everyone in their group, Audra let him. She let him wrap his arms around her, because they felt good. Because if it was all for nothing, then what did it matter? They could only do the good and right things.

"Thank you," he whispered into her hair.

"For what?"

"For sharing what we all needed to hear."

"It's what Ziv told us with his life," she said into his chest.

"But you gave it words."

Audra's tears flowed freely and did not stop for a while.

*　*　*

The salt dried on her neck and collarbone as Audra returned with the others. She walked past the mess hall again, diverting her eyes, not able to bring herself to enter - those men fending off Lisa with just a chair. It could happen again. When? Weeks from now? Days?

Audra looked back at the gate, which was now shut. But the forest beyond their chain-link fences called to her. Maybe she'd go back out. Lose herself in the fall leaves. Before she could decide, her escape was thwarted.

"Hi Jack."

He and his father were allowed temporary heavily-guarded stay while Audra decided what to do with them.

"It's Peter. Peter Bren, Jr." He offered his hand. Audra lifted her hand to meet it. "I assume Satomi explained who my father is."

"Yes, but why don't you tell me?" They sat down on the limestone wall. Audra stretched out her legs, crossing them at the ankle. She propped herself up with her hands.

Jack's - or Peter's - eyes went shiny. "Dad's a scientist. Worked for Lysent in D.C. He knew exactly what was going on when the outbreaks started, stockpiled the antiviral. We had it made, considering. Then, it stopped working, or never did work - I dunno. So Dad decided to modify it. He thought that if he turned the zombies into soldiers, we'd be better protected. He even tried to enhance us. He started with himself - you can see that didn't work out well."

Audra listened, staring at the little grasses cropping up around the cracked concrete. Her own memories were very different from the start, and yet, here they were.

Peter continued, "Dad was the scientist, but I was the builder. I built the moving convoy when Dad got sick. We figured we'd seek out other Lysent scientists. Maybe they could continue Dad's work. I guess we got out of hand. The names. Our stupid plastic thrones. The fighting. We just assumed everyone out here was bad, deserved it, I guess. Jill's idea to burn that zom. Figured they're incurable anyway and it'd scare Satomi." His voice honeyed as he talked about his sister.

"If you knew your army wouldn't really be cured, why'd you surrender?" asked Audra. It was something that had been bothering her.

"We were... unprepared for you. Greenly came too fast. It was over before I knew it. Evelyn was dead. I realized I just wanted my dad - as flawed as he is - as flawed as Evelyn was."

Evelyn was flawed. So was Audra. They'd both tried to rely on destruction, and look where it had gotten them. She thought of Satomi's mission statement, those Latin words that directed her path, and she thought of Ziv's reluctant but correct choices. She knew what to do.

"You can stay if you want. We don't have a lot of free space. Our enemy has a virtually unstoppable army. And we're an outbreak waiting to happen... but we can live together. Help each other."

"Thank you. I don't mind tight quarters. I can bunk with my dad."

Audra understood. If she had family left, she wouldn't let them out of her sight either.

"We'll ask Satomi if she'd like to help with your father," she said, standing up and stretching.

They both knew she would.

Audra brushed through the gate. She started with a slow jog to prevent any protesting muscles, and so that Osprey Point didn't think she was fleeing, even if that's how she felt. As soon as she was out of eyesight, she light-stepped into the woods. She preferred it over the road. You had to dodge and juke. You had to be clever with your steps, else get caught up or slip. Her cadence increased and her speed picked up. The lighter wisps of loose hair moved this way and that against her neck with her rhythm. It was a rhythm that made Audra feel in sync with both nature and herself. She felt more her, the farther she ran.

She would not get to run long. The sun danced around the trees at eye level, threatening to go under as Audra flirted with dusk. She looked up to see orange and red cresting the sky. What should have been a pleasant sunset seemed to be an omen of blood to come. It pushed her forward, faster and faster. She careened through the woods, jumping over logs, skidding in leaves, light branches scraping her face and chest. She'd continue. She'd keep going. Just as she was doing now.

Audra would have loved to run as far as she could in one direction, set up camp for the night, and be alone. She would have loved to gaze at the stars and watch the satellites fly by. She'd pretend she could be as distant as those satellites, so far away that she could only see peace. No warring factions, no wandering sick, no desolate cities serving as harsh growing grounds for the weeds. Instead, she'd see green, and blue, so much blue. Audra wondered what the ocean looked like now. She hadn't seen it since she was oh so very young. How blue was it? Had it changed now that man was basically gone? Would man eventually be gone?

Running until night overtook her was not a viable plan at the moment. They needed her to be present in Osprey Point. Audra reluctantly turned back around. She started toward her community, with all its flaws and with all the trouble they were in. She ran towards her home, whether she considered it that or not.

Home would have Belinda. It would have family.

Belinda, it had not. Family, possibly.

20 Lysent's Announcement

It turned out Audra didn't need to reach out to Lysent. As she and her small core group approached Lysent headquarters, an announcement was already in progress. They hung outside the fences, just within earshot, a place Audra was familiar with. Audra recalled Greenly's previous announcements - the cure, the tagging program, their stance on rebellion as they executed Vesna. Greenly's announcements always changed her life.

And this one wouldn't be any different.

Larange Greenly stood in front of the Lysent plaza. Her mahogany podium shined with polish. Audra tried to decipher what was different. Greenly was sandwiched between two guards, different from ones Audra had seen previously. And the protesters. They used to be a permanent fixture for these announcements and were nowhere to be found. Vesna's execution must have put an end to that.

"I have grave news today," Greenly's voice carried to them. They continued to hide in the brush. "You may be familiar with the group to the southeast of us. They are a small group who stole the antiviral from our trains, antiviral meant to go to one of you. You may have heard that they are curing people without regard to financial status, which I'm sure will hurt them come winter time when they find themselves stretched too thin.

I have done my best to protect you from them. One of their leaders had to be executed on this very stage."

Audra felt the heat rise to her face. Her blood was boiling. How dare Greenly talk about Vesna up there as if any of that was a favor to anyone.

"Unfortunately, their experiments have not ended there. They have stolen other things from us, performed genetic therapies that typically would have been vetted by a review board in times before the infection. Without that oversight, without our oversight, they have done reckless things."

She hesitated, then continued, "At times, I wonder if they weren't doing these irresponsible experiments before the outbreak which led to our troubles today."

"Wow," said Gordon, and he lightly punched Audra in the arm to get her attention. "Did she really just blame us for the zombie plague?"

"I think she did," replied Dwyn, picking some berries from the bush he was behind. "It's smart. If we come out with our proof that Lysent started it, we're pulling papers from OUR laboratory. She'll say, it wasn't Lysent, it was us."

Gordon swore. "Is this what it's all about?"

"I don't think so," said Audra, wishing they would all hush. Greenly didn't assemble her people just to poke holes in an old story.

"Our scientists have discovered the group out there has experimented too carelessly. They pushed forward with a supposedly 'temperature-stable' antiviral. My scientists avoided this unnecessary upgrade because the proteins show subtle deterioration. Their nonperfect replica seems to be malfunctioning, leaving trace, dormant amounts of the virus in the host. We haven't been able to measure it in any blood test; however, for reasons unknown for now, the viral load can increase and take the host back over."

Greenly knew.

Murmurs and cries filled the plaza.

"I want to be clear!" shouted Greenly over the din. The trained crowd quieted.

"I want to be clear. Anyone cured through Lysent proper is not in danger. The antiviral works, just not the bastardizations found via the black market. The group to our southeast is an outbreak waiting to happen. Their entire community is a ticking time bomb. If you live with anyone cured by one of these underground means, know that you are living alongside a zombie in sleeping.

That's the danger of doing this on your own. That's the danger of no oversight. That's the danger of awakening people without due process!"

"She's blaming us for the whole damn thing," said Dwyn. His berries fell from his hand, forgotten.

"That she is," Audra muttered. She backed even farther from the fence. Suddenly, she didn't want to be seen.

"Holy crap. Do you think she's right?" Gordon asked.

Audra wasn't sure how to answer that.

"She could be lying," she said thoughtfully. "Ja- Peter said they had the same problem."

"Isn't that a dangerous lie to tell your community?"

"Do you think she cares?" countered Audra. "She just has to keep up the charade until she sows enough discord."

"Enough discord to do what?" asked Dwyn.

"Prime her people for war. To look the other way or cheer when she wipes us out," Audra explained.

"So we're the villains," concluded Gordon. "If I'm the villain... I can't go greet my daughter. I can't approach my family."

It seemed to be sinking in for Gordon. Audra had wondered when it would.

"What do you mean?" asked Dwyn.

"I'm a zombie, in waiting. There's no reason to tell my family I'm here and safe... because I'm not."

Audra's heart crumbled to pieces and her stomach felt pitted. She had been trying to help everyone. Was Lysent right? Was their antiviral flawed? Had they rushed something that shouldn't have been rushed?

"But maybe you can tell them?" asked Dwyn. "Maybe they'd want to know even if... you know, you're still sick."

"I can't! Don't you see! I could turn and destroy everything and everyone near me. I'm a - what did she call me? - a ticking time bomb. I can't be anywhere near my daughter. Ever. For the rest of whatever life I have left."

The others fell silent. It didn't really matter what else Greenly had to say. They had come to warn her, but now there was nothing to do here. Greenly had beat them to the punch. And she had punched hard. It was time to go and mop things up at Osprey Point. And prepare. Prepare for war.

*　　*　　*

Her legs couldn't carry her back from Lysent fast enough. Audra was ready to get back. Running was now just for transportation - nothing could be achieved by it. No longer would she be out searching for zombies to cure. That was on hold indefinitely. They could be on the verge of a massive outbreak, a wave across the country where survivors and zombies were pitted against each other once more. Were they ready this time? With no cure in sight, how should they treat the sick?

More leaves softened her path than shaded her from the sun. Lysent was correct on another point. Winter was coming. And they needed to be ready. With the crunch of leaves, Dwyn finally asked the question Audra dreaded.

"Do you think it's true?"

"Do I think what is true?" she asked to buy time. Was it true that she had lost or would lose everyone she cared about? Was it true that all of what Audra had lived for was worthless, dying, or dead?

"Do you think that those cured by Lysent are OK?"

That wasn't what he was asking. He was asking if he was OK. Was he on borrowed time? Would he turn on his family?

Audra had no answer for him.

CHASING EXTINCTION

R.M. HAMRICK

1 Courier

The oak leaf litter, muddled browns and rich blacks, muffled Audra's footsteps. But the bare trees did little to shield her approach as her short, lithe frame climbed through the Georgian brush. Pearl skin and speckled green eyes flashed underneath a thin hood which she adjusted over her hair. Although summer's coppery highlights were fading back to their chocolaty auburn, it remained in sharp contrast to the colors of a bleak winter.

Audra felt the outline of the scrawled letter through her threadbare jacket. She'd have to remember to put it in her pack if it rained. She hadn't delivered mail in a long while. Not since a simpler time. But, it allowed her to do the one thing she could do.

Run.

Darting through the forest was Audra's specialty and priceless in this world where escaping a zombie's bite meant you lived another day. Audra's life had centered around running. First, running for Lysent Corporation as she tried to secure a cure for her bitten sister. Then, she ran for Osprey Point to secure a cure for everyone.

Both failures on her account.

No one in her group could make sense of the formerly cured people turning back into shambling shells. Their treatment for the z-virus did not seem permanent. While Larange Greenly of Lysent blamed it on Osprey Point's 'reckless incompetence', Jack from Washington DC reported Lysent's antiviral was just as temporary.

Gordon had just located his family, but now with the risk of reversion hanging heavy, he refused to reunite with them. Instead, Audra carried his letter — a notification he was currently alive and thought of them often, and also a goodbye.

Audra wasn't sure why she should be running anymore. It was all for naught, just lies she had believed. Just lies she had told herself.

Audra's stomach grumbled.

Winter wasn't a lie.

She surveyed the ground for something to settle the churning in her gut. Tracks of a nearby animal to hunt was asking for too much. She'd dig up some acorns buried by squirrels or dandelion roots sleeping through the winter — anything to make her salivate and lie to her stomach that food was on the way.

She should have packed rations for her journey, but splitting their stores between Osprey Point and their new quarantine location had made it startlingly clear there was not enough food for either group's winter. As they divvied up their fall harvest of hickory nuts, chicory roots, and the like, it was clear winter foraging would be a daily task.

She couldn't take from their supplies.

But, she had also forgotten the difficulties of blazing a trail. This wasn't walking through her well-worn paths around Osprey Point or Lysent rail lines. This was navigating to a town far from the Lysent network with no clear route. Audra had forgotten how much energy it took to keep in the right direction and hike through the brush. Maybe she'd risk taking the roads back. But unfamiliar roads meant unfamiliar people and possible traps. Easy moving might turn into easy dying.

Audra moved from maple tree to maple tree, pulling the shriveled winged seeds from branches, shaking off the cobwebs. Flavors would differ from tree to tree, but winter declared they would all be bitter. Still, snapping the wing off and popping the seed pod into her mouth — it was better than nothing.

Audra recalled Gordon's directions to find the town. It had to be close. Maybe not close enough. Or maybe she was lost. The sky's grey whiteness vaguely lit the forest, but also hid the time from her. She pushed forward. The cool day would lead to a cold night she wouldn't want to suffer in her flimsy summer tent. She needed walls. Shelter.

While she was sure the letter would find its way in, she wasn't so sure if she'd be allowed to accompany it. Audra and Osprey Point no longer had anything of value to offer. She'd cross that bridge when she came to it. For now, she just wanted to find the small town before the sun tumbled from its hidden perch.

*   *   *

Audra all but stumbled upon her destination. She had been sure she was lost, but the small main street with its defunct traffic light popped up in the wood. A few shops barely justified it being called a town before. Now, it was tired and ghostly. It would be like any other small hub for farming neighbors, except for the giant chain grocery store just on the outskirts which had seen its demise before the world's end. Audra imagined that the store had gone out of business just as quickly as it had popped up, leaving a parking lot that would never be filled and a building much too large for anyone to utilize. Until now.

The curb against the road had been stacked with overturned grocery carts, creating a barrier of materialistic waste from the droves. Every defense against the zoms risked drawing the attention of marauders. This wall of coated metal carts was a shiny beacon for those looking to take. Audra refused to underestimate them and took caution as she scooted through the opening in the carts.

A few feet onto the concrete parking lot were parked cars, lined bumper to bumper. The path to the green sedan in the center looked well-traveled. Audra found the driver's door to be unlocked and most of the interior gutted. Audra slid through to the other side, where she opened the passenger door and slipped out. There, another line-up of cars, this time an opening between two of them. She looked over the row to find more vehicles, all positioned purposefully.

Settled dust on hoods and roofs indicated the residents carefully walked around them for their ingress and egress. Maybe to shed doubt on the store's occupancy, or perhaps to keep scent trails intact. It was a maze or a queue, really — a way to slow small groups of wanderers. It wouldn't stop a large herd though. They'd just flood over the cars.

Audra pulled a rag out of her bag. It wasn't white but it would have to do. She didn't want to be mistaken for the sick. Holding it over her head, she walked the circuitous path.

When in Rome.

As she finally reached the store front on the other end of the parking lot, she heard a throat clear above her. She looked up to see a long rifle pointed at her from the roof, steadied on a rusty security camera. 50/50 the rifle was loaded. 20/80 he could shoot and wasn't just up there for show. Behind the rifle was a ruddy face with a bulbous nose.

Audra waved her little raggedy flag once more.

"I'm Audra. I've got mail for someone inside."

"Mail?" the man pulled his face away from the rifle, and used a hand to scratch the back of his head in thought.

"Yeah, for Haleigh and Eliza Bottman," she said as if postal work was common. "Do you have anyone here by those names?"

His round shoulders shrugged. "Do you have any weapons on you?"

"Just my blades."

He nodded his head towards the entrance.

Her word was enough?

Guess he didn't think much of her. Audra had assumed defenses would be tight, considering their flashy entrance. Instead, Audra couldn't find reason this place was unmolested. Seemed they let anyone in.

Either side of the windowed front wall had been reinforced with freezer units filled with cash registers and other worthless machines. Audra walked through the entrance. On either side lay the previously sliding doors and boxes to support them for closing up for the night.

A woman with short curly hair streaked with silver, and deep lines in her bronzed face approached Audra and without introduction, she brusquely patted her down. Her hands ran down Audra's body. They paused at the knives, feeling size and features. Guess they wouldn't take her word for it after all.

"Where ya from?" she asked, folding her arms over an oversized army fatigue jacket.

"Osprey Point. It's a —"

"We know Osprey Point."

"You do?" Audra was surprised.

"Is it true you have a cure?" she asked curtly. Her flinty demeanor cracked as her brows furrowed into one. She stared down at Audra with one hip cocked, waiting.

Audra found she couldn't voice the words. She shook her head. They had no cure. The woman didn't need to hear it out loud. Her face settled back into its grim features and stiff expression.

Now, bad news was just news, but still its delivery wasn't Audra's forte. She hadn't even fully entered the establishment, and she already wished to be done and gone — despite winter's nightly bite.

"Do you know where I can find Haleigh and Eliza Bottman?" Audra asked.

The woman gave the same nod as the man outside had. "Black woman and a little girl? They're in the produce section."

The answer confused her for a moment before she recovered and copied their nod. The dimness of winter came through the store's skylights, illuminating grocery store aisle signs. Faded in color, they hung from the ceiling, outlasting the time when shelves upon shelves were stocked with cardboard- and plastic-wrapped food.

Now those shelves had been arranged to create stalls for the living. Some of the families appeared to be in transit. Others, as if they'd been here for several years. Audra walked toward the back corner previously for produce. Some of the cubiclees had curtains. Others had not managed such privacy. But in each cubicle, the soft glow of lanterns unsuccessfully fought the bleary evening.

A group of children giggled, danced, and skipped past her, ignoring the gloom of the weather. Audra wasn't sure if Eliza was in the short-statured crowd, but they all appeared healthy and washed. The place did feel a bit like a sanctuary with its tall walls and ceilings, but Audra couldn't help but consider it was only protected by a wall of shopping carts, a few cars, and a man on the roof. What would stop a group from coming in and robbing or killing them?

In the produce section, the display coolers had all been removed, leaving dark scuffs and electrical outlets where they once stood. Audra tried her best to casually glance into stalls for a sign of Haleigh or her daughter. Toward the corner, she spotted a woman with dark hair pulled back by a kerchief. She was tall and slender. The woman, as if she felt eyes on her, turned. She wore long flowing slacks cinched tight around her waist, and a soft jersey tank underneath a moth-eaten sweater.

"Haleigh Bottman?" Audra asked.

Her brown doe eyes blinked as the skin around them wrinkled a bit.

"Yes?" She wrung the scrap of cloth she was using to dust.

Audra had spent most of her hike rehearsing ways to tell this woman her 'long-dead' ex-husband had written them a note. None of her approaches seemed great. She'd go for simple.

"I'm Audra. I'm carrying a letter from Gordon for you."

"Ta— what?" she stuttered. Her arms came out in surprise, hitting the LED lantern.

Despite her ill-fitting clothes and some security vulnerabilities, Haleigh had a good setup here. And if Gordon's reconnaissance was correct, she also had a husband. It crossed Audra's mind that Haleigh might not want to read the letter.

In the swinging light, the woman found her way to her cot and sat down.

"Is he—?" she whispered.

Audra didn't know how to answer that. He hadn't written it years ago if that's what she meant.

"It's complicated. I'm sure his letter explains," she said as she reached for the letter from her coat.

Audra was surprised by her body's own frailness underneath the layers. Winter was making everything bare. No matter.

Haleigh's intentions for the letter were made clear as she snatched it from Audra's hands. Audra gave it freely.

Haleigh's eyes swept the handwriting before she clasped it to her chest. Large orb tears rolled down her cheek. She whimpered again before she pulled the letter back into her sights. Audra wondered if she could even read it with the glassy tears distorting her vision.

Audra felt a rare amount of social awkwardness as she waited for Haleigh. She looked from side to side of the aisle, but there really wasn't any place to go. She settled on sitting against the edge of their stall wall, her back toward Haleigh. Audra refused to see the fall of her face as she reached the letter's conclusion. Audra would never have written a letter like this. Why give them possibility just to rip it away again?

A tall, gangly girl whipped around the corner with a giant smile overtaking her face. Her hair flew behind her, the coils bouncing to a stop on her shoulders as she skidded to avoid Audra. The girl had some of Gordon's features, although Audra couldn't name them. Eliza's dark brown eyes darted from Audra to her mother and back to Audra again, flashing with accusation. Audra had done something to make her mother cry.

"Please, leave us alone," she whispered in passing.

Audra's eyes followed the girl as she wrapped her mother in her small arms. The gray cot sagged under their combined weight. Even though Eliza was only eight, Audra imagined she had a good sense of how to read and comfort her mother. Audra understood the dynamic well; emotional stability of your family dictated your survival. At eight years old, Eliza was an expert.

"I don't think I understand," Haleigh confessed. The wobble in her voice echoed in the cubicle.

Audra stood up, peeling out of her pack and leaving it on the cracked tiled floor. Back in their alcove, Eliza had weaseled herself between the letter and her mother, as if to protect her from it. Eliza stared down at the words, although Audra wasn't sure if she could read.

Did they have schools in this place? From the giggles and shouts, it sounded as if they had enough children for it.

"Earlier this year I went with some scientists and cleared out a laboratory, the one your husband worked at."

"Ex-husband. And 'lived at' would be more accurate." Her comment more matter-of-fact than bitter.

"Ex-husband," Audra corrected herself. "He'd been bitten. We treated him with a replicated antidote we stole from Lysent Corp. He was healthy again and was looking for you. But, it turns out the cure we gave him wasn't an enduring treatment. He's going to turn back into a zo— sick."

"Is there anything you can do for him?" Her chin rested on her daughter's head as she held her close.

"We're trying to figure out what went wrong so we can fix it... There's a lot of unknowns. It might take some time. It might be impossible."

She nodded, unsurprised. Outside of Lysent, many people hadn't heard more than rumors about a cure. And what sounded too good to be true, usually was.

With the crux of her mission complete, Audra needed to tend to other necessities. "I'm sorry, it's getting dark. Would it be OK if I slept on the floor of your... establishment... for the night?" she asked.

"Oh yes, of course." Haleigh rose immediately, letting her daughter fall to her feet. "And some food. Eliza, get the girl some food. Oh, I'm sorry — what's your name?"

"Audra."

"Thank you for doing this for us, Audra. You are kind to go out of your way in the winter to deliver a letter."

"Anything for Gordon. He's saved my life more than once. I wish there was more I could do."

In fact, Audra wished there was anything she could do. When it came to beakers and protein markers, Audra was at a loss. She couldn't even figure out why Satomi always reprimanded her for calling it an 'antidote'.

Eliza offered Audra some brown fruit leather. After thanking her, she couldn't help but tear into it. She was so hungry. The sticky sweet stuck more to her teeth than landed in her stomach. Still, she was grateful. She worked pieces down with her tongue.

"Thank you," said Audra, feeling her lips stick to her jaw with each word. "I'll sleep here tonight. That will give you a chance to write your response, if you'd like. I'm sure he'd love to hear from you."

"It will give us a chance to pack," said Haleigh simply.

Audra raised her eyebrows. To pack?

"You will take us to see Gordon," Haleigh explained, riffling through a box of supplies.

Audra hadn't read the letter, but she was pretty sure that's not what it said. Gordon was clear. He didn't want Haleigh and Eliza to watch him turn into a zombie.

Next to the box sat a pack — large enough for a woman and a girl in times of transition. Audra wondered how many times they'd run. If they didn't start with additional guards on the perimeter, it might come again soon.

"Don't you have ties here?" reasoned Audra, noting at the same time how small the cot in the cubicle was. Was Gordon incorrect on the fact she was remarried?

"Kayle is dead," she said as if Audra had known his name. Her eyes seemed to recede, lost in grief's shadow. "Happened last week. On a run. I'll have to take his place."

Take his place on the run?

Haleigh's voice became distant and hollow. "I don't want to. What if something happens? What will happen to Eliza?"

Audra didn't have answers for Haleigh, except that her own volatile community wasn't the place for a young orphan. It wasn't really a place for anyone. Audra hadn't given much thought to how much more difficult life would be with a child.

There hadn't been many to remind her.

"I don't remember my dad," said Eliza, looking Audra in the eye, her mouth small. Audra could tell she was collecting information. Her mom's thought on death, for one.

"He remembers you, love. But he's sick. You can't go see him." The first half for Eliza and the second half to benefit her mother.

"We need to be there for him," said Haleigh. "No one should do this alone."

She mindlessly moved things around, waffling in her packing. Audra felt restless in the stale air. She had only brought trouble to this small family.

"We were alone," Eliza said, pulling on her mother's sleeve.

"He's not alone," assured Audra. "We have an entire quarantine area," she offered dumbly.

Haleigh ignored Audra's comment. Her long fingers danced in the girl's hair as she spoke to her. "We had each other. That is never alone. And your father needs someone too."

To hell with that. There was no way Audra was removing them from the produce section. Gordon's fate had haunted their dreams for years, but they'd never be able to discard the real sight of a cold decrepit shell and the shallow gray eyes. Audra's dreams were testaments to that.

Eliza's eyes were bright and sharp.

They would remain that way.

"I cannot take you," Audra said firmly. "Thank you for the food. I'll come by for your letter in the morning." Maybe hinting that she'd leave would settle the matter.

"No, please, stay," resigned Haleigh. Eliza's eyes slanted at the request, but she said nothing as her mother turned her to the small pail in the corner to wash up.

Audra appreciated the conversation's end. Her legs felt like they might collapse under her weight. She pulled from her feet the pieces of leather which once resembled shoes, before she slumped against a shelving wall. The air didn't feel quite as stale from her resting position. In fact, the warmth and humidity of a community enclosed in walls was almost comforting. Audra didn't have to worry about more pleas, she was fast asleep before they could fall on her ears.

2 Complications

Satomi lay on her hay-filled mattress as she finished counting the imagined rows of tiles on the ceiling of her dark room. She stared at them so often, she felt she could see them even when the sunlight faded and her lantern burned out. The edges glowed, burned into her sight. Maybe she could see them.

Her long black hair created a nest for her head on a pillow filled with folded worn clothes. She barely turned her heart-shaped face, fearing movement would chase away any sleep to be had. The window now in view, her almond-shaped eyes found nothing but soft moonlight filtering in.

Satomi surrendered to another night of sleeplessness by finally moving from her static pose. Her arm silently swept the blanket beside her.

No one.

Ryder had left for the quarantine location, leaving Satomi to work on the antiviral. Satomi didn't want to be apart from Ryder. More so, she didn't want Ryder in a place where its inhabitants could become driven to eat their roommates. The virus was dangerous again — not containable. And Ryder wasn't as scared as she should be.

Satomi felt Ryder's missing panic rising within herself. Her separation from her partner at least allowed her to sink into distress without an audience. A couple months had passed since she was penned in a police car like an animal, but still the fear and restlessness remained like a massive entity attached to her being. It left no room for others, isolating Satomi from friends. It loomed over her and threatened to expand so much that there'd be no room left for Satomi either.

Her skin crept and crawled underneath the blanket until she was convinced something was in the bed with her. Throwing off the blanket, she sat straight up. Sweat beaded along her hairline and fell in droplets off her legs. Breathing in the room's stagnant, musty air gave no relief.

She jumped out of bed, grabbed her jacket, and raced to the door. There, she came to an abrupt stop, willing herself to move with quiet composure. No need to wake anyone. Nothing was actually wrong, right?

That's not the way it felt.

She slipped into the hallway and followed the light of the lobby. The sounds of her feet were deadened by the rough nylon carpeting. The coolness of the tile floor preceded her escape out the door. There, cold air bit into her face. Outside, she heaved as if she'd been holding her breath for the moonlight and dew.

Maybe she had.

The ragged concrete felt cool on her feet. Weeds wrestled through the cracks and tickled whatever they could reach. Satomi walked from the sleeping quarters toward the center of the industrial park. The park's fence and laboratory had been invaluable at the start and the scattered one-story buildings had been re-purposed for their community. When Satomi had first arrived here with the other scientists, she was filled with hope. Now her hope had dried up like the cracked fountain sitting in the plaza.

Satomi sat on the ground against the fountain's walls. Her arms began to prickle, her jacket unworn beside her. Her olive skin had paled and yellowed with the winter, and the moonlight reflecting off the orange-hued limestone walls gave her an odd glow. She couldn't see the osprey statue in the center of the pool from her spot, but she imagined it diving down for its kill.

*   *   *

"These systems didn't work last time," she had urged while she and Ryder squared off in Osprey Point's laboratory.

The aging fluorescent bulbs flickered with the solar power illuminating the linoleum-lined floors and aisles of counters. The front lobby's door was closed, as was the door to the windowed conference room. The coldness of metal and glass waiting for scientific work usually pleased Satomi, but with doors closed and Ryder threatening to leave — the laboratory felt more like a prison than a sanctuary.

Satomi had seen it before — the terror of outbreaks in a large populace. Even though she hadn't entered the medical field at that time, she surmised any protocol short of complete isolation of healthy and complete extermination of the sick was no match for the infections that avalanched into cities. And even then.

"We know things we didn't know then. We're better prepared," had said ever-optimistic Ryder. "We will make it work. We have to make it work."

Ryder's supply of hair gel had finally been exhausted and her ash-brown hair was now being groomed into a flat pixie cut. Little silver rings lining her ears, pale pink skin, and an upturned nose validated Satomi's suspicions that Ryder was an otherworldly, mystical beauty. However, Ryder currently sounded more like a politician than any fey entity, combating reality with a determined positive attitude. Satomi expected her to stand on the counter and chant slogans at any moment.

Ryder had been nestled in Lysent Corp for the outbreaks. She didn't understand that the supposed cure had allowed survivors to regroup just to break down again, sending waves of infection out into the world. Ryder could remain optimistic, here at Osprey Point.

"You're not sick. Please just stay where you're safe," said Satomi, her dark eyes flashing darker under her tresses. "Dwyn is going. He's more than capable of caring for them."

Ryder shook her head, silver jewelry swaying underneath her ear.

"We don't know if Dwyn's cure will stick either," Ryder replied in a hushed tone as if speaking the possibility of failure at full volume made it more probable. Then more loudly, "but maybe you're the one that should be going — they need a doctor."

God, it was like talking to someone from a different world. On Ryder's planet, apparently the sick population she had irrevocably failed would welcome her continued medical expertise. In the real world, Satomi didn't even consider the possibility that Lysent's results were equally short-lived. No one had even heard rumor of reversion before Satomi's antivirals had been spread far and wide. And although it remained unspoken, Satomi knew they all blamed her. It was her fault. She knew it. They knew it. She had developed the temperature-stable antiviral. She had declared it safe and effective.

Satomi had doomed all the people in her community. The treated would turn, then consume. Precious Ryder would be torn apart by Satomi's deluded efforts to save the world. The defeated doctor settled in her stool and buried her head in a text book. A thick curtain of hair separated her from Ryder. Perhaps it would be easier if she couldn't watch it all fall away.

* * *

Satomi donned her jacket, but the goosebumps remained. She rubbed the offending extremities with her hands, but it wasn't just the cold wind or the wet dew on her bare feet. Her body was rebelling against her. Her head felt hot and stuffy, like it might explode. Nothing seemed in sync. Nothing made sense.

Satomi looked behind her toward the gate. The two figures standing on the scaffolding, watching for outside threats, ignored the threat that remained inside the fences. The one who had damned them all. Her eyes followed the chain links down to the sedans lining the inside of the fence. Rebar windows flashed in her mind and sent her stomach spiraling.

Satomi turned back around and tried to fight the rising tide inside her. Cold, damp air in her lungs to cool the frustration and shame. She would win against it, at least tonight she would. Satomi stared at the trailing cracks in the concrete and pretended she could count the invading blades of grass in the soft moonlight.

Some time later, Satomi caught sight of the sun peeking the tiniest pink rays, shadows on stars. She retreated back to her room, ducking into the darkest shadows, so no one would know her crime of sleeplessness. Her pant hem was soggy on the tile and back onto the carpet. She crawled into bed, which lay directly on the floor. The pillow pushed her long hair around her. It was wet from the morning and created a small cool environment around her racing mind. She imagined Ryder lying next to her; her soft skin pink with sleep. Satomi almost rolled over to caress the imaginary face before closing her eyes. Sleep was good. Ryder was good. She only wished she could be there, and not lost in the dew.

* * *

Satomi sat in the small two-room building that served as a mess hall and adjoining kitchen. An eclectic collection of tables, chairs, and benches had accrued in the space, but almost all were empty in the early morning hours. While Satomi hadn't been able to recognize the guards on the scaffolding in the darkness of late night, Branson and Tess had now been relieved from their shift and sat at a picnic table for a small meal before napping through the morning.

Branson's pearly brown hair was tied back with elastic. His blue eyes twinkled with every laugh from Tess. Even sleep-deprived, they had no trouble keeping up with their constant flirting. Tess flicked her white blond hair off her shoulder, only for it to return again. While Satomi hadn't the energy to keep up with the latest gossip, it seemed Tess was still keeping Branson at arm's length, if only to protect her two young children from possible confusion and heartbreak.

Satomi appreciated their self-absorption. They made no mention of her nightly wandering and her subsequent status as a lump on a log. She tried to ignore the fact that they were sitting where Katie had lashed out at her weeks earlier. Katie's girlfriend Lisa had been the first to turn and attack her friends. Before Katie was sequestered at the motel for her own potential to revert, she had told Satomi it would have been better if she and Lisa hadn't been cured at all. They never would have found each other and lived in false hope.

Satomi wondered if Tess's and Branson's relationship and her own would suffer the same ends. Not wanting to be bothered with starting the communal fire, Satomi ate her serving of soupy grain corn and beans cold. Corn and beans weren't her favorite, but she knew they'd be eating foraged food before long. Watercress and mushrooms if they were lucky. Pine bark after that.

The mess hall door opened and someone took the long way around Satomi and her table. She hid underneath a frame of hair and eyed her half-full bowl. She couldn't just up and leave. Branson and Tess halted their banter.

"Hi," said the man, standing in front of her table, hand on chair.

Another swallow of food. This one had a bit of crunch. Satomi looked up and stared at him without saying a word. An invitation to sit down wasn't coming. She understood having Pete Jr. — or Jack as they'd taken to calling him — stay was Osprey Point's best strategic play, but it didn't mean she and he needed to be on friendly terms.

Even if Satomi had stood up, Jack would still tower over her, his blue eyes constantly looking down to speak to others. In response to the dwindling supply of hair gel at Osprey Point, he had shaved his hair short — an odd decision as winter came rolling through. It emphasized the strong angles of his face, something he got from his father and had shared with his sister.

Jack and his family had controlled a hybridized infected army, brainwashed men with the resilience afforded to those sick with the z-virus. With their army lost to the Lysent Corporation, Osprey Point couldn't afford Jack joining Greenly's ranks. His potential to command the army under Greenly would secure Osprey Point's demise. Their only option was to welcome him into the fold. And he seemed to have a lot to contribute. However, he had also previously held Satomi captive for several months.

Jack held out a palm in half surrender. Satomi fought the urge to recoil. Without his leather armor, he was less intimidating, but she still connected his scent, his voice, and his mannerisms to the man who sat on a lawn chair throne and allowed his sister to be fiercely cruel to her and the community he now lived in.

"I'm sorry. With so many gone to the motel, I've only got so many people who will even acknowledge me…" he started.

Satomi wasn't surprised her cold stare was considered an acknowledgment. Jack and Jill had launched their army into Osprey Point upon first meeting. Satomi glanced over to Branson. His clenched jaw and vice grip on his spoon revealed he had not forgiven Jack for the death of a fellow guard, Lionel, during that proceeding.

"…My dad's refusing to eat. I'm at my wit's end," said Jack, his voice scratchy as if he too hadn't gotten much sleep.

"I'm not responsible for your father not eating. That's on you." Her voice tensed.

When she had first met Jack's father, Peter, she thought he suffered from some neurodegenerative disease. She worked to help him regain lost mental function until she learned he was involved in the development of the z-virus. He had manipulated the virus to create his army, and even his dementia had been triggered by one of his own experiments gone awry.

"Totally agree," he said hurriedly. "It's just he keeps asking about you… Evelyn and Eli too."

Sharp pain burned at the edges of her chest and throat at the mention of Eli's name. Her jaw clenched. Eli wouldn't be coming to see him. Jack's sister — Evelyn, Jill, whatever — had bled Eli out after he tried to protect her. Eli had been their loyal companion as they convoyed through the eastern states, and she killed him in anger. Shortly thereafter, Jill was killed by Larange Greenly's men.

"He'll forget. He always does." She brushed him off.

"No, he remembers you. And it doesn't help that Evelyn is gone. It's just me and he finds me boring." Jack grinned.

Satomi wasn't sure what was funny.

Jack sighed, giving up on the humor. "You don't have to be OK with me. I get it. But my dad doesn't understand his circumstances. He just knows he's sad and he misses you."

The man was suffering. Given his hand in the global mass extinction, maybe he should. However, Satomi's responsibility as a doctor tapped her on the shoulder. Satomi sighed. More than clear ethics for medical care and experimentation, she wanted Jack out of her face.

"I'll think about it," she conceded.

Jack breathed a thanks and left the mess hall without breakfast.

"You don't owe him anything," Branson announced.

Satomi said nothing, her spoon scraping the sides of the bowl to finish her meal. Another unsettling crunch as she chewed. She didn't blame Peter one bit for refusing to eat this gruel.

3 Quarantine

Sunlight scattered through the skylights before Audra stirred. That stirring quickly brought to her attention an ache emanating from her tail bone. Cracked linoleum over concrete was not a forgiving surface. Audra assumed she'd be paying penance for the rest of the day. She arched her back and listened to the satisfying pops before twisting laterally for the same results. On her way around to her left, she glanced at the cot in Haleigh's and Eliza's cubicle. Just a small lump, barely moving the covers. A swath of dark hair peeked from the blanket's edge.

Audra stood up quietly and calculated the odds of being able to leave without argument. Haleigh's bag remained on the ground, half full. At least she hadn't continued packing. On top of the rotting cardboard box sat a thick sheet of handmade paper. Audra attributed its color and texture to food containers, something a grocery store would have in abundance. One side presented a monochromatic stick figure drawing. She turned the paper to find thinner ink, letters looping and curving. Haleigh's letter.

Audra averted her eyes. It was none of her business.

She pulled a large-mouth bottle from her bag and made sure no water still settled in it before she gently rolled the art for its protective sleeve. She did scan the contents of the box underneath the letter. Along with spare socks, a pair of eyeglasses, and the crayon she saw two more pieces of fruit leather. A jar of flour. And a cup of unshelled pecans.

This couldn't be everything. Some had been packed.

But still.

Audra wondered what they had traded for the paper. There was nothing else like it in the box.

"Mom said you could have another piece of fruit leather," Eliza's lilting voice escaped her rough blanket.

"Oh, no, I'm not hungry," Audra lied.

Straight arms protruded from the top of the blanket and came crashing down to the girl's sides, flipping the blanket off her face.

"Everyone's hungry."

Audra was almost sure that was true. Eliza was still younger than Audra was when the outbreaks occurred. She still remembered the oak dining room table, matching plates, and her mother's soft voice chiding her for spooning out more than she could consume.

"Where's your mom?" she asked. Surely Eliza wasn't left here by herself.

"Running. She has to do it now. Now that Kayle's gone." Of course she was left by herself. What else could her mother do? "Maybe Gordon could come and do the runs?"

Audra really hadn't dealt with such innocence and youth in a long while. Not since Belinda, who although older, was more like a child than a supportive figure.

Eliza climbed off the cot. Her shirt rode up, too short for her thankfully growing body. She grabbed a dented tin pail and walked out.

She hadn't expected an answer.

Audra left as well, returning after trading a couple wares in her bag for a few days' rations. Neither of the space's occupants had returned. Audra wasn't sure how long this community's runs were. Could be hours, days, even weeks.

Audra slipped all the newly acquired food into the family's box. And after searching their bag, tucked her tent in its main pocket. How safe was leaving these things unattended? Audra scanned the produce section's population. Several older women huddled together on a mat, knitting and mending.

"Looking for someone?" a woman with wiry hair and an equally wiry voice asked.

"No, I have something for Haleigh and wasn't sure if I should leave it or just wait." Audra didn't even want to say it was food, although anyone could look into the box and know.

"Thieves don't last long here," the woman laughed, transferring her darning needle to her other hand before brandishing a butterfly blade.

Audra could find no reason to doubt her.

With her pack a little lighter, she abandoned Haleigh's cubicle. Bodies stopped and eyes stared as she headed toward the front of the store. They must not see too many venture out solo during the winter months.

The woman who patted her down was by the door again.

Audra addressed her in a hushed voice.

"I'm not sure how this place is still here, but you need more guards on duty."

The woman cocked her head and raised her eyebrows at Audra.

Audra had a million other things to do before raiding a camp of families. "No seriously. Your cart wall out there is a flashing neon sign that people live here."

"That's how we trade, dear." The woman's condescending tone was clear.

Audra also had a million other things to do besides argue with a stranger over safety concerns. She promptly rolled her eyes and exited the damp grocery store.

Yesterday's overcast had been replaced with sunny coolness. Audra kicked herself for waking so late. It would throw off her entire journey. At least she didn't have a woman and her child clinging onto her legs, trying to prevent her escape.

Audra weaved her way through the maze, feeling the exterior guard's eyes on her back. When she reached the entrance, she marveled once more at the grocery cart wall. The bottom had been staked down deep. Ties and supports had been twisted through to keep them from toppling.

Use what you have, she guessed.

Still, she felt a little unsafe under its shadow. They were metal carts on wheels after all.

The edge of the asphalt crumbled as she stepped onto the faded road. Wide, sweeping cracks filled with tall weeds encouraged the deterioration. This main street once had a quiet life. Now it was even quieter. The rusted gas station's pumps had been wrenched over. The pharmacy had been clearly raided many times over, its windows broken and nothing standing upright inside. The neighboring bank appeared untouched. Although maybe it was missing its chained pens and paper slips.

This was hardly a town. Why this chain grocery store had been placed here in all its magnificence was a mystery. And why it still stood now with just two guards taking most shifts was another. Not her problem, her mind recited. Still, she feared for Haleigh and her daughter.

Osprey Point and the quarantine location were south. Audra couldn't resist surveying the opposite direction. The road rambled into a fallen neighborhood of modular houses, and from there, fields.

Osprey Point south. North not.

Audra felt the pull. Almost like a panic. She wished for something else, anything else. And north was that.

If she returned to Osprey Point, she'd only watch her friends lose their last battles. Battles against the horrendous virus that had taken out so many. Family losing family. Friends. Lovers. She held Haleigh's and Eliza's correspondence in her bag, but she didn't need to read it to know it was just apologies, sadness, and regret. Eliza's drawing would just wrench the father's heart in two. It was better off undelivered. Their act of writing goodbye was for them — so they could move on.

What if Audra moved on?

Who would she find? Who could she be? Lost in the questions, not in the answers, Audra inhaled dry cold air and exhaled clouds of moisture. She stole another glance in the direction Osprey Point did not exist.

She would go there.

After Osprey Point's defenses fell and the quarantined consumed themselves, it would all be gone. She'd have no choice but to leave and never return. Current temptation be damned. The inevitability provided a certain amount of comfort.

She didn't have to go now.

She'd be going later.

She began her jog south, enjoying the tattered road to her temporary home.

*　　*　　*

With the safety of the light, and then the cover of darkness, Audra risked the roads back. She enjoyed the opportunity for straight, undeterred running. She flew through the day and far into the night, only stopping for watercress and accessible oyster mushrooms to fuel her. In her journey, she had purpose. She knew at her destination it wouldn't be so clear. So here, despite her race, she rested.

Audra took the overgrown exit ramp for a trucker's rest stop: a gas station and a motel for those who could no longer maintain their lane. The sun peeked over the pines — the time when drivers would leave motels like these, not arrive at them. She slowed to a jog as she turned the corner, giving a wave to the figure atop the gas station.

A quick-thinking resident had fenced the motel's parking lot when the outbreaks began; however, that hadn't saved its occupants from threats within. Soon zombies wandered freely inside. Audra had scouted out the motel many times before, as had many others. They had come to the same conclusion she had — clearing the parking lot, picking all the locks, and disabling everyone inside would be an intense feat.

But when Audra needed a place to separate their healthy from their potentially sick, it became necessary to finally clear the old motel of its zombie inhabitants — if only to replace them. And clearing wasn't nearly as difficult as convincing the previously infected to migrate the few miles from Osprey Point. It was an especially hard sell for those who had received their treatment from Lysent. She, like all the others, hoped Lysent was truthful in their claims that their antiviral was unaffected, but the risk was too great. Overlooking Lysent-cured could cause Osprey Point to fall like all the others.

Audra pulled on the heavy gate. It screeched, metal against concrete, like a rooster's strangled call just before the sun's arrival. She estimated the distance and slipped through the gap. Her pack caught on an aluminum barricade panel, sending it rattling in the cold air. So much for a quiet return.

Hushed voices paused as Audra made her entrance. The light hadn't quite slipped over the fences, but Audra saw a small wood fire going in the modified grill. It cast shadows on two women.

The parking lot held a few moldy chairs and rotting tables from select rooms, and scattered blue plastic water barrels. Audra smiled at the new addition — a metal picnic table, no doubt collecting dew. The two-story motel formed a U shape around the lot with each room's exterior doors facing the center.

Apparently recognizing but not acknowledging Audra, their voices started up again, heated and arguing. Audra recognized Ryder's sharp angles of ears and jewelry. Her petite figure with minute curves was also telling. Bradley's broad shoulders shook with emotion.

"I run high in the morning," Bradley pleaded.

"You didn't run high yesterday morning," retorted Ryder. Audra was surprised by Ryder's abrasiveness. Her diplomacy usually earned her few arguments.

"That's because I was up for a few hours before breakfast time. I just rolled out of bed. You can't take my temperature right after I roll out of bed…" Bradley trailed off, her voice souring. Perhaps she was realizing there was more than breakfast at stake.

"Good morning, what's up?" asked Audra, placing herself between the warring women. She ran her hands along her pack's straps before deciding to put it down.

"She has a temperature of a hundred-and-one," said Ryder coolly, washing the offending thermometer.

Bradley had journeyed toward Osprey Point alone when she was bitten. Audra found her just one mile off with a note in her pocket. Audra couldn't help but think she might need to write another note soon.

"And I'm telling her I always sleep hot. I'll cool down in a couple hours - well, unless you guys rile me up!" Bradley's face looked rosy, from her fever or anger Audra wasn't sure. But Bradley knew the protocol. Keep all doors closed. Temperatures taken every morning. Fevers stay in their rooms.

"A hundred-and-one doesn't sound like sleeping hot, Bradley," said Audra softly. "How do you feel?"

"Scared that you're going to lock me away because I came to breakfast too soon!" she shouted.

"OK, OK, look," said Audra, throwing up her hands in surrender. Tensions in the motel were high enough without people waking up to a yelling match. "It's just one reading. If you are sick — any kind of sick — maybe you shouldn't be out here. Get your breakfast and take it to your room. In a few hours, we'll take another temperature. No biggie. We just want you to be healthy and we want to keep germs — all the germs — to a minimum."

Bradley huffed but began picking her rations. Audra didn't address the fear in her eyes. Bradley just needed to come to terms with what was happening. The group didn't claim to know much about the reversion process, but Lisa had been sick for a few days before she turned and attacked people at Osprey Point. They hoped those were measurable symptoms heralding a reversion. It also could have been just a coincidence.

"How are things here?" asked Audra dumbly.

Ryder's narrow shoulders fell to an even sharper angle. The rising sun illuminated the bags under her eyes. She reached for a ring in her ear, spinning it around.

"Both Jia and Mary are sick, like bad sick. I think we're about to confirm the virus's reversion course. They were also the medical assistants. So now, all of this is on my and Gordon's shoulders."

And eventually Gordon would be gone too.

"Satomi?"

"She won't come. Also, she's better off trying to solve this from the lab. We're a lost cause here."

Ryder was far from the bubbly engineer who had hiked to an abandoned laboratory to save the world. Her optimism had fallen away to reveal someone very human. Ryder inspected her medical accoutrements, neatening their perfect rows along the table.

Audra couldn't draw up any words of comfort, just, "I'll let Gordon know to run blood work on Bradley."

Pulling the bottle from her pack's main pocket, Audra didn't bother to take her bag to her room. Truth be told, she couldn't recall which room was hers at the moment. Instead, she climbed the concrete exterior stairs to the second floor. From there, the sun glared but didn't warm the air. It would be another cold night this evening. Audra knocked on the door marked 13. No one else had wanted the room. Gordon thought it seemed apt.

"Come in," came his distant voice, husky and muffled.

Finding the door unlocked, Audra opened it and flooded the room with soft light.

"Audra!" shouted Gordon, jumping from the small bucket where he was rinsing his face. "Did you find them?"

Gordon bounded over to her, his squared face wrinkling in both excitement and worry.

"Yes, yes I did —"

"Are they OK?" he asked before Audra could add anything to her answer.

Her nod yes sent his knees dropping to the floor. He was still almost as tall as Audra in that stance. His tawny skin matched the color of his thin-framed glasses, which turned askew as he pulled his large hands to his face. Audra unscrewed the canister and wiggled out the note. He immediately straightened his glasses, ready to receive the note, choking back tears.

Audra busied herself by pulling the curtains open as he read. All the rooms looked the same. Faded peeling floral wallpaper in greens and yellows. Defunct flat-screen TV. Dressers in various states of decay or destruction from their previous zombie tenants. Out of the corner of her eye, she saw Gordon's fingers run over the smoothness of his daughter's drawing.

"Are they safe there?" asked Gordon, not looking up from the drawing of his family together in a grocery store.

Audra waffled long enough for Gordon to turn his attention to her.

"What's wrong?" he asked, his voice deep.

Audra explained the scarcity of guards and Kayle's death. She also told him of the women who look after their section of the store, coloring them more as caregivers than knitters with knives. Honesty while not inciting Gordon into rushed action. Truth was, Haleigh and Eliza had survived this long without him. Audra was fairly certain they could continue to do so.

"Maybe they could live at Osprey Point? I could visit if just for a while." His half question, half wish hung in the air.

"They wanted to come see you," admitted Audra.

Audra had considered the option, but with Larange Greenly marking Osprey Point as the poster child for the rebellion, it was no safer than here. Best not to get them involved in any way.

Gordon's lips quivered with a small smile at her words. He frowned as Audra answered his question with a shake of her head. He didn't push the subject.

Audra hated to pull him back to reality, but duties remained. "Bradley had a fever this morning. We told her we'd check it again in two hours, but I imagine she'll need to be added to the list for regular blood work."

"Bradley. Got it," he replied with sad resolution.

4 Turned

When Audra exited Gordon's room, she noticed the sun had finally decided to grace the entire complex in light. She also noted that she was approaching twenty-four hours without sleep. A dull headache had settled in the back of her skull. She knew it would radiate upward the longer she stayed awake, until it wrapped around and impacted her vision. She would rest. Later.

Ryder was busy with breakfast screenings, trying to get temperatures before the early risers consumed hot beverages. Marcos appeared to have fallen back asleep on a half-padded chair. It was difficult to tell with the waves of rich black hair that framed and often covered his face. Audra joined the tiny mob around the grill and managed a generic motel mug filled with pine needle tea and a scratchy blanket that had been warmed by the fire. Initially Audra hadn't been sold on the motel, but its amenities were surprisingly helpful.

With more people awake, the gate didn't sound quite as loud as Audra slipped out with her sights on the gas station. Audra had worried their location was too close to the highway. And really, it was. But the neighboring gas and convenience store with its flat roof had convinced her security could be manageable.

When she and Dwyn were scouting and first climbed up the metal cage surrounding the ladder and reached the pea gravel roof, the space felt oddly vacant and even otherworldly. It had taken a moment for Audra to realize why.

The space was untouched.

The interior of the gas station had been raided several times over just as the rest of the world. But the roof had remained a spot the end hadn't touched. The last person up there had been experiencing a different universe. Maybe his biggest concern was greasing a stuck vent. In his world, the sick didn't walk around and consume their brethren. The sick stayed home, ate soup, and watched TV.

Undisturbed as the world fell, places like this had become rare.

And Audra thought most unfortunate.

An unused resource was a reminder that someone else hadn't made it to that point. Perhaps if the roof had been more accessible, someone could have escaped a herd. They could have enjoyed a few more quiet nights with a warm fire and a chance to gaze at the stars. Instead, the unmarked roof showed no history of campfires and the gravel remained unfussed. Anyone nearby had found another means of evasion or had been overrun.

The roof was an excellent watch spot. From the vantage point, Audra and Dwyn could see inside the motel's fences, its gate, the highway, and both ramps.

"This will do," Audra had said.

And finally the resource was used.

Having found the key to the ladder inside the gas station, it was now easy to traverse to the top. Audra managed the metal rungs one-handed. Her peace offering was in the other hand. The roof was still a mostly empty and serene place, but now the white gravel had been marked up with campfires, and some weather-resistant odds and ends were scattered about.

Wisps of chestnut brown hair peeked out of a bundled blanket wrapped tightly around curves. On a birch log by the fire, Katie sat on guard. Audra offered the white ceramic mug and the woman's knobby hand emerged from cloth to receive it. She pulled the tea close and let the steam warm her face. Katie, like everyone in quarantine, drank copious amounts of pine needle tea, hoping its vitamin C would ward off any illness. Audra draped the second blanket over Katie's shoulders, which fell gently with the added weight.

Audra sat on a milk crate next to her. The road and forest were quiet. It seemed the birds and few small animals left in the area were sleeping in. Audra cleared her throat and asked the obligatory question.

"How's Lisa?"

Lisa had sent Audra into a panic on two separate occasions. The first was their meeting, when Audra stumbled upon her in the woods. Infected, yellow blond hair, and formerly blue eyes — wandering, lost in the world, she looked just like Audra's sister Belinda. Audra had brought her in as their first outreach and cure. Then later, she was the first to revert. She infected three other people before Audra contained her.

"In pain," she said, exasperated.

The infection was not a passive thing. Those cured recounted sensations of burning bones and joints that sent shocks of pain with each degree of rotation.

"Sometimes I wish I'd go ahead and revert. Join her. Maybe time would pass more quickly." Katie tipped her cup and watched some of her tea pour out onto the roof.

So much for her peace offering. Katie's eyes shot daggers at her. And Audra was out of platitudes, having given them all to Gordon. She had already promised them hope when she brought them to Osprey Point. She couldn't promise again at the motel.

Audra knew her frustration. She had carried it and the accompanying guilt for years. Your loved one rots in pain. Your progress to save them excruciatingly slow. And some days, you don't even bother. And that's the scary part. Katie watched her girlfriend revert and infect others, somehow not getting caught in the scuffle. And now she had nothing to do but perform her guard duties and wait for her dormant virus to take hold. Idle and emotional hands.

After a few moments of foggy silence, Audra stood up to leave.

She would go check the snares. A dinner of meat would improve morale. It always did, until the residents remembered flesh-eating conversion. Then the game wouldn't settle as well in their stomachs. And their minds would churn as well.

But Audra had nothing else to do either.

*   *   *

If Audra had been more clear-thinking, she might have realized speaking with Katie in both their sleep-deprived states would be counterproductive. But, Audra didn't plan to stay at the motel long. And she knew if she delayed the meeting, she'd find a way to leave before it occurred.

Audra promised herself sleep. After she checked the snares.

The cool air dulled the forest smells, but the expanse still felt isolating and peaceful. She knew Katie was watching her from above. Probably pouring out the rest of her tea. But it didn't matter, Audra would be deep in the woods soon. Her figure fading into pines and oaks.

Four snares then sleep.

Noise at the first snare did not sound like the flailing of a delicious animal. It sounded like a dumb human.

Not another.

But when she approached the area, she recognized Dwyn's height, his dark curly hair flying in multiple directions. He turned, surprised, then a large toothy grin expanded over his face.

"I thought I'd check them for you. Figured you'd be asleep."

"No, the snares are my job," she said curtly, communicating her displeasure.

His dimples disappeared with his grin. He dug his toe into the ground, submitting to her.

If the last twenty minutes had been a bad time to interact with others, these minutes would be worse. She hadn't meant to be rude in her greeting; she had just hoped to be alone out here. She hadn't even seen him enter the woods.

"You don't have to take it all on your shoulders, you know."

While she deserved a rebuke, there was much more kindness in it than Audra was comfortable with. She knew he meant more than the snares. It's what Haleigh had said about Gordon.

No one should do this alone.

Audra bit her tongue and instead of replying, started to the next snare. She neither encouraged nor discouraged his following.

He followed as she knew he would.

The next was up over the hill. Her boots treaded softly on the dank pine needles, the crunch of the amber needles gone with fall. Dwyn's footsteps followed almost as muted. No words between them, she could dismiss his noises as a zombie following her climb. She followed the ridge of the landscape, the dry breeze making her face feel tight. Her headache rumbled toward the crown of her head.

Audra had done it alone for so long. Even when she'd carried her sister, she was alone.

A gust of wind grabbed at her hair and continued over the edge and into the valley, swaying the brush and small trees. It wasn't difficult for Audra to imagine the movement in the woods below as that of the dead, drifting like sea currents over the earth. An ocean of hands and teeth.

So many gone. And yet, someone was still to be last.

Maybe chance would choose her. Maybe she was destined to do it alone.

Then, she'd stand last. Until she decided not to. She'd lift the burden from her shoulders and chase it into the sea. She'd leave the world to its fate. Devoid of higher humans. Devoid of higher purpose.

Dwyn and Haleigh were right.

No one could do it alone. Least of all, she.

"Who is that?" called Dwyn behind her.

As if her thoughts had conjured him, a figure climbed the hill towards them. He scrambled uncoordinated, but in using all four of his extremities, he would cover the distance in short time.

Audra held out her hand in caution. Dwyn's curiosity always got the best of him. He'd be stutter-stepping down to meet the danger head-on. She wasn't sure what it was yet, much less who.

This far from Osprey Point's perimeter, roaming rotters were more common, but the thing scaling the hill was more man than rot. Arms, legs, torso, and neck all held proper angles. Well-preserved, not even weather-torn, he could be a half zom scout with many brethren to come. Audra looked past him into the valley and beyond, fearful for a second that her sea of death wasn't a dream. Nothing of the sort. For now.

As he pulled himself up to Audra's and Dwyn's level, Audra recognized the slack-jawed demeanor of a freshly turned, but full-fledged zombie.

And it was just a kid.

Audra sidestepped as she inspected him. No scruff on his paling face. Ash brown hair fell to his shoulders. He was fourteen, fifteen tops. A thin arm reached toward them, its hand ripped open by teeth and now filled with brambles from his climb. He let out a snarl from the corner of his mouth. Audra tried to recall where she knew him from.

She pictured him with shorter hair that didn't cover the green eyes or the freckled cheeks.

"Kip," she said. The zom's head jerked in her direction. More likely in response to the sound than his name.

"He lives in Uno. Or, did."

Uno was the last township on the Lysent rail line. Kip had approached her a few years ago, even more so a kid. He asked her to teach him how to tag. Audra told him no. Told him if he lived in the townships and didn't need to cure a loved one, he should just count his blessings and stay home.

He should have stayed home.

"Help me leash him so we can get him back."

"To Uno?" asked Dwyn.

Audra looked around and realized she didn't have her pack. She had left it at the motel. Her headache shot a bolt of lightning between her eyes. She wouldn't be able to get him back to Uno today. He'd have to come with them.

"Home first. Do you have anything we can tie him up with?"

"What if Uno doesn't want him?"

Dwyn had a point. Even if the corporate cures worked, getting them had become near impossible and a null point. People could barely afford food, much less the treatment for someone who would also need to eat during the winter months and beyond.

And did the corporate cures work? Audra didn't want to think about it. Didn't need to think about it. She would return Kip to his responsible party. They could decide his fate. This was finally a decision Audra didn't have to make.

Audra pulled some dying vine off a tree. Dwyn hadn't offered anything of value.

"That will cut into his wrists," said Dwyn.

What the hell did it matter? Despite it not being her decision, she guessed he'd never be cured. She didn't reply.

Dwyn got behind and held the boy's arms straight out. Audra bound them together.

"What do you think he's doing out here?" asked Dwyn.

"You mean, what was he doing out here," corrected Audra. She reached into the boy's coat pockets.

"That's stealing," explained Dwyn.

"Maybe it will tell us why he's out here. Or, maybe he has a snack to share with us, since we're being so kind to travel with him."

Dwyn shook his head, but didn't argue.

Audra pulled a folded paper from his back pocket. It was machine-pressed, not something a teenager in a Lysent-outskirting town would typically possess. Perhaps he was delivering a letter? Her face crinkled as she scanned its contents.

"What does it say?" asked Dwyn, his curiosity winning over any thoughts of keeping the zom under control.

Audra gave it a hard kick in the back and it tumbled halfway down the hill. It would take time for it to come back up.

"Hey, be gentle," reprimanded Dwyn.

"Hell with that," said Audra as she shoved the letter into Dwyn's chest and slumped against a ragged pine tree, watching their zom climb back up on feet and elbows.

Dwyn read over the form.

"I don't get it," he said. "They're looking for zombies?"

"It's a bounty list offered by Lysent. It's got tag numbers, names, and last-known locations. A hundred and fifty credits redeemable for fuel and food per head."

"So, he's a —"

"Tagger." Kip had apparently gotten his wish. "Check out the name at the bottom of the list."

"Yours. Gordon's on here too."

"Along with half of Osprey point," added Audra. "I recognize all the names. They're looking for MY zombies."

"But they're not all zombies."

"No, but Lysent could make the argument that they were all given faulty cures and will turn."

Audra picked up a stick and dug it into the soft dark ground, spinning it in a screwing motion.

"But why?"

"Who knows," she said. But she knew. Greenly had her army. And she wasn't content to just go in for the kill. First, she'd destroy everything around Audra. She would hurt anyone Audra had ever interacted with. And after Audra watched everything burn, Greenly would grow bored like a cat playing with a mouse — and she'd either end Audra's life or worse, not.

Alone. The last.

Kip arrived back to them.

"What are you going to do with him?" worried Dwyn. Audra threw the stick in her hand. The zombie lurched, following the motion like a dog. The idea this young man could capture anyone seemed laughable, but Audra knew there would be more capable opportunists. "Are you taking him back to the township?"

"No, who's to say they won't grab me and turn me in."

"I could take him."

"He was going to turn us in for cash! He doesn't deserve to go home. He deserves what he got."

"None of us deserve this."

And Audra knew he believed that. But she wasn't convinced that she didn't deserve it. What did she think was going to happen when she took on Larange Greenly and her massive corporation? She should've minded her own damn business. Now, lots of people were going to get hurt.

Audra fought the urge to kick Kip again. Instead she stood up and took a less-steep route back to the motel. Kip and Dwyn followed, other snares forgotten.

5 Restitution

Satomi walked past her room, no longer feeling the high anxiety that had led her to flee earlier that morning. Her eyes flitted from the carpet's worn and blurred geometric patterns to the two tin mugs of liquid she balanced. Peter's room was farther down the hall and to the right.

Jack hadn't even formally given his request during their conversation when Satomi had decided to visit Peter. He was the one person who didn't know what awful things she had done — the false hope she had shared. He didn't even know what awful things he had done. The death toll was in the billions.

His door had a chain installed on its exterior to keep him from wandering. Satomi used one hand and arm to hold the cups of pine needle tea, and the other hand to pull the chain as discreetly as she could before knocking. Satomi was uncertain if Peter remembered or even knew about the chain. She certainly didn't want to explain it.

She gave three firm knocks and listened to the long session of shuffling behind the door. If he took a while it was due to confusion, not physical limitations. Soon, the door opened a crack and its owner didn't even peer out to identify the caller.

"I don't want any food, thank you."

"How about a friend, then?" she asked.

Peter let the door open to a wider angle. His silver hair was combed and parted. He wore a denim shirt tucked into his denim jeans. A neat black belt separated the two. Satomi gave a smile and Peter's blue eyes brightened.

"Evelyn!" he said as he swooped in for a hug, his arms under hers. Satomi held the teas out at length to avoid burning him or herself.

"Satomi, remember?" she said into his ear, her chin resting on his neck. He pulled back immediately, another jostle to her frame and to the teas. He stared hard into her face. His brow furrowed and she wondered if he might throw a tantrum.

"That's what I said," he said. He welcomed her inside.

His room was a poor substitute for the studio apartment on wheels Jack had built him. A straw mattress much like hers, sat in one corner of the room. A table and chairs were the only real furniture. An interior office meant no windows. Along the wall stood a stack of books. Peter spent a lot of time reading.

"Tea, tea," he said, looking around his room. There was no stove to make tea.

"I brought tea," she said as she placed it on the wood veneer table and motioned for him to sit down.

"Oh yes, of course," he mumbled. He sat down, folded his hands in his lap, and waited. He cut his eyes at her. Satomi was sure he had forgotten who she was, but she wasn't sure if it was momentary or if Jack had brought her here under false pretenses.

Satomi slid the cup across the table to Peter. Satomi liked her tea strong and unsweetened, which worked well in the new world of pine trees and dandelion roots. She had resorted to stealing honey from Ryder's stash to temper the tea's sharp taste for Peter. He sipped it and smiled up at her at its sweetness.

Satomi sat across from him and shared his smile. It was easy to like Peter and almost impossible to reconcile the meek and pleasant personality with the person who created a slave army. Satomi wished she knew the truth about his character. If he gained additional mental function, would he be a different person?

"What are you up to, today?" he asked jovially.

"Oh, work, you know."

In truth, probably fumbling around in the laboratory, pretending she had even the first clue how to save her friends from a terrible disease. Her chest tightened at the thought. Helplessness and stress were not benefactors to Eureka moments. And she needed a big one if she was ever going to make progress.

"What kind of work do you do?" he asked.

"I'm a doctor… well, a scientist I guess, at the moment," she stumbled through her words. She wasn't sure if being honest was a good idea but she found a need to talk to someone. She guessed she hadn't much gotten the chance with Ryder being out.

"Oh, I'm a scientist too!" Peter said, his chest puffing a bit. "It's a very noble field."

Satomi couldn't suppress her eyebrow raise, but she did offer a small smile.

"I work with nasty bugger viruses," he started. "Research and development — can you believe that? We actually develop viruses."

"That sounds dangerous," led Satomi.

Working with the original z-virus, he must have some insight. Did his broken mind hold the key to her Eureka moment?

"Yeah, well, I figure it's better to have a finger in the pie. It's my only chance to know what's going on. I don't want to get stuck in the crossfire."

Billions dead.

While it was unfair to blame a middle-management scientist for Lysent's fatal direction, he had realized the risks in his work. Satomi couldn't be sure of the end result if she returned Peter to his former glory in his 'noble field'. But for now, other matters were easier to settle.

"Speaking of pie, I hear you're not eating, Peter."

"Do you have pie?" he asked, looking up from his cup.

Satomi laughed at her mistake. She didn't know anyone who wouldn't be happy to eat a sweet, buttery pie right now. "No, I'm sorry."

"You know they don't feed me," he announced.

His face settled into a worried almost fearful look, as if he really was having trouble getting people to feed him. Satomi imagined his current hunger might be enforcing these thoughts. Did old Peter assume the role of a victim too? Did he ascribe his awful choices to just trying to keep his family alive and well?

"That's awful. If I go get you some food, will you eat it?" she asked.

"Oh yes, thank you. I'm really quite hungry," he said, and smiled.

Satomi wasn't sure what her punishment should be for failing in her antiviral work, but this was definitely Peter's restitution. He had a great mind and little access to it. He had become a burden to the son he was trying to save. Lost a daughter and couldn't mourn her. If Satomi could release him from this mental purgatory, would he deliver the remaining population from his past sins or would he continue to pull strings for personal gain?

Peter's eyes swept over the dreary, windowless room. "Also, I'd like to go home."

Satomi nodded. She gathered the empty cups and promised to return with food for her friend.

* * *

Finally feeling tired, Satomi purposefully marched past her room after successfully getting Peter to eat. If everyone else was kind enough to not mention her insomnia, she would also pretend it didn't exist. She walked through the plaza, around the fountain where people mingled, chatting and laughing. Since the previously cured had been sequestered, Osprey Point had become guiltily relaxed.

Satomi walked through the laboratory's lobby, which now only contained some spare medical equipment and a tremendous pile of telephone cords tangled in a corner. The dark paneling on the walls remained, but desk, chairs, and even waiting area reading materials had been usurped by other community residents.

On the other side of the door lay the reason they were here at Osprey Point. Vesna had helped them locate this isolated laboratory forgotten by Lysent Corporation. It had seemed like a gold mine with its lab equipment and scientists to cure and recruit.

Now, it sat empty. Everyone but Satomi sent to quarantine.

Sure, the equipment was still there. Three rows of counters with cabinet space underneath. Refrigerators against the back wall. Microscopes sat uniformly in a line. Beakers and notebooks scattered with a day's work before its scientists were ushered to a motel. With these items and any available solar power, Satomi was supposed to prevent the extinction of the human race.

Satomi had pushed them to swap the populations. Let those not at risk for reversion go to the motel. They'd have a larger population of scientists working in the appropriate space. But, it was decided the laboratory itself was too valuable for it to be lost in an outbreak. No, Satomi would remain.

Remain to do what, she wasn't sure.

Since she had let go of First, do no harm, decisions had become difficult. Now she was plagued with questions as to what the right direction was. She thought when she saved Ryder from that zombie and held her close that everything would fall into place, but it hadn't.

Ryder refused to stay where she was safe.

Peter didn't deserve to be cured.

Osprey Point depended on her to work diligently in her laboratory until she stepped out with a vial of miracles. Instead, Satomi sat on a stool and stared at an empty space on the counter. She didn't have the slightest clue what was wrong with the antiviral.

A noise behind her startled her. Satomi gave a little yip before turning around to see.

"Sorry to surprise you," said Marla, poking her head in before entering completely into the laboratory. She pushed her black-framed glasses higher onto her nose, which was softly freckled. "I just wanted to see if I could help you today."

Marla was Ryder's junior engineer. She hadn't any formal education, but she did have a knack for figuring out how to fix things. Ryder had taken her under her wing and taught her engineering principles. Together, they were building the infrastructure for a better Osprey Point. Satomi could only wish her work were as tangible as theirs.

"No… no," Satomi hesitated. She wasn't sure what she was doing, much less what someone else would do to help her.

Marla sat down on the stool next to Satomi. She leaned with her hands on the seat between her legs. She looked to Satomi earnestly, sprigs of red hair tucked behind her ears.

"I know it sucks we're all separated," she said. "But, once we figure this out, we'll be able to reunite with everyone."

Once I figure this out… Satomi knew she meant well, but this wasn't helping. Just a reminder of the stakes that were avalanching on top of her, paralyzing her.

"Maybe if you explained to me what you were working on, something might come to you?" Marla suggested.

Satomi shook her head. "I could use more fuel, though. I can't get my materials hot enough with the solar energy."

Marla nodded eagerly, jumping off the stool, believing Satomi's lie. With her exit, Satomi suddenly missed her presence. Unhappy with people. Unhappy without.

Satomi opened her composition notebook and looked over the numbers again, hoping they would offer her some hidden insight on the thousandth viewing. She had measured the viral load in the patients she treated for the z-virus. With each treatment, the load decreased until it wasn't measurable. Then, she continued to test for over a month, to ensure the virus was eradicated from the person.

But the blood sample from Lisa showed the virus had burgeoned in her body. It had not only been reintroduced into her system; it had come back with a vengeance. The viral load was so massive, the three people she bit turned almost immediately.

The virus's return reminded Satomi of bacteria developing resistance to the drugs used to combat them. If this was simply acquired resistance, treating those who hadn't been previously cured should also become more difficult, but it hadn't. And besides the viral load, she saw no difference between first and second infections. She was missing something.

Something that Peter might know. But was it fair to spend precious time curing the person who had put the world in this predicament? Could he fix what he had broken? Peter might just make things worse.

Satomi wished Eli were here to help her decide, or at least keep her company. While he had helped keep her prisoner — standing large at the door of Peter's mobile lab — he was a good man. Despite not having a foundation in science, he was curious and always gave her his undivided attention as she spoke. His warm smile would make his russet face glow, especially when he comprehended a concept Satomi was explaining. He had died protecting her from Jill. To save Peter, her father, felt like betraying Eli.

Eli wasn't here… maybe that was her fault.

Satomi pushed the notebook to the back of the counter. She bent at the waist and let her forehead touch the cool vinyl counter. Her hair fell down at all sides and created a small space of darkness.

She wished to be gone like Eli.

6 Strategy

The morning had gotten late. Audra knew those allowed to be outside their rooms would be when they arrived. Audra grabbed a handful of the back of Kip's shirt as Dwyn wrenched the gate open. Everyone stopped what they were doing and stared at the two's prize.

Katie leaned over a water barrel marked 'Laundry'. Apparently, sleep was escaping her as well. Marcos was fully awake, splitting wood in the far corner. Several others were eating breakfast or otherwise keeping busy in the daylight.

"Who is that?" asked Ryder. She rose from a table scattered with tools and broken contraptions.

"Someone from Uno. He followed us home."

"Then let Uno take care of him," Katie called over.

Kip purred at the sight and scent of Ryder approaching. Her eyes were wide and her voice was hushed. "I don't think this is a good idea."

"He can't go back to Uno. I'll explain later. But this is quarantine. And he needs quarantining." Audra wasn't sure what the big deal was.

"It's just… these people don't need reminders of what they're struggling with." She eyed the young man, pulling like a junkyard dog, t-shirt stretching. "This guy lived in Lysent towns? Let them deal with him. We've got our own to care for. This is bad for morale. You're not here all the time. You don't realize how delicate these people are."

Audra really didn't give a shit how delicate they were. They were turning their backs on a form they were destined to inhabit. If they had red expiration dates stuck onto their foreheads, they'd read 'tomorrow' and 'past due'. They could easily be the next on a leash, foaming at the mouth.

Audra pushed Kip through the parking lot. If anyone had a problem with it, they'd have a physical fight on their hands.

"This is ridiculous. We don't want him here," said someone from the picnic table.

It took a moment for Audra to locate him since he didn't have the courage to meet her eye. It didn't matter. They all needed to hear it.

"What you don't understand is he is you."

Audra scooped up her bag. She wasn't going to pitch a fit over where Kip would stay. He could stay with her. Kip tripped on the curb, slowing their departure. Audra hoped it wouldn't dull the sting of her last words.

They were pretty good last words.

Once inside her room, she walked Kip over the low-pile carpet and released him into the bathroom. Closing the door, she pressed her forehead on it for a moment, listening to the teenager wander the small space. She wouldn't abandon him.

She had done enough of that.

*   *   *

After blessed sleep in which Audra was sure she hadn't stirred a bit since falling face first into the mattress, she woke to fumbling noises in the bathroom. The light bordering her curtains told her it was evening. Audra wondered which evening.

Wiping the sleep from her eyes, she checked her pack for anything needing to be replenished or replaced. She would need extra rope. And she'd need food, but that still wasn't something she was willing to take from the motel.

After washing with a rag and bucket, Audra put on the spare clothes from her bag. Her jacket on top of that. She balled up clothes to take across the way to wash. Resisting the urge to say goodbye to Kip, she stepped outside. Her skin, being recently wet, prickled with the cold underneath her loose clothes.

Dusk was well on its way. The sky was pink with streaks of gray clouds. People were eating supper before the sun dipped and left them in the dark. Audra washed her clothes in the laundry basin and silently waited for the majority of the residents to retire to their rooms. She wanted to meet with the core group, and didn't want the whole motel butting in.

After hanging up her articles of clothing to dry, and hopefully not freeze in the night's air, she invited Dwyn, Gordon, Ryder, and Marcos to meet in her motel room.

Marcos and Gordon brought their own chairs of wood and worn padding in. They sat along the round table with Dwyn. On the bed nearby, Ryder sat with legs crossed and feet tucked under. Audra joined her. Despite their disagreements, they could still remain amiable.

Each had brought in an LED or lantern with homemade fuel (thanks to Ryder's engineering skills) which created patches of light on the wallpapered walls and on the serious faces of the group.

"Should I let Kip out to join the meeting?" Audra teased. Everyone shook their heads 'no,' in case she planned to push the joke further.

They knew her too well.

"Dwyn says there's a list?" asked Marcos.

Without ceremony, Audra pulled out the Lysent directive. They all took turns reading it under their light of choice.

"It's safe to say Lysent is trying to draw you out," announced Ryder, her arms resting on her crossed legs. She glanced at Audra's bag, which was not unpacked. "Are you going to be drawn out?"

"I don't see how I can not go. They're my tags. If I don't help them, no one will."

"A lot of these names are here at the motel," Dwyn reminded softly. "You're not responsible for everyone on this list. You're on this list too, y'know. You need to stay safe."

"The people here are safe. Everyone still thinks this place is overrun. It's the people I left behind. I need to help them."

Ryder shook her head in disagreement.

"I'll go too then," said Dwyn. Audra knew he would offer.

"No, I need you to go to Lysent."

"Wait, what?" he asked, taken aback.

"We don't know if the corporate cures are working. We don't know what she plans to do with her half-zom army. We're in the dark here."

"And how am I supposed to shed light on any of that?"

Audra stopped pulling on a snagged string on her bed's blanket, and mustered the courage. "Corette."

"What! Corette doesn't want to see me!" His face balled up in confusion or pain. "She refused to see me when I was cured. She doesn't want anything to do with me."

Corette and Dwyn were engaged when the outbreaks started. They survived together until Dwyn was bitten. Corette eventually found Lysent, married another, and was able to pay for Dwyn's treatment.

"You really don't get it, do you?" asked Audra.

The wrinkles atop the bridge of Dwyn's nose remained as he tried to decipher her meaning. The others waited awkwardly. Audra was sure some of them had figured it out as well. She hated having this conversation with Dwyn in a group setting, but she wasn't sure if she'd have the guts to tell him otherwise.

"She married him so she could awaken you! She doesn't hate you. She loves you."

Audra's love for Belinda had led Audra to signing her life to the only entity that claimed a successful awakening process. Audra was sure Corette had also signed her life away to save the person she loved. And she signed it with an 'I do.'

Despite the overall shades of jealousy Audra felt for Corette's successes where Audra had failed, Corette could have connections who would be able to give them critical information — attack plans, virus protocols, or more.

"You're grasping at straws," he said with more than a touch of bitterness.

"We need all the straws we can get," said Audra.

And she knew they weren't straws.

Vesna had protected many secrets in her life, but in one instance she hinted that Dwyn had a second connection to the rebel network. When he finally spilled his story months ago, Audra understood.

"I wouldn't even know how to contact her."

"Rosie can connect you. She'll know. She handles all the awakening accounts."

Rosie worked the front desk in Lysent's main building. She was the first person you saw, and as Audra had heard from reports, was still the first person, despite having helped Audra. She had kept Belinda safe from being executed with Vesna by never submitting Audra's release request. She then warned Audra about the impending attack on the laboratory.

Pain shadowed on Dwyn's face. It was obvious he still loved Corette and didn't appreciate the ripping open of an old wound in the name of reconnaissance.

But, they were in desperate need for any sort of advantage. Without it, they'd die. And if Greenly was lying about the efficacy of Lysent-sponsored treatment, lots of others would die too.

"OK. I will talk to her if she will see me," he said as he gave in.

When Audra heard those words, a sharp pain glanced her heart. Images of Dwyn and another girl flashed in her mind. All of a sudden Audra wasn't sure if she had won or not. But it did not matter. Only her people mattered. Not her. Not her vacillating feelings for the annoying man she refused to call Wilfred.

"I'm on the list," said Gordon as if everyone else had missed it.

"Yes, I'm sorry about that," Audra mumbled.

When Gordon had first started looking for his family, Audra had scanned his DNA with her biometric reader. It hadn't told them much, just that someone at some time had inquired about him. Big whoop. However, it had also transmitted the information to Lysent Corporation as the reader was company property. Just another tentacle of the ever-reaching company.

"Don't be. I'm worth food and fuel."

"You're worth credits," she corrected. "Lysent controls the pricing of food and fuel. They could call inflation or whatever the hell they wanted and say you're worth one night's meal."

"That's one more night. Promise me. When I turn, you'll surrender me to Lysent and give the bounty reward to my family." Audra balked. "It's the only way I can provide for my family now."

Audra chewed on her lip. She knew she'd have done the same for Belinda.

Even if she was worth just one night's meal.

Gordon couldn't let Haleigh and Eliza go hungry or be cold, especially if he was mindlessly wandering a remote location as he had for years before.

"OK, I promise," she declared, releasing her bottom lip. Although Audra knew if she could provide for his family another way, there'd be no need to surrender his body to the cold marbled building that was Lysent.

"Ryder, Marcos, keep them safe here. Forage, but don't go far. I don't want anyone getting snagged by a tagger."

"I still don't understand why Lysent wants us — me," said Marcos.

"We live outside their system. Lysent thinks we're a threat. And hopefully we are. Any word from Satomi?" asked Audra.

"No," said Ryder. "And we haven't figured it out here either."

Another reason Audra should leave. She couldn't help them here, but she might be able to outside their fences.

"Things are going to get bad… real bad, before it gets better," said Gordon.

And they might not get better. But moping in a candlelit seance circle wasn't going to get them anywhere. They hugged and said their goodbyes in the small calm before the storm.

7 Goodbye

Dwyn slept on the second floor with his curtain open, so he'd wake with the rising sun. He knew Audra would be getting an early start. She wouldn't stay for goodbyes. He'd have to be outside and in her way to see her off.

His heart had beaten heavily in his chest at the mention of Corette's name from Audra's lips. Worlds colliding. Corette's name stirred a firestorm of pain and confusion. When he was bitten and the virus coursed through his body, all he felt was pain. Then, he suddenly awakened to find he couldn't return to anything he knew. Anything he loved. Corette refused to see him. While Audra ran as a means to escape, Dwyn started running and working for Vesna to fill his life with — something.

Then, he found Audra. A woman who didn't put up with shit in a world full of shit. While his heart involuntarily fluttered in every moment they shared, more than a romantic relationship, he wanted Audra to feel comfortable around the people she defended so intensely. She built a community. Two communities. And refused to live in either one.

The picnic table felt like ice on his rear as he waited for Audra in the morning chill. Could she be right? Corette had married to cure him, not because she loved another?

It was presumptuous.

It was nice to think about.

Even if Audra wasn't correct, she still had a point. Corette at least had felt obligated to make sure he didn't rot in that sedan. If he could speak with her, maybe she'd be willing to share some information that would avert disaster. Or at least, let them know when and what was coming.

Audra looked surprised when she stepped out of Room 2, her pack already on her back.

"You didn't think you'd be able to leave without saying goodbye, did you?"

"One could only hope…" she replied.

It was always difficult to know when she was joking.

Dwyn's knees popped as he got up from the cold seat. While he hadn't aged much during his infection, it still seemed to be catching up to him. He thrust out a bag of shelled pecans, dried fruit, and oatmeal bars with a straight arm to signal his determination that she have it.

"I'm not taking from the stores. They need it here. I can find food while I'm out there."

"Please take it just in case you run into trouble. It's not from the stores. I gathered it while you were sleeping yesterday," he lied.

Fortunately, Audra took the bag without looking at its contents. She shoved it in a side pocket of her pack. Still not saying goodbye long enough to take her pack off. They both walked to the gate.

"And trouble? When have I ever gotten into trouble?" she asked and smiled.

"Only every time you run headstrong into it. So just don't, this one time," he grimaced.

"I'll see how I'm feeling," she said and shrugged with a smile. She was joking this time. Maybe.

Audra tucked her arms underneath his and snuggled her face into the layers of corduroy and flannel on his chest. He kissed her softly on the top of her head. If they could be like this forever, that would be OK. Better would be Audra stopping for just a moment to realize she didn't need to go running off to save people who had never known her, just because Greenly had put them on a list.

He opened the gate for her and she was gone.

Dwyn trudged back to his room to begin packing for his trip. He hadn't done it the night before, because the temptation to help Audra tag would have been too much. It would have been like old times, running maneuvers in the woods and fields, branches and teeth snapping.

*　　*　　*

By the time Dwyn had prepped his bag and stepped out of his dim quarters, the place was bustling with people. Most of them were lined up to get their temperatures taken so they could line up again to get breakfast. The door next to him opened and Gordon emerged from his own poorly lit accommodations.

"Morning — where you going?" Dwyn asked, eying Gordon's khaki-colored pack.

"With you," he said with a smile.

"I appreciate it, Gordon. But they need you here."

"Nah, they don't. Ryder's pretty good at drawing and testing blood now. Marcos is organizing the food-gathering trips."

"I still think you can do more here," suggested Dwyn. It wasn't that he didn't want the company… "I'm probably just headed for a dead end."

"You and me both, brother." He gave Dwyn a small punch on the shoulder. "I'm going to surrender to Lysent. Get that bounty."

Had they all gone crazy?

"Audra promised she'd take you there if you turn."

"And you believe that? She's not going to take me. She's never given up on anyone."

That wasn't true.

Dwyn hadn't known Belinda. Audra wasn't really open to talking about it — or anything really, for that matter — but he knew the two had been on their own for the longest time. The Audra he knew now had emerged from that relationship's tangled roots.

Gordon opened his canteen, which steamed with citrus and bitter pine. He tipped the mouth of the container toward Dwyn. "Besides, it's not if – it's when. I have a fever."

Dwyn felt his heart drop lower in his chest. It just wasn't fair. Gordon's health was deteriorating. Lysent's stance was that Gordon deserved it for not having the financial means to go through 'proper' channels, that Dwyn was safe because he was well-connected. But neither of those things was in Dwyn's or Gordon's control.

What was in Gordon's control was a decision to trade his body in for food and fuel for his family. And soon, he would lose that opportunity as well.

Dwyn gave a nod and a flick of his eyes for Gordon to join him. They topped off their canteens with more tea before heading toward the rail line and its easy navigation to Lysent corporate headquarters.

*　*　*

After having navigated to the grocery store, Audra appreciated her half broken-in trails. She opened her gait and coursed through the woods.

Endless pines, oaks and sweetgums crowded the trail, giving Audra a bit of camouflage as she pushed toward the highway.

I-16.

She and Dwyn had left several in cars along the highway. They would be easy to check on, gather, and bring home. The rest were spread out. They would take time.

Audra had time.

This was something she could do. She couldn't cure the z-virus. She couldn't medically tend to the sick. But she could round them up before bounty hunters did. She could keep them safe until the world could be made safer.

The chill in the air kept her body temperature down, allowing her another level of speed impossible to sustain in Georgia summers. Dwyn had wanted to come, but he never would've kept this pace for the hours Audra would. His top speed was always faster, but she had the endurance to run for what seemed like forever.

Audra's breath caught in her chest, not from her exertion, but from thinking about Dwyn. It wasn't lost on her that she had sent him to speak with his ex-fiancée after assuring him the woman still had feelings for him. Dwyn's feelings for Audra were earnest, but she had pushed him away so many times. A relationship would demand Audra communicate emotions and vulnerabilities. It was easier to stay closed off. It was easier to run. She just wasn't sure how easy it would be to watch him move on.

Hours passed before Audra popped out of the forest and onto the highway. Large swaths of wire grass had died and fallen. Their brown streaks matched the rust of the decaying cars, shoved and overturned by Jack's old convoy. That convoy was sorely missed now. If they had managed to hold onto those vehicles, they could've gotten the hell out of Dodge, leaving Greenly and her wrath behind. Or, even she could've just gone and escaped the punishment of watching her mistakes snowball into another outbreak.

No matter as it was all wishful thinking. Without vehicles and a reliable source of fuel, they were locked in.

It didn't appear any vehicles had come through since the convoy. No bustling cars. No terror here. She raced down the highway on foot, pine straw and empty plastic bottles crunching underneath her feet. Despite the throes of winter, human touch was being eaten away by vegetation, streams, and trees. The median and the other side of the highway were indistinguishable from one another. Their phase on Earth might be snuffed out before it ever got started again, the remainder of them just a second round of fertilizer for a new, peaceful world.

Audra ran until things almost looked familiar. She slowed to a walk, peeking into shattered windshields and warped windows. With the highway changing and yet the same mile after mile, it became one thing to remember she'd left a young girl in a sedan and entirely a different thing to remember which sedan. Audra's mind began playing tricks on her. Had she missed her or was she gone? The attack she suffered on this highway clouded and crowded her memories.

Just as Audra convinced herself she needed to backtrack, she caught sight of the cherry red, now rusty red, vehicle parked at an odd angle on the shoulder of the road. The antenna had been bent into a zig zag at the top. Her mark. Approaching the rear passenger door, she wiped the filth off the window with her sleeve to get a better look. Her heart dropped to her stomach.

The little girl was no more.

The door handle gave with a creak. The familiar odor was not overpowering, just a part of her world. The body slumped against the opposite window and door. She pulled the decaying body down until it was lying on the seat cushion. Her skin had mottled with green and gray hues.

Audra walked around and opened the opposite door, ignoring the bodily fragments left behind. She forced the girl's eyelids over the emptiness. Audra pulled the yellow tag off the brown ear — a tag she had left when she abandoned this girl. She wiped the flesh off the tag against the back of the passenger seat before putting it in her pocket. Her breath stuck in her throat.

As she climbed out of the car, she looked around for something to leave her. No flowers to be seen. Just winter and death. Audra walked through the drainage ditch and into the forest, climbing a tree to cut down some boughs of evergreen. The somber woman folded and braided, scratching up her arms with the sharp needles and protective bark, until she had a half wreath for the girl. She crawled back inside with the bones and sinew to wrap the head in a green offering.

Audra gently shut the door. She turned around and she finally broke, her knees buckling, her back scraping the crustiness on the door. She let fat tears roll through her hands to her knees underneath.

Audra had found that girl alive, and instead of helping her, she had checked to see if she could use her for gain. When she couldn't, she trapped her without any way to get food. Lysent said they would round them up and keep them safe. Lysent lied. And Audra knew Lysent lied. She had left her there to starve and rot.

It seemed those were the only options left — starve or rot — but in trapping that girl, she was no better than Lysent.

Wiping the tear-filled grime off her hands, Audra pulled out the list of names bountied, really sentenced to death, because their paths had crossed Audra's. A heavy burden of grief settled over her as she realized she had knocked out half of this list herself. Many to ash in the trailer she had traded Greenly. Lysent needn't even bother. She was doing fine killing them all on her own. And their faulty cure — that would do the rest.

Despite the barrage of death, Audra climbed from the ditch where she sat. If this tag was untouched, then there was a chance the others on the highway were also undisturbed. She tightened the straps on her bag, and marched on, determined to help at least one person on the list. Her list of failures.

8 Tagging

Audra braced herself with a deep, heaving breath before she approached the black car. Her stomach twisted in knots. Would the teenage boy she and Dwyn left in there be dead? Gone? Audra hoped for the latter over the visual confirmation that another had died.

She muttered a little prayer as she used her sleeve, nasty from the red sedan and her breakdown, to clear the window. The black-brown muck didn't allow itself to be removed as much as it simply shifted to the sides. Audra fell back in surprise as a mass charged at the window. Teeth snarled atop receding gums. They smacked the glass with a clunk. Gray orbs for eyes bulged. Audra's ass hit the asphalt and she laughed in surprise before more closely examining her captured tag. He had already sunk back in his seat, having depleted the energy available to him. The teenager's papery skin had a sheen of grease. His stomach and lower legs bloated and no fat or muscles to speak of, but he was alive.

Audra poured water through the partially opened window, noticing rain stains along the interior of the door. Carcasses of a few rodents lay on the floorboard. Rats seeking rotting flesh to find it wasn't quite dead had sustained the teenager — Link Culpepper as the bounty list had reminded her. Link lapped up the water, his swollen tongue scraping along the filmy surface of the window.

Pushing into the woods, Audra searched until she found a small rodent den. Building her snare with sticks and a wire, she baited it then repeated the process at another den. She wished her traps luck. Hopefully she'd catch a mouse. Even better, two. One for Link and one for herself. Hedging her bets, she foraged before setting up her tent within visual range of Link's vehicle. She wanted the opportunity to protect him if another tagger came by.

Soon she had a rat for her pal Link. She bled it, letting the rich liquid flow down the window for his consumption. She then fed him bits at regular intervals late into the afternoon. Link revived with a new energy. The virus was a curse and a blessing for the resilient human body. She yanked the rusty door open and Link fell out. Getting to his feet, he followed her just as he had when she first met him. However, walking was slow. His feet dragged and twisted underneath swollen ankles. Audra forewent the leather mask. Link deserved the full experience of a change in scenery.

When she approached her next stop along the highway, she tied him to a yellowing side view mirror a few cars away. She knew what she'd find. She braided another bough of pine greenery before approaching the car. She laid it gently around the elderly lady's bones. She picked the tag off the seat where it had fallen and put it in her pocket with the others. At least no one else would try to make money off of her body.

Audra had done enough of that.

Monetizing the sick. Monetizing the dead. She and everyone else had survived only to betray the last of humanity. They deserved whatever was coming. A second outbreak. A wiping out. An extinction. They had failed spectacularly.

Audra distracted herself by searching the ground as she led ambling Link. Lars and Lindon would have covered these miles after attacking her and stealing her pack. Besides being hungry for a few days, Audra had lost several personal mementos. While she knew chances were slim, her eyes swept the road and her feet kicked over loose debris. A carved figurine. A discarded photograph with Belinda's smile. Seen just one more time. Audra yearned for a reminder, but not for the person. Belinda would be out of her mind with terror if she had to face the looming threat of reversion. Where Belinda was, fear could no longer wrap its claws around her.

Better than a physical memento, that was something to hold onto.

The tautness and angle of the leash changed ever so slightly behind her. Only years of pulling zombies allowed her to sense the change, even if she couldn't explain it. Link looked straight ahead, but not at her. Beyond her. Audra's eyes followed but saw nothing. She pulled him off the highway in any case. He sensed something she didn't.

A pack of men tromped down the road past her and Link's hiding spot. Eight men she didn't recognize. Either travelers or just venturing from the safety of Lysent townships. Were they hunting tags? Hunting her? If so, they'd continue on the highway where they'd find boughs decorating dead bodies. She hoped they'd let them rest.

Audra decided to continue on not using the roads. Link would move even more slowly, but they'd move more safely.

* * *

The residents of the motel tensed as Audra entered with Link. The few tables were filled with people, playing cards or eating. Always eating. Ryder stood over a pot of steaming stew. Audra hoped there was at least one group out foraging for food to replace what they'd eaten today.

"Another one?" a man with deep ocher skin and slick black hair said around the food in his mouth.

"Yes… I'm bringing him here because it's quarantine," Audra said slowly as if they were kindergarteners forgetting yesterday's lesson.

Ryder stood back, not supporting Audra's idea of quarantine or pointing out the man's hypocrisy.

"I just don't see the point. We have no doctor. No cure. Just this dusty motel to die in," he said, having swallowed his food.

Audra felt heat rising over her collarbone and creeping up her neck. She covered half the distance to the table. Link pulled ahead on his leash, limiting her movement.

"I didn't clear out this entire place for you to die here," she answered with a cold calmness.

"No, I think when we turn, you'll go back to Osprey Point. This is just your dumping ground," started another person at the table. "And we don't want them here."

Audra launched forward, grabbing Link by the back of the shirt before barreling toward the table and stopping just short. The Snow White derivative — jet black hair, unnaturally white skin, and lips splattered with rat blood — did his part by pulling and snarling. Link acted like Audra felt.

"What the hell!" came shouts, which just riled Link further as the complainers tumbled off the bench, trying to find distance. From the corner of her eye, Audra saw Ryder rushing over. She didn't have much time before the situation would be yanked from her hands.

"While he looks like a monster to you, this boy's name is Link Culpepper. His family was evacuating the coast when he succumbed to his illness. We will keep him safe until a cure can be found. And when you get sick, we will do the same for you. Even though I don't like you as much as I like Link."

Audra pulled Link away from the table. She heard Marcos stifle a giggle from the corner. Ryder stopped short of intervening, shock on her face. The people stood up and brushed themselves off.

"This isn't a dumping ground. You're welcome to leave if you don't like how we do things." She waited for the woman who called it such to make eye contact with her. "But you should know. Lysent is hunting those who have lived outside their system — you. You will not be treated well if you fall into their hands."

"Why? We didn't do anything wrong."

"Apparently they believe in us more than we believe in ourselves. They see us as a threat that needs to be eliminated. So let's trust each other to outlast this bad break and see each other through — turned or not."

"Where will you keep him?" asked Ryder, hesitating and mousy. "We don't have any more spare rooms."

"In mine," she answered.

"Where will you stay? Surely not in there with them."

"I'm not staying," she said plainly as she escorted Link to her room.

"She sure does like the young boys it seems," giggled someone from another table.

Audra ignored him.

With Link deposited into her room, Audra immediately turned about face and began to head out.

"If anything happens to Link or Kip, I'll make sure the same happens to you," threatened Audra. There were nods all around. Apparently she had gotten through to some, or at least scared the heck out of them.

Ryder walked with her to the gate. "I know you want to help them, but aren't there more important things to do?" she asked softly so the others wouldn't hear.

Audra reeled around, "There is nothing more important! I won't sit back and let my tags be scooped up for slaughter. I won't."

At one time Ryder felt a duty to the sick and vulnerable. Now she argued for safety. What did safety matter if they lost their humanity for it? She let the gate bang open in the crisp air and didn't stop to close it.

They were good at that.

9 Sisters

Dwyn and Gordon decided to meet up with the rail line and follow it to Choros, the township housing Lysent corporate headquarters. While it wasn't the most direct route, it was the least complicated. Not having the years of Audra's experience in traipsing through the woods, they didn't want to chance getting lost before completing their tasks.

They gave Uno a wide berth when they neared it. As a township that had sent out taggers, they couldn't be trusted. If anyone recognized Gordon, he could be detained and sent to Lysent. And while that's where Gordon wanted to end up, he didn't want anyone besides his family benefiting. Dwyn promised he'd trade the credits for food and fuel and deliver it to Haleigh.

For the first hour of walking, both men were wrapped in their own thoughts. But Dwyn realized he'd work himself into a frenzy worrying about all the worst-case scenarios of his current venture. He imagined Gordon felt the same in his contemplation. Dwyn decided an effort toward small talk was necessary, if only to keep out of their own heads. Gordon must have had the same idea.

"So, you were a tagger when you met Audra?" he asked abruptly.

Dwyn laughed. "Audra wouldn't say so. I was uh, pretty green."

Dwyn remembered his fumbling attempts to scan zombies before Audra had taught him the ropes.

He recounted his job placement. "After they woke me up, they explained to me that during the outbreaks, many people were 'misplaced' in the chaos. Taggers reunited the sick with the healthy. It was a crock, but I was required to have employment and 'Lysent goon' didn't have a lot of appeal."

"You think this bounty is a crock?" asked Gordon. His face flushed with either the exertion of the hike or with his illness. Dwyn himself felt a little warm.

"You'll get something, but nothing worth your life."

It was Gordon's turn to laugh. "I'm not sure my life is worth much. I wasn't there for Haleigh and Eliza at the onset. I was in that damn laboratory, and what did I accomplish? Nothing. And now, I can sit in my room and revert, or I can give them something."

Dwyn hated it but it was Gordon's decision. And it wasn't even a horrible one. He was sacrificing himself for his family. A decision many had made over the years. Audra tagging for her sister. Vesna's fatal push to dampen Lysent's rule. Ziv to cure the half zoms. And maybe Corette. What was his sacrifice? And whom was it for?

"Is it weird going to see your ex?" asked Gordon, pulling Dwyn from his reverie.

"Well, yeah. Audra could just be talking shit because she thinks this is the best play. Corette could hate me. Turn me in for a few bucks."

"What was she like before? Hell, what were you like before?"

Dwyn realized he hadn't really discussed it with Gordon. Their past lives were so different, they didn't really seem relevant. But then again, maybe he hadn't changed much.

Dwyn blinked and instantly could smell her lavender perfume. "She was a dancer and I was head over heels. I couldn't believe she agreed to marry me. We were so young." He paused. "After all this, I thought maybe I had loved her more than she had loved me."

"Young and idealistic. Me too — I thought by staying in the lab, I was going to save the world."

"Will you hang back until I feel things out at Lysent? I mean, uh, how sick are you?"

"Low-grade fever still, but it's just a matter of time, right? Lisa has already reverted and I was before her. But yes, I can try."

"A low-grade fever? Dude, you got time. What if we took a little detour after I meet Corette?"

"Detour? We'd already be there."

"I'm just thinking, you could go up and see your little girl. I'll watch out for you, make sure you get where you need to be. Keep everyone safe. I am after all, a tagger."

"You'd do that for me? Don't you need to get back and… save the world?" Gordon looked at him in earnest.

"I'm saving my part," he assured Gordon. "Plus, if I can buy some time, maybe I can convince you not to sign yourself over to the corporation."

"I'm not sitting around."

"I know, I know," Dwyn assured him.

But those weren't the only two options.

Dwyn raised his arm and ran his fingers along the silver links of the fence. He could almost make out the melody. A small song in the woods. Dwyn thought of Corette's sweeping lines and wondered if she still danced.

* * *

Dwyn showed Gordon a spot by the creek outside the Choros fences. When Audra had business in Choros, she was often here instead. He smiled as he remembered Audra running off with his clothes when he was bathing there one day. She and Vesna had really taken him under their wings. They introduced him to this new world and showed him that it wasn't that bad. Only the people who lived in it and made it bad were the ones that soured it. And Vesna explained that could be fixed. They could eventually overthrow Greenly and Lysent. And he, in turn, had convinced Audra. But did it all start here with Corette? Was she the first one in his life to take a stand against Lysent's principles, so that he could do the same?

Even though he hadn't made a name for himself as a tagger, rebel, or anything in between, he still felt nervous standing at the gate. Tall, bulky guards stood in front of the massive timber block gate. They had upgraded since he was last here.

The two men, almost identical in size and color, said nothing to him. One waved his hand, a signal to someone hidden. And mechanical noises accompanied the opening of the gate. Dwyn cautiously stepped inside, but no one stopped him. It seemed Choros had become so confident that they were open to public business.

Dwyn took a deep breath, fighting against his shoulders arching into his ears. He wasn't sure if it was being so close to Lysent headquarters or the possibility of seeing Corette that was making his entire body tense. He stiff-marched up the main drag, which had been dressed in cobblestone. It seemed that being close to headquarters had its perks.

No one paid the man any attention as he entered the gated plaza, rounded the fountain, and walked up the tall white building's steps. The tall windows glistened and when Dwyn entered the marbled lobby, he thought the combination magnified the light. No matter the weather outside, it was just brighter in the Lysent building.

A mahogany desk sat center, like a sentinel protecting the administrative keep. A woman with round cheeks and dark hair that fell in coils sat behind it, her fingers deftly separating paper from file. Her brown eyes matching her desk looked over their papers to see him standing there.

"Dwyn!" she said, taking no time to recall his name. "How is she?"

He knew whom she spoke of. While she remembered Dwyn's name, it was Audra who held a special place in Rosie's heart.

"She's doing well. We're all doing well. Thanks to you," he said with a somber smile.

Rosie had saved Belinda from being slaughtered with a simple paperwork error. And she'd saved the entire laboratory by warning them about an incoming attack.

Rosie gave a soft smile as if these things were basic duties in her line of work. Then the smile turned mischievous and her eyes sparkled.

"Are you two…?" she asked.

"No ma'am."

Rosie shook her head. Her soft curls echoed the movement. "It's not good for a person to grow up alone out there like she did."

"She had her sister," reminded Dwyn. Audra could make connections. Belinda was proof.

"She had a burden," Rosie corrected unapologetically. She straightened a thick stack of papers, and then immediately placed a larger, more disordered stack of papers on top. "So what can I help you with, tagger Dwyn?"

"I was hoping you could connect me with someone."

"Isn't that the job of a tagger?" she asked, amused.

Dwyn smiled. If he was still tagging, the fact he hadn't seen Rosie in the last year did not bode well.

"Corette Ku—" her maiden name of Kuzma trying to roll off his tongue. "Corette Godin. She awakened me. I'd like to say thank you."

Rosie squinted thoughtfully. "I do think it's time." Dwyn wasn't sure what that meant, but at least Rosie seemed willing to help. Rosie straightened in her chair as if returning to her administrative duty. "I will arrange a meeting for you, at the creek, outside the fences, tomorrow morning."

"Thank you, Rosie."

"No problem, dear. Don't give up on Audra, all right? She's been through more than most."

Dwyn nodded, already anxious to see his Corette.

*　*　*

Audra ran. More, she sprinted until she was out of sight of the motel and even the highway. Sooner than she was ready, her lungs began to burn and her legs slowed without her permission. Sweat stuck inside her shirt, pulling her skin. The space between her nose and lips moistened.

Her tags would die, just like those in the semi-trailer, the open roof billowing with smoke, ash, and flame. She pumped her arms ever harder to get the last of her sprint until her feet stumbled. Her face careened into the pine needles, scraping the high of her cheeks and neck.

She lay there for just a moment. The silence. The constant silence. Just her heavy panting into the dirt, the heaviness of her pack, and nothing moving within earshot.

All dead.

She snapped off her bag and rolled over. Dark branches scratched through the overcast. Dead leaves. Dying earth.

When her breath settled in her stomach and slowed, she pulled herself up against a small poplar. Pulling out the list once more, she tried to ignore the names of those already lost. At least others would be searching for bodies gone. Instead, she racked her brain to remember all the tags she had left in secure locations, locations where they'd have been able to survive.

Audra used the poplar tree to pull herself up. She needed to hurry. Time would kill anything Audra couldn't reach.

Hours of running led her to back roads that slipped through overgrown fields. Green tractors, sweeping arches of irrigation systems, hay balers and their decaying rolls scattered along the farm land. These places supported the food supply for thousands when thousands was just a drop in the bucket.

It wasn't good tagging grounds though. It seemed those who fed people didn't get much in return. Most families from this area couldn't afford to awaken their loved ones. By the time the awakening process was set up, farmers had already shared all their knowledge and skill to help others survive. They had nothing left to trade.

A fallen sign for Hunt Drive signaled to Audra to turn from the asphalt road to a gravel road. She peeled the sign from its tangled nest and chucked it into the field. The ground was evidently disturbed, but at least undeniable confirmation of the spot had been removed.

Audra traversed the lengths of a couple of fields before she reached the head gate on Hunt Drive. A metal sign hung a good ten feet over her head. Hunt Farm. No way she'd be chucking that sign. She walked underneath the graying archway.

The large two-story house had probably looked imposing before, but now that the exterior was falling apart, it seemed even more intimidating. Its sunken wrap-around porch, jagged like teeth. Shutters falling off hinges as sagging facial features. Audra tiptoed on the floor joists of the porch. An open front door allowed anything to come and go, animals and spirits alike, but also offered rain water and vermin to any occupants within.

Kaci and Sofi Hunt were high school-aged daughters of the Hunt Farm apparently abandoned when they turned. Audra wasn't sure what would push the Hunt parents to leave such an advantageous spot, but then, she had also never lost offspring to a gruesome disease. A storm must have passed through to leave the exterior in such disaster. The interior was otherwise intact.

Audra stepped into the foyer and waited. She hadn't made much noise, but for hosts that hardly ever had visitors, it would be enough. Moisture from the elements had crept into the space. Where tile protected the floor, shoes lined against the wall rotted underneath damp fallen jackets. The hooks on the wall remained stalwart, but the walls were stained and pitted.

Audra was surprised no one had come to greet her. She looked up the stairs, following the wrought iron rail up to the second floor and its balcony hall. Past the stairs were several doorways. A large kitchen with an island bar, breakfast nook, and butcher table. A dining room with the furniture perfectly aligned — never used before or after. Audra entered the open living area with a double fireplace, dried-up throw pillows, and intact couches. And sleeping bags. And camping supplies.

Audra finally heard someone approach, but it wasn't decaying twins coming with a pitcher of lemonade and neighborhood gossip. It was boots on the porch joists and the rattle of a door unsticking from the tile on the floor.

Shit.

Audra stepped softly but quickly into the back end of the kitchen, out of view of the foyer. Opening a door, she found the laundry room as well as Sofi and Kaci. Their buttery blond hair crept down to their waists, blending with their pearly skin with a jaundice tinge. They had the same sharp noses and even tilts of the head as they turned to look at Audra. Audra left the door open a crack. She might need a diversion.

She heard cackling laughter bouncing in the foyer as she slipped into the walk-in pantry. The door creaked open but closed with a dry click. She hoped the twins hadn't caught sight of her entering her hiding place.

"What was that?" Audra heard a thump of two bodies and the laughter ended.

Audra was left in the dark. She hadn't even seen the entire interior of the pantry before she closed herself inside. Afraid to shift her feet, she pulled out her dagger and bent her knees, ready to strike if someone opened the door.

They were silent and she was silent. Then Audra heard the rasp of labored breathing as the women migrated across the kitchen.

"Oh hell, the twins figured out doors," a deep voice announced. Heavy boots met the women's barefoot steps and ushered them back into the laundry room. A scraping sound as something was braced against the laundry door. The back wall of the pantry backed into the living room and Audra could hear two other people – which matched the number of blanket piles Audra had seen.

"That'll keep 'em," the voice gruffed in the kitchen.

It would keep more than just them. Audra's eyes adjusted to the light coming through the bottom of the door and saw the pantry floor clear. She allowed herself to shift her feet.

She'd be here awhile.

"Wanna try to fish?" asked a voice in the living room. "It's been warmer these last couple of nights."

"Yeah, yeah," came a voice which shifted with the owner's movement through the house.

"I don't know why anyone'd leave this place," laughed someone else, matching the grating laugh that had first traveled through the front door.

"Well we're gonna have to, to take these girls to Lysent. I'm thinking we stop by Osprey Point on our way there. Maybe we can grab someone else."

The three rummaged around and bantered for a bit before she heard them pass through the kitchen for the back door. Audra recalled a pond out back. Laughter was right. This would have been a wonderful place to bring Belinda. A modern home where she could pretend the world was normal minus the Internet and cable television.

Audra gave the men time to settle in their fishing spots. She didn't want someone retrieving something they'd forgotten while she was out of her hiding spot. With the house continuing its silence, Audra opened the pantry door. It gave with a low-volume, but high-pitched complaint.

Audra paused again to assess for sounds that were not her own before she slipped out into the kitchen. Tall windows and a windowed patio door looked out to the pond a hundred feet away from the house. Audra decided they'd have trouble discerning motion inside with the glare and refraction.

As Audra tried the doorknob of the laundry room to verify it hadn't been locked, the chair placed against the door slid then clattered to the floor. Audra didn't see any reaction from the men outside. Inside, the girls faced each other and rocked from foot to foot in sync with each other. Audra had never seen such behavior. Had they inadvertently hypnotized each other? Audra didn't have time to think about it. She wrapped her silk cloth around the wrist of each, attached a lead, and walked them out of the kitchen and into the foyer.

After navigating the broken porch and crossing underneath the Hunt Farm sign, Audra helped them pick into a run. With good form (for zombies) and coordination to stay upright, the girls could have been track stars. They left laughter and fishing in their dust... although Audra did laugh herself as she thought about the men trying to understand how the girls had mastered the barricaded door and escaped.

10 Connections

He waited. He didn't know if she would come. He hoped she would come, even if it was just to tell him to leave her alone. Then he'd know. But he wouldn't know if she didn't come. If she didn't come then maybe she was too scared, or was stopped, or didn't trust. God, he wasn't making any sense.

Dwyn watched the water flow over the river stones. The bright blue sky reflected in the water, making it appear clearer than it was. After long runs, he and Audra would soak their feet in the cool water, rubbing their blisters and hot spots on the smooth river rocks, massaging sore muscles. It was one of the rewards of running — the pure relaxation that could follow. He wished he could reach that place now, but instead his stomach twisted in knots and his heart danced around, even though he commanded that it slow. He was here to ask for her help in upending a corporation, not for her hand in marriage.

He remembered when that had happened too. He had taken her to a fancy dinner. She loved to dress up and eat a three-course meal with white tablecloths and where the server placed the napkin in your lap. Dwyn always found the places rather impersonal, but he liked to watch her there. She could be so sophisticated with her sly smile. Dwyn didn't even remember dessert. They had two options, and he didn't remember which one he had. He was too nervous. He paid for dinner. He must have, else they wouldn't have let them leave, right? And now they were walking down the sidewalk. He gave her his jacket. She said she didn't want it. It was quite warm.

Oh, so it was.

"Can we walk through the park before we leave? I really like this park."

"It's a little dark," she remarked.

Was it?

"That's OK – let's just go to the fountain. It's lit up. I want to make a wish." He smiled broadly.

She smiled back. "OK."

She didn't complain that he was making her walk in her nice heels. Later they'd realized the leather on the back of one was ruined after getting stuck in a crack between two concrete insets. And when they got to the fountain, it was beautiful. The prism of colors from the lights flashed and made the fountain look much prettier than it actually was. They had spent many an hour here, making wishes, and spending time with each other.

He kissed the penny and tossed it in, but instead of making a wish to the fountain, he knelt down in front of Corette and held out a velvet box with a ring.

"Will you?" he asked.

"I will," she said.

And his wish came true.

Or, no it actually didn't. He had forgotten that for a second. His wish had not come true. Months later instead of leafing through their wedding planning book, they were running for their lives. It was a different hand in hand. It was a nightmare.

"Is it you?" someone asked of his back.

He was sure he was doing something, but he wouldn't remember what later. He turned and saw her. She looked just as beautiful as when they had first met, although she had matured much more. Dwyn was behind a few years for all his slowed metabolism. She hadn't had that experience, instead she had experienced much more. Subtle wrinkles accentuated her dark eyes. Her thin nose leading down to lips and perfect teeth were just as he remembered, but her dark brown hair was sprinkled with fine gray. She had worried, struggled, and fought to survive. And she had. She had even carried Dwyn through to this new place and world. She was the reason he was there. And he was so thankful.

"It is. I… I… thank you," was all he could muster as the tears flowed.

"What?" she approached him cautiously.

"Thank you for curing me. I have all of this because of you."

"It's not much. I'm sorry I couldn't give you more," she said with a concerned smile.

"It's so much. I have a chance out here."

"May I give you a hug?" she asked.

Corette walked toward Dwyn. Her steps were so graceful. Long legs creating perfect lines.

Wrapping his arms around her, he found himself wrapped in that familiar lavender scent.

He couldn't help himself. It burst from him before he knew it. "Do you love me?"

"It's not that simple."

"I know that. Boy, do I know that. But, I just need to know what happened between us."

"Nothing happened between us. It happened to us. You got bit. I had to survive on my own. I found someone else."

The last sentence stung Dwyn.

"Do you love him?" he asked.

"I couldn't find it in myself to kill you after you turned. But I mourned you as if you were dead. Eventually I met Hiram. And yes, I do love him."

Dwyn let go and nodded his understanding. He was thankful for what he had, but it turned out, that was all he had.

"I'm so sorry about Vesna." It was her turn to burst out.

"What do you know about Vesna?" he asked, confused.

"I knew her. She recruited me, same as you later. I swear I didn't know what Greenly had planned."

Dwyn's head was spinning. "Wait, you're part of the rebel network?"

Corette nodded, her light skin paled.

Dwyn's face broke into a giant grin. At the same time, his eyes teared up.

"How many of you are there? In Lysent?"

"Just a handful, but we've all worked to key positions. I work in the armory. Clyde has access to the entire campus."

"Your husband, Hiram?" Dwyn tried out his name.

Corette shook her head. Dwyn didn't push.

"Do you know if the corporate cure is still working?"

"No, I don't know. I've tried to find out. Something is definitely going on, but they're keeping it under wraps."

Dwyn wasn't sure if the non-answer was better than confirmation he was at risk for reversion.

"Do you know what she has planned?"

"I know she's gathering her forces. Training the zombie soldiers. I think she's going to war, but I don't know who against."

Dwyn smirked. "Probably us."

Corette's eyes went wide. She hugged him tightly.

*   *   *

Satomi jumped in surprise with the whine of the lab's door. She thankfully landed back on her stool, not falling to the chilly floor.

Satomi finger-combed her hair and hoped Marla hadn't noticed she was sleeping. She couldn't sleep at night, and she couldn't stay awake during the day. The only consistency was her inability to get anything done.

"Sorry to bother you," said Marla.

Marla didn't appear to have sleep problems. Her eyes shined brightly underneath her dark spectacles. Her wavy red hair was pulled into a fluffy ponytail.

"What is it?" Satomi rubbed the warm spot on her forehead, which was probably red and wrinkled from its pressure on the counter.

"There's… there's someone at the gate."

Satomi's eyes went wide. She could hear the worry in Marla's voice now. What was Satomi supposed to do about someone at the gate? Audra and Ryder, their capable leaders in war and peace, had left. Satomi was more apt to hide than to answer the call of a stranger.

Crap. What was she going to do?

"Is Jack around?"

"He was out gathering. I don't know when he'll be back."

There wasn't much she could do besides climb the scaffolding and speak for Osprey Point. Satomi somberly stood up and pressed the wrinkles from her long lab coat before taking small steps to meet Marla at the door.

Several people were already outside with melee weapons, waiting for some signal to attack or scatter. Across from the fountain and atop the scaffolding, Satomi saw the brunet and blond pair of Branson and Tess, arrows nocked. Satomi couldn't recall ever climbing up there.

She gripped the rough pine sides and worked her way up, trying not to rock the structure. She trusted Ryder's engineering skills, but heights were another matter. Positioning herself between Branson and Tess, Satomi put her hand on the edge of the solid metal barricade positioned on the fence. It rattled, echoing in the forest. Pulling her shaking hand back to herself, she peered over the fencing.

Three men stood below. A long-faced man with blond dreads kept two horses. A large man with a wiry red beard kept Jack, blue knit hat askew and his arms bound behind his back. He looked up at Satomi with an apologetic grimace.

The redhead cried out a greeting. "Hallo good scientist!"

Satomi blinked. She didn't recognize them, but apparently he knew who she was. Or maybe it was just the lab coat.

"Hello. What uh, can I do for you? Why do you have my…" it was hard to say it, "friend?"

"Well, he was out here all by his lonesome! Haven't you all ever heard of the buddy system?"

"Of course, we just don't have a lot of hands to go around," she said before realizing her mistake.

Tess snickered next to her. Jack hung his head. Satomi wondered again why they had no one better to stand up here. She should not be up here.

"Well, that's a shame," said the man with the two brown mares. "We're here for your turn-backs."

"Turn-backs?"

"Ex zombies, gonna-turn-agains, I don't care what you call them. Whoever's sick or is gonna get sick again," he explained impatiently.

"We don't have any of those," said Jack, helping Satomi. "They hit the road. Didn't want to be here when they… y'know." Jack shrugged his shoulders to accompany the end of his sentence.

The redhead's voice grew raucous. "Hey, I'm getting them off your hands. They're going to turn any day now and you're going to be behind the walls with them, running for your life. I'm just making this easier. Taking them to headquarters where they can get treatment and safety."

"Are they also going to get some cotton candy and a pony?" asked Jack from the corner of his mouth, but loud enough for Satomi to hear.

The broad man tugged on the bindings, throwing off Jack's balance in response. Satomi didn't need Jack's comment to know their proposal wasn't favorable. They were rounding up the sick for Lysent, but why?

"Look, you can either let us in, or I'm going to kill Blondie here." He used his leverage to rock Jack by his bindings once more.

Jack looked up and met her eyes. A few weeks ago, Satomi would not have been bothered by such a threat. It was not lost on her that Jack was now in the same position he had forced her into just months ago. His family had brought a great amount of fear into her life. But, she could not wish the same for him.

"Please, don't," was all she could manage.

"OK, then we'll just come in."

Satomi heard an electronic beep before a clap of noise. Metal plating and chain link flashed in her peripheral as the east side of the fence was tossed and scattered. The scaffolding swayed. Marla and several others lay on the ground, stunned.

"Now we've got one more of those planted along your place," said the same but distant voice. "Bring out your dead — soon-dead I guess — and we'll be on our way without destroying another thing."

Satomi's vision blurred with panic. Everything seemed to be tumbling down. "I'm telling you!" she screamed. "WE DON'T HAVE ANY HERE!"

The man shouted back, ragged and angered. "Then we'll take YOU, Peter Junior here, Peter Senior, and Audra! You guys are worth more than turn-backs anyway. I'm tired of talking shit with you."

Satomi wasn't sure where it came from, but a sick laugh erupted from her mouth. "You think if Audra was here, that you'd be talking to me?"

Hot stingers of tears collected in the corners of her eyes. Why did Lysent value her life? How was she a threat? She understood that Greenly must've run Evelyn's DNA and figured out who the family was — creators of the army she had confiscated. And Audra was a big pain in their butt, but why Satomi? And why turn-backs? If Satomi's antiviral was the only faulty version, why not just let Osprey Point revert and die off?

Maybe she had missed something.

And maybe it was too late. Maybe Peter's creations were about to march in and cut them down.

What was she going to do?

* * *

Heading to warn Osprey Point of marauding taggers, Audra wasn't far when she heard the explosion. She considered dropping the sisters' leash to reach the community faster, but if they were taggers, the sisters would be of high value. Instead, she pulled out her knife and reached back, making a shallow slice into the back of her shoulder. She felt warm liquid trickle into the small of her back.

Now they were moving. The sisters became frenetic. The growls and snapping kept pace behind her as they raced down the road toward Osprey Point. Three men and two horses stood at the gate, and they turned to address the tiny stampede careening toward them.

"Oh, ho ho, Blue. There she is!" The man with curly red hair laughed.

Audra pulled to a stop, but the zoms, having spotted and smelled the sweaty horses, continued forward. Audra set her feet and held on like an owner with eager dogs.

"Oh, and she's got some for us," said Blue. His cowboy hat hid his dark beady eyes.

Audra recognized them both. Manny and Blue, two of Greenly's zombie shepherds.

"They aren't for you," countered Audra. "Haven't you killed enough of them?"

Audra had escorted them to her trailer of sick and they had set it aflame. The next day after the fire had burned out and the metal had cooled, Audra dropped down into the chalky remains, breathing in the ash, helping the last of them pass.

"Now, we do regret that. Mostly cause now they're worth money."

Jack's eyes were wide at the sight of Audra's pets. Manny kept an arm around him. A large knife swung from his belt.

"Everyone OK in there?" she asked of Satomi, who was perched atop the fence.

"Um, they blew up part of our fence. Say they got another one ready if we don't surrender some people."

"Did you tell them you didn't have any tags?" she asked as she wrestled with the leash. The horses whinnied and stomped worriedly.

"Yes, told them all the reverting left so we wouldn't be in danger. But now they want me, Jack there, you… Jack's dad."

"And those," the shepherd reminded her again.

"These are mine. I've tagged them — now more than once. Finder's rights, you know?"

Audra's anger settled as flames flirting with her collarbone. It wouldn't be the first time she had to defend her tags.

"Well, then I guess that makes Peter Junior here ours," laughed Manny. "You're out there tagging again?"

Audra didn't answer, which gave him his answer.

"Then maybe we can strike a deal. You give me the duo and I'll leave you guys alone for a bit. I'll even hand over Jack here. He can help you tag. When I return, you hand over more valuable zoms or that scientist. I don't really care which. Call it rent, protection, whatever."

Blue smiled at the proposal.

Audra thought it over for a moment. "These two for Jack?" she asked to clarify.

"Sure. For now."

"And what if I don't?"

"We set off the other explosion and take everything."

Manny and Blue both cocked their heads to wait on the answer to their offer.

Audra's pair continued to pull toward the large sources of meat as if they were eager to go. It would be easy to hand the girls over. Arguably, Jack and the others inside were worth more than the forgotten Hunt sisters. Osprey Point's inhabitants had lives to live. This duo didn't.

And yet, she couldn't push the burning trailer from her mind. Those lives lost were on her. And so would these be.

It wasn't worth it. Her heart — her soul — couldn't take another death.

"Take me instead."

11 Trade

"I know there's a bounty on my head. Am I worth more than these two?" she asked.

"Quite a bit," said Manny, nodding. He appeared to think it was a good deal.

She was sure it was. If Lysent had decided that she was this important, then maybe she'd make good on their evaluations. She heard murmurs of disagreement above her.

"Audra, you don't have to do this," said Jack. "We can fight them."

"There's no need." She wasn't going to let the shepherds have any more of her people. She wasn't going to let Lysent dictate what happened here. "It's time to end this."

"Audra, stop. I'll go," pleaded Jack. His eyes were wide with surprise.

Greenly having the half-zom army's controller. That was the last thing she needed.

She ignored him. "You'll let my zoms go into Osprey Point." She couldn't very well lead them to the motel and the jackpot of tags who lived there. "And I'll come with you."

Manny untied Jack and pushed him toward the biting zombies. "Take 'em," he grunted.

"What the hell's going on?" asked Jack in a rough whisper as he took the lead from Audra. Audra tucked the folded bounty list in his front jacket pocket.

Manny placed Jack's bindings on Audra. Jack straightened his beanie and met Audra's gaze one more time. His eyes asked if he needed to make a play. Audra gave a small shake of her head. She knew he wouldn't interfere without her permission. Dwyn would have been another story.

Audra gave a nod up to Satomi, Branson, and Tess, hoping they wouldn't worry. She then departed with Manny and Blue, who had not mounted the horses. Too much distance from Audra and they'd get arrows in their backs.

After removing themselves from range, the men hopped into the saddles. Manny put his hand out for Audra. She didn't accept it. She'd rather walk. He didn't mind. He laughed.

He allowed Audra a long lead to follow behind them. Even with the space, the horses kicked up dust and grit into Audra's nose and mouth. She worked her kerchief from her neck onto her face with shoulder shrugs and neck contortions. Still, it was better than being hip to hip to these shepherds. She remembered their crude behavior. She'd keep separate from them as long as possible. The rope scratched and scraped her hands and wrists. It was nothing like the cloth ones she used for her zombies. The horses smelled of sweat and manure. Or, maybe that was the men.

With the bounty list, Audra hoped Satomi would be able to piece together why Lysent was intent on scooping up zombies and scientists alike. They needed more time, and she was giving it to them. But that wasn't her only reason for trading herself.

Audra thought of the dead in sedans, the ash of the trailer, the angry, lost, and sick at the motel. She and Larange Greenly had something in common. Everything they touched — they ruined. Perhaps they should meet their matches.

Audra had no delusions she'd survive Greenly, but if her scorecard had anything to show, Greenly wouldn't come out of it alive, either. And that she could deal with.

Manny and Blue continued down the road, joking with each other and passing a flask back and forth. Audra assumed it wasn't water. She used to have that life. She didn't have a horse, but she had a flask and the joy of a good cash find leading up to a fine fire, good spirits, and a good night. Audra knew they wouldn't make it to Lysent headquarters before sundown at this pace. That gave her time to come up with a plan. Greenly would meet her. She was sure of it. But she'd still have her guards with her. Audra wouldn't be able to do much to Greenly.

Whatever she did, it would have to be quick. And life-changing.

Perhaps she could sneak a blade. She imagined plunging it into Greenly's carotid. What would Audra do as the woman bled out? Smile? Laugh? It'd be easy to watch someone who created such chaos be put in their place.

A slow light rain highlighted the scents on the trail. Despite the overcast, it'd be a beautiful time to run. But for now, her hair stuck to her face with the moisture. Brushing it away with her bound hands just scratched her face with rope.

After hours of walking, they reached a boarded-up gas station. While the weeds, scattered vehicles, and debris made the place look abandoned, the fact that all the windows and doors were closed and secured, was a sure sign that someone was using it. The bright reds and blues of the brand had faded to oranges and grays. Manny and Blue dismounted and began walking the horses to the back. There they found a ratty wooden fence, but a fence nonetheless. It slanted and swayed. Several boards were missing or broken. But the gate worked, sort of. Manny pulled up on it to get it to move. They led the horses in and tied them up. The wire grass inside had been flattened — the horses had been here before.

Blue lifted his shallow chin toward the back door. The metal handle had been knocked off the heavy door. Audra looked at him expectantly, but did not move to go inside. She wasn't going to go in first or second. Hell, she wouldn't even go in at all if she could help it. In there, she'd be trapped.

"Get in, girl," pushed Manny, his growl devolved into a thick cough.

She cut her eyes at him, trying to size him up. He was still large and grizzly. More than she could handle. She remembered what he had told her when they first met. She'd better watch herself.

She might never see Greenly.

He opened the door and Blue pushed her in. So much for holding her ground.

For its boarded windows and front door, the inside was still not as dark as she had expected. A large hole in the one-story ceiling was to thank for that. Audra looked at the floor where the hole made a spotlight. She saw the markings of past fires underneath, old coolers on their side around it to sit on. Against the windows, shelves stood as a secondary barricade, much like at Haleigh's community. Prepackaged food items were long gone, but their discarded wrappers littered the ground, gathering dust and decomposing even more slowly than their dying consumers.

In the corner, blankets sat. Their beds. Audra didn't want to investigate them any further. Besides the obvious, the bedding seemed to be crawling with thin roach-like bugs.

"If I agree to get on the horse, we could make it to headquarters before it gets dark," suggested Audra.

"Nice try. It's gonna get dark fast. And 'sides, we don't need to go just yet," Manny added suggestively.

Audra didn't have any preconceived notions she'd be treated well. It didn't matter as long as she had enough strength to kill Greenly in the end. If it saved the reverted, made a difference, even better.

"Don't scare the girl, Manny," said Blue. Then to Audra, "We know what you did to those shepherds, but your payout at Lysent is worth much more than getting revenge for the two SOBs that couldn't survive a little girl." He smirked.

Audra wasn't sure if that was true or if there was a bit of respect there.

"Then why don't we go to Lysent?"

"Cause their listed bounty for you is shit!" he laughed.

Negotiation. Audra understood. She sighed. She didn't have time for these petty greedy transactions. She needed to get to Greenly and end it. At this point, if she'd had any credits to her name, she'd pay them to deliver her to Greenly. Preferably with a weapon in hand. But she in fact had a very large debt in the Lysent system. It hadn't seemed to matter much, until now.

"I'll head out in the morning and talk to 'em," said Blue. "Manny will stay here with you."

Manny wiggled his eyebrows.

Audra flopped her butt onto the ground and let the two build a fire for them.

*　　*　　*

Satomi volunteered to help in the repair of the fence at Osprey Point. Marla nervously pulled on her shirt's hem as she directed people. It was her first project without Ryder and she had her work cut out for her. The explosive wasn't just a scare tactic. It had taken out support beams and Osprey Point didn't have much in the way of supplies. This side of their home would be weaker for many months to come.

"We can add a set of cars on the exterior. They can help support the fencing for now, but I'd like to cut trees and perform the repair sooner rather than later," Marla said, scratching her head between waves of curls and looking down at her half-scribbled plans.

Satomi helped dig out the remainder of the telephone posts that hadn't been blasted away. Another shovel contributed to her work with Jack sidling up to her.

"Hey, I'm sorry I got caught like that."

Satomi shook her head. She dived her shovel's point into the hard dirt. "That's why we don't go out alone," she lectured.

The potential to be grabbed or held hostage wasn't the only reason to not go out alone, but in this moment she allowed it to be so.

"Thank you for not letting them kill me," he said and smiled.

"I didn't do anything," she said. Anger directed toward herself and a particular dirt clod. She wasn't quite sure what to do with the thoughts churning in her head.

"No, no," said Jack, dropping his shoulder and put his hands lightly on her arms. "You kept them talking. You kept them from killing me. You had a choice. You could have taken one look at the situation, laughed, and gone back into your laboratory. You don't need me. You don't like me. I did… awful things." He let his arms drop.

Satomi tied her hair up into a ponytail with the elastic from some old clothes, giving herself time to think. As much as she wanted to hate Jack and punish him — she couldn't.

"I couldn't let them kill you. You're not a bad man," she admitted more to herself than him.

Jack had made horrible mistakes, but since his sister's death, he busied himself caring for his father, defending the community, and working harder than many of Osprey Point's original inhabitants. Satomi considered the mistakes she had made. She wasn't 'bad' either.

Jack gave a nod and started back digging.

"After this, I'll go out and search for Audra." He sighed. "We lost her."

Satomi gave a small smile. "I doubt that woman's out just yet. She's either got a plan in mind or she's at least giving us an opportunity."

While Satomi had beaten herself up for mistakes still unknown to her, Lysent didn't seem to hold the same mindset. They didn't want her working. And if that was the case, then that's exactly what she should be doing.

Jack wiped the sweat from his brow. "Opportunity for what?"

"To do what Lysent doesn't want us to do. Cure your father."

*   *   *

After helping with the fence, Satomi stepped into her laboratory. It felt like an entirely new place. She was thankful to be there, to have a chance to work. And with her decision made, she no longer felt lost.

Satomi pulled open a drawer and removed the notebook she had kept under her shirt when Audra came to negotiate her release from Jack and Jill. It contained the protocol for creating a peptide that might not only bring Peter back, but would also be the first beneficial application of the z-virus. Satomi opened the refrigerator to confirm the medium for building the peptide remained untouched. It might have been useful in working on the antiviral. Instead, it would be helping the father of the virus.

Jack coughed at the door to not surprise her. She jumped anyway.

"Sorry," he said.

She gave him a look and he apologized for his apology. She had asked that he stop apologizing so much. She was ready to move forward.

"I'm going to escort Audra's zombies to the motel," he announced. "Is there any message you want me to deliver to Ryder or anyone else?"

Satomi's eyes moistened at the thought of getting a message to Ryder. She'd be pleased to know Satomi was working toward something to help them. She only hoped her friends still thought she was capable. She ripped a sheet from the back of the notebook and began trying out the pens for ink.

"God, Dwyn's going to be super pissed, isn't he?" asked Jack. "She disappeared on my watch."

He rubbed the back of his neck.

"She didn't disappear. She chose to go. But yeah, he's going to be upset," she said, not looking up from the start of her letter.

"Maybe we can form a search team, try to find her, try to back her up. Whatever it is she's doing."

Satomi had learned a long time ago Audra never asked for permission or advice before running headlong into things. Satomi wasn't the same.

"I'm glad you came in, I need your express permission to treat your father." She paused. "I don't think he's lucid enough to understand and give consent. I will be injecting the z-virus into his body, which we currently don't have a cure for. This treatment is highly experimental. It could kill him, maim him, or otherwise infect your father."

Jack thought for a moment. He gazed at the beakers on the counter, the lopsided microscope on the table. Jack never thought they had a cure to begin with.

"My father was a risktaker. If there was a chance he could become whole again and useful, he'd do it in a heartbeat."

Satomi couldn't help but ask.

"Was your father... a bad man?"

Jack huffed at the question, leaning on the back of a stool. "I don't really know how to answer that. He's my dad. I never thought of him as a bad man. He worked at his job. He did what he was told. When things started going to shit, he knew exactly what it was. Shit they were working on. He did what he could to protect us. Always. And so did Evelyn and I after that. I don't think we're good people — not like you guys. We're just... surviving. I think my father would help with the cure if he could. It drove him crazy that he couldn't figure it out on his own. I think he'd help you."

Peter was a pleasant man now, but that did not mean he'd remain that way. He could become less than cooperative, combative, with his intelligence back. That wouldn't be her fault though. Peter had done wrong, but it wasn't Satomi's place to judge him. Only Lysent held back treatment based on agendas and selfish protocol. Satomi would no longer do the same.

She finished her letter to Ryder and started pulling supplies off the shelves to take the treatment from paper to injectable serum. It was time to take action.

12 Reconciliation

Dwyn picked up a long, straight stick along the path. Its bark stripped, it had already done time as a hiking companion before it had been discarded. Dwyn used it to provide support as he climbed root systems that wove over the surface of the hill like a waterfall. The steepness required some amount of focus, so he was allowed to not speak to his partner constantly.

Instead, Dwyn tried to wrap his mind around a world in which his ex-girlfriend plotted for a corporate downfall and secretly recruited him. There had been some amount of deception in bringing in Audra. He was naive to think that it wasn't the same for him. She could also be lying. Pretending to be on the inside to get information from Dwyn.

But then, why wouldn't she lie about loving her husband? Why be honest about that, when it could turn him away?

As if waiting until they crested the hill, Gordon asked, "What if they hate me?"

"Audra said they loved your note. They're going to love you all the more," encouraged Dwyn as he considered dropping the walking stick. It could help someone else down.

Dwyn looked behind and saw Gordon slowing down.

"I don't know if I deserve to see them."

Gordon stopped.

Dwyn backtracked to him. It was obvious something was bothering Gordon. Dwyn nodded toward a couple of fallen logs and swung his pack off. Gordon did the same, plopping down on one of the logs.

"Haleigh didn't tell me she was pregnant with Eliza until after the divorce was finalized. She said she wanted me to decide on her as a wife, not as the mother of our child."

"Whoa, that's rough, dude," was all that Dwyn could get out.

"I was too focused on my career. I got the job at Osprey Point shortly after we got married. I was publishing papers. Working with our largest client, Lysent Corporation. I didn't put time into our relationship.

I was angry when I learned what she had kept from me, but more so I was embarrassed. It had seemed easier to let her go than to change my ways. I figured what was the harm."

Gordon kicked at a rock, which rolled over. Tears streamed from his eyes.

He sighed. "It's taken pandemics, world restructuring, and a god awful long time for me to realize what really matters. I should have fought. I should have fought before the divorce. After the divorce."

"And now," recommended Dwyn.

"And now. So even if they hate me… because they have every right to… I'm still going to go and fight for them, for us."

Dwyn placed his hand on Gordon's shoulder. People's problems weren't erased by the z-virus. In fact, at times they seemed highlighted by it.

"Ready to go fight?" Dwyn asked with a grin.

Gordon wiggled back into his pack.

"We're not far. That was the last big hill," Gordon stated as he kicked the gray rock off to the side of the trail.

Dwyn leaned his stick against the logs for someone else or perhaps his future self.

It wasn't far at all to the tiny town. Dwyn couldn't imagine a giant grocery store here. It must have landed here after someone in corporate fed data into an algorithm, no one actually bothering to scout out the site.

"It's down this way. Across from the bank," Gordon said, picking up the pace.

Dwyn started in a trot to follow him. As they turned a corner, the store came into sight. By the road, a couple hundred grocery carts lay scattered and tossed.

Dwyn guessed the carts were not where they were supposed to be. It sent Gordon into a frenzy. He ran headlong into the mass of carts, hopping, tripping, and climbing. Dwyn followed more carefully. He noticed some carts were tied together when they fell. They created odd pyramids and ramps over cars.

Gordon cleared the carts and leapfrogged over them, yelling Haleigh's name all the way through the parking lot.

Gordon pushed his way into the store and disappeared into its depths. No one stood atop the store. Inside, trash, supplies, and debris lay scattered on the ground. Blood. No one in sight.

It didn't bode well. Dwyn pulled out his knife and waited at the door.

Deep guttural sobs started from the produce section of the store, moving through the aisles. It seemed to shake the entire core of the store.

There wasn't enough blood on the floors. And there were no bodies. The carts had been trashed.

Where was everyone?

What had happened here?

*   *   *

Audra's shoulders ached. Besides breaks for the bathroom and a single meal, both her wrists and ankles remained secured. And yet, Audra refused to ask for reprieve. She didn't want to owe Manny anything and she didn't want to be touched any more than what was necessary. She just needed to survive the next few days. Then, she'd be delivered to Greenly.

Two nights passed at the gas station before Blue sauntered in and slid onto a moldy cooler.

"Sup?" asked Manny, tossing Blue a bottle of water.

Both Audra and Manny were anxious to know the results of his negotiation. Audra for its time frame. Manny for its monetary value. Blue spat tobacco onto the chipped linoleum floor, shaking his head and a few days' worth of scraggly facial hair.

"She's drawing it out, Mann. Doesn't want to pay up." He kicked a stone into the fire. Sparks flew and died.

"She don't care about money. Why she stalling?"

"I been thinking. Maybe she doesn't need her, just needs her out of the picture."

"Out of what picture? Osprey Point?" Audra couldn't help but ask.

"Sure, she wants your whole crew," said Blue. "But they don't seem so difficult to round up, especially with you out and the group split between there and the motel."

Greenly knew about the motel? Audra felt adrenaline building in her body as she realized she had left both locations vulnerable.

"Take me to Greenly," she demanded. She needed to finish this.

Blue raised his eyebrows. "Why you so eager to die?"

"You promised you'd take me to Greenly! I'm going to kill her."

Audra fought against her wrist bindings. Her shoulders burned in protest, but the rope-made creases had gone from numb to raw. At Osprey Point, she felt useless. Here, she felt like a ticking time bomb.

Both men watched her and laughed. Manny finished with a hacking fit.

"You doin' all right, Mann?" asked Blue, passing the bottle of water back to Manny.

"I'm fine," he grunted, wiping spittle from his beard before taking a sip from the bottle.

"For now," his friend mumbled.

Audra paused from her temper tantrum.

"You were cured?" she asked.

"Apparently not," said Manny, his voice dripping with bitterness.

She'd have known if they had cured him with their faulty antidotes. They hadn't.

"What do you mean?" she dared to ask the giant man. She needed confirmation.

"Turn-backs. Folks everywhere turning back."

Jack was right. It wasn't just their stock; all the antidotes were bad.

"Does everyone know?"

"No, Lysent's covering it up — blaming you guys for having sleepers in the townships…"

By blaming Osprey Point, none of the townships would be taking proper precautions. Greenly wouldn't be able to keep up the lie indefinitely, but until then, Audra expected many townships to fall. All the Lysent-cured were at risk.

Dwyn.

Dwyn had been cured by Lysent.

Audra struggled to not be sick as she considered it. Dwyn's face going ashen, drool in the corners of his mouth, reaching out to her with bony fingers. Dwyn was on borrowed time.

Audra realized she was too. She was being held ransom, and just because they had shared information didn't mean they were helping her. It just meant they didn't think it would matter soon. Audra pushed the rising panic down.

Killing Greenly wouldn't fix this.

"You need to let me go."

*   *   *

"We have to find them," Gordon said, his voice rife with panic.

Dwyn stood frozen for a moment at the store's entrance, not sure how to say what needed to be said.

"We will," he started. "But we can't, right now."

Gordon's face contorted in anger. Dwyn considered the possibility that his friend was about to punch him out. He took a step back, but Gordon fell to his knees.

Dwyn approached to comfort him, but Gordon waved heavy arms out to maintain his space. Then, his hands went to the floor to support him as vomit spilled from his mouth.

Gordon was getting sicker.

He sat back and wiped his mouth with his dark jacket sleeve. He leaned against some boxes.

Dwyn knelt down to him. "Something went down here, but I don't think they're dead." Gordon whimpered. "They moved, or they were moved. But we're just going to have to trust Haleigh to do what she's done for years — keep herself and Eliza alive. I promise we're going to get to the bottom of this. We will find them, but for now I have to get back with my information, and you're getting worse. If you stay out here, you'll turn. Then you'll never find them, or worse, you will."

Gordon didn't move or respond.

The mess on the floor stung Dwyn's nose. He wanted to get some fresh air, but knew he couldn't leave Gordon alone.

"I'm so sorry. But let's write them a note in case they return here. You found them once. We can do it again."

He pulled Gordon up and they went to find something for a note. After what seemed like a long time, they finally made their way around the carts outside.

Gordon looked back. His eyes swept the store front.

"How could I have run out of time?" he mumbled.

But it had been a long time coming.

*   *   *

Satomi decided against bringing Peter to the laboratory for treatment. It was an unfamiliar space with familiar objects. She didn't want him to be upset or scared, nor did she want him to latch onto latent memories that might pull him in a bad direction. Who knew if that's how it worked. It was all experimental.

Instead, she prepared a tray with sets of syringes for a house, or room, call.

Jack had returned from dropping off the sisters whom Audra apparently considered of equal value to herself. He delivered Satomi's letter and notified Ryder and Marcos of Audra's latest excursion. He sat with Satomi as she worked.

"OK, I'm not reneging my consent or anything, but if I'm being honest, I don't see how infecting my father with the z-virus is going to make things better."

Jack then began to spin on his stool, so Satomi wasn't sure how serious he was in his statement.

"Well, what does the z-virus do?" she asked.

He reached out a hand onto the counter to stop his motion. "It turns you into a stupid brute that eats people. Like I said… not an improvement."

"What else does it do?" Satomi asked as she put a pot of water over her Bunsen burner to boil.

"Well, it makes you hard to kill."

Satomi nodded. "This virus is the most pervasive and the most enduring the world has ever seen. Upon infection, it replicates and hijacks the body and mind, shutting down higher thought processes and stimulating hunger in the presence of other potential hosts."

"Yeah, the feeding… You're not selling me on this." He gave himself a single rotation around as his reward.

"— the other part of its success, is that it protects the host. It boosts the brain's natural defenses and repair functions because the longer the brain stays intact, the more opportunity the virus has to spread. That's the feature we're exploiting. I'm hoping it will repair the present damage and restore your father's mental capabilities."

Satomi took the pot off the burner and poured the water into the teapot filled with pine needles she had collected this morning, and dried mint and ground dandelion root.

"Those upgrades only come after the virus replicates and reaches a tipping point in the body. The peptide I synthesized will signal to the virus it has already reached that tipping point, starting its protective processes. If we can keep a certain level of the peptide in the bloodstream, it should curb viral replication so it can't get out of hand.

And if we develop a cure, we can completely eradicate the virus from your father after it's cleared out all the damaged cells."

"And the mindless cannibalism?" Jack asked.

"Hopefully not so mindless."

There was an awkward pause before Jack realized it was a joke.

"Funny. But, really."

"Really, the viral load in his body should be so low that he won't develop any of the unwanted characteristics."

Jack spun one more time, his head back. "My dad, the zombie."

Satomi arranged the treatment series on the tray and added honey to one of the tea cups.

First, Satomi infected Peter intravenously with the z-virus. No matter how Satomi rationalized it, it went against everything she had vowed when she took on the title of doctor. If her highly experimental treatment did not work, Peter's body would become infected with a virus that had no cure. He would lose the little but crucial amount of brain function he had left.

Peter was cooperative for the first injection, but when Satomi informed him that the rest of the syringes were also for him, he began to get suspicious. Jack held him down as Satomi introduced into his blood the peptide that signaled to the virus it had replicated to capacity.

The peptide was something the virus naturally produced whenever it replicated in a host. As the peptide built up in the body, it slowed viral replication, giving the virus a form of self-regulation so it wouldn't overwhelm and kill the host. By synthesizing and introducing the peptide earlier, Satomi was attempting to use the virus's own systems for the host's benefit. She only hoped it would work.

13 Transitions

The next day, Satomi didn't notice much of a difference in Peter, except that he had fewer angry outbursts. It could have been her imagination, but if not, it indicated an increase in his ability to cope. Even if that was all that came of the treatment, it had possibly improved his quality of life and hadn't turned him into a ruthless cannibal. But still, hoping for more, she and Jack said nothing to each other. They both stayed silent, as if speaking of the possibly imagined results would make them disappear.

Turned out, they could have discussed it loudly for days on end, because it was working. Satomi treated Peter with the peptide until the levels in his blood matched the levels in fully infected individuals. Short-term and long-term memory was recouped. His working vocabulary increased. He followed complex trains of thoughts and had his own.

Not all returns were pleasant. Soon, Jack and Peter were huddled together in tears over Evelyn's death. Peter pulled at his hair and mourned, really mourned, for his daughter. Peter hugged his remaining child tightly. They cried together, laughed together, and cried some more.

Satomi gave what she hoped was an appropriate amount of family time before knocking on Peter's door. She was called to come in and she quickly joined them around the wood veneer table.

Peter actually physically looked different. The hard lines in his brow and jaw had softened. His posture relaxed and his shoulders slumped. He still wore a buttoned shirt, but the collar was loose and Satomi noticed a couple of wrinkles in the shirt. Perhaps all that neatness had been an attempt to find order and peace. Satomi hoped he was now content, and wouldn't press forward with absurd experiments.

"Hi Peter, do you remember me?" she asked.

"I don't have any memories of you before my illness," he said, his eyes searching. "But I know you now. You drink tea with me." He nodded his cup to her.

"Yes, I do. I'm also a scientist and a doctor."

"I was sick, but I feel better than I have in ages. Did you give me something?"

"I did."

He jumped up from the table, his chair falling to the floor. Satomi found herself wrapped in a huge bear hug. So far, so good.

"How did we meet?" he asked, all smiles, still holding her in his arms.

"…your children kidnapped me."

A giant backhanded blow hit Jack in the jaw.

"I'm sorry, Dad. I didn't know what else to do!"

"You got your sister killed and you kidnapped this lady! Is she still captured?" he asked incredulously, looking around to verify if the room was a jail cell.

"No, no," Satomi explained. "Your son released me. I brought you both back to my community, where we're trying to fight the epidemic."

"Oh," Peter said, looking down at the ground. "That."

"Yes, that. Were you working on it too? Is that how you got sick?"

Satomi gave him a moment. Peter returned to his chair and uprighted it.

He shook his head and let out a low chuckle. "I got sick because I tried to vaccinate myself. I knew the cures weren't working and I couldn't get it to work. I figured the next best thing was to bolster our immune systems so that we wouldn't catch the damn thing."

"That didn't work," encouraged Satomi.

"No, it didn't," he confirmed.

*   *   *

Audra pushed soot around on the ground with her boots. They were still bound, and the movement kept her feet from going numb. Despite involving her in discussions, Manny and Blue still didn't trust her.

They were giving her too much credit.

The combination of her self-initiated stagnancy while Greenly planned her strike and the poor ventilation from their indoor fires left Audra feeling dumber with each passing day. Blue had left again to negotiate payment for her head. Apparently, Manny wasn't allowed in

Lysent headquarters due to his preexisting condition, which was an appropriate policy given that Manny's health was precipitously declining. The stupidity of it all made her want to scream. She stomped on the ash.

"Need to go out, little dog?"

She ignored the question. Even the dimness of the remaining evening couldn't hide the fact that Manny didn't look so good. Sweat poured from the crevices of his red face.

"Manny, you're turning. Let me help you," she said, willing her voice to remain steady.

Manny exploded in anger, shouting, "You can't help me, you stupid little girl." He grabbed a metal rack and threw it against the shelves. It made a clattering noise that echoed off the wall of refrigerators. He wiped his brow with the soaked sleeve of his jacket. "No one can."

It wasn't the first thing he had thrown that day. At least nothing had been directed toward her yet — ricochets excluded.

"That's not true. We have scientists working on it. We're taking care of the sick until we can cure them."

She needed him to see reason before reason became impossible.

"Ha! You can't pull this shit again. Lysent already fooled my folks. They're in debt up to their eyeballs for my first cure."

"…That's why you're selling me," she realized aloud.

"I want to at least pay back my worth before I turn back."

He flopped down on his bedding, sending a scurry of generic insects in multiple directions.

"Please, let me go. Neither of us has to die from this."

Audra couldn't think of a more pointless death than being eaten by Manny the Zombie. Stupid.

"That's where you're wrong, pretty. I've held you hostage for days. If I let you go, you're gonna kill me or keep me for your weird collection. This way, we're both dying from this."

"I won't take revenge," she promised. "I don't want it."

"OH HELL YOU DON'T! Why else would you offer to be delivered to Greenly?"

"I thought she was only hurting Osprey Point to get to me."

"Her plans are bigger than a grudge," laughed Manny. His red hair stuck on his head with sweat. He leaned against the browning plastered wall.

"I know that now. I need your help. I can't do it alone… no one can do it alone." She recalled Dwyn's constant reminders.

Manny hacked into his sleeve. Looked down at it. His nostrils flared with surprise and fear. Was he coughing up blood? Manny was going to turn and Audra would have to watch, arms and legs bound.

"Too bad you are alone. So am I." He slumped over and was quiet for a few minutes before he began to snore. His body heaved with the effort of his breathing, and convulsed periodically with fevered sleep.

Audra felt her eyelids grow heavy. She responded by adjusting her shoulders and sending searing pain down her back. As she listened for the snores to end and the snapping of teeth to begin, she searched the thrown debris for something to cut her binds. Eventually she settled for the sharpest rock bordering their fire circle. She finagled it behind her back and began scraping against the rope. If nothing else, it was something to do.

*　　*　　*

As the sun faded, Manny didn't stir to build their nightly fire. There wouldn't be much time before their abode was enveloped in darkness. Audra risked standing up, balancing with ankles tied. She hopped, scooted, and pivoted until she reached the door.

It was jammed up.

Audra started on the windows, pushing the shelving with her shoulder to see what, if anything, gave.

"What are you doing?" asked a voice behind her.

She turned in surprise.

"Just trying to find a way out of here before you turn and eat me," she said coolly.

"Sit down. I'm not gone just yet." His voice scratched.

She backed around him and returned to the cooler where she was sitting. The rock still hidden in her palm.

"Drop the rock."

She dropped it without a word.

He came up behind her again and this time Audra gagged from the smell of his yeasty sickness. She felt her ropes tighten then loosen. They fell to the ground. Her shoulders cried in their sockets as she brought her arms forward.

"Build a fire," he said.

Audra did as she was told, but kept a close eye on him. He was leaning up against a shelf, slouched partly over. He pulled out a flask and drank heavily from it. She figured he had been saving it all for this night. It was not a night for savoring, but a night to die. She hoped it wasn't hers too.

In leaning the logs, Audra's hand dragged across a large splinter of wood. Risking the noise, she snapped it off as she positioned the kindling. She peeled some off the end to crudely hone the tip to sharpness. She'd only get one chance to stab something vital. She tucked the shiv into her sleeve and started the fire with one of the matches.

Matches.

What an odd thing for these shepherds to carry. Why carry matches instead of flint or another reusable fire starter? Modern conveniences must die hard.

A large belch emanated from the corner as the fire sparked up. The flask lay on its side, done. He started to bob his head up and down, the sickness and the alcohol making his eyes float in his head. Audra didn't ask about her bindings. And he didn't seem to remember them.

"Anything I can do for you?" she asked. There wasn't much that could be done. Bind his hands? Ha. Sing for him? God, she hoped not.

"Not a thing, honey. No one can do nuthin' for nobody. We're alone here. It's been a long time coming."

"I'll at least boil some water so you can have some to drink."

"Have some to throw up, you mean."

That was true too. But she imagined that the moonshine he downed would be enough to vomit for a bit.

She poured water from the bucket of unboiled into the pot. She set it up against the flames. The guys hadn't bothered to find a grate or anything to cook upon. They subsisted on barely boiled water and jerky and protein bars provided by Lysent. All of their supplies, she thought of the matches, were bought from Lysent. She bet the shepherds were kept on a pretty tight financial leash just as the taggers were.

"You put me out of a job, you know. Now she got that army, she don't give a shit about the herds I push around. Now they just rotting in the corrals. Worthless like me." He spat just inches from himself.

Audra hadn't really thought about how she had turned the system upside down. Shepherds. Taggers. Zombies. She had caused a lot of trouble, but right now, she found she just wanted to help Manny. Give him some moments of peace and keep him company. Something her sister didn't have. Audra repositioned the pot to get it into a warmer spot. She wanted it clean and cooled off for him. It was the least she could do.

It was one thing to turn once. It was another to know it was coming again.

Audra's body threw itself onto the hard floor without her permission as the explosion rang out, shaking her bones.

When the echo in her ears subsided, she could feel the coldness of tile on her cheek and the silence. The smell of copper reached her and she turned her head to peek.

There he lay flat, not far from her. A large crater formed at the top of his head. Blood and wads of soft material splattered on the floor. A sawed-off shotgun between them.

Audra stood up, her teeth rattling. The sight wasn't all that unfamiliar, but the explosion of noise and the fact that he was there — and then he wasn't — sent adrenaline coursing through her body.

He was alone.

And so was she.

A shocked, bitter laugh escaped her lips. She couldn't convince Manny he wasn't alone any more than her friends could have convinced her. With Manny gone, she could still make her way to Lysent. She could surrender to Greenly, try to kill her, hope this madness stopped.

Or, she could stop demanding to be alone.

Audra heard the creaking of shelves and plywood.

She reached for the shotgun, but her arm jolted in large twitches. Instead, she kicked the weapon underneath a shelving unit.

God, what poor timing. She could have been gone.

"Audra?" called out Dwyn, his voice brittle and shrill. "Are you OK?"

"I'm OK!" she responded in both relief and panic.

"We heard a gunshot. Are you OK?" came Ryder's voice, clear and slow.

"Yeah," she said. She hadn't realized they were nearby.

"We're going to get you home," Dwyn said through the door, while he pulled and pushed.

Home.

Before the water started bubbling in its pot, Audra was in Dwyn's arms. As the adrenaline faded, her upper body rang out in sharp pains from her former bindings, but the steady pressure of his body brought comfort and the sure sign she was no longer alone. She breathed in his musk and tried to settle her ragged breath. Ryder searched and retrieved the shotgun, but found no extra shells on the body.

"How did you know to look for me?" Audra asked.

"Ryder found out from Jack," Dwyn whispered into her hair as he kept her in the hug. "We were looking for you."

Audra nodded into his chest. His hands were on her back, strong and steady. She felt their strength and imagined them curling as they ripped into her spinal muscles and dug between her ribs. Audra abruptly shook out of the embrace. Dwyn took a glance at the body of her captor and began to lead her away.

"Why did he do that?" asked Dwyn. Audra shook her head. She didn't want to tell him yet.

Ryder smiled and took her by the shoulder. "Let's go home."

"Wait," said Audra.

She poured the water from the pot, extinguishing the fire. Then inside the pot, she dropped five yellow tags. She hoped when Blue redeemed them, he'd split the cash with Manny's family. They didn't deserve the hand they'd been dealt.

14 Returns

In the darkness of night, the trio hiked to Osprey Point. Adrenaline and the worry Blue might return kept them moving forward against passing desires of sleep. The cold fresh air and the familiar motions helped Audra shed the lingering dread from the recesses of her brain and the shock from her frame. She appreciated that Ryder and Dwyn didn't push her to talk. Conversation would be more tolerable within Osprey Point's fences and underneath the morning's rays.

In the passing time, Audra tried to compose herself and she arrived at Osprey Point all business. She marched to the blown fence to inspect it, despite the fact that darkness still encompassed them. Ryder tried to reassure her that Jack and Marla had reinforced it and nothing needed to be done before morning. Audra took the hint and dismissed her for the night.

Ryder raced off to wake Satomi from what was probably a great night's rest. Something she hadn't had for a long while. Dwyn remained at her side, near the vague form of the fence. With the flashlight pointed at the ground, she more felt his presence than saw it. His body was warm, broad, and strong.

"People will still be asleep for a bit. Now would be a good time to wash and rest up," Dwyn suggested.

Audra noticed the way he phrased it — focusing on efficiency, rather than a reminder to care for herself. She'd let him think she bought it.

She gave a nod and followed him to the sleeping quarters. Their rooms would still be vacant. Space was aplenty again there with the potential sick staying at the motel. That's where Dwyn should be.

Audra surprised herself when she followed him into his room rather than retreating to her own. If Dwyn was surprised, he didn't show it. They both took off their boots, leaving them in the hall. Dwyn reached for a bucket of stale water and a couple of rags. He let Audra clean her face, then he helped her wash the wounds of rope against skin. It was a quiet moment between them until Dwyn began his scolding.

"What were you thinking?" he asked as they sat face to face.

He blotted the wet cloth along her neck and shoulders. The water felt cool against her hot skin.

"I thought maybe I could end it by myself," she answered distantly.

"In that gas station?"

Audra laughed. "Pretty stupid, I know."

"Pretty hardheaded."

"Have you come to expect anything less from me?"

His lips smiled in return. He stopped moving the rag, and rested his arms on her shoulders. His fingers playing with loose strands of hair on the back of her damp neck.

Audra bit her lip and looked away.

"What's wrong?" he asked.

"I'm so sorry," she muttered as she untangled from him.

She walked to the other side of the room. Dizzy, she leaned against the wall, afraid otherwise she might fall. Dwyn slowly stood up and carefully approached her.

"You don't have to be sorry. You've just been through hell. And you didn't even want to be with me before. I'm just glad you're safe and you're my friend."

Audra wiped hot angry tears that pooled on her cheek bones. She pushed them into her hair, but didn't will them to stop.

"Dwyn, Manny killed himself because he was reverting."

Now Dwyn looked like he was the one that would collapse, his knees buckling. Audra rushed her arms around him, grabbing his ribcage tightly and holding him upright. He said nothing, but he did wheeze a slight bit.

"I'm so sorry," she said again, as if that lessened the blow.

Audra felt all the things she had pushed back for so long. Dwyn had been her rock even when she wasn't accepting. He had been her comfort, even when she didn't want to get close.

Dwyn coughed and Audra pulled back in surprise.

"No, you were just squeezing the air out of me," he choked.

Audra laughed through her tears.

He gave her a small smile. "It's OK. I'm not special. Loads of people are in this situation. I know the scientists will find a cure. It's just a little scary."

And a little like fate.

"I feel fine." He almost sounded convincing.

"I have to clean up again," said Audra. Her tear-streaked face felt hot and tight.

"Why? I like the proof that you care about me!" He said, wiping her cheek with rough fingers.

Audra punched his arm. Dwyn lost his balance for a moment, but pretended he didn't. He ruffled her hair, and got his hand stuck in it.

"What do you expect? I've been held hostage for days."

Dwyn removed his hand as delicately as possible. Then, they remained close. Closer than they had been in a while.

"If you kiss me now, how will I know it's not because I'm dying?"

Audra smirked. "You'll just have to figure it out."

She leaned even closer, pressing a soft open kiss into him as she pushed away her own whys and wherefores.

It felt good to be home.

*　　*　　*

Satomi pulled out of sleep and sat upright. She wasn't sure why until a rapping on her door sounded softly. It mustn't have been the first. Her eyes refused to adjust to the moonlight as she stumbled to the door. Her sleep must have been deep. She should have cured Peter a long time ago. It would have saved her all those sleepless nights.

Opening the door a crack revealed a bright smile encased in thin pink lips.

Ryder entered the room and even though she was small, she was strong. Satomi couldn't see much for her own hair flying into her face as Ryder picked her up and spun around. For a moment Satomi floated in the air, held up by her love. Ryder tossed her gently onto the mattress pad, quickly following behind her.

"Oh, I missed you too, Ry," giggled Satomi. She was being kissed all over.

Ryder smelled of pine and sweat. Her nose, fingers, and toes were cold, but were quickly warming up. Neither woman could stop smiling. Or kissing.

Ryder tucked Satomi's hair behind her ear. "I'm sorry I left the way I did," she apologized. "They needed me... but so did you."

Satomi shook her head and let the hair fall back. "I was lost. I found my way."

"I'm glad you're back."

"We were in different places, in more ways than one, but I'm here now," Satomi confirmed. And here, they could be together.

"Well, there's much to be done," Ryder said, each word punctuated with a kiss on her skin.

Satomi giggled and sunrise came too soon.

*   *   *

It was late afternoon before the group collected themselves and absconded to the conference room adjacent to the laboratory. Audra shut the door and relished the temporary peace and security. She imagined it was something no one had really felt in a while. The size of Satomi's smile was only eclipsed by the tightness of her embrace.

"I'm glad you're OK. I'm glad you're back." Satomi's eyes moistened with tears.

"I'm sorry if I wasn't supposed to tell them," interjected Jack.

Audra patted him on the back. "I'm glad you did. It really wasn't going as planned," she admitted.

The crew found spots against the walls, among the boxes of papers and broken equipment. Ryder hugged onto Satomi. Dwyn patted a spot on the ground next to him. Audra rolled her eyes then tempered it with a wink before sitting down across from him, against a defunct copier. Jack sat with his father, Peter. Peter sat with legs crossed on the floor with the limberness of his son. Audra didn't pretend to understand Peter's treatment, but he carried himself like a different person. And most importantly, Audra had been assured that he now had access to all his memories concerning the z-virus and the soldiers.

The group all left space in the middle, as if the conference table still existed. Audra's thoughts flashed back to Gordon's awakening, tied to the table and coming to after years of infection. That was a different time then. They thought they were pushing toward a reborn world. But now it seemed the catalyst for that might be their extinction.

"Greenly knows about the motel. It isn't safe, just like here. The shepherds I was with thought she was organizing some sort of strike against us. And I bet it's not going to be just a herd of rotters again." She caught Dwyn's grimace out of the corner of her eye. "I mean sick," she ended dumbly.

"Did Corette know anything?" Audra asked.

"She didn't know what Greenly was planning, but she made it pretty clear that she and several others in Lysent are ready for a change in leadership."

"That could really help us. Did she know where Greenly keeps the half zom army?" remarked Ryder.

"That doesn't matter," spoke up Peter. "They can never be used against us."

"A failsafe?" asked Ryder.

Peter nodded. "I programmed a safety word. As soon as the army arrives, I can disable them."

"What is it?" asked Audra.

"Earl Grey," Peter shared. "But since I programmed it, it will be most effective if it's relayed in my voice."

"Could they be used against Greenly?" asked Audra.

"Technically yes, but I've come to realize it was wrong of me to create them. I took away their free will, just to keep my family safe. I don't feel comfortable using them."

"Neither do I," added Satomi.

A round of nods confirmed that those who didn't choose to fight, wouldn't fight.

There was another point to discuss. Audra sighed before diving in.

"Something's wrong with all the antivirals. One of the shepherds I was with got really sick and said he was reverting. He said it's happening all over — called 'em turn-backs. I can't confirm his story though. He killed himself before he turned, but I can't see that being a ploy."

Satomi had already been told, but everyone else involuntarily looked at Dwyn. He gave a small wave.

"I'm OK for now folks, but yeah, I'm glad I've been staying at the motel."

"Could the treatment you gave Peter help those reverting?" asked Audra.

"No, the peptide is already present in Dwyn's blood. And what's more, Lisa's reinfection seems less receptive to the peptide. It's not a cure, just maybe a preventative measure if given quickly after initial infection."

"So what else you got?"

Peter and Satomi glanced at each other, before Satomi answered. "We need the original virus."

"What do you mean, the original virus?" asked Dwyn.

Peter clasped his hands together. "For years, Lysent was experimenting with viruses of mild to moderate illness severity, high morbidity, low mortality. They'd disperse them into the population, then sell vaccines or treatments to bolster the medical sector. It made a lot of people a lot of money. Unfortunately, the z-virus mutated almost immediately upon release. It crossed the blood-brain barrier, which had… unintended consequences."

"Understatement of the apocalypse," muttered Audra.

"So the crossing of the blood-brain barrier and shutting down high brain function wasn't intentional?" asked Ryder.

Audra thought Ryder had a good joke too, but eventually realized she wasn't being sarcastic.

"Goodness, no. It was just supposed to be a flu-like virus. When it did that and kept the hunger response active. Wow, I didn't think a virus could really evolve to spread like that."

"Why not? It's pretty effective," replied Satomi.

"Why not, indeed," he repeated.

"So, if the virus mutated, why do you need the original?" asked Audra, ready to get to the point.

"They never modified the antiviral. They just rolled out the stockpile they had. Unmodified, it does a pretty decent job of clearing out the virus, but it doesn't cross the blood-brain barrier like the virus does. As such, the virus sat dormant in the brain and then, I assume it's mutated enough to become resistant to the antiviral. Lysent sold these treatments as a bandage for a much bigger problem."

Audra stared at Peter, refusing to repeat her question.

Satomi intervened. "Peter and I think if we have the original virus and can follow its mutations, we'd have a better shot at making the correct modifications to the antiviral."

"But there's no place that has the original virus, right? Everyone's been infected with the mutated stuff," Jack said.

"Lysent would have it," said Peter. "We had it, but I didn't think to grab any of it before we left DC. Why would we? I thought the virus was already abundant. But they had both, virus and treatment. They had to disseminate it, before they cured it."

"Do you think Lysent would have held onto it?" asked Audra.

Ryder nodded. "Yeah, they hold onto everything."

"If they have any idea of its value, I'd say yes," agreed Peter.

Satomi looked to Audra. "We need that original virus. Otherwise, we'll continue to lose this war."

"And what about Greenly?" asked Jack. "Do you think she's really going to attack?"

"We'll be ready for them," said Ryder.

"Actually, I think we'll bring this fight to Lysent," announced Audra.

15 Regroup

Katie met Audra at the gate of the motel parking lot. 'Defeated' was the first word that popped into Audra's head. Katie's hair hung limply, unwashed. Bags hung underneath her eyes. But the fixed look of pain was the worst.

"There's no one at the gas station?" asked Audra. If Greenly knew of their occupancy here, they couldn't slack off on watch duty.

"We don't have enough people."

Audra's eyes swept the parking lot. There was no one else around.

"How many have turned?"

"Twelve and most of us have fevers. I didn't think it would be prudent to have someone outside the fences."

"Do you have enough food?"

"We have plenty of food," Katie answered flatly.

Audra thought she heard thunder following behind the rain beginning to fall. But it was the sick in their motel rooms, crashing into things, damaging their bodies, and falling back into decay. A prison of slow death. It felt strange to come here to recruit. These people were sick. But, of course, if they didn't win this fight, then they'd remain sick forever. These people had the most to lose.

"Whoever is healthy enough and willing, we're marching on Lysent."

"I will go… for Lisa," she volunteered. "Marcos and Sara will want to come as well."

"Gordon?"

Katie shook her head.

Audra walked softly up the stairs, hoping not to disturb too many trying to get rest or wandering restlessly. She stood in front of Room 13. The noises sounded distant and she dared open the door.

Audra's eyes adjusted to the darkness of the room. She saw the TV broken on the ground, and his bucket of water upturned giving the place a damp smell not unlike the rainy environment outside.

The groan discordant and husky preceded the large looming figure. Gordon's rectangular face looked wooden, like Frankenstein's monster. Besides spots of glistening drool and sweat, his skin was a flat grayed khaki.

He shifted weight on straight legs as he walked toward her. As if he knew Audra was supposed to accompany him to Lysent headquarters.

"I'm sorry, dude. It's not going to happen."

He grunted, and kicked the TV as he made his way across.

"I'm going to find your family. We're going to cure you."

Gordon's mouth more fell open than he made any effort to work his jaw. A small cry scratched its way out of his throat. He was in pain. Audra had denied it for so long, pulling along her sister as if all was all right.

"I'm sorry. Just hang on," she whispered as she shut the door on him.

The door vibrated with a THUNK.

Audra fought the temptation to slide down against the door and cry. Instead, she climbed back down the stairs.

"When do we leave?" asked Katie. She had changed out her shirt.

"Not just yet. Get some rest. I need to take someone home."

*　*　*

His dark hair might have thinned a bit and his coloring dulled, but Kip still appeared to be an (otherwise) energetic, healthy young man. After pulling him from her motel room, she escorted him at a slow pace, so he wouldn't damage his extremities.

While this boy had been out to hurt Audra and her friends, in the end he was just a kid. Kids needed family. They shouldn't — no one should — go it alone. Winter hadn't been mild, and Audra was sure his family thought the worst.

Audra couldn't feel the tip of her nose by the time Uno's gate came into view. She approached cautiously. Audra wasn't sure if she'd be considered friend or foe. Back in the day, they had been friendly enough when she brought mail. She often brought them news others wouldn't bother to take so far, seeing as they were the farthest from Choros and Lysent headquarters. But this wasn't 'back in the day' and at least one tagger had originated from their fences.

"You got a sick?" called out the guard from atop the gate.

"I do, but he's one of yours. I've seen him around here. His name's Kip, right?"

The guard squinted to see. "Eh, let me get Moe."

"Tell him it's Audra."

Moe's rounded belly preceded his round face as he opened the gates and ushered her in a few minutes later.

"Well I'll be damned. You're still alive. Why you never come around anymore?"

Moe had kept on as mayor and bootlegger of Uno for years. They knew each other well. He looked more spherical than ever. A short scraggly thing patched on his red face. He couldn't nurture a beard like he could a bottle.

"I quit the good stuff… and Lysent," she replied. "Is this one yours?" She pointed to her friend.

"Shit, Kip."

"Yes, it seems that he got bit out in the woods."

"You don't say?" said Moe, eyeing her.

"I didn't set it up. I found him like this, but I do know what he was up to."

Moe sighed, "Now, now, he wasn't out on official township business. I don't condone his actions. But a few of our young men took the opportunity. Winter's cold. They were hoping to get food and fuel for their families."

"At the expense of others," said Audra.

"Well, that's why we're short in the first place," he said. "At the expense of others."

"Lysent takes much more than it gives," said Audra.

"And the townships too," he said.

"What do you mean?"

"We're the last on the rail line. The rations go through every township before ours. You can imagine that some take more than they should — until we're left with the scraps. Lysent refuses to start down here, work their way up, even just once a month. Greenly favors the first towns. They're closer to her. Do stuff for her, I guess. We get the short end and always will."

Another way Greenly set the towns against each other and kept them separated. It made it difficult for the townships to band together and demand fair treatment.

Audra tested the waters. "What if Lysent was convinced to turn itself around?"

It was his turn to ask. "What do you mean?"

"Greenly is blaming my scientists for the reversion—"

"Reversion?"

"Cured no longer being cured?" she tried.

"Oh, the turn-backs. We don't got any cured here. No one could afford it."

"All the cured are susceptible. Her lies and unfair policies are going to kill us. We're marching on Lysent headquarters to overthrow Greenly. It's our only chance to use the company resources to develop a permanent cure and distribute it."

"That's ambitious. We're just trying to last the winter," Moe admitted.

"Us too, but I think this is the only way we do. Would you guys be willing to fight? How about the other townships farther out like you?"

"Well, there is still the rebel network. We're a big part of it here. Some in other towns too."

Audra nodded. She had intense feelings of mistrust after Vesna's membership in this mysterious network hadn't saved her from being executed. She didn't know Corette or many of the others who claimed to contribute. But unfortunately, suspicions didn't supplant Audra's need for more hands and weapons.

"Greenly refuses to admit her cure doesn't work. She's going to sit back while our friends revert and we have outbreaks all over again."

Moe looked at Kip. He shook his head. "I don't want my kids running around trying to care for their families. We should be getting rations for our contributions. Cures should have been free a long time ago. If you're going to fight, we're in, but you know she has an army now. Some sort of robot soldiers."

Audra would have laughed at the description, if she hadn't been the reason Lysent had that army.

"Yes. They're some sort of hybrid. But, we may have a way to disable them."

"May?" asked Moe, raising his eyebrows.

"There's an 'off command', but they've been under Lysent's control for months now. Who knows if they've managed to reprogram them."

"So they are robots… What are they like?"

"They're as coordinated and agile as humans, but must be killed like zoms. Their skulls are hard, so you have to get soft spots, eyeballs, ear canal, temples, even the nose. The back of the neck starting at the base of the skull and coming up through the spinal canal—"

"I know how to kill a zom," he interrupted.

"Yeah, besides soft access to the brain, you could also bash their heads in if you have enough force," Audra added, fighting the temptation to demonstrate on Moe's round one.

Two boys ran from the center of town, rushing Audra and Moe. Both had dark hair like Kip. They took hold of his lead, keeping him at arm's length.

"Did you bring him back?" asked the taller of the boys.

"Yes, he shouldn't have been out by himself."

The shorter one kicked the taller one. "We knew he'd do it with or without us. We shoulda gone."

"Maybe, but now you're here and healthy," responded Audra. "You can take care of him."

"Until what?" scoffed the taller one. "There's no cure."

Audra dug her shoe into the dirt. "I'm trying to fix that."

The boys shook their heads unconvinced and walked off with their brother.

Audra hoped they wouldn't kill him. Although, with the pain the infected felt and no cure in sight, what was the best thing to do? She thought of Gordon recounting the wicked flames that wrapped around his bones. Maybe it was more merciful to let the infected die, but Audra couldn't let go of the possibility of healing and life.

"Let's go talk," said Moe. "Over a drink?"

"Talk, yes. I have a few questions about this train…"

16 Uno

Back at Osprey Point, Dwyn hugged Audra tightly, his face buried in her hair. She took a moment to rest and enjoy the quiet peace before saying another goodbye.

"Be careful," she finally said. "We need the network, but I don't trust them."

Dwyn was going ahead of their gathered forces to organize Corette and her people. A two-pronged attack.

"They're against Greenly. What else do you need?" asked Dwyn.

"It's just, I don't get it. They've spent years benefiting from the system. Why do they want to help us?"

"They're dealing with the broken antiviral. Same as us," he reminded her, pulling up her chin with his hand. Audra thought his hand felt warm.

Dwyn gave a little cough.

"It's OK!" he said. "Just a tickle in my throat."

Audra nodded, ashamed that she was looking for signs.

Dwyn coughed again.

Audra's heart sank a little lower.

Their goodbye was interrupted as reinforcements from the motel arrived. Six. Six people. Audra wondered if the six people could even make up in fighting power what they had lost in morale seeing just six return to Osprey Point. Tears were matched with questions and answers. Katie told them Lisa was holding up. She just needed a cure. Bradley was confined to a room without furniture as she kept injuring herself. Gordon down. And so many more friends and family.

* * *

The next morning, when Audra and her group arrived at the gates of Uno, she saw the guards there had doubled. They looked professional, much more than her own, despite their similarities. Both Osprey Point and Uno had zombies to deal with. They had to hunt and gather outside safe boundaries. They all-around had to survive a harder life than Lysent's more favored counterparts. But Uno looked much more prepared. Perhaps because those at Osprey Point were comebacks, relatively new to the world again. Or perhaps because Audra had mistakenly kept them hidden and safe.

The gates opened and her thirty or so flooded into the township, some for the first time. Audra directed them to a small building up against the platform for the train. The track looked modern and sleek, much unlike the world they lived in, even in the townships.

Moe pulled her to the side. "I thought you'd have more people."

I thought you'd be skinnier with less rations. "A lot of us have turned."

"Should've brought them too."

Audra sighed. She never saw eye to eye with the townships. There was no point arguing now.

"We have more waiting at Lysent. Tell me again about the train," she requested. She was used to hearing Dwyn repeat reports and strategies over and over. It no longer felt right to do differently.

Moe gave her a patronizing look. "Always one guy at the helm. Fifteen unmarked cars. Each with a guard and randomized cargo. I wonder whose fault that is…" he trailed off.

Guards in every car. Audra had prompted that policy when she stole antivirals off the automated and unmanned train.

Hijacking the train would give them transportation and the element of surprise. They'd be able to roll right into Choros, picking up anyone they wanted on the way. They'd arrive at Lysent's doorstep — together and ready to fight.

Would Lysent roll over or would they battle their own people? Audra knew the Choros residents would side with whoever promised them safety and security at the end. They wouldn't fight. Instead they'd wait with their heads in the sand.

"When does the train get here?" asked Audra. She already knew, but she was beginning to feel nervous. She wanted to be out of sight when it came barreling into the train station.

"3:30 Lysent time. The cold things are no longer cold. In the summer, the meat goes bad. Greens are withered."

"And these are the people that are usually here?" Audra motioned to the men on the deck.

"Yes, some of our strongest men help us unload the boxes. Makes for a quicker transport trip. Works well for us, huh?" said Moe.

Audra nodded. She could almost feel the ground vibrate or maybe hear the hum emanating from the tracks. Whatever it was, it set her hairs on end. Audra looked at the clock which hung from an A-frame. It was early — not by much. She squinted down the tracks until it appeared into view. Audra gave Moe a big slap on the arm, unable to reach his shoulder, before she stepped off of the platform. She'd be back soon enough.

Inside the buildings were teeming with people ready to board the trains. They quieted as the silver bullet of a train swept into the station. It slowed to a stop and with a gentle high-tech bing they could hear nowhere else, all the doors to the cars opened on both sides.

Moe's front line pulled back. They had expected boxes and guards. Instead the cars were packed to the brim with people. They all wore potato burlap sacks and smelled of sewage.

Half zoms.

Shit.

Two barreled out of their car and were on Moe before Audra could consider a strategy. He was on the ground with a mouth over his neck. The blood squirted at an inconceivable height even with Moe's most likely high blood pressure. The second repeatedly stabbed him in the stomach, guts coursing. The other half zoms emerged more slowly out of the train, but Uno's first line had frozen, taken aback by the screaming and crimson of the rotund man.

"Jack, Peter, come now! Half zoms!" Audra shouted into the crowd.

Lysent knew. Someone had betrayed them. The coup could end before it even got started. Audra pulled out her dagger — it seemed small when regarded next to these soldiers. There was no way. She looked for a melee weapon and saw Jack and Peter moving through the crowd. Jack gave her a quick nod and escorted his father toward the station.

"Earl Grey!" Peter shouted as soon as he faced his army.

The soldiers continued forward.

"EARL GREY!" he tried again, squaring his shoulders to air confidence with his command.

Nothing.

Jack tried. Why wasn't it working?

Peter ran up to a bulky man. He yelled into his face. The man only grabbed him back. Audra felt sick. Jack raced over and ripped his father from his fanged creation.

"I'm so sorry!" Peter yelled out as Jack fireman-carried him away.

Audra had known it was a long shot. The soldiers had been reset somehow. Leave it to Greenly to brainwash the brainwashed. Now they were left with only one option.

Kill.

Audra yelled out directions concerning soft spots as people finally began to rush out with weapons drawn. She ran toward the front cab which had the driver's compartment but found she couldn't ignore the half zoms consuming Moe. They pulled at greasy flesh, drawing out the feast. Audra knew others would falter at the sight. She raised her bat and swung down with all her might. It gave a mighty crack before the half zom collapsed over him.

Moe shook with eyes wide, but most of his body was gone. The second zom stood over him and brandished his knife against his smile. Audra didn't give him a chance. She knocked the smile off with her bat, his face contorting and his jaw dislodging. She raised her bat again.

"Herro?" he called out, much to Audra's surprise. Was that a hello? He shook his head as if to cast off the stars floating in his vision.

She didn't have time to decide. She swung. This time higher than his jaw. She knocked him down and swung and swung. He emitted sounds of pain, human pain. He was crying out. And Audra felt herself begin to sob as well.

He was human. He wasn't human a moment ago, but he was in this moment, this moment of death. Audra had knocked the sense into him only for him to experience being clubbed to death in some unknown place by some unknown woman. An electrifying shiver shook through her. She thought she was going to be sick. But she couldn't. There was no time. She looked up to see people fighting the half zoms, some successfully, some less than successfully. Blood sprays and screams seemed to meld together on the train's stage.

Audra pushed toward the cab. There was no way Lysent had planned to give them this train, filled with half zoms or not. She needed to stop the train from returning to Lysent without any of them on board. If that happened all of this — all of this death — would be for nothing. She reached the cab and its closed door, the only closed door. Inside, the conductor messed around with the keys and buttons on the control stand. Audra guessed he was more familiar with herding zoms by horse than driving trains. Otherwise he'd have cleared out already.

Testing the bat against the window did nothing but alert the conductor, bounce back, and threaten to knock her out. Audra had enough sense to not try again. Instead she searched the exterior of the cab. Ahead, people fought on the tracks. Safety protocols wouldn't allow the train to move with obstructions on the track. Audra had taken advantage of that protocol during her first heist.

There had to be a way to manually open the doors in case of emergency. Underneath, she didn't see any levers or any eye-catching red or yellow. Getting up, she saw some of the fighting had moved away from the tracks. She didn't have much time.

On the back of the cab, several panels were inlaid, but Audra couldn't reach. She stepped onto the connection between the two vehicles. The train jolted and Audra's body fell into the back of the front car. She put her hands up to regain her balance. The train was trying to make its getaway. It lurched, and then stopped again.

Her hand fell near a bright red lever. While she couldn't tell what it was, she imagined it wouldn't help the train go on its way. Audra braced herself with her foot and pulled. It crept down with a deep grinding noise. She heard the beautiful high-tech beep and then a gentle swoosh. She had done it.

When Audra stepped inside, the man hadn't figured out he wasn't the one who had opened the doors. He frantically re-pushed the buttons he had just pushed. He looked much larger when Audra stood in the car with him. Maybe she should have called for backup. When he realized Audra had joined him, he searched the console again. This time Audra figured for a weapon.

With the bat in one hand, she pulled her blade from her holster and jettisoned it toward the grizzled man. She followed with her bat, covering half the distance between them. In that time, he yanked her knife from his shoulder with a primal growl. He passed the weapon to the injured arm, a small advantage.

The odds were against her. She was so much smaller. But perhaps she could keep distance or buy time with her bat. He charged at her. Audra tried to picture his round head as a baseball for her bat to meet, but she missed.

Her miss still managed to move her out of his path. He almost went straight out of the train, but he stopped himself with his hands on either side. As he shifted his momentum to bring his head and torso back inside, Audra struck the space between his shoulder blades. He only turned at the waist and wrapped one large hand around her weapon. Audra took the opportunity to wrench his injured shoulder, whipping the bat out of his hand. She pivoted on her heels and smashed it into his back.

This time he dropped to his hands and knees. She swung at his head again, again, again, until the only movement was the splashback from her bat.

A muffled static noise came from the floor of the train. A small overturned radio by the conductor's seat.

"This is Dunnbreak Township, relaying a message for Lysent Corp. You're to have departed already. Please clear the track for your return. What is your status, Blake?"

There was no telling what Blake had already told them. In front of the train lay bodies. The train wasn't going anywhere anytime soon. Audra stomped on the radio with her boot and climbed out of the car.

Her feet had barely hit the ground when they were ripped out from underneath her.

Claws grabbed her ankles and pulled them underneath the train toward ripped lips and rotting teeth. His ears bled. Her fingernails dug into the concrete but flaked, serving as failed brakes. As her boots got close to the face, she kicked upward. Her foot freed and met his chin. His head smacked the bottom of the train and Audra hoped he saw stars. She used her free foot to stomp his face and his other hand. Prying her other foot away, she quickly backed up, hands and feet scurrying.

He did the same, backing out on the other side. Audra sprinted through the cab to the opposite door. She made short work of him with her recovered bat. Audra took a gasping breath. Her arms shook, making the bat rattle in her hands. All this death. She had just wanted to board the damn train.

Her victim's ears were crusted in old blood. Surveying the train stage, she saw he wasn't the only one.

They had emerged from the train and attacked with mouth and blade, but they hadn't been given any defensive measures. The uninfected workers of Jack's surrendered convoy would've verified the half-zoms followed Jack's and Jill's verbal commands. Despite that knowledge, she apparently couldn't figure out how to reprogram the soldiers to follow her.

So instead, she had deafened them.

The fighting was dying down, but the violence hadn't. All around, weapons whipped through the air, the thunks, and shlunks, and the sound of wet bloody impacts. The train, station floor, and her people splattered in sick garnet.

17 The Train

Audra avoided glancing at the pools of sticky blood and fragments of flesh that decorated the station floor while she directed the people. Bodies sorted and adrenaline fading, energy levels were plummeting. Audra recognized their need to regroup if she was ever going to convince them to board the train.

She encouraged them to wash up, to change from their blood-soaked clothes, and to eat as much as they could handle. Marcos circulated drinking water. Satomi treated the injured. And Ryder organized barricades to keep the train from being recalled. Jack and Peter were nowhere to be found.

After baths and clothing had been distributed, Uno citizens disappeared into their homes, reappearing with coverings and trinkets to dress their deceased. Even in a place where possessions were so few, they surrounded their lost with respect. Survival had been the only focus for so long, but they had returned to keepsakes and giving. They couldn't go back. They had to fight for what they had achieved.

Atop one of the covered bodies sat a small wooden elephant. Audra touched its trunk. While they had to push back toward keepsakes, Belinda had never wandered from them. Her days were spent whittling her animals, leaving them here or there for others to find. Audra didn't allow herself to consider if this was one of hers.

There was work to do.

With all gathered around, Audra reported on the obvious, "Somehow, Lysent got word of our attack. Someone either here or elsewhere — another township maybe — betrayed us."

"How 'bout your boy in Lysent?" asked a man in the crowd.

"Possibly his connection there," Audra conceded. "Lysent sent these half zoms to destroy us. But they didn't. We're still here. Now, we need to make our move before the traitor has a chance to report back."

There were murmurs. Some showed agreement. Most did not. They all sounded tired.

"I know you all fought hard. We will have reinforcements. We just have to pick them up. They'll have our backs. They'll help us."

A few more nods.

"Lysent sent those half zoms to us. They didn't send them evenly throughout the towns. They sent them ALL here. You know why? Because they're scared of you. They're scared of Uno. They know they've treated you wrong and they know you're a threat. Are you?"

"Yes!" came the cries.

"If you're willing to fight more to get what we need, let's gather the weapons, some food for the road, and board this train. You know the horror you felt this morning? Lysent will know that same feeling. They sent half zoms to destroy the thing they fear most — us."

The crowd cheered and readied themselves. And Audra hoped she was doing the right thing.

Within thirty minutes, they were boarding the train. After saying goodbye to loved ones, they settled on stray crates and on the floor, which unfortunately smelled of urine and moist flesh.

Audra and Marcos pulled the barricades off the track and joined the crew in the cab. Ryder pulled on a lever and they began moving forward. She eased them up to speed, sights set on the next township.

They had found Jack and Peter, and they sat in the back of the cab. Audra tried to explain to Peter why his safe word didn't work, but she got no response — just unfocused eyes and periodic I should have never's and so sorry's.

Audra's next objective was to not get sick. She had never moved so fast before. Well, she guessed she had in cars years ago, but she could hardly remember that. It didn't feel like this. Her stomach sloshed. Her head spun. Satomi wretched in the back, which made Audra follow suit.

"Can you slow it down?" asked Audra.

"This is the slowest operating speed. It's an express train, you know," Ryder answered.

If the next township wasn't surprised by the arrival of the blood-streaked train, the outpouring of people doubled over with motion sickness guaranteed their confusion.

"Oh heavens! We knew something was wrong when the train flew by without dropping off any goods and completely off schedule..." one man rambled as he gave hugs, touched arms, and shook as many hands as he could. He called out to others even while he continued.

"We sent a scout? Did he arrive? We were going to all come to your rescue if we heard there was trouble. We're so glad you're here. How did you take the train?"

Audra was surprised to hear a small pause where the lithe man was actually expecting an answer. She explained to them in a few short sentences what had happened.

"We need to get going," she said.

"Wait! It's still on?" His blond curls bounced on his head.

"Yes. They won't expect it. They'll assume those half zoms wiped us out and we'll regroup to possibly fight another day. They won't expect us blazing in on this bloody train."

He nodded vigorously and barked commands behind him. "Let's go fellows! The war is still on!"

There was a hustle and bustle as the people began filing out with their weapons.

"Do you have any citizens that disagree with this?" asked Audra. She knew with each township the fighters would become increasingly the minority.

He made a half shrug. "As soon as they saw someone Lysent-cured go mad, they lost the argument. They might not come with us, but they know it's the right thing to do. We all know it's the right thing to do."

Audra nodded and then helped the men pile things into the train.

"No women wanted to come?"

The man suddenly turned reticent. "We're not sacrificing our women."

Audra's eyes shrank as she assessed him. She didn't know what to make of him and she really needed him on her side.

"Do any want to come?" She pressed. "Other women from the other townships are coming." She tried not to point out the obvious.

"That's the other townships' problem," he said. His eyes flashed with ice. He wasn't going to budge.

Audra really didn't have time for this. She nodded and went into the buildings to help others. While there, she spread the word that anyone who wanted to come was welcome and could sneak onto the train.

With each trip to carry stuff onto the train, she saw new messages painted on the train's silver sides.

Down with Lysent.

Uno Forever.

Stand with us.

In the next township — half of them had no idea what was happening.

"Are you infected? Where are the goods? What happened to the train?" the people asked on high alert.

And only half of those who knew, wanted to come. They hadn't even reached Dunnbreak yet and dissenters were becoming few and unwilling.

"Skip the rest of the towns. If they want to fight, they're not far from Choros," she told Ryder. Over the intercom, Audra warned her passengers of Dunnbreak's actions and their probable sellout.

"What do you think we'll find at Choros?" asked Ryder.

Audra wished she had the slightest idea.

*　　*　　*

Ryder approached the train station at Choros, Lysent's home, slowly. Audra had been sure that Lysent had been informed of both the results of the half zom attack and their movement to Choros. How could they not? Their shepherd had stopped reporting back and the bloody train streaked down the rail line.

And yet, the two guards who stood over the perimeter fence made no action against them. And now within their fences, the train sighed to a stop in front of an empty station platform.

Audra decided to immediately let the people out. The rail could be boobytrapped, and even if not, the sooner they got fresh air, the better. The station was a short distance from Choros proper. Past there, Lysent headquarters.

Audra and Peter were the last to leave the cab. He had composed himself since the encounter with his army. With steady breaths and the ability to maintain eye contact, Jack no longer felt it necessary to be at his immediate side and helped others off the train.

Before exiting, Audra opened the top pocket of her backpack. She pulled out a syringe intended for her sister. She had kept it safe for many days and months afterwards, to save someone else. Now, she hoped, being as worthless as it was, that it would actually save them all.

"What is that?" asked Peter as Audra put the antidote in her pocket. "You know those don't work anymore, right?"

Audra giggled at the joke. "It's how we get to Larange."

Peter's eyebrows rose, but he did not pry.

Audra jumped down and signaled for everyone to follow her to the Lysent plaza. Just inside what would be considered the township's line, where the buildings began, sat Dwyn. He rested on the dusty ground with his back and head up against the wall of a building.

"It's about time," he said, jumping up and worried.

"We got delayed. You know how trains are."

"No. I don't," he said, not excited that she was joking at a time like this. They shared a quick hug. He was warm. Too warm. She made no mention of it as he walked with her and all their people.

"Corette? The network? Anyone?" she asked in whispers.

"Yes, some. They are ready when you are. I'll send the signal." Dwyn gave a sharp-keyed whistle. One they used often in the woods.

Audra stopped herself from asking about Corette's motivations and Dwyn's intentions. It really wasn't time for such trivial matters.

"I need a favor from you," she started.

She couldn't let down her people. And they wouldn't understand, but this was how they got Lysent to bow without battle. She had never intended for them to fight. They'd lose a fight, even if they won. They'd lose people and that wasn't acceptable to Audra. She was here to save her people. And that's what they were now. In these final moments, they were her people.

"Anything," he said.

She spoke in a hushed voice. "I need you to bite me."

Dwyn stopped in his tracks and stared at her, deciding if it was one of her jokes. "Hell no," he said, finally understanding.

"Shh! Please. I need to infect Greenly. It's the only way to convince her to work on a cure — when she needs it herself."

Dwyn gave her a hug. "You don't have to do that."

"You don't understand, Dwyn."

"I do," he said. "I'll do it."

"I can't ask you to do that."

"You're not." He reached for her hand. She let him take it and he put it against his face and neck to let her in on his feverish secret, which she already knew. She felt tears prickle in the corners of her eyes.

You don't have to do it alone.

That's what he had told her. That's what she had told Manny. Now it was time to accept it, even if it meant risking Dwyn's life instead of her own.

They walked in silence for a few moments. Peter coughed behind them and drew up closer.

"Hey, I want to talk to Greenly," he requested. "Maybe she'll cave when she finds out she isn't the only surviving manager. Maybe we can pull corporate on her."

Peter had seemed so broken up over what he had done. Audra wasn't sure how stable he was now. She barely knew the man. "She rattled their eardrums. It's not your fault. We don't blame you."

"Oh, but you should. I created them. That's why they are out in this world. I didn't see hope, so I made things worse. But you continue to strive toward a cure. You've always made sure people are treated as people."

"Not always," Audra's voice broke. "But I try now."

"Me too," Peter replied.

As they reached the township, many people watched through windows. Some opened doors and stood outside to watch the small mass of people with weapons quietly march toward Lysent. No one had ever seen so many people convene in the township, not even for major announcements. There were lots of murmurs and discussions, but at least no one was pulling weapons on them. They were more curious than anything else of the people who lived in townships they'd never visited.

"Why are you here?" asked a man, standing on a business stoop.

"We're requesting Greenly work on a cure," stated Audra.

"There IS a cure," the man scoffed. "Why don't you just play by the rules?"

"We didn't mess up the cure. People everywhere are regressing. Lysent needs to stop telling you lies and start trying to help for once."

Some joined their ranks as they continued down the main drag. Many others followed just to see what would happen. And several more tucked away, fearing the outcome of a meeting between an overbearing government and ungrateful constituents. The adults told their children to stay home as they promised to be back. Just another boring announcement, they told them.

18 An Audience

They marched down the main road to the wrought iron fencing surrounding Lysent Corporation proper. Lysent Corporation was a campus of buildings, which to Audra's knowledge, had not closed a single day during the pandemic. When things went to shit, Lysent just kept its employees inside. Over the next several years, the township of Choros developed at Lysent's front door to serve as a public market and to house a farming community.

Larange Greenly seemed to be expecting them. The tall decorative gate had been swung completely open and no one stood at its perimeter to modulate the flow of guests. An open gate, an invitation. Lysent had not confronted them at the station, because it wanted to confront them here.

Audra led over a hundred people into the plaza. Directly across, past the cherub-covered fountain, sat Lysent's primary building, often called headquarters. The pristine, unbroken windows towered on the face of the white mansion. Pillars and a long veranda graced the facade. The front often served as a stage for Greenly. Even now it had a podium placed in its center.

Before they even had a chance to settle and wonder what to do next, the massive doors opened to a petite woman. The woman could never resist an opportunity to tell her constituents they were ungrateful. Large bulky guards moved in front of her as they exited onto the veranda. They moved to either side when Greenly settled behind the podium.

Audra could not imagine a tighter bun of hair. It not only flattened crow's feet, but went as far as changing the shape of her eyes. The salt and pepper was more salt than Audra remembered. Was it age or the stress incurred by building an empire around an ineffective cure? Otherwise she looked well-rested. She had probably slept well knowing she was sending a disposable army into the heart of the rebellion.

She wouldn't sleep well tonight.

Larange Greenly looked directly at Audra and spoke to her from her perch. "Did I not tell you that you were not allowed in this place?"

"I don't remember. Did you?" she couldn't help but answer. Ryder gave her an elbow. This apparently wasn't the time.

"I see you brought friends," she waved her hand dismissively over her community, people she should know as fellow survivalists.

"Yes. You'll see that your towns all want the same thing. To be safe."

"And how is stampeding into my corporation safe?" she asked a little too fast. Audra knew her temper was already simmering at the surface.

"It's not the safety of your corporation we're worried about," she explained.

"May a few of us could come up there? It is difficult to yell."

The guards, who Audra didn't think could tense up any more, did.

"And why would you come up here?" she asked. "Do you want to kill me?" she laughed.

Audra did want to kill her, but she thought it better not to speak the truth on that one. For now, she'd settle for a conversation and possibly a conversion.

"I want to discuss this, leaders to leader. I don't want there to be a disagreement. We just came to show you how serious we were. We are."

"You do not want to fight?"

"No."

"That is very smart of you. Yes, you may come up and negotiate your surrender."

"We want to fight," Ryder whispered hoarsely. "We are willing to fight."

"I know, but maybe we don't have to fight."

Audra stepped toward the stage. Peter and Dwyn joined her.

"Please remove all weapons. They are not allowed on the stage," a guard barked.

Audra raised her hands in a surrender motion. "Of course, of course." She gingerly and slowly pulled weapons off her, being clear with her actions. Dwyn and Peter did the same.

Afterwards, Peter cleared his throat. "I know you have the original virus, Larange. All the corporate branches received virus and antivirals for distribution." His tone was professional.

"Who are you?" she asked.

"I'm a Lysent scientist from the Washington, DC branch."

There were murmurs in the crowd, both in her group and those watching. Peter gave them credibility. Suddenly there was another corporate voice outside of Larange Greenly and her direct employees.

Greenly kept her cool. "We distribute the antiviral in a sustainable way. You don't have a say without knowing our economic system."

"You're providing an antiviral for the original virus, but it's not effective for the current virus rampaging through your region. We request that you give up the original virus samples you have, so real work can be done to help the people. Otherwise, you're taking advantage here, selling snake oil for food."

Voices began to rise from the crowd, even from behind the fence. Audra hid a smile. The townships loved authority, and Peter was displaying a lot of it — at Greenly's expense. Even if you didn't care — especially if you didn't care — about the antiviral, you didn't want to trade your food for it. The basis of Greenly's empire was crumbling to a hungry winter and a down-talking official.

Pink splotched Greenly's papery skin. Her left eye twitched.

"Get off my stage!" she screamed, rushing toward Peter, waving her hand as if to shoo him away.

As Greenly closed the distance, Dwyn leaped in a forward tackle. He almost made it, but a large fist came up by Greenly's ear and met Dwyn's face. A hollow crunch and Dwyn's task was left incomplete. And yet, Greenly's screech, shrill and panicked, still filled the stage.

Arms, legs, and fists flew.

A guard pulled Peter off Greenly, not the other way around. A small spray of blood. Twice as large as Peter, the guard plowed his heavy fist into the elderly man. Peter fell back and didn't move. Audra tried to enter the fray. The same strong arm struck her gut. Lower ribs stung as her small body was thrown off the veranda onto the concrete below.

Blood.

Blood had flown before Peter's jaw broke. Audra didn't understand.

The guards pulled back revealing Larange, who sat awkwardly on the ground in her black pencil skirt. Her hand covered her left cheek. Crimson blood flowed, a stark contrast to her pale skin — which paled further.

Still holding her cheek, she screamed, "Search him!"

One of the men began ripping clothes off the unconscious body. He held up a thin arm, its flesh shredded. A grievous injury.

Peter hadn't flinched when they patted him down. Audra hadn't even recognized when it happened. He had gotten up in his soldier's face. He had done it on purpose.

"Kill him! Kill them all!" Greenly raged.

Jack rushed the stage, followed quickly by Audra. Larange backed away, but Jack moved to his father's body. He held him close to his chest and tried to wake him. Greenly's face went from pale to fuchsia. She jumped on the guard, physically trying to pull him into action. He brushed her off like someone would a small child.

"Kill them now!" she yelled again. The guards traded glances before continuing their stillness.

Frustrated, she turned to go inside, but the doors swung open before she reached them. She stepped back in surprise as thirty employees filed out.

"What is this?!" she called out. Steam could have risen from her diamond-studded ears.

"We all want the same thing. Safety. From the virus. You created," said a Ukrainian woman Audra assumed to be Corette.

Audra noticed Clyde and Rosie among those standing on the veranda. Clyde's thick sun-worn skin in soft white robes. Rosie's black ringlets shook in anger. The crowd was angry too.

Shouts for Greenly to be killed.

"We all just want the same thing — all of us," said Audra. She pulled the syringe from her pocket. "You can take it, and you'll be safe for a while. Then, we can all work together to make it permanent."

Greenly turned pale again before her eyes darkened and she spat at Audra. Muscles glistened from her cheek.

"You ungrateful bastards!" she shouted into the crowd. "I used that make-shift cure to build this place — a safe place! None of you deserve to be cured. YOU CAN ALL ROT!"

She then stood up straight and smoothed out her suit. She cleared her throat. "I'm sorry you haven't been able to see what I've provided here," she said as she reached into her pocket and pulled out a device.

Audra and Dwyn rushed her at the same time, but Greenly's hand had already pressed and released. A smile tore through her face.

* * *

How they hadn't noticed the smell, she wasn't sure. Maybe the lingering scent of the half zoms and the train had disguised the smell of the herd. The wind was just right. Or, they were just all distracted by the woman on the stage.

The gate rattled and twisted with the pressing force of bodies funneling into the plaza. Fresh and long decayed alike. A thousand at least. The shock almost moved Audra's stomach to upend itself.

This was the purpose of the corrals.

The corrals were never to keep the townships safe. They were never to cure when life improved.

They were Greenly's contingency plan.

Plaza exits blocked with zoms pouring in, Greenly rushed inside the mansion. Audra fought the urge to give chase. It wasn't just her now.

"Follow her! Get inside!" Audra yelled to the crowd unnecessarily as they pressed into the narrow entrance. She jumped down and helped people over the stage. Arms and legs and panicked panting.

As the stage filled with bodies, Audra fought the flood to place herself between the people and the zoms. She pulled on the arm of a woman on the ground.

"No!" the woman screamed out. "This is our punishment. We know these people. We know them. And now they'll know us!" she babbled.

Audra let go of the woman's arm violently. She didn't have time for such nonsense. Her words were words Audra had repeated so often. Those healthy were not exceptional in any way except for their obligation to help those in need. But they turned their backs on them — and now their backs were probably going to be consumed.

She had never seen such a herd. Their skin dripped from their facial bones. Flesh barely clung to arms and legs. Torsos pulled apart. There was nothing to them and yet they were still moving, jagged infectious bones, claws, and teeth. Some bodies seemed to have merged, pressed together by the mob, masses moving like a rushing current.

"Do not engage! Go!" she yelled even as she sank her recovered knife into an empty eye socket. The body fell off Audra's knife and onto the ground. There were hundreds more. One down in a sea of a thousand.

"Don't close the doors!" someone cried. The edges of the tall doors wavered into sight as people pressed against others entering.

Audra swore under her breath. They'd all be able to escape inside if they could pull themselves together. Even staring into the depths of ripped flesh and jutting bone, she almost preferred its company to those she was protecting. She moved with the crowds as the final retreating and protective line. A bag of flesh staggered to Audra. With a swift kick from her boot, its entire skull gave way like a deflated ball. It fell to the ground and did not get back up.

Two down.

Lysent hadn't even managed to maintain their zombie hordes. Exposure had left them soft and dying. Their bone spongy. But to these people who had been sheltered, it was a horror, stuff of old nightmares that clung to their brains in the darkest of nights.

The zoms surged over and around the stage. The podium fell and disappeared. The zoms close to her tripped on the steps, but she couldn't risk any more kill strikes. She'd get overwhelmed.

Audra jumped onto the veranda, through the zoms, and sprinted as the last living person outside. The doors nipped at her heels, sending her flying into the marble lobby. Hallways branched off on the first floor but Audra knew all exits only led to the now-buried plaza. Marcos and Dwyn ran by, pushing Rosie's solid mahogany desk, slamming it against the front door. Rosie stood where her desk had been with an armful of papers and a stapler. She added them to the pile atop the filing cabinet, but it was quickly whisked away as well, sending papers flying.

"I never..." she muttered. Her eyes bulged as she stood alone in the chaos.

Audra escorted the woman to the stairs, placing her paper-worn fingers onto the railing. Rosie followed the stream of people seeking higher ground. Along the edge of the stairs, a steady flow of melee weapons passed hands.

Audra slipped her wrist into the leather braid of a sharpened machete. It was a weapon too large for her, almost unwieldy, but favorable in this choke point situation. Ryder sheathed a hunting blade, attaching the belt to her waist. She held a clawed hammer in her hand.

Even though they were hidden from sight, the tide's trajectory could not be changed. Bone, flesh, and death smashed against the walls and windows with increasing velocity and increasing height as bodies piled upon the building. The glass heaved and let out high-pitched complaints with the pressure. The door bulged with the heaviness. The furniture jolted.

Audra directed all those with weapons to stand adjacent to the future entryways. She didn't have to count heads to know that the majority of her defense line was composed of Osprey Point, not Uno and most surely not Choros.

The ever-illuminated lobby went dim as the windows filled. With pops and hisses, the glass shattered. Pressure, not individual exertion brought the zombies forth. As they passed through, jagged window pieces created tangled threads of flesh. Audra brought her machete down like a guillotine parallel to the window's frame, slicing off portions of emerging faces.

The clots and clogs of zombies multiplied and bulged. The cracking of glass, wood splintering, and the groan of office furniture signaled the impending swell. Audra pulled her group. They retreated to the next floor as the sick crept in like unwanted water.

19 Chasing Extinction

Audra had never been on the higher floors of Lysent headquarters. A large parlor met her at the landing. A mahogany desk, identical to the one in the lobby, stood adjacent to a double door with elaborate carvings. Larange Greenly's office, no doubt. Audra weaved her way through the trembling men who hadn't helped defend the first floor, and she slipped in to see if the CEO was in.

The rectangular office faced the plaza, filling the office with beautiful natural light that made this building a favorite of Lysent. Audra wondered if the second-story windows would also be eventually carpeted by the dead. The wall to her right had inset shelves lined with books. Old tomes of business law, calligraphic fiction titles, and everything in between, stocked to the high ceiling. Opposite, a three-dimensional map of the world hung on the wall. Thin metallic continents seemingly floated on their ocean-blue canvas. Gold pin heads scattered on the map, locations of Lysent branches, Audra assumed.

And in the center of her windowed wall, the manager of this particular branch paid her no mind. Small shoulders over straight posture, she had remade her silvery bun. The hair swirled into itself like a nautilus. She stood at the window, overseeing her advancing infected troops as they attacked her keep.

"Did you want to go down with the ship?" Audra asked her coolly.

"You brought down this ship," she said without turning.

Osprey Point and the townships had requested medical care, else a change in government. In turn, Greenly had unleashed hundreds of zombies to wipe out the population. How the latter wasn't to blame for the sinking ship was beyond Audra's understanding and she assumed, beyond even Greenly's capacity for explanation.

"You have shepherds out there," Audra said.

No answer from Greenly.

"They could lead these zoms out. You've made your point. You're willing to see this whole place destroyed before you give up power, but is that what you really want? Do you want to die here?"

Greenly turned, wine red blossoming along the tissues of her wound.

"Yes, if it means I get to watch all of you die first. You've brought this on yourselves and me. You're right. The cure is no more. You've sentenced me to death, and I'm carrying out that sentence."

Audra maneuvered around the marble-capped desk.

"It doesn't have to be a death sentence. You could clear this place out and we can go back to normal business, studying and working toward a cure."

"For whom? Like you'd give it to me." A muscle in her cheek twitched.

"You think I'm like you?" asked Audra, disgusted. "Picking. Choosing. Selling cures? I would gladly provide you with any available treatment. It would give you time to be tried for your crimes against your people."

Greenly digested Audra's proposal.

"I have the upper hand," Greenly replied. "I have the zombies."

In Audra's hand, she had a dagger.

The zombies below couldn't prevent Audra from digging a claw deep into Greenly's bun, pulling to expose her wrinkled neck, and bleeding her out. Greenly didn't have the zoms. The zoms had them. Soon, all of them, in hungry, horrible ways.

Greenly continued despite the nearby blade, "I had high expectations for you — fiery and angry — a great combination, one I'm intimately familiar with. But you're weak," she spat. "You've always been weak. First it was your sister. You dragged around that corpse baggage for years. And now it's these people. Like me, you don't need them."

Greenly thought Audra's connections made her weak. By wiping out the masses, the ones left standing would be stronger. But what would really be left? Dwyn believed no one should go about this life alone. Audra considered the place she stood, on a precipice overlooking an undulating sea of the dead. She'd never want to be the last. And she didn't have to be.

Like me.

For someone facing death, Greenly was disturbingly calm. Her palms and collar dry. Her breathing deep and rhythmic. Audra followed Greenly's eyes. She no longer looked at the masses of gray rot surging below them. She looked beyond them. Just beyond Choros.

It was quiet there.

Audra began kicking around the room, snooping for Greenly's escape. The bookcases, although promising based on memories of weekend morning cartoons, did not demonstrate any secretive features. No trap door underneath her desk. Audra pulled the map sculpture off the wall. Behind it, a stepping stool and safety harness sat in a hidden shaft. The shaft's built-in ladder led up, Audra assumed to the roof.

"When were you going to go?" asked Audra.

"I was going to sneak away when things got chaotic. I still might, darling. Looks like they're coming up the stairs…"

"Chaos, huh?" Audra confiscated the safety harness then swung the office doors open. "She's in here," Audra called.

As Greenly was dragged into the parlor, Audra checked on the status of the first floor. The first floor could no longer be seen. Zombies ebbed and flowed on the stairs, working their way up then being pulled back down by their own. The sounds and scents would eventually draw them up like the tide.

The townships had always traded freedom for protection. Now it was time to stand on their own. Audra directed them to protect the second floor where they currently resided. After grabbing a coil of rope from the armory, she called Ryder and Dwyn into Greenly's office. Satomi followed tightly on their heels. The safety harness and Greenly's speech of solo endeavors hinted that her escape was not one for the masses. But if the zombies could be redirected, they all might survive another day.

Audra climbed up the ladder first, the safety harness slung on her shoulder. She pulled on the latch at the top and light streamed through. Climbing onto the flat roof, Dwyn followed right behind her.

"Come on up," she directed down the shaft. She heard Satomi and Ryder share a kiss before one of the women started up the ladder.

At first Audra only saw electrical cables. If Greenly was going to use them to escape, it would have been an escape of a different kind. One came from the lines that ran along the town. And there was another that reached to a lower building, as a secondary supply. No one had bothered to wire the building up to the main supply? Why not? But no, they had. The one that actually held power to deliver to the building was partially hidden from view by trees.

As Audra approached it, she realized it was only disguised as electrical. It was no such thing, but just a line anchored from building to building.

Audra walked to the edge of the roof. She looked down at the expanse of zoms that filled the plaza. It was like a slow-moving and foul-smelling fire that had them retreating to higher ground.

"Oh my," whispered Ryder.

Audra stepped into the harness and began to pull it up when clanking steps sounded in the passageway.

Larange Greenly's mussed gray hair came into view. She raised one of her hands in surrender as she continued her way up. Her face had drained of color except the crusting darkness that lined it.

Audra was impressed with her gall and surprised she had escaped the others. They must have been more worried about their survival than about the malefactor.

Audra felt the same. She pulled out her knife.

"What are you doing up here?" Audra asked.

"I'm here to bargain. You can have the original virus in return for allowing me over that line."

Audra stepped out of the harness. Greenly moved to accept it and Audra kicked it to the side.

"We're going to get the original virus anyway. You're done," said Audra.

"But you're done too." Greenly tilted her head at an almost maniacal angle, even more disturbing with the rip in her cheek.

Audra blinked in disbelief. Greenly was willing to sacrifice this entire corner of the world, just to say I told you so. There was no helping this woman. And without help, she wouldn't be able to escape the roof. Because no matter what Greenly thought, she couldn't do it alone.

Audra pivoted to pick up the harness. Small feet pitter pattered behind her on the gravel. Audra spun around in time to receive the small woman. Greenly hadn't turned, but she might as well have. She snarled and snapped. Spittle fell on Audra's face.

Audra grabbed the woman's shoulders. They felt thin and decrepit. Muscles separated from bone. Larange really wasn't that powerful after all. Audra threw the woman off her. She skittered on the gravel, her feet off the building's edge.

Audra walked over to the woman who had watched the world fall then kicked it again. Larange had so many choices. She could have celebrated the fences, instead of bartering them. What if Audra had pulled her sister into town and Greenly had provided treatment? What if she had worked on a cure from the beginning, instead of doling out false hope to get ahead? Maybe, they would have survived.

Greenly scrambled to stand, but struggled to do so. Mouths below undulated in the background.

"You've killed us all," admitted Audra to the woman in black.

A cracked sneer broke on Larange's face. "Good," she giggled.

Audra's boot smashed into Greenly's spotted face. With a hard push, she slipped farther off the roof. She didn't call out for help that wasn't coming. Greenly's fingers dug deep into the gravel for a moment before straightening, the woman's arms and torn face falling from sight.

The feeding frenzy roared like a wave.

*   *   *

Without a word to the others, Audra returned to the safety harness and stepped inside it.

It wasn't her fault Greenly had refused to call it quits.

Satomi's hands shook as she latched the buckles, and pulled the straps tight. Having last been tested on Greenly, the straps didn't require much adjustment from one small figure to another. Audra tied the rope to the harness so it could be retrieved for Dwyn's use. She then used the harness's accoutrements to attach herself to the anchored cable.

She got close to the edge. The sea of zoms, the smell, the heights. Audra pulled in a deep breath and swallowed the bile that threatened to make itself known. Pulling herself onto the cable, she crossed her legs over. She moved her arms in the back and forth motion to carry her across, focused on the crisp blue above.

The cable sagged with her weight, but it had to be fine, right? She pretended there were no zoms below her. She pretended that she was floating through the sky. She was going down and down and the cable felt like it was falling unnecessarily low. The roaring got louder as she caught the attention of zoms.

She knew they were clawing at the air and at each other, trying to reach her. Their muscles straining tight and snapping against bones. All it would take would be a zombie with some hops, and she'd be torn from her hook. Bitten and chewed, her insides sprawling on the ground. And, as Audra remembered from so many times in her childhood, it would take forever — absolutely forever — for the person to die. She'd watch her body being parceled out before death caught up.

"You're there, Audra!" yelled out Dwyn. "Feel around with your feet!"

It went against her instinct to take her feet off the cable. She lowered them slowly, so slowly, until she felt something solid. Pea gravel. The roof. She dug her heels in and pulled her body farther onto the roof. She didn't feel safe until she had ass on gravel.

She unbuckled her harness and let Ryder pull it back along its route. Soon Dwyn was hooked up and began his descent. The cable sagged even more with Dwyn's weight, the heavier of the two, and Audra almost cried for him to stop and turn around, he was so close. The zoms snatched at the air right below his back. They could almost grab him. But Audra knew she had gotten through, and it probably looked scary as well. Ryder didn't seem to have any fears, so Audra stayed quiet, but murmured small prayers to no one.

With Dwyn's ass safe on the gravel, Audra jumped onto his body, pressing into a deep kiss.

"It's not because I almost died just now, is it?" he laughed, nervously.

"No, it's because you don't make me weaker. You make me stronger."

Audra finally knew her reason. Home didn't have to be a place to run from.

"You in?" she asked.

"Until the cows come home," he assured her.

Audra glanced down at the mob.

"And after," he added.

On the single-story building, the zombies pulled even closer. They reached to them. Their eyes wide and their mouths gaping. They were rotting inside and out. They would soon be gone from this world, but not soon enough. Audra picked her favorite non-zombie side of the building. She lowered herself down, and then gently dropped the rest of the way.

Dwyn followed.

"Grab my pack from the train," Audra directed Dwyn as they landed in Choros.

"Where will you be?"

"In the market," she yelled over her shoulder as she raced away.

Audra found her destination deserted save a couple of zoms distracted by the same reason she had come. Bags of bones and skin reached into the hog sty. One had fallen in and was slowly shambling around the pen. The animals rested until it got close, then ran off. Run. Rest. Run.

Audra jumped in, dodging both the zom inside the pen and the mouths and arms hanging onto the perimeter. She rushed and dove, trying to grab a hog — hopefully a small one she could carry. She thought of all the zoms swarming and how everyone was going to perish as she ran around chasing pigs. She lunged again, and this time caught the small one. Dwyn had returned with her pack. He jumped in and helped her tie the hog up with the rope from her bag. Knots she had taught him.

Toting the pig, they marched back to the plaza, positioned themselves at the gate. The masses had their backs to them. She pulled two noisemakers from her bag.

Audra dragged her knife through the pig's body. The pig squealed an awful sound. Organs slipped. Drenched in hot blood, she turned on her noisemaker, sirens blaring. Dwyn did the same. They stood there, waiting, steeled to stay as long as they could to collect as many as possible.

Heads turned, bodies followed. It seemed to only be a small movement at first. As the first approached, Audra and Dwyn took a few steps back, dragging the screaming animal by the rope. They stared down the horde with its slowly turning tide. Audra saw Dwyn shiver. She put a hand on his arm, leaving a smear of blood.

"Oops," she said.

Dwyn shook his head and smiled before they began their backward jog. Just moments later, they had to turn and sprint. Their following had become less of a crowd and more like an avalanche, threatening to swallow them whole. The narrow drag created a funnel pushing zombie atop zombie and still climbing. They were fast. They were falling. They kept moving.

"You got this group?" she asked.

Dwyn's eyes widened as he realized why she was asking.

She pulled the pig rope out of his hands and threw it on the ground, abandoning their bait. Now Dwyn could run faster. And Audra peeled off.

They hadn't pulled off the loop-de-loop maneuver in so long and never with this many zoms, but it also kind of felt like home. Knowing they were partners, she finally allowed him the first wave. She no longer had to do everything herself.

Audra let the dreaded crowd pass as she cut back behind other buildings. She approached the plaza once more. All the zoms that were leaving had left. Those inside were left inside, not getting enough stimulus from the plaza to find their way out.

A smear on the ground indicated what remained of Greenly. Physically, she was gone, but the damage of her reign remained. Audra had imagined killing Greenly often and in so many ways. But now, she only felt a burden on her heart for all the work left to be done. Greenly had dealt them a hand they might not be able to survive.

Crunching sounds above told Audra she wasn't alone. All her people stood atop Lysent's headquarters, safe from the zombies inside.

"You all OK?" she asked.

Ryder replied. "Yes, no problem here. Take your time."

Audra tied her last noisemaker to her bag before stepping deep into the plaza, toward the building's now-many openings. Picking up an abandoned piece of lumber, she broke all the glass left in the Lysent windows.

Space and noise.

She couldn't do anything about the desk and filing cabinet that partially blocked the door, but they had found their way in, they could find their way out.

Audra returned to the center of the plaza, not far from the bloody intersection of concrete and remains. She turned on the noisemaker and lit her flare. Sound rang from one ear to the other. Chemical smoke touched her lungs. And the fleshy undead wandered toward her. Her head spun. How long had she been fighting today?

Somehow she realized it would be dark soon.

Audra put her hands on her knees and let herself be sick. She was so tired. She waited the last possible moments, covered in the blood of the undead, of swine, of enemies. Layered in her own vomit and tears. Now, she'd just have to run. After all the hard work, she just had to run.

Or you know, get eaten.

Audra turned, but someone snagged her bag. Faces flashed in her mind. A haggard Greenly rising up, forcing her to take notice. A gaunt Belinda, willing her to see. Audra jerked away and freed herself. She couldn't play to the visions invading her mind. Even if they were so inviting. It was appropriate that the many faces of the lost would run her from town. She hadn't been able to save them.

What would be left in the wake of these zombies? Would they survive, find a cure? Or were they slowly dying like their brethren, corralled by their mistakes?

Audra sprinted out onto the road as the sun was setting. She wouldn't have to answer these questions alone.

And that was a start.

Epilogue

It took Audra many weeks to find her small pop-up tent out in the woods. She breathed a small prayer before calling out. Thankfully, it was answered.

A large organized group had pulled apart the community at the grocery store, taking all their food and fuel. From the description, Audra wondered if it was Lysent goons. Everyone had scattered to find their way. Haleigh and Eliza were on the run once again.

But Audra had made a promise.

"Thank you," said Haleigh for the hundredth time.

Audra acknowledged her and handed Eliza a piece of jerky to walk with. She felt it necessary to warn Haleigh again. "You understand we've made good progress, but it's not done. It might take some time."

Haleigh giggled. "You understand that we thought he was gone? Gone for years. We're happy to see him in any state, in any part. If you cure him, wow… fantastic. If you don't, we'll still have seen him, been with him. We'll no longer be alone."

Audra did understand.

They stopped frequently for blisters and snacks. Audra carried Eliza when she tired. And they camped just off the road for the night. While she tempered Haleigh's expectations, she had full confidence in her scientists. With the original virus retrieved from Lysent's labs, they had quickly found mutations that needed to be addressed. They were going to get a cure.

Gordon would be cured.

Dwyn.

Lisa.

Late in the next day, Audra paused.

"We have to get off the road now, and go through the woods," she said to the pair.

"Is that OK, Eliza?" Audra knelt down to ask.

Eliza shook her head. Her eyes wide. "I'm scared. The woods are scary."

Audra looked into the woods and while she usually saw glittering light, obstacles to dodge, and a chance to move freely, now she saw what Eliza saw. It was dark, gloomy, scratchy, and full of unknowns.

It was what Belinda saw.

"It is scary, but sometimes you have to do scary things. Sometimes they end up not being scary. Sometimes they are. But if you don't move forward, you'll never know."

"Will you be there with me?"

"I will."

"And mom?"

"Until the cows come home." Eliza gave her a confused look. "Yes, she will," Audra clarified.

"That's enough then. We can do it together."

Accepting support while moving forward. Audra couldn't force, but she could help.

Eliza took Audra's hand as they stepped into the woods.

Zombie Tagger Edition

This compendium Zombie Tagger edition is dedicated to my Zombie Taggers who have supported me for years on Patreon, Ream, and beyond. Thank you! You've made this possible.

Zombie Taggers
Stephen Hamrick
Austen Rodgers
JJ Falco
Barbara Casaceli
Richard Casaceli
Nirvana Yoga

Atalan Crew
Alledria Hurt
Carmen Loup
Darkwood
Max Daemon
Steph B
Sharon Hamrick
We Have Issues Podcast
Zack Loup

Thank you for following Audra and me through the Georgian woods and the zombie apocalypse. If you enjoyed these books, please consider reviewing them on your favorite bookselling platform.

Lastly, while the suicides in this trilogy are fictional, suicide is a very real and tragic part of our lives. Please know if you need help there are people waiting to talk to you. You can reach free and confidential emotional support by calling 1-800-273-TALK (8255) or texting HOME to 741-741 in the US or calling 116 123 in the UK.

About RM Hamrick

Despite not completing algebra in high school, R.M. Hamrick escaped Georgia Tech with a degree in Biomedical Engineering. She uses this degree to invest time and money into broken appliances before throwing them away and to repair her car every other month. She is the author of the zombie-steeped sister saga *The Chasing* trilogy and the wacky all-female space opera, *Atalan Adventures*.

Currently partnered with a tantrum-throwing tortoise, she loves board games, craft beer, and odd numbers—the author, not the tortoise. The tortoise loves strawberries, tomatoes, and other red food-stuffs. They both live in central Florida where alligators, armadillos, and Publixes roam freely.

Linktr.ee/rmhamrick